THE SKY CALLED HER HOME

THE SONG OF STARS TRILOGY

BOOK I

B.J. WILDE

Duskae Press

The Sky Called Her Home

Publisher: Duskae Press

ISBN (eBook): 978-1-7641287-2-8

ISBN (Paperback): 978-1-7641287-0-4

ISBN (Hardcover): 978-1-7641287-1-1

Cover design by Alexandra McLaughlin

Map illustration by Chiara Noemi Monaco

First Edition

www.bjwildewrites.com

To the dreamers and the ones brave enough to follow what calls them with passion, devotion and joy.

And to my husband, who, despite all my protests, told me to just write the fucking book—I love you.

NYMERIS
MAP
THE LIGHTBORNE BARRIER
VIRELLIN
DUSKRIDGE HOLLOW
SKAEDO CREST
NYVAR RANGES
THE BLACK STREAM
LYSSAR TEMPLE
THE FRAEL FOREST
MOUNT LY
TANNERY
THE UNDERBELLY
THE BARRIER DISTRICT
DRAV
THE VIRELLIN SLUMS
VYRH
THE NAMARAI SEA

CAELORIA
THE SEA OF SEVERED TIDES
THE KNOWN REALMS
BY THE ARCHIVIST
CINDRALIS
THE SHADOW WASTES
THRESHOLD TO THE FORGOTTEN
THE DECAY
THORNEWOOD
KRYNTAR
RIVERIAN JUNGLE
STARLIT GROVE
THE JOINING
AEVRYN
N
W
E
S

She doesn't know it yet, but she was never lost.

Only hidden—to all except me.

— The Shield of Dawn

File type: Intercepted missive
Found: Smuggler's tunnels at The Joining
File under: Letters to decode, Vault of Elarion
Notes by: The Aevryn Archivist

PART I

FATE

CHAPTER ONE

I take the route I've traced thousands of times through the slums of Virellin that allows me to slip from shadow to shadow with practised ease—this time, not for thieving or raiding, but for Ronyn.

I glide across thatched roofs, down walls blackened by soot, slowly making my way through narrow alleyways that twist like veins through a corpse. I need to get to The Black Stream markets—they stand between the slums and The Barrier District.

The Black Stream is notoriously difficult to cross—oily, enchanted, corrosive. It's the sole access to the other side, and the unspoken boundary between the privileged and the forgotten.

After dark, The Black Stream markets are a pit of anguish. Smoke curls in the air, clinging to my skin as desperately as I cling to survival, and the murmurs of deals for lives, steel, secrets, and flesh drift between the shadows. I keep my hood low, my hand hovering near the hilt of my favorite blade at my thigh, and my gaze steady and scanning for a way across the bridge. The Black Stream churns below, dark and venomous, a warning to anyone reckless enough to cross without permission.

Fortunately, I'm reckless. And the thought of Ronyn in danger is all it takes to steel my resolve.

Then I see it—a line of wagons, heavy with crates and covered cages.

One wagon inches forward, its caged passengers unmistakable beneath flickering torchlight. The faces of women, their eyes hollow, their lips pressed into silent fear. My stomach twists, but this is what The Black Stream markets are known for, and it is also my only chance. There's no other way across. Not unless I want to swim through flesh-eating sludge.

The wagon master is easy to spot—a hulking man with a shaved head, a jagged scar splitting his left brow. He moves with the arrogance of someone who trades in things he doesn't care about—lives, virtue, innocence. He's standing by the lead wagon, counting coins that clink against his ostentatious rings.

Fitting.

I adjust my cloak, pulling it lower to reveal the curve of my collarbone and the swell of my breasts. My heart pounds, but I shove the fear down. I've been prey before; this time, I'll make them believe I'm willing.

I walk seductively towards Jagged Scar, forcing confidence into my voice. "Good evening, sir," I lilt, fluttering my eyelashes and averting my gaze. "I hear you're heading across the bridge tonight."

The man doesn't even deign to glance up. "And what of it?" He sneers.

I drop my voice, lowering my hood just enough to show my face. I graze my teeth lightly over my lips—just enough to look tempting. "I'm looking for passage. A face like mine could fetch a fair price, don't you think?"

That gets his attention. His head snaps up, his indecent eyes locking on mine. They roam over me, slow and deliberate, and I fight the urge to flinch and recoil.

"You think you're clever, don't ya, girl? Listen up—they won't care about your face, love. I'm not selling faces. I'm selling bodies. You hear me?" His voice is thick with disdain. "I'm lookin' for girls who can spread their legs. Clever gets girls killed around here."

I let out a soft laugh and draw my cloak lower, exposing more of my frame, letting him know I am no stranger to what he is selling, and that I consent to it—not that my consent is a prerequisite for him. "I'm not here to be clever. I'm here for an opportunity. Take me, and you'll have one more beauty to sell."

The silence stretches, his suspicion hanging in the air between us. I hold my breath. *Don't blink.* If he says no, I'll have to find another way—and fast.

But finally, he grunts, his lips curling into a smirk that makes my skin crawl.

"Fine. Climb in. But if you cause trouble, I'll throw you in the stream before the guards even get a look at you."

I nod, keeping my face neutral as I move toward the last wagon. My hands tremble beneath my cloak, but I don't let him see.

Inside, the air is suffocating. The women glance up—wary, dulled by resignation. I take a seat in the corner, folding into the shadows. The wood beneath me is splintered, digging into my thighs through the thin fabric of my trousers.

A girl next to me—I doubt she's seen sixteen summers—leans closer. Her voice is a shaky whisper. "Did you come here... willingly?" She drops her voice even lower. "Like them." She tilts her head subtly to the others.

I glance at her—her cheeks are hollow, her wrists thin enough to snap, and her eyes are a mirror of every nightmare I've had. I lower my voice. "No. I'm here for passage. What's your name?"

"Tess," she whispers. "My father sold me. Said the money would feed my brothers."

My jaw tightens, the urge to run my blade through every man near this wagon rising hot and sharp in my chest. But I force my voice to stay soft. "Stay close to me, Tess. Don't speak. Don't make a sound."

She nods, her small hands trembling against her lap.

The wagon surges forward, and the creak of wheels mingles with the steady clop of hooves. The bridge is close, I know it. I close my eyes, the reek of smoke and sweat clogging my lungs, willing myself to stay still. Stay calm. Just get across.

I note the change in sound of the hooves as we move from cobblestone to wooden bridge, and exhale. *I'm on my way, Ronyn.*

The wagon draws to a stop. *We're here.*

My breath catches as voices rise outside.

"Open the wagons," a guard demands, his voice gruff. "We need to see what you're haulin'."

The driver grumbles, but the sound of boots climbing onto the wagon silences everything else. A torch swings into the air, throwing flickering light across the faces of the women. I shrink deeper into the corner, pulling my hood low, trying to avoid attention.

The guard grins. An invasive grin that makes my skin prickle. "Well, what do we have here?" His gaze sweeps over us, landing on me, but swiftly moves to Tess. "This one's new. And young. Probably still intact, eh?"

The other guards laugh, as if he's just told a light joke at the tavern over a pint of ale. *Pig.*

I stiffen as he steps closer, his boots thudding against the wagon floor. Tess whimpers beside me, and I press my hand gently over her leg—a silent plea to keep quiet.

The torchlight flickers over our hoods, illuminating the edges of our faces. He leans down, close enough that his acrid breath blows a strand of hair out of Tess's face. My hand moves to hover over my blade out of instinct, and I hold my breath. If he places a single hand on this poor girl, I won't lose a single moment of sleep over his death.

"Pretty thing," he murmurs, his voice low and vile. "Bet you'd fetch a good price behind The Barrier. What do you say I test you out first? Break you in, eh?" His hand slides up her thigh—clammy, deliberate—and something inside me snaps.

Before I've even registered the decision, I'm moving—blade out, hand steady. His blood is warm as it runs over my fingers, blade embedded in the side of his neck.

It happens so fast, the scream never even forms in his throat. I swiftly sheathe my blade back at my thigh with the din of laughter from the outside guards nothing more than background noise.

No one has seen the blood yet. *But they will.*

"Oi!" Jagged Scar barks from the front of the wagon. "What's going on in there?"

The guard stumbles, clutching his throat, eyes wide with shock, so I help him along with a firm boot to the chest.

My eyes meet Tess's as I urgently whisper, "Stay quiet. Follow my lead. Keep up!"

Her eyes are wide and wet, but she nods. I pull my hood back up, and launch out of the wagon, stumbling and screaming hysterically whilst pointing towards the wagon in horror.

The guards attempt to climb in against the current of screaming women trying to get out, and I use the chaos and clambering to disappear into the market crowd, hoping to every god I've never prayed to that Tess has heeded my advice and kept up.

My heart hammers louder than the screams, the chaos battering my thoughts as I force my feet to move.

But I have to move—Ronyn needs me.

I vanish into the shadows. Because tonight, I'm the hunter.

CHAPTER TWO

I MOVE LIKE DARKNESS INCARNATE. IF ANYONE KNOWS HOW TO GO
unseen and take what they need, it's me. A daughter of the slums,
raised on deception, swaddled in secrecy.

On this side of The Black Stream—closer to the King's magic-
forged barrier that seals the sky and keeps the Starborn in and the
Earthbound out—the only people who move freely are Starborn
nobles chasing illicit release, far from the prying eyes of their kin.

I tighten my cloak, hiding the threadbare clothes beneath, grab
a discarded bottle off the street floor, and nod for Tess to follow suit.
If the streets have taught me anything, it's this: appearances are
everything. I wrap my arm around her shoulder and start swaying and
stumbling, prattling about Stars know what. Tess looks confused and
uncertain, but joins in when she sees the guards' eyes lingering on
her a little too long.

I slur my words just enough to make my performance
convincing and call to them, "You boys on offer tonight?"

They share a brief look between each other before eye rolling
and dismissing me, "Not tonight, love. Move along."

Only when they pass do I realize I've been holding my breath. I hastily pull Tess into a quiet alcove in The Barrier District's bustling marketplace. The thin crowd around us dabbles in secret dealings and conversations, but so far, we've gone mostly unnoticed.

I knock on the door we rest against, our chests heaving with the intensity of escaping the wagon and evading attention—three sharp knocks in quick succession, followed by two booming knocks spaced three heartbeats apart.

I wait. And wait. *And wait.*

And just before I move along, the heavy wooden door cracks open just enough to see a sliver of a harsh face looking down at me.

"What could two lovely ladies possibly want in The Underbelly?" he asks with suspicion.

"I'm here to see Gellesk. Tell him Iskara is here and I've come to collect on a debt he owes me," I snarl, all traces of the inebriated fool I'd played gone in a heartbeat.

"Fuckin' Gellesk and his Starsdamned debts," the man grumbles.

The door slams in my face. *Fuck.*

But just as I think the man has shut me out, the door retracts fully to reveal a big-bellied man, strapped head to toe in steel. "Follow me," he states gruffly with a wave of his hand, and leads us through the abandoned shopfront, and we descend into the bowels of The Underbelly.

If it's outlawed, this is where you'll find it. Navigating these labyrinths underneath The Barrier District is a rare skill. *I have it.* The depravity and sheer ruthlessness of the vendors and clients that inhabit this place are enough to make the Royal Guard look the other way. In The Underbelly, everything's for sale, and it always goes to the highest—or darkest—bidder.

I can see Tess's face contorting in discomfort, and her eyes averting from the afflicted nobles high as Stars on moonshade and voidroot stumbling through the corridors.

The deeper we descend into the depths, the darker the deals in shadowed alcoves, and the more clearly I see what the Virellin Kingdom is most afraid of: challenges to their power and threats to the tight leash they have on us.

That's the thing when you take everything away from people; they will resist, and they will find a way of life that pushes against the cage they get put in. Of course, it doesn't look like a threat. It looks like hushed voices, secret handshakes and stumbling recipients.

The Underbelly is crawling with contraband: The Lunar Codex, a banned book said to contain forbidden rituals, Obsidian Shards that grant the drinker a temporary ability to hide from magical detection, and Memory Orbs that contain stolen memories, from where, no one will say. But perhaps the most unsettling are the shadowhound beasts that can be used in battle, but are more often than not used for entertainment and coin in fighting pits.

The relics here speak of histories I've never been taught—symbols no one remembers, names that vanish the moment they're spoken aloud. Sometimes I wonder if we've forgotten on purpose. *Or if someone made sure we did.*

But the real reason this place exists? Every type of state-altering elixir one could imagine—eclipsium, moonshade, voidroot, souldrift.

It smells like regret and shit down here—a heady mix of voidroot smoke, unwashed bodies, and whatever passes for food around here. Tess clings to my side like I'm her last hope, which, in all honesty, I probably am.

I spot Gellesk at his usual stall, haggling over what looks like a pile of moldy fabric and maybe a cursed relic or two. He's gesturing wildly, his face already flushed with whatever temper tantrum he's throwing.

Perfect.

I stride up to his table and rap my knuckles on the wood. A few of his precious vials wobble, one teetering dangerously before I catch it. I give it a deliberate once-over before setting it back down.

"Still running this sideshow, Gellesk? I see quality control isn't your strong suit," I sneer, an arrogant smirk lifting the left side of my mouth.

He freezes mid-shout, his head swiveling toward me like a startled owl. "Oh, for fuck's sake. Iskara? Stars damn it, what do you want now?"

I smile sweetly. "I've come to collect." My tone is lilting.

His face falls, all theatrics replaced by genuine concern. "You wouldn't dare."

I lean forward on the table, dropping my voice so only he can hear. "Oh, but I would. Let me jog your memory: voidroot overdose, no pants, and an angry noble who very much wanted to see your head on a spike. And then there was me, rendering him unconscious, saving your very visible ass."

He groans, throwing a hand over his face. "For the last time, I wasn't overdosing. I was... experimenting."

"You were drooling on yourself and begging for mercy." I raise an eyebrow, "From the furniture."

Gellesk glares at me, cheeks reddening. "And you just had to bring that up. *Again*. I said thank you, didn't I?"

"Oh, yes. Thank you, Iskara, for saving my life while I was naked and covered in voidroot ash," I mock, pitching my voice higher. "Thank you, Iskara, for keeping me from being skewered by a noble after I slept with his wife and stole his jewelry."

He bristles. "I didn't steal his jewelry. She gave it to me. *Freely*," he tries his hardest to convince me.

"While you were naked and drooling," I remind him, my tone saccharine sweet.

He opens his mouth, then closes it, clearly losing the battle. "Fine," he snaps. "You saved my life. *Once*. Are you happy? Now, can we move on to how I'm clearly a reformed man?"

I smirk. "Reformed? Gellesk, you're still peddling moonshade nectar cut with ash and passing off tin charms as Starforged relics," I scoff a laugh.

"They're decorative," he grumbles. "People should read the fine print."

"Enough small talk," I say, leaning closer. "You owe me. I'm here to collect."

He groans again, long and loud, like I've just asked him to chop off his own arm. "Iskara, you can't just show up and—wait, who's the kid?"

Tess shifts uncomfortably behind me, and I put a hand on her shoulder. "This is Tess. She needs a place to lie low, and you're going to give it to her."

Gellesk's jaw drops. "Me? Oh, no. No, no, no. I'm a business-man, not a babysitter," he gestures to his table of knock-offs and trinkets.

"She's not a baby, Gellesk. And you're barely a man," I retort.

He slaps a hand on his chest, feigning indignation. "How dare you! I am the most sought-after trader in The Underbelly. My goods are legendary."

"Your goods are mostly counterfeit," I say while flicking a frail piece of tin off his table.

"Details," he huffs. "The point is, I'm too busy to——"

"You're not too busy to chug voidroot and gamble away your profits," I cut in. "You'll take her. And while you're at it, you're going to tell me where Ronyn is."

Gellesk shifts on his feet, his bravado fading as his gaze flicks to the edges of the corridor. Always the cautious one——when he's not high on voidroot, of course. He leans forward, lowering his voice.

"Alright, fine. I'll tell you what I know, but don't go pinning this on me," he mutters. "Your arrow-slinging idiot of a friend got himself caught."

I cock an eyebrow. "Caught? By who? Let me guess——someone smarter than you, which, to be fair, isn't a high bar." *Fuck.*

"The King's guards," he grumbles. "Well, not the fancy types. More like the rejects who couldn't make it to the palace. They were stationed at The Black Stream depot. My sources say Ronyn was sniffing around a supply cache during a raid. He got too close, and they dragged him off to The Tannery before he could wrangle that oversized bow of his."

I swallow my panic, and take a step closer, looming over him just enough to remind him who's in charge here. "And The Tannery? How hard is it to get in?"

He groans, throwing his head back like I've asked him to part the Stars themselves. "It's a low-level op, alright? Not palace guards

—just a couple of Starborn grunts keeping watch. Bloodbonds, maybe Aetherstrides if you're lucky. They'll sense you, and they won't stay down for long. These guys are ruthless and mean. Like you, only with less charm."

I smirk. "You think I'm charming? Careful, Gellesk. People might start to talk," I say with a wink.

He groans louder. "Why do I even bother? You're just going to storm in there and make a mess, aren't you?"

"Probably. But don't worry—I'll make sure it's a memorable one," I say, patting his shoulder. "Unlike your last big mess, which involved no pants, drool and a very angry noble."

"I'm never living that down, am I?"

"Not as long as I'm breathing," I reply cheerfully.

I glance at Tess, hovering behind me like a nervous shadow. "Speaking of big messes, you're going to take Tess here off my hands. She needs somewhere safe."

Gellesk stares at me like I've just told him he's been conscripted into the Royal Guard. "Me? I've got a business to run!"

"This," I scoff, pointing at his miserable table of trinkets, "is not a business. It's a scam. And Gellesk," I look at him with intensity, "her father sold her into The Flesh Circuit."

Gellesk's face drops. He may be a shitty businessman running a counterfeit operation, but he *is* governed by *some* level of morality. He refuses to trade in people. He looks at Tess, and for once, his expression softens with something like genuine care. If there's one thing I know about this goon, it's that he draws the line at The Flesh Circuit. "Come here, love. Uncle Gellesk will sort ya out."

I tell myself Tess will be safe here, with his counterfeit charms and dusty codes of honor. But I've learned not to trust safety—not in Virellin.

As I turn to leave, feeling a modicum of assurance that Tess will be okay, Gellesk's grumbling follows me. "One day, Iskara, you're going to push me too far."

I glance back with a grin. "And one day, Gellesk, you're going to grow a backbone and a legitimate business. Let me know when it happens. I'll bring cake."

I hear him mutter something about Starsdamned women and their impossible demands as I disappear into the shadows.

The Tannery is waiting. And something in my blood tells me this won't just be a rescue—it'll be a reckoning.

CHAPTER THREE

THE TUNNELS REEK OF ROT AND SECRECY. I DON'T MOVE THROUGH the darkness—I become it, slipping through like a blade through silk.

I check the blades at my thighs—sheathed, secure, ready—and move swiftly without making eye contact with anyone in The Underbelly. Stars know I'm one lingering gaze away from a knife to the ribcage.

There's only one thought echoing as I climb back to ground level—*I'm utterly fucked.*

Low-level or not, I'll be facing Starborn magic. Alone. It won't stop me—nothing ever does. But it gives me pause to consider my best approach.

Stealth or an all-out attack—these are my options.

I keep to the rooftops, moving through the shadows like smoke. My chest tightens, and a strange lightness swells behind my ribs— dizziness, maybe, or something else. I tell myself it's hunger. But the feeling lingers, hot and consuming. I press on. Food can wait. Taverns here are more likely to serve you a blade than a meal. In The Barrier District, Starborn nobility come slumming for a taste of darkness—whorehouses, fighting pits, gambling dens. The air hums with moans, grunts, and the scent of sweat and coin.

The reality of life in Virellin's slums is that even if I weren't thieving and raiding—which I absolutely am—nothing guarantees your safety. Innocence in the slums means nothing to the Royal Guard, who have been indoctrinated to see us as subhuman, and therefore, not worthy of their morality—if they even have any. Guards raid homes, take from those who already have so little, and abuse the Earthbound—all because we were born beneath a blank sky, untouched by starlight, unchosen by any of the constellations that grant magic.

We have all grown accustomed to the reek of ale on soldiers' breaths, wandering eyes and liberal hands, our meagre belongings being taken, and the innocent being found guilty of whatever it is the guards need to offload blame for—an occurrence now almost routine.

Despite my tight chest, I urge my legs and lungs to carry me farther before swiftly climbing down an abandoned side street. I peer around the broken building on the corner, assessing how in the Stars I'll get across the open ground. The Barrier District night trade takes place here—the merchant wagons line up for inspection before being granted access beyond The Lightborne Barrier into the inner sanctum of Virellin nobility. In other words, it is absolutely crawling with magic-wielding Royal Guards who would love nothing more than finding an Earthbound street thief here. Being found on this side of The Black Stream would get me a public lashing at best, or a noose around my neck at worst.

I'm quite skilled with a blade—Revryn has honed me into more than just a street thief—but being perceptive has always been my real weapon. Growing up in the slums, I've learned to notice *every-thing*. Perceiving subtle movements—the twitch of a finger, the clenching of a jaw, the shifting of feet. Without it, I would've been dead years ago.

The smell hits me before I even see it—the sickly sweet, cloying stench of voidroot. Only one person in Virellin manages to make even voidroot seem dirtier than it already is. Sure enough, I spot a familiar face in the lineup—*Jeks*, one of Gellesk's lackeys, leaning lazily against the side of a merchant wagon.

The wagon is overflowing with burlap sacks, the faint glow of voidroot seeping through the coarse fabric. Jeks is chatting with another lackey, laughing at something stupid, no doubt. No doubt some tall tale that never happened.

I duck back into the shadows, watching as the wagons inch forward toward inspection. There's no way I'm slipping past unnoticed with this many guards around. I'd bet all the coin in Virellin that I would make a lovely prize for anyone in this area to turn into a bountiful payday in one way or another.

My gaze flicks back to the voidroot wagon—a plan starting to form. Gellesk always said his wagons were untouchable because no one in their right mind would risk the King's wrath over voidroot smuggling.

But Gellesk isn't here, and I've never been accused of being in my right mind.

I creep closer, keeping to the shadows as I slide a flint from my belt. The plan forms quickly: set the voidroot alight, watch the chaos, and slip across the open space while everyone's busy trying not to choke on the acrid smoke. It's not elegant, but it's effective— and honestly, it feels a bit poetic.

I edge closer to the lineup, ensuring I blend with the shadows. Jeks doesn't even notice me as I crouch behind the wagon. He's too busy regaling his friend with some story about how he once "outsmarted" a rival group. Judging by the fact that Jeks is still alive, it's probably true, but Stars fucking save me, the man is insufferable.

I glance at the sacks, noting how the glow seems to pulse faintly in time with the rancid fumes. Voidroot doesn't just burn—it *explodes.* And that's exactly what I need.

"Gellesk's going to kill me for this," I mutter as I strike the flint.

A spark catches, and I press it against the edge of a sack.

A moment. A hiss. Then—fire.

A thin plume of smoke curling into the night.

"I'm coming, Ronyn," I say softly, stepping back into the shadows. He'd better be alive—S*tarsdamned fool.* I didn't risk my life several times in one night to let him die in a place like this.

It doesn't take long for the fire to spread, leaping hungrily from sack to sack. The faint glow turns into an eerie orange blaze, lighting up the wagon like a festival bonfire. Jeks notices just as the first bag of voidroot bursts with a loud *boom*, sending up a cloud of thick, choking smoke.

"What in the holy fuckin' Stars?!" Jeks yells, coughing as he stumbles back from the wagon.

The guards are on high alert instantly, shouting commands and pointing fingers. Some of the merchants scatter, while others try to save their goods from the spreading flames. The chaos spreads like wildfire—quite literally.

I don't stick around to watch the fallout. Using the rising smoke and the confusion as cover, I dart across the open space, heat blazing at my back, my boots silent against the cobblestones. The guards are too busy dousing the blaze to notice a lone figure slipping through the shadows.

As I reach the other side, I glance back at the chaos. Jeks frantically tries to smother the flames, but it's a losing battle. Gellesk is going to be livid, and the thought sends a surge of satisfaction through me.

Gellesk may have to become a legitimate businessman after all.

With a smirk, I turn away, slipping into the alley that leads to The Tannery. My chest still feels tight, and I grab it out of instinct, but I feel a flicker of accomplishment. One problem down. Only a dozen more to go.

The Tannery looms at the edge of The Barrier District, a hulking structure of decaying wood and soot-streaked stone, its towering chimneys setting off plumes of acrid smoke into the night sky. The air here is thick, tinged with the unmistakable stench of rot and chemicals used to strip hides of their flesh.

As I step closer, the ground beneath my boots grows slick and uneven, stained with years of runoff from the vats inside. The faint glow of torches dances behind grime-covered windows, casting distorted shadows. The warped wooden door is reinforced with rusted iron bands, its surface scarred with deep gouges, as if someone—or *something*—had tried to claw their way out.

I pause in the shadow of a broken barrel, letting my eyes adjust to the dim light.

The walls are lined with massive wooden racks, each one hung with half-cured hides in various stages of decay. A prickling heat blooms under my sternum, and my skin feels like I'm being branded. The fallout of my hunger and the tension of Ronyn's safety weigh on me, which simply spurs me on to make quick work of this.

The warped wooden-planked floors are riddled with gaps that reveal shallow pools of foul-smelling liquid beneath. Every step is a gamble—too much pressure, and I could plunge through the rotten boards into the sludge below. If I slip, it's over. If I charge, it's war.

In the center of the main room, gathered around a low-burning fire, sit four loud and burly guards—likely Bloodbonds based on the sinewed muscles and protruding veins—on old crates who have clearly had too much ale. They seem wholly engrossed in a conversation about last night's fighting pits, and I decide that stealth will be my best approach—best to leave the pigs to their ale and camaraderie.

In the far corner, mostly obscured by shelves filled with tools and devices, is a door guarded by two men who look sleep-addled and relaxed—the arrogance of men who assume no one would be stupid enough to even come close. *But they haven't met me yet.* I need to get beyond that door, because I imagine what's lying beyond it is precisely what I'm looking for—Ronyn.

I trace the perimeter on silent feet and pull my favorite blade from its sheath in preparation for what I can only assume will be violence. As I round towards the back of the building, a wooden door is left ajar that takes me directly to the side of those sleepy, arrogant guards.

Stealth is definitely the plan.

I am silence incarnate. My hand slips around in front of the first arrogant guard's face and falls across his mouth; my blade drags along his throat, silencing his protest before he's even thought about doing so. The warm spray of his blood is a reassurance that I can do this—I've done this before. I unfold him onto the ground, and move swiftly to the next guard, who turns to face me just in time. I slash his throat, the shudder of muscle giving way, and shove him back onto the crate he came from, his head lolling like he's slipped back into the dreamscape he never should've left.

I check the ale-riddled guards around the fire have continued their conversation, and when I'm confident they haven't heard a thing, I push through the once-guarded door to whatever lies beyond. A cluster of holding cells stands apart, their iron bars blackened and warped as if they've absorbed The Tannery's misery. The captives inside are little more than shadows, their faces obscured by the low light and their movements sluggish, weighed down by exhaustion, chains or worse.

This place isn't just a tannery; it's a purgatory. A place where things—hides, people, souls—come to be stripped of their essence and discarded. And if I'm not careful, I'll be next. I move along the strip of cells to check if Ronyn occupies one of them.

His wavy mop of chocolate brown hair is the first thing I see—his face is marred with bloody cuts and mottled bruises. He looks up at me with his signature lopsided smile that I'd recognize anywhere, and says, "About time you showed up, Isk. I was just about to start composing a tragic ballad about my untimely demise."

Thank the Stars. I loose a breath of relief, and I can't help but allow myself a silent chuckle. "What in the Stars happened, Ronie?"

"Perhaps we could debrief on my errors when we're not in enemy territory, Isk? I think the first order of business should probably be getting me the fuck out of this cell."

"*Obviously,*" I scoff.

The cell door rattles, and I curse the sound. I jab my dagger into the lock, desperate, reaching, but have no luck. Frustration and urgency get the better of me, and I jab my dagger in again. "For fucking Stars sake, Ronyn, you couldn't pick a cell with a normal fucking lock?"

"Sorry, next time I'm beaten and snatched, I'll request the deluxe suite," Ronyn shoots back, leaning casually against the bars despite the blood on his lip and bruises darkening his jaw. "You know, maybe one with snacks and a key under the mat."

I roll my eyes and look around, trying to come up with a plan before huffing and grunting in frustration again.

"You know, Isk, I don't know if you'll be able to huff or grunt the lock open, unfortunately," he quips.

"Shut up and let me think! What if I—"

"Uh, Iskara?" Ronyn interrupts, his tone suddenly sharper. "We've got company."

"No shit," I hiss, scanning for a plan for this Starsdamned lock. But before I can move, a low, amused voice interrupts us from behind.

"Struggling with a lock? How... *quaint*," the voice muses.

I spin, my dagger flashing in the dim light, to find a man stepping out of the shadows. He moves too quietly, as if the darkness itself bends to his will. A hood obscures most of his face, but the smirk glinting beneath it is infuriatingly visible.

I size him up—smug, too confident, too clean for this place. A wolf at the edge of the campfire.

"Who the fuck are you?" I demand, keeping my voice hushed and my blade steady.

"Kael," he says after a pause, like he's deciding whether to lie. Like his name should mean something to me. His tone is as maddeningly casual as his posture. "And if you don't keep it down, you'll have the entire guard down here."

There's something in his tone—a quiet confidence that feels too practised, like he's holding secret agendas and hidden motives behind that infuriating smirk. My instincts scream at me to keep my guard up, but right now, curiosity wins out.

"You know," Ronyn pipes up. "If he hasn't killed you yet, he may actually be helpful."

Kael glances at Ronyn briefly, as though weighing him up. "Your friend's smart—perhaps you should listen," the man, Kael, says, pointing at Ronyn with the gleaming tip of his blade.

"I'll decide who I listen to," I snap, pointing my own dagger at

Kael. "You've got about five heartbeats to explain why you're following me, or you'll find this blade somewhere uncomfortable."

Kael's smirk deepens. "You're cute when you're threatening."

Ronyn snorts. "She's not cute. Trust me—she's decidedly grumpy in the mornings."

"Ronyn," I growl. "Shut up before I leave you here."

"You'd miss me," he says, but he shuts up—for now.

Kael crouches beside the lock, ignoring my glare. "Enchanted," he says by way of explanation. "You'll need more than brute force. Lucky for you, I'm feeling generous."

"No one is generous without an agenda around here," I say, watching him pull a strange device from his belt.

He glances up, his dark eyes gleaming with a challenge. "I'm not from around here." Well, he's not lying about that—his accent is definitely not from Virellin.

Before I can probe, he presses the device to the lock. A soft click, and the door creaks open. Ronyn steps out, rubbing his battered face. Seems this man doesn't want us dead—at least, not yet.

"Remind me to send you a thank-you card," Ronyn says, dusting himself off.

I huff a laugh at his infinite optimism. "You've looked better, Ronie," I say, taking in his injured body. "But I'm happy to see you," I say with a genuine smile, squeezing his arm.

Kael's gaze lingers on me for a moment before he says, "Happy reunion, lovers. Now, move. Quietly, if you can manage it."

"We're not— Never mind," I roll my eyes and huff in irritation, but we fall into step behind him. We barely make it three steps before the door at the end of the corridor slams open. Four guards pour in, magic gifted from The Crimson Hydra constellation they were born under flaring red in their eyes. Their blades are at the ready, a snarl twisting their mouths. Their leader—a hulking brute with a face like a badly smashed anvil—looks directly at me and licks his lips, as if preparing for a tasty meal.

"There's nowhere to run, darlin'. Slum rats like you won't make it three heartbeats," he snarls.

"Care to make it interesting, *darling?*" The last word drips from my mouth like a seductive invitation, and I see Kael smirk from the corner of my eye at my flagrant cockiness.

"Iskara," Ronyn hisses, already reaching for a dagger sheathed at my thigh, seeing as he's unarmed. "Maybe don't provoke—or enter into a wager with—the murder squad?"

"Wouldn't be me if I didn't," I lilt. The tightness in my chest turns molten. Not fear. Not hunger. Something else. Something waking. I unconsciously clutch my hand to it—the sudden, searing heat beneath my ribs is too much to bear. Kael notices my discomfort and nods slightly, stepping forward to edge in front of me.

He snarls with primal fury, and I can practically feel the killer instincts dripping from him.

Without warning, he unsheathes the twin swords from their scabbards across his back in a single, seamless motion, the blades glinting with a dark, deadly sheen even in the dim light. I don't know what his swords are forged with, only that they're beautiful. *Lethal.*

He moves like a predator—silent, calculated, and terrifyingly fluid. Every step, every pivot, is a dance honed through years of training or battle, or both—a symphony of razor sharp precision. His muscles coil and flex beneath his armor, the sharp lines of his body mirroring the cutting edge of his weapons. The swords blur as he wields them, each strike a masterpiece of controlled power, each feint a whisper of death.

Kael cuts down two guards with ruthless ease, his blades blurring into arcs of muted black, and his dark gaze locks on to the third as if daring him to make a move. The final guard—a broad-shouldered thug with a snarl carved across his face—skirts the clash of swords and fixes his eyes on me. Claiming me. *Branding me as his kill.*

"Ronyn, run!" I scream, my voice raw.

"I need my bow and the ledger!" He screams back, his voice hoarse.

That fucking ledger. He's not wrong—we do need it. Without the supply routes and guard rotations it contains, we'll starve.

"GO!" I scream again, shoving him into motion as the thug charges.

Ronyn hesitates, clutching the dagger I gave him, but he knows it won't do a damn thing against the Bloodbond brutes—their magic for battle fury, regeneration, and enhanced stamina renders our blades useless unless we can kill them with a clean slice through the throat or heart. He bolts around the other side of Kael, disappearing into the chaos of The Tannery.

The thug charges, his rotting teeth bared in a feral grin. "Aww, I get you all to myself. How sweet," I taunt, dropping low at the last moment. The slick floor burns against my thighs as I slide beneath him, my blade slicing clean through the tendons behind his knee.

He roars, collapsing for a moment, but he moves faster than I expect. His good knee slams into my stomach, driving the air from my lungs in a gut-wrenching wheeze. I lash out, dragging my dagger across the thick muscle of his arm.

"That won't do much, girl," he snarls, baring his teeth in a sadistic grin as his wounds begin to stitch together before my eyes.

He's regenerating. My dagger might as well be a spoon.

Fucking Bloodbonds.

I claw for the dagger in my boot, but his massive hands close around my throat, cutting off my air. My vision blurs, and my arms flail, desperate to pry his fingers free.

Stars help me. I can't die here—not like this.

His weight presses down on me like a boulder, pinning me to the floor. My fingers finally close around the dagger, and with the last of my strength, I drive it into his ribs. He barely flinches, his focus still locked on choking the life out of me.

The burning in my chest explodes into agony. Heat pulses under my skin, and before I can move, blinding light floods the corridor, searing through the cells and walls. My body curls instinctively, arms wrapping around my legs as the light devours its path.

Searing light erupts—it stills time, consumes thought, hijacks my senses.

The heat behind my ribs recedes, leaving a hollow ache in its wake. The light around us begins to fall, evaporating into the air as if it never was. I look down at my own body, light glimmering and glowing under my skin, illuminating me in a fine dusting of what looks like starlight falling around me.

The heat ebbs, the light fades, and the world around me sharpens into focus. The thug lies next to me, skin disintegrating before my eyes.

I scramble back, horror coursing through me.

"Wh— What is happening?" I stammer the words, struggling to sit up.

"Isk!" Ronyn rushes over, pulling me into his arms. "What in the fucking Stars *was* that? Are you okay?" His eyes roam my body, searching for wounds, but I know he won't find any. "You just turned that Bloodbond to fucking dust!"

His expression is unreadable—a mix of fear, surprise, and relief.

"I'm... okay," is all I can manage.

"I have a *lot* of fucking questions," he says, pulling me tighter.

I don't know what to say. I don't know how to say it. So I say nothing at all.

As the light clears, my gaze sweeps the room. The guards lie dead, twisted and broken, dissolving into nothing but ash before our eyes.

But my magic is bound. This shouldn't be possible. Unless... my magic is fighting back.

Kael leans casually against the cell door, his twin swords sheathed, arms crossed, not a single strand of his perfect hair out of place. His smirk sharpens as he steps out of the shadows, his eyes cutting through the ash and dust like a blade.

He leans down just slightly, closing the gap between us.

"Hello, Lightborne," he says, his voice low and heavy with meaning.

My stomach drops, blood draining from my face.

He knows who I am.

Fuck.

CHAPTER FOUR

THE DISTANT POUND OF BOOTS ON COBBLESTONES CUTS THROUGH
the air—sharp, urgent, relentless. Orders are barked. Rein-
forcements.

They must've seen the light. *My light.*

Shit.

Kael doesn't move. He leans against the cell like he has all the
time in the world, smirk etched on his face.

Ronyn's eyes stay fixed on me, wide and expectant. "Are we
gonna discuss this, Isk?"

"Not now," I snap, pacing the corridor like the motion might
help me claw together a plan. "We need to get back across the
bridge before they lock it down."

Think. *Think, damn it.*

The footsteps are closing in. I can *feel* them pressing in on The
Tannery from all sides, tightening like a noose.

"I have my bow and eight arrows," Ronyn offers, but we both
know it's not enough. Not against what's coming.

"It's not enough," I bite back, sharper than I mean to.

He drags both hands through his hair in frustration but doesn't
argue.

Then Kael clears his throat, utterly unbothered. "If you'll follow me." He gestures toward the exit like he's inviting us over for tea.

Ronyn and I exchange a look—equal parts suspicion and desperation.

We follow.

"And where, exactly, are you leading us?" I ask, tone clipped.

"I'm a Shadowweave," Kael says simply, as if that explains anything. "I'll take care of it."

I stop dead. I know next to nothing about Shadowweaves. Though I've spent my entire life separated from the Starborn, I'm no stranger to their skills. Especially Aetherstrides and Bloodbonds who guard, hunt and raid through the slums and The Barrier District. But Shadowweaves—they remain an enigma. Rare, coveted, and the full range of their skills elusive. "A Shadowweave?"

"Magic of the Obsidian Serpent constellation," he explains. "Sentient shadows, illusory strikes, cloaks of darkness. You know?"

I stare. "No, I don't *fucking* know."

He turns to face me, sighing like I'm the difficult one. "It means the guards won't see us until it's too late. A cloak to hide us. Phantoms to distract them. Sound simple enough?"

Not in the fucking slightest.

I glance at Ronyn. His face is tight with scepticism.

Kael's calm is infuriating. His certainty even more so.

"This better work," I mutter, stepping in behind him, anyway.

Kael isn't wrong. We are blanketed in the cover of his magic, moving through The Tannery like wraiths. The first guards burst into the main space, their torches casting wild shadows against the walls. They look around us, their eyes scanning the room. No—they look *through* us.

"I can feel magic," one guard snarls. "Strong magic," he adds, crouching low as he moves across the space like a predator tracking prey. *He has to be an Aetherstride.*

"There!" Another guard shouts, pointing at a broad-shouldered man near the corridor. He charges, sword raised, and slices clean through thin air. The illusion flickers, its edges distorting like ripples on water before vanishing.

It's not just illusions. It's intentional misdirection—Kael's playing puppet master while we slip by like ghosts.

Another projection takes shape behind them, then another, and another—each one more lifelike than the last, their faces twisted into cruel sneers. The guards falter, disillusioned, their shouts turning frantic as their blades meet nothing but shadows. The air thickens with confusion, chaos, and a building sense of terror.

The guards lose all sense of reality, unable to determine what is real and what is a trick of the eye. It's unsettling. Horrifying. But right now, we need this. Or we'd be outnumbered, unprepared... and probably dead.

We don't stick around to watch. Under the shroud of Kael's magic, we sprint for the bridge, the sound of guards' boots and panicked cries echoing behind us. He moves like a piece of the night itself, eyes never catching on his shape. My chest burns—not from the effort, but from the cold wrongness of his magic. The shadows snake around me, alive and unnerving, their icy tendrils slithering across my skin.

I push the thought away.

We don't have time for doubts.

Not now.

The blockade at the bridge is nearly set, torches flickering as guards bark orders and position themselves. We've arrived at the perfect time—any later, and we'd be trapped. The faint clink of armor and low murmurs drift from the guards stationed at both ends. My muscles coil with the instinct to run, but I force myself to stay silent, each step deliberate as we weave through unseen.

When my boots finally meet the familiar dirt of the slums, I exhale a breath I hadn't realized I was holding. The tension in my chest doesn't fully leave, though. Not until we follow Kael's lead to an abandoned warehouse on the outskirts of The Black Stream markets.

Inside, the moment his magic lifts, it's like something slithers off my skin. Like stepping out of an oppressive cloak I didn't ask to wear.

"Did you just remove the cloak?" I ask, my voice sharper than intended.

"Yes. Now you'll have to go back to moving through the shadows like before," he replies, amusement coating his tone.

I narrow my eyes. "How do you know how I moved before?"

Kael turns, the muscles in his jaw tight. He closes the space between us in a few strides, "I was born in the shadows, darling," his voice comes out a low rumble. "I've made a home in them, and they've welcomed me." His voice is heavy with unspoken meaning, as if daring me to dig deeper.

"Were you following me? Why?" The accusation in my tone is impossible to miss.

"When I saw you moving through The Underbelly, setting void-root wagons ablaze, I was... *intrigued*," he says with a note of sincerity.

My jaw tightens, and I ball my hands into fists. "Intrigued? I'm not some puzzle for you to solve, Shadow Boy."

"Shadow Boy?" He chuckles, low and unhurried. "You'll have to do better than that if you want to wound me, Lightborne."

The way the name rolls off his tongue—Lightborne—sends a prickle down my spine. I grip the hilt of my dagger, though I know it would do little against a man who can bend shadows to his will.

"Whatever your game is, I'm not playing."

Kael steps closer, his gaze fixed on mine. "That's where you're wrong, Iskara—if that really is your name. You're already playing. You just don't know the rules yet."

"Enlighten me then," an invitation I'm not entirely sure I'd like him to fulfill.

"Look at your chest, Lightborne."

I look down to see a faint imprint poking out above my threadbare tunic. A shimmering imprint of a constellation that spans my entire chest, the Stars reaching out to the tips of my collarbones.

It's the Eye of Lireal.

I'd know it anywhere.

The constellation of the Lightborne. *My constellation.*

The threads shimmer like starlight beneath my skin—threads of silver fire etched across bone. Not ink. Not scars. *Light.*

It pulses under my gaze—like it knows I'm looking.

"What in the Stars..." Ronyn gasps, eyes wide. "And can we come back to the voidroot—"

"You are the Lightborne from the prophecy, whether you're ready to admit that or not. '*Her skin shall glow with threads of light*'—I know you've heard that before," Kael looks at me with an intensity that unsettles me.

I have heard it. Of course I've heard it. It's been my mantra for twenty summers.

"Isk... is what he's saying true? Are you... *her?*" He steps forward, softer. "Hey. Breathe. It's still you in there, yeah?"

Still me. But everything feels too tight. Like my skin doesn't fit anymore. Like I'm standing in someone else's reality. Like I'm watching my own nightmares take form.

The weight of it slams into me. Prophecy. Destiny. Skin that glows like the fucking Stars. My breath comes too fast, too sharp. This isn't happening. This *can't* be happening.

"I can't do this right now! I need to go home. I need to see my little sister. *Leave me alone!*" I *snarl* the last words, thick with venom, the kind that leaves your throat raw. My chest flares with light, and I clutch at my skin, beating my fist across my chest, urging it to go away. To beat it into submission.

I must look crazed, because both men remain silent. Ronyn watches me with trepidation, but Kael takes a step closer, as if moving to touch me. I recoil, before regaining my composure and turning on my heel.

"If you'd like more answers, I'll be at the old outpost at the edge of the Frael Forest at daybreak," Kael calls to me. "Bring your weapons. Your questions. I'll be there." All signs of the arrogant Shadowweave from earlier are gone, and I feel the spark of something genuine. *Something real.*

"You're wrong—*I'm no one.*"

But even as I say it, something in me knows—this is only the beginning.

CHAPTER FIVE

I can't breathe. My lungs seize, desperate for air.

The shock claws at my chest.

He knows.

Ronyn heard him.

Kael knows.

The truth—*Lightborne*—echoes in the hollow spaces of my mind, louder than the chaos that still lingers in the dark warehouse. My head spins. My chest heaves.

I'm no one. Just a thief. A shadow. A scrappy girl from the slums of Virellin.

But I am also someone—someone fated, marked, destined.

My name was written in the Stars the moment I was born. Under a rare constellation that hasn't graced the heavens since King Thalmyr himself—*The Eye of Lireal.*

For twenty summers, I have carried that prophecy like a secret, a promise, and a curse. *The Lightborne.* I have whispered those words to myself in the quiet moments when the darkness of the slums threatened to consume me. They have kept me alive. They have fueled my every step, every choice, every dream of vengeance.

Twenty summers ago, conscription and prophecy brought the

Royal Guard to my door—to take me, to use me, like they do to all Starborn children of Dravara. But they didn't want to stop there—they wanted to abuse my power, to remove me as a threat.

Twenty summers ago, they murdered my parents in cold blood. I was just a child—five summers old—when the world collapsed around me. Their screams, raw and agonized, have been the fuel on the fire of my nightmares ever since. I hear them still, echoing in the darkest corners of my mind. Not even sleep offers reprieve.

I'll never forget the way my father stood between me and the guards, unyielding even as their blades tore into him. I cannot forget the way my mother clutched me close, whispering her final words as blood soaked her hands. *"Live, Little Star. You are our only hope."*

I am the only child in Dravari history to escape conscription. But it cost me everything—my parents, my name, my magic. It's still bound with the ancient spell they put on us at birth. But I've felt it stirring—rebelling against its constraints like a caged animal.

Even now, there are pieces missing from that night. From the past. Not just from me, but from the world around me.

Questions that never get asked. Histories no one remembers. As if someone took a blade to our past and carved out the truths too dangerous to leave behind.

Sometimes I wonder what else they stole—what else we've forgotten.

But I refuse to forget them.

Their names—Salvis and Lesara—are my prayer and my battle cry. Every night, I fall asleep whispering them like a mantra, their memory the only light in the endless shadow of my grief.

Salvis. Lesara.

Salvis. Lesara.

Salvis. Lesara.

Their deaths *will* matter. One day, their names will be the last words the King chokes out before I end him—just as he ended them.

They say having a Starborn child is an honor for parents in the Kingdom of Dravara—or so they want you to believe. A blessing bestowed upon them by the Stars themselves, who have deemed them worthy of wielding magic—and paying for the privilege with a lifetime of service to the crown.

Even the Runewrights—Starborn under the Amber Forge constellation—end up drunk on the King's doctrine. Sweet, scholarly children with a flair for language, crafting and logic become beasts who carve violent runes into weapons without flinching.

But I can see the truth: service is just another word for obedience, and honor is just a prettier word for sacrifice. But that sort of thinking gets you hanged for treason around here.

I have hidden in plain sight, a phantom in the gutters of Virellin. I have thieved and starved, fought and survived. Revryn has given me shelter, trained me, and kept me alive, but the hunger for justice—no, for vengeance—has been my true sustenance.

And now, the Stars have called me to collect on their promise.

I clutch at my chest, squeezing my eyes shut against the brutal reality crashing down around me. The Lightborne mark burns beneath my skin, searing with a light that refuses to be ignored. My fingers dig into my shirt, desperate to claw my fate free, to tear it out and cast it away.

But there's no running now. No hiding. My destiny has found me, and it demands that I face it.

The warehouse looms around me, its shadows heavy and oppressive, threatening to swallow me whole. The air is thick with the lingering stench of blood and smoke. My chest flares with light once again, a cruel beacon that pierces the darkness. The burning is relentless, a reminder of what I am and what I cannot escape.

I fall to my knees, gasping as if I could extinguish the light inside me with sheer willpower. My hands tremble in recognition—my time has come. The Lightborne mark pulses beneath my palms, a brand that feels too heavy to bear.

"Breathe, Isk. It's okay. Shhhh," Ronyn soothes. His voice cuts through the haze, low and steady. His hand finds my back, rubbing slow circles against my spine. His touch is firm but careful, anchoring me to the moment when I feel like I might shatter.

"You're okay," he says softly, his tone so at odds with the chaos within me that I almost believe him. "I'm obviously shocked, but listen to me—you're still you. And I'm still me. We'll figure it out, okay?"

I open my eyes, my vision blurred with unshed tears. Ronyn's face hovers just inches from mine, his expression raw with concern but unflinching.

For a moment, the weight in my chest eases, and I focus on the steady rhythm of his hand against my back. He's always been there —through every scrape, every scheme, every impossible situation. And even now, as my world shifts on its axis, he's here.

"Let's go home, Isk," he says, as if nothing has changed at all.

"Elyssara," I correct him with a whisper, because *everything* has changed.

CHAPTER SIX

Her excitement hits me like a burst of light, sharp and over-whelming, after the darkness of The Tannery. Before I can take a full breath, she barrels into us, pulling us into a tangle of limbs and nervous energy.

"What happened? Were there guards? What happened to your face?" she asks, her words tumbling over one another in a rush. "Oh, Stars, you were gone for so long I thought—"

"We're fine, Little Star," I interrupt softly, brushing her hair back the way I always do when she's worked up. "See? Safe and sound."

"Well..." Ronyn drags out the word, edging away just enough to dodge my elbow intended for his ribs. "Safe is maybe pushing it a bit. Sound? Debatable."

I roll my eyes, scoffing.

He grins at me, all teeth and mischief. "What? I'm just saying, your rescue methods could use a little... finesse."

"Rescue methods?" Seren pulls back, blinking up at me. "What's he talking about?"

Before I can stop her, she turns toward the trapdoor and shouts, "Revryn! Get up here! Something happened!"

Revryn appears at the top of the ladder, his arms crossed and an eyebrow raised. "I take it you didn't stick to the plan?"

"Define 'plan'," Ronyn says innocently, dropping onto one of the blankets strewn across the floor.

"The plan," Revryn says dryly, "where Iskara gets you from The Barrier District quietly, without raising half the city's guard force."

Revryn used to serve in the Royal Guard—back when swordsmanship, not the constellation in the sky when you were born, earned you a place in the ranks. Swordsmanship is a skill. The constellation you were born under? That's just luck. After King Thalmyr's decree that only Starborn could serve, he was cast aside like so many others. For twenty-five summers now, he's worked the forges in the slums, crafting weapons for the same crown that exiled him.

"Ah," Ronyn says, scratching his jaw. "Yeah, no. Definitely didn't do that."

Revryn sighs, pinching the bridge of his nose. "Alright, someone explain. *Now*."

I shift uncomfortably, avoiding his gaze. "Ronyn got caught."

"Hey, in my defense," Ronyn says, holding up his hands, "It was a very high-level operation—I was practically invisible."

"Invisible?" I say, incredulous. "Must've been a hell of a trick, considering they saw you, caught you, and locked you up."

Ronyn grins, unbothered. "Details, Isk," he winces as he says my name, but pushes past it. "Don't get caught up in the details."

Ronyn and I have always squabbled like siblings. I met him in the slums of Virellin when I was twelve summers old and had just learned how to steal without getting caught. He, on the other hand, had not.

I was crouched in an alley, keeping low and waiting for the right moment to snag a loaf of bread from a baker's stall. It was my first chance to eat in two days, and I wasn't about to mess it up. But then *he* came barreling through, all gangly limbs and wild chocolate brown hair, with two very angry traders hot on his heels. He nearly tripped over me.

"Move!" he hissed, glancing back at the men chasing him. "Unless you *want* to get stabbed."

Even then, his tone was more cheeky than panicked, though I could see the fear in his eyes. I almost let him keep running—he was a walking disaster, and I didn't need the extra attention—but something about him made me hesitate. Maybe it was the way he was clutching a stolen bag of dried apples like they were the only thing keeping him alive. Or maybe I just knew, somehow, that this fool was about to become my problem.

So I stayed. Waited until the traders rounded the corner, then shoved a broken barrel into their path. The bigger one tripped and crashed to the ground, swearing loud enough to make a merchant across the street jump. The other stopped to help, giving us just enough time to disappear down the twisting alleyways I knew better than anyone.

When we finally stopped, both of us breathless and filthy, he gave me a lopsided grin—the same one he still flashes now, like he's the Stars' gift to the world. "Thanks for saving my life," he said. "Want an apple?"

I should've walked away right then. But instead, I took the apple and sat beside him in the shadows, eating in silence.

That night, we didn't talk about why we were alone or how we'd ended up stealing. I didn't tell him about my parents, and he didn't tell me about whatever he'd lost either. But by the time the moon reached its peak, we were a team.

Ronyn was loud, reckless, and impossible not to care about. And as much as I hated to admit it, he made surviving a little less unbearable. He taught me how to laugh again, even when there was nothing funny about our lives. I taught him how to move quietly, how to listen, how to fight.

Now, more than a decade later, he's still loud and reckless, and I'm still saving his ass. Some things never change.

Revryn interrupts my nostalgic thoughts, "So, are you gonna tell me how you got out of there?"

"It involves a magical device, a mysterious Shadowweave, and *her*," he jabs a finger in my direction, "setting a voidroot wagon ablaze. Are you sure you want to know?"

Trust Ronyn to lead with the most outlandish parts of my plan.

"Holy fuckin' Stars, you two. You don't do things by halves, do you?" Revryn drags a hand down his face, exasperated by us and our... *adventures*. "Okay. Start from the beginning."

"Well, I arrived at The Barrier District and couldn't find Ronyn. I knew Gellesk would know—he has eyes everywhere throughout the district, and he owed me a favor—"

"Not that counterfeit crook, Isk. You know better than to dally with street criminals," Revryn sighed.

"Rev, I *am* a street criminal. Anyway, I went to The Underbelly —I needed to drop off Tess somewhere safe, but I also knew he'd know where—"

"WHO!?" All of them interject at the same time.

Oh Stars. "Long story, everyone. Tess. Her father sold her to The Flesh Circuit, and I just... couldn't leave her." Rescuing women— *girls*—from The Flesh Circuit is our unspoken law. I met Seren being loaded into one of the Flesh Circuit wagons when she was just twelve summers old. I used the blade I commissioned from Revryn at The Black Stream markets to send the wagon master back to the Stars, and Seren and I haven't been apart since.

Seren's eyes widen, and her hand floats to her chest in under-standing. "Anyway, I got a bit... *stabby*."

Ronyn snorts. "When aren't you?"

I smirk—he's not wrong. "He told me Ronyn was being held at The Tannery with Bloodbond guards, but I needed to get across the zone of wagons, so I," I bite my bottom lip, preparing myself, "Kind of blew one up and used it as cover to get across." I grimace, knowing this will set Revryn's paternal instincts into overdrive.

Revryn sucks in a breath, seemingly speechless, so I continue.

"I fully intended to rescue Ronyn with stealth as my method, but ahh... the plan changed. Anyway," I draw out the word, "I... disabled a couple of guards—"

"With a knife across the throat," Ronyn interrupts with pride, as if slashing weapons across necks is commendable.

"But I couldn't find a way into his cell. The lock was *enchanted*, of sorts," I say cautiously.

"Enchanted?" Seren's curiosity piques at that.

Revryn doesn't say anything—just closes his eyes in exasperation.

"And that's when Shadow Boy arrived," Ronyn quickly adds.

"I'm gonna need more than that. Isk? Ron?" Revryn is barely able to keep a leash on his need for answers.

"Shadowweave. Bends shadows to his will. Cloaks people in darkness. Creates terrifying illusions. Yeah, anyway... he helped," Ronyn offers nonchalantly. "He had a magic device that unlocked the cell, and proceeded to help us escape under the concealment of his shadows, and well... here we are!" Ronyn claps his hands together, as if that's the end of the conversation.

"I'm obviously very relieved that you're okay, but who is this Shadowweave, and why did he help you? Why was he at The Barrier?" Revryn's questions tumble out frantically. "There is only one Shadowweave in all of Virellin, and he is the right-hand man to the King, far behind The Lightborne Barrier. What do we know of this person?" His scepticism is palpable and hangs in the air.

I have known for my entire life that this conversation was inevitable. I have carried this moment with me, heavy and unrelenting, like a stone in my chest. I have known that someday, I would have to stop pretending.

Pretending that I am just Iskara, a street thief with sharp knives and sharper wit.

Pretending that vengeance isn't the fire that has kept me alive for twenty summers.

Pretending that the blood on my hands hasn't always been a means to an end.

I glance around the room, at the faces of the only people who have made me feel like more than a mouth to feed. They've made me feel like someone—someone who matters. Revryn, with his gruff but unwavering guidance. Seren, the little sister I never had. And Ronyn—Starsdamned Ronyn—who looks at me now with curiosity instead of judgment, as if he can already sense that whatever I'm about to say will change everything.

My chest tightens, but this time it's not from fear. It's the mark. The Lightborne magic clawing its way to the surface, demanding to be acknowledged. The faint warmth beneath my ribs flares, a cruel reminder of what I've hidden, of what I am.

But I'm not ready. I'm not ready to see their trust splinter into doubt, their love twisted into fear or anger. I'm not ready to be cast out of this fragile thing we've built together—a life that feels like safety, even if it's an illusion.

Revryn's voice pulls me back. "Well?" he presses, his eyes narrowing. "What aren't you telling us, Isk?"

The use of my name—my *false* name—stings. It cuts through the protective walls I've spent years building, laying them bare.

I take a deep breath, my fingers tightening into fists at my sides. I want to run. I want to hide. But there's no escape from this moment, no delaying what's already begun.

"I think..." My voice falters, barely above a whisper. I swallow hard, forcing myself to meet their eyes. "I think he was looking for me."

The room falls into a heavy silence.

"Looking for you?" Seren echoes, her brows furrowing.

Revryn straightens, his arms crossing as his expression darkens. "Why in the Stars' name would a Shadowweave be looking for you?"

Ronyn, trying to dispel the rising tension, quips, "Maybe he heard about her knife tricks. Very impressive."

"Ronyn," Seren chastises, voice sharp enough to silence him.

I force a smile, but it crumbles almost immediately. My hands tremble, and I clasp them behind my back to hide the weakness.

"I..." The words stick in my throat, heavy with twenty summers of secrets. "Because I'm not who you think I am."

I see it then—the shift in their expressions. Revryn's calculating gaze hardens into something unyielding. Seren's curiosity flickers into uncertainty. And Ronyn... Ronyn just stares, his grin fading as realization begins to dawn.

"I..." My voice breaks, and I hate it. I hate how small I sound, how vulnerable. But there's no stopping now. The truth presses against my ribs, a dam about to burst.

"I'm Elyssara," the words tear from my throat like a confession, sharp and shaking. "Elyssara the Lightborne."

The silence that follows is deafening. My chest burns, the mark flaring again as if to punctuate my words.

"Elyssara," Revryn repeats my name, his tone unreadable. "The Eye of Lireal. The one from the prophecy."

I nod, unable to look at him.

"And you never thought to tell us this?" Seren's voice trembles—not with anger, but with hurt.

"I couldn't," I whisper. "If you'd known... if anyone had known..."

Seren's hands twist in the fabric of her tunic, her knuckles white. She doesn't speak at first—just watches me with a kind of wounded understanding, like she's sorting through every moment we've shared, every lie I didn't tell but also never corrected.

Her voice, when it comes, is quiet but steady. "I always knew there was something more. But I thought... I thought if you ever needed to tell me, you would."

She doesn't say it to accuse, but the hurt is there, tucked beneath the calm, soft as snowfall, but no less cold.

"Then what?" Revryn demands, his voice rising. "Do you think we would've turned you in? Do you think we'd abandon you?" He shakes his head like he's hurt.

In my darkest moments, yes. I was afraid they'd turn me over.

"I don't know!" The words explode from me, raw and desperate. "I don't know what you would've done! I just... I couldn't risk it. I couldn't lose you."

"When they cast me out," Revryn says, his voice lower than I've ever heard it, "I didn't stop loving my wife just because she was Starborn and I was Earthbound." He closes his eyes, dredging up memories he's tried to bury. "Our differences can't stop love. It's not about the sky you were born under, it's about who you are in there," he taps my chest gently, eyes welling with tears.

Revryn was loyal to the crown until the day it betrayed everything he loved. His wife was a victim of the unchecked aggression and debauched culture of the Royal Guard, and made the choice to send her own soul back to the Stars. Even before that, their daughter had already been conscripted—born under The Widow's Crown constellation and claimed by the crown as a Venomshade. Venomshades are rare. Alchemists trained to blend poison and starlight—infusing blades, potions, darts, and even breath with death.

"They've taken everything I've ever loved," he says, his voice a rasp. "Until the three of you." I choke out a sob. "I won't lose another child."

The room is heavy with unspoken words, with the weight of twenty summers of lies. Raw emotion crackles through the loft.

Ronyn is the first to speak. "You're an idiot, you know that?"

I blink, startled by the levity in his voice.

"You think this changes anything?" He steps closer, his familiar grin creeping back on to his face. "You're still you, Isk. Or Elyssara, or whatever name you want to go by. You're still the same girl who saved my ass in an alley and made me share my apples."

"Ronyn..."

"No, seriously. You're still my favorite pain in the ass. And honestly? If you've got some kind of prophecy hanging over your head, that just makes you more interesting."

The tension in my chest loosens, just a fraction.

"He's right," Seren says softly. "This doesn't change who you are. It just... explains a lot." She steps closer, her fingers brushing my sleeve. "Next time you're carrying something that heavy..." And I wonder, briefly, what weight she might be carrying too. She lifts her eyes to mine, steady and luminous. "Let me help."

Revryn doesn't speak at first, his sharp gaze fixed on me. Finally, he exhales, running a hand through his hair. "You're going to have to tell us everything. No more secrets. No more half-truths. Do you understand?"

I nod, my throat tight. "I understand."

For the first time, I feel the weight of my truth lift, even as the light of my destiny shines brighter.

Revryn steps forward without a word, his arms wrapping around me in an embrace so solid it feels like a shield. I collapse into him, sobbing into his chest as the weight I've carried finally spills out.

"You're safe, darlin'," he murmurs, his voice steady and soft. "You've always been safe with us."

I feel another presence at my back—Seren, her gentle hands gripping my shoulders. "You're still you, Isk," she whispers. "This doesn't change that."

Ronyn presses a kiss to the back of my head. "Still gonna need some clarification, though. Like, on a scale of one to Starsforsaken, how doomed are we now?"

A laugh bubbles up through my tears, shaky but real.

Revryn pulls back just enough to look me in the eye, his hand firm on my shoulder. "You never had to do this alone," he says. "You're my daughter—not by blood, but by choice. And nothing, not a prophecy, not a kingdom, nothing, will ever change that."

The dam breaks completely, and I sob into his chest again, my tears soaking into his shirt.

Ronyn clears his throat. "Okay, this is very touching, but can we talk logistics? Are we overthrowing the King now?"

Seren swats him lightly on the arm. "Let her breathe, Ronyn."

Revryn chuckles, his gruff voice breaking the tension. "Let's start with food. No one tells a good story on an empty stomach."

Ronyn grins. "I vote pie. Prophecy revelations deserve pie."

We all chuckle, the laughter lightening the air. And for the first time in twenty summers, I feel the weight in my chest shift—not gone, but lighter, shared.

We're laughing. But beyond the laughter, the Stars are calling me home, and I'm answering.

I am the Lightborne.

CHAPTER SEVEN

THE LAUGHTER FADES, LEAVING A STILLNESS TOO FRAGILE TO
disturb. My family—the only people I've trusted with any piece of
myself—sits around me, their faces lit by the soft glow of the
lanterns. It's not just curiosity I see—it's something deeper. Something raw.

They're waiting. For answers. For the truth. For the pieces of my
life I've guarded like a fortress in my heart for all this time.

I grip the edges of my cloak, my fingers trembling. For so long,
I've hidden this part of myself—even from the people who mean the
most to me. But I can't anymore. The mark won't let me. The
prophecy won't. I won't.

Slowly, I remove my cloak and pull at my tunic, exposing my
collarbone, my shoulder, and finally, the etched Lightborne mark
that revealed itself tonight, almost blinding everyone in The
Tannery.

I've seen it only once before, in the heat of chaos and pain—as
if the mark responds to my distress, rising against the chains that
seek to bind it. Perhaps the magic thrumming through my veins isn't
just a force but a living thing, a spark of defiance pushing back
against its submissive bond. Even now, as its faint shimmer dances

across my skin, I feel it—a pull deep in my chest, like a fire begging to be unleashed. It's mine. And yet, it feels like it belongs to something far greater than me.

The mark is faint, not presently glowing, but its intricate lines almost imperceptibly shimmer with a silvery-gold hue that seems alive. The Stars stretch over my chest, the faint lines that connect the constellation glimmering softly from star to star.

The lantern light flickers across my skin, dancing with the Stars that have kept me in the shadows.

Seren gasps softly, her hand covering her mouth. She steps closer, her delicate hand hovering near the edge of the mark as if afraid to touch it. When her fingers finally brush my skin, her voice is barely a whisper. "It's beautiful, Elyssara," she breathes.

My name on her lips steals the breath from my lungs. For the first time, she knows me. It's no longer a curse or a burden—but something sacred. A quiet vow between family.

Ronyn sits up straighter, his usual bravado slipping as he stares. Revryn doesn't speak, his gaze fixed on the mark as if it holds every answer he's ever sought. Finally, he exhales, his voice low and steady. "Darlin', I've always known you were something extraordinary. I just didn't know the Stars would make it so... literal."

"This is why they came for me," I say quietly. "Why they killed my parents. Why I've been running ever since."

I reach into my boot, pulling out the piece of parchment I've carried for so long it feels like an extension of my soul. The edges are frayed, the ink faded, but the words are still legible—still seared into my memory. I could recite them without looking.

"My mother gave me this the night she died," I continue, unfolding the parchment with careful hands. "She said... she said it was my destiny. My vow. My purpose," I say, voice thick and weighed down from years of holding all of this alone.

I pause, the weight of that night pressing down on me like it always does. I glance at Revryn, his steady presence anchoring me, then at Seren and Ronyn, whose wide eyes remind me why I'm doing this.

"She said these words would guide me when the time came.

That I'd know when to act." My fingers trace the edges of the parchment. "I've been waiting twenty summers to feel ready. But I never have. And now... now, I don't think I can wait any longer."

I place the parchment on the floor between us, letting them see it for themselves. The prophecy, penned in my mother's elegant hand, gleams faintly beneath the lantern light:

> *"In the twenty-fifth summer beneath Lireal's Eye,*
> *The Lightborne shall rise where the Stars deny.*
> *Bound to the Sky, yet free from the flame,*
> *She carries the light—and an unspoken name.*
>
> *Five keys await to unbind her light,*
> *Where shadow and star must share the night.*
> *Beneath the temple where fears take form,*
> *The blade ignites and the veil is torn.*
>
> *On starlit peaks where the heavens sigh,*
> *The compass rests 'neath the watcher's eye.*
> *In shadowed depths where roots entwine,*
> *The crown reveals the path divine.*
>
> *Her skin shall glow with threads of light,*
> *Each relic found will burn more bright.*
> *Piece by piece, the Lightborne wakes,*
> *To bend the dark, the veil it breaks.*
>
> *Where ruins burn and the Flame-heart sleeps,*
> *The dragon stirs in the soul it keeps.*
> *And in the skies where wild winds sing,*
> *Beast and bond form a timeless ring.*
>
> *The Lightborne and Sky must tread as one,*
> *Their union unlocks what must be undone.*
> *Vengeance shall blaze to balance the scales,*
> *And justice shall rise where all else fails.*

When relics awaken and powers combine,
The chains will fall, and the Stars shall align.
Her destiny looms, unknown and untamed,
To balance the world or shatter the frame."

The words hang in the air, heavy with meaning.

"I've read it a thousand times," I whisper, my voice barely audible. "But tonight, for the first time, I feel it. The mark—the prophecy—it's calling me. And I don't know how to answer."

Revryn leans forward, his expression softer now, though his voice remains steady. "You're not answering it alone, darlin'. You never were."

Seren nods, her hand still hovering near my shoulder. "We'll figure it out, Isk—Elyssara," she corrects gently. "We're here."

Ronyn finally speaks, his grin returning, though it's tempered with something almost reverent. "Yeah. Besides, how hard can it be to save the world and take down a king? Sounds like a regular Tuesday."

The laughter that follows is shaky but real. I might not have to carry this weight alone.

The Stars have called me home—and this time, I'm ready to answer.

CHAPTER EIGHT

REVRYN SITS CROSS-LEGGED ON THE FLOOR, MAPS OF DRAVARA scattered around him in a chaotic constellation of parchment and ink. The weathered prophecy lies beside him, its faded lines catching the faint lantern light. Seren, ever the scholar, has barricaded herself behind a fortress of books, her fingers already tracing through pages in search of answers to what the Stars might demand of us next.

Revryn has lived in Virellin his entire life, but his time as a weaponsmith in the Royal Guard has taken him across the kingdom. He sourced steel from the volcanic forges of Vyrhal and traded designs with the artisans of Galreth. If anyone can decipher the locations of the keys or relics in the prophecy, it's him.

For as long as history has been recorded, maps have been among the most valuable weapons of war. They hold the power to shape battles, conquer empires, and protect borders. And nowhere is this power more desperately guarded than in The Shadow Wastes.

Some say The Wastes are preparing for war. That the fragile trade agreement with Dravara has fractured, perhaps even cracked clean through. But here in the slums, war's been at our door for years. This just makes it official.

No map of The Shadow Wastes exists in Dravara—not a single line of ink, not a whisper of terrain. Their realm has been shrouded in secrecy for centuries, its boundaries marked only by rumors and fear. All we know is that it's a land cursed by the Stars themselves— a barren, burning wasteland left ravaged after The Endless War between their people.

The border where Dravara and The Shadow Wastes meet— The Joining—is a battleground without end. For centuries, King Thalmyr has stationed Dravara's most grotesque and beastly border lords along its expanse, creating an unyielding line of defense. It's the only shred of gratitude I hold for him; whatever else he's done, he's kept The Wastes at bay.

Between The Joining and Virellin, Dravara's capital—home to The Lightborne Barrier and my own home in the slums—lies the Frael Forest. A mythical stretch of land filled with creatures, beasts, and nightmares, it is an unrelenting second line of defense against any Shadow mercenaries who breach The Joining.

I've never dared to enter the Frael Forest, only observed it from the edges. For those of us born to the slums, the Frael Forest has always been more than a boundary. It's a legend, a living nightmare whispered about in the flickering glow of oil lamps. Our parents, and their parents before them, tucked us into bed with stories of the forest's perils—not to soothe us, but to scare us into obedience. Don't stray too far, they'd say, their voices low and trembling. The shadows will take you. The roots will trap you. The beasts will devour you before you can scream.

Those stories weren't just warnings; they were laws, as binding as any royal decree. And we believed them. Better the peril you know than the horrors waiting in the Frael Forest. It kept us nestled in the slums, trapped in the predictable cage of poverty, but spared from the terrors beyond.

Even standing at its edge, the forest feels alive. The air carries an unnatural stillness, a silence that isn't empty but charged, as though the forest itself is watching. The Frael Forest is as much a mystery to me as The Shadow Wastes beyond it, but one thing is certain—if the prophecy takes us there, survival will not come easily.

Kael's words slice through my thoughts, sharp and inescapable.

If you'd like more answers, I'll be at the old outpost at the edge of the Frael Forest at daybreak. Bring your weapons. Your questions. I'll be there.

I look up from the maps to my family. "I know where to begin," I announce.

Ronyn stretches lazily, his grin sharper than usual. "Do enlighten us, El," he says, my real name rolling off his tongue with a casual ease that sends a flicker of warmth through my chest.

"The Frael Forest." My voice lands firmer than I feel. Like I believe it—because I have to.

Revryn's eyebrows shoot up in immediate protest. "The Frael Forest? Elyssara, I know you're the Lightborne, but that feels like walking into certain death," he scoffs.

I meet Revryn's gaze, steady despite the storm churning in my gut. Then I shift my focus to Ronyn, directing my next words at him. "We need to meet Kael," I say simply, though there's nothing simple about him. There's something in him—a pull, a dance, intrigue. Something that makes my magic stir. "He knew me. He *felt* me. If anyone can answer the questions we can't, it's him."

Ronyn's grin falters, just for a moment, before it returns—softer this time, edged with curiosity. "So, we march into the forest of death to have a chat with Shadow Boy. Sounds about right."

Revryn exhales heavily, dragging a hand down his face. "The Shadowweave from The Tannery?" His voice is sharp, tinged with the worry of a parent watching their child edge too close to danger. "Elyssara, please. Think this through. We'll find another way."

"I can feel it in my chest, Rev," I reply, the words shaky but resolute. I press a hand against the Lightborne mark, its faint heat a constant reminder of what I am, of what I can no longer ignore. "The marking... it responds to me. It's calling me." I take a breath, steadying myself. "This is as certain as I can be."

The fire in my chest thrums quietly, but with an intensity that demands to be heard. "The Frael Forest is where it begins. And if we want to survive this prophecy, we need answers. From him. He said he'd be at the edge of the forest—at the old outpost. At daybreak. We have to go."

Revryn's jaw tightens, his eyes narrowing as if weighing every possible consequence. The silence stretches, thick with unspoken fears and reluctant acceptance.

Finally, he exhales, his voice low and steady. "Get some sleep, then. We leave at daybreak."

CHAPTER NINE

I RUB THE HAZE OF SLEEP FROM MY EYES, THOUGH THE STING
lingers—an unwelcome reminder of how little rest I've managed.
We didn't descend to our bedrolls until well past the moon's peak,
and now, with daybreak fast approaching, the promise of more sleep
feels like a distant luxury.

We pack what little we can—dried meat, a handful of withered
fruit, and a meagre wedge of cheese. It's not much, and it won't last
long. Soon enough, we'll have to hunt, steal, or forage. But scarcity
is an old companion, and the gnawing uncertainty of our next meal
is as familiar to us as the air in our lungs.

I load my few belongings into the same canvas pack I've carried
since I was a child. The fabric is frayed and patched from years of
wear, the stitches a map of my life. But I can't bear to part with it. It
was my mother's. A rush of nostalgia washes over me as I remember
her vibrant, wide smile, deep green eyes full of defiance, and the
mess of russet and caramel hair that swayed across her mid-back as
she moved through The Black Stream market's bustling day trade.
She wore this very pack strapped across her body, her stride sure
and steady, as if she weren't starving, thirsty, and barely surviving.

I glance down at my own mess of hair cascading past my waist, though mine is a vibrant auburn that can't be missed—the same tattered pack now slung over my shoulder, and I know I have her eyes. The way they seem to glow like the Stars themselves, full of fire and defiance—the same she always carried. I can almost hear her voice, soft and insistent, whispering the destiny she believed I would fulfill. For a moment, the familiar ache of grief and heartbreak doesn't come. Instead, I feel something unexpected: pride.

I was born for this.

"I'm scared, Elyssara." Seren's voice pulls me from my thoughts. Sweet Seren, looking up at me through the wild curtain of her golden hair, her wide, innocent eyes brimming with unshed tears. Her bottom lip trembles slightly, and her voice wavers. "I'm not strong, and I'm not brave like you and Ronyn. I can't wield a blade or a bow, and I'm terrified I'll slow you down. Hold you back. Get us killed."

A lone tear escapes, tracing a path down her plump, rosy cheek and across the dusting of freckles that make her look far younger than the years she's survived.

"It's okay—we're probably going to die, anyway," Ronyn cuts in, grin lazy, timing as horrendous as ever.

"Ronyn!" I hiss, shooting him a glare sharp enough to draw blood. He shrugs, unapologetic, but at least has the decency to stay quiet.

Turning back to Seren, I crouch so we're eye to eye. "Little Star," I begin gently, using the nickname that's always soothed her—the same nickname my mother gave me. "I've been preparing you for this for years—I've always hoped you'd come with me when the time came. You are more ready than you realize. Your strength isn't in blades or bows." I press my fingers to her heart. "It's here." Then to her temple. "And here." I wipe the tear from her cheek with my thumb and squeeze her shoulder, letting my words settle into the space between us.

Her voice is a whisper, her hope fragile but growing. "Wh— What do you mean?"

"What have I asked you to read about over all these years?" I probe.

"Ah..." Her brow furrows as she searches for an answer. "Well, a lot of damn temples, that's for sure," she says, a wobbly smile tugging at her lips.

"And what else?" I prod gently, coaxing her along.

"Mountains, peaks, forests, villages, hunting... magic, of course. And the constellations," she rattles off the topics I've urged her to study.

"Good," I say, my voice steady but warm. I reach into my pack, pulling out the parchment that holds the prophecy. Its edges are worn from years of careful handling, the ink slightly faded but still clear. "Now, Little Star, read the prophecy."

Her fingers tremble as she takes the parchment, her eyes scanning the words at a speed only Seren could manage. She doesn't speak as she reads, her expression shifting from apprehension to dawning realization.

"I've been reading about the prophecy," she breathes, awe lacing her tone. Her eyes meet mine, her earlier fear replaced by something far stronger. "The locations, the keys... how we'll survive!" Realization dawns on her.

"That's right," I say, pride swelling in my chest. I watch as her back straightens, her shoulders squaring. The resolve blooming on her face is unmistakable. She's beginning to see her place in this— her gifts, her value.

"Not all wars are won with steel, Little Star," I say softly. "We have to be clever, too."

She nods, her fingers tightening around the parchment. The flicker of confidence in her eyes has become a steady flame, and I know now that she's ready. Or as ready as any of us can be.

"That reminds me," I unloop the leather on my satchel and pull out a single lunafleur to hold it in her line of sight. Lunafleur blooms exist only on dining tables of nobility behind The Lightborne Barrier in Virellin for just two months during the summer. "It's just like you," I say, pushing back her unruly curls and tucking the purple bloom behind her ear. "Beautiful. Sweet. Vibrant. And it hates the cold."

"Oh my flaming Stars!" She squeals, reaching her fingertips to the petals and gently smoothing her hair behind them. "It's magnificent," she breathes, then her eyes settle on me. "I can do this. I can guide us through this prophecy," her voice strengthened with resolve.

"I'm counting on it," I say with a wink.

"Great, now she's smarter and braver than me. Thanks, El. Way to raise the bar before we've even started." Ronyn, of course, swoops in to turn a beautiful moment into exasperation.

I can't help but let a smile tug at my lips. These people are my family. Wildly different paths have somehow converged here, and together we're about to leave behind the only thing we know better than anything else: the slums. This moment will mark both a beginning and an ending, and the weight of that is not lost on me.

I scan the loft, ensuring that we are somewhat organized— packs, water skins, bedrolls, food—but my gaze catches on Revryn. He's standing at the edge of the room, his eyes already on me, steady and unwavering. But something is off.

I glance around, suddenly noticing the absence of his belongings. My chest tightens. "Why aren't you packed?"

He shifts slightly, his gaze dropping to the floor for the first time. "Darlin'," he says softly, "I can't come with ya."

The words hit me like a blow. "What?" My voice is sharp with disbelief. "Why not?"

"The Royal Guard will know something is amiss as soon as I leave," he says softly, his voice laced with a weariness I've rarely heard. "They may still respect me, but they sure as hell don't trust me. I never leave the slums, and they know it. And..." His gaze finally lifts to mine, his expression solemn. "I'm too old for this journey. You need to forge this path on your own."

"But—" My throat tightens, the words tangling on the way out. "But, Revryn, I need you."

"No," he says firmly, stepping closer. "You don't. You never did. You've always had what you needed to survive—your strength, your grit, your heart. You've been more ready for this than you realize, Elyssara."

Tears prick at my eyes, but I refuse to let them fall. "I'm not ready. I—I can't do this without you."

"Yes, you can," he says, his tone soft but unyielding. "You're the best fighter I've ever trained—better than any Royal Guard I ever served beside. Too smart for your own good. And dammit, you're more beautiful than all the Stars in the sky. This is your destiny, darlin'. Yours to fulfill."

"But I don't want to do it without you," I whisper, the words escaping as a plea, a whimper, a truth.

Revryn places his hands on my shoulders, his grip firm and steady. "I've taught you everything I know. You carry it with you, in every strike, in every step. And when you're standing on the other side of this, victorious, I'll be right here, waiting for you to come home."

The dam breaks, a single tear slipping free as I lean into his touch. His words fill the cracks in my resolve, bittersweet and steadying.

"Now, go on," he says gently, his hands falling away. "You've got a world to save."

CHAPTER TEN

Ronyn, Seren, and I stand ready—or at least, as ready as we can be. Our blades are strapped, our bows slung, our nerves frayed. The weight of what lies ahead presses heavily on our shoulders. Readiness, I think, is something else entirely, but the sky is still cloaked in darkness, and daybreak is too close to linger any longer. It's time to leave.

Revryn pulls us into one last embrace, his arms strong and steady as they gather us close. His voice, gruff but filled with warmth, carries the weight of years and love. "I'm so proud of you. All of you. I love you like you are my own flesh and blood."

"Alright, alright, old man," Ronyn says, his lopsided grin in place, though there's a flicker of something softer in his eyes. "Let us be off before you start crying."

Seren steps back just enough to look Revryn in the eye, her voice trembling with sincerity. "Thank you, Revryn. For taking me in. For showing me what fatherly love should look like." She pauses, her hand briefly gripping his arm. "We'll see you when we come home."

Revryn's smile is small but full of pride. "You will," he says, his voice quiet but certain. He looks at each of us in turn, his gaze lingering on me last. "Move like the night, my loves."

On his final words, we slip out the window and into the darkness, the faintest whisper of his presence still clinging to the air behind us.

The perimeter of the slums is seldom guarded. It doesn't need to be. The Frael Forest, with its beasts and whispered tales of gnarled roots and death, is deterrent enough. Even the boldest slummer knows better than to test its boundaries. No one goes in, and no one comes out—a truth as ironclad as any law, enforced not by soldiers, but by fear itself.

We move silently through the thinning streets, our footsteps muffled by the dirt paths that give way to the tangled outskirts of the forest. The faint glow of the moon filters through the sparse forest to our right, casting ghostly shadows on the ground—the remnants of the slum's dirt streets still apparent on the forest's edge. My heart pounds in my chest, every beat echoing louder than I'd like against the oppressive stillness of the night.

Ronyn, ever the hunter, takes point, his movements swift and quiet as a shadow. Seren stays close behind me, her breathing uneven but controlled, while my senses remain razor sharp, scanning every flicker of movement, every sound that could betray an unwelcome presence.

The fraught silence of the forest edge carries an unsettling weight. The air is thick, charged with an almost predatory stillness, as though the forest itself is holding its breath, waiting to see if we dare cross its threshold.

Ronyn freezes suddenly, his hand shooting up in a signal for us to halt. My stomach clenches as I strain to see what's caught his attention, my eyes narrowing against the dim light, and I draw two blades from their sheathes at my thighs. There's a figure standing just ahead, half-shrouded in shadow but unmistakably there—a man, tall and broad-shouldered, leaning casually against the crumbling remains of an old stone outpost.

Kael.

Even in the dim light, I can make out the sharp lines of his jaw, the faint gleam of steel strapped across his back, and the air of calm command that clings to him like a second skin. My stomach twists despite myself. Stars, he's... striking. Broad shoulders tapering into a lean, powerful frame, every inch of him exudes the quiet confidence of someone who knows exactly what he's capable of. He's not just handsome; he's arresting in a way that demands attention. A warrior. Dangerous. And yet, despite the raw power in his stance, there's an elegance to him—a kind of predatory grace that makes it impossible to look away.

It grates on me. He *knows* what he looks like. I can see it in the way he tilts his head, in the deliberate calm of his gaze as it locks on to mine. *I'm not staring,* I tell myself. *I'm assessing a threat.*

But something else catches my attention—a second figure, emerging from the shadows at his side. Taller, leaner, but no less imposing, with a quiet intensity that seems to radiate from him like heat. His presence is a stark contrast to Kael's measured stillness—dangerous, coiled energy barely restrained beneath a calm exterior.

"Who the fuck is that?" Ronyn mutters under his breath, his voice barely audible.

"I don't know," I murmur, though my eyes stay locked on Kael. He hasn't moved, hasn't so much as shifted his weight, but I can feel the intensity of his gaze on me, sharp and unyielding, and I return the same.

Ronyn doesn't wait for an answer. In one fluid motion, he draws an arrow from his quiver, nocks it, and releases it with deadly precision—all in the span of a heartbeat.

"Ronyn, no!" The words tear from my throat too late.

The arrow slices through the air, missing Kael's head by less than an inch, heading straight for the second figure, but he almost imperceptibly moves at the last moment, and the arrow embeds itself into the stone wall behind him with a resounding *thunk*. Kael doesn't flinch. Not even a blink. He tilts his head slightly, his gaze flicking to the arrow before sliding back to Ronyn with a calm that's far more unnerving than anger.

The second figure moves then, lightning-fast, stepping forward with a hand already on the hilt of his blade, his sharp eyes scanning us like a predator assessing its prey.

"Easy, Therion," Kael says, his voice low but laced with authority. His companion—Therion, apparently—hesitates for a moment before releasing the hilt, though the tension in his posture doesn't ease.

"Interesting way to greet an ally," Kael drawls, his gaze settling on me now, dark and unreadable. "Though I suppose I can't fault your instincts. You've kept yourself alive this long."

Ronyn bristles, clearly unrepentant. "Maybe next time don't skulk around like a fucking shadow."

"Maybe next time aim better," Kael replies, his tone so even it takes a second for the insult to register.

"Enough," I cut in, stepping forward before Ronyn can escalate things further. My voice is steady, though my heart is racing. "We're not allies. You said you'd meet us. We're here. Let's not waste time."

Kael's expression doesn't shift, but I catch the faintest flicker of something in his eyes—approval, maybe, or recognition. He gestures toward the outpost with a tilt of his head. "Inside, then. We've got much to discuss."

CHAPTER ELEVEN

WE ENTER THE CRUMBLING OUTPOST, DEVOURED BY TIME AND THE elements, as the dawn sky begins to lighten, revealing us more clearly to one another. The space is stark—stone walls worn thin, a fractured ceiling allowing slivers of golden sunlight to pierce through. Dust swirls faintly in the still air—a calm contrast to the storm raging inside my chest.

The silence here feels heavy, as though the walls remember every word ever spoken within them. Forgotten words, for a forgotten place. But then again, so is everyone on this side of The Lightborne Barrier.

Ronyn leans against the wall, his bow slung lazily over his shoulder, though his sharp gaze flicks back and forth between Kael and his companion, Therion. Ronyn doesn't trust either of them—and I can't blame him.

Seren stays close, clutching her worn book like a lifeline. Her eyes dart toward Therion too often, brows furrowed, as if she can feel the weight of his gaze, his lingering attention.

I turn to confront him, my lips parting to ask what in the Stars he's staring at, but Therion speaks first, his graveled voice slicing through the silence like a blade.

"Let's skip the niceties," he says, leaning against a cracked pillar. His tone drips with disdain, as though our very existence offends him. "I see three people who wouldn't last a day in the forest—let alone The Wastes. You can't fight, can't lead, and from the looks of it, you react on impulse." He jabs a finger at Ronyn.

The words sting sharper than I'd like to admit. Ronyn stiffens, jaw tight, but I step forward before he can speak, my voice sharp as steel.

"If we're truly so useless, go on without us," I say, my glare piercing his like a blade through armor. "It is you—or rather, your companion—who requested to meet us here. If we're not dignified enough for your delicate sensibilities, quite frankly, Therion"—I let his name curl like a curse—"you can fuck right off. I don't see you fulfilling the prophecy in my stead."

I hear Seren's sharp inhale of breath beside me.

For a heartbeat, I wonder if I've pushed too far. Therion doesn't flinch. Instead, the corner of his mouth quirks upward, faintly amused, like a predator who's found its prey interesting.

"You're bold, Lightborne," he murmurs, voice low, eyes shadowed. "I'll give you that. But bold doesn't mean capable. Words won't stop greedy kings from tearing you apart, no matter how sharply you spit them."

Ronyn pushes off the wall, knuckles white around his bow.

"We've handled worse than the likes of you," he snaps.

Therion doesn't even blink, his gaze sliding to Ronyn as if he's nothing more than a mildly bothersome fly.

"Pride kills faster than steel," he mutters, more warning than threat.

I open my mouth to retort, anger simmering, but Kael steps forward. His voice cracks through the tension like a whip.

"Enough."

We freeze. There's an irrefutability in his tone, as if even the air bends to his command. Therion stands down, his silence a reluctant surrender, and I hate the way it only amplifies Kael's presence—commanding, effortless, unshakable.

"So, you are the Lightborne," Kael says—a statement, not a question. His gaze cuts through me, stripping me bare. I can feel it —like he sees my thoughts, my soul, my *secrets* laid bare before him.

I lift my chin, forcing my spine straighter. "I am," I say, though the words don't carry the strength I intend.

Because it's hard to feel like a prophesied savior when you're standing in a tunic and linen pants that have been worn for seven days straight. My clothes are threadbare and filthy, held together with Revryn's stitching. I feel naked. Exposed. Ill-equipped to bear this title—or fulfill this destiny.

My destiny.

A knot tightens in my chest. Doubt whispers its poisonous truths: *You're not ready. You're not enough.*

But as if answering the unspoken question, the mark on my chest flares. Heat blossoms beneath my ribs, and a burst of golden light spills through the fabric and lights up the outpost for barely a heartbeat—a flare of power, of defiance, that silences every doubt.

It burns beneath my ribs. Not a flare of magic—but a claim. One I can't run from anymore.

I am the Lightborne.

Kael's gaze flicks to the light spilling from my mark, lingering for a moment before returning to my face. His eyes are piercing, scrutinizing, as if he can see into the depths of me. There's something there—recognition, curiosity—but it's gone as quickly as it came.

"How did you know it was me in The Tannery?" I ask, unable to keep the edge from my voice. "You helped me before my mark flared. How could you tell?"

He hesitates, just enough for me to notice, and when he speaks his voice is measured, deliberate. "I could *feel* you," he admits. "Your magic, your presence—it's unlike anything I've sensed before. It's not just power. It's *alive*. Fighting to break free."

"But how?" I press, my frustration bubbling to the surface. "My magic is bound. I've never felt it—not even a flicker—except for the two times my mark has flared. I can't wield it. *At all*."

Kael's expression doesn't shift. "I'm a Shadowweave. My magic is connected to our darkness, what lurks within. That's the best explanation I have. I sensed you before I saw you—your magic was... *different*. When I saw you in The Underbelly, I followed you."

"Followed me?" I echo, my irritation sharp. "Why?"

"Because I thought you might be who I was looking for." His tone is infuriatingly calm, as if that explanation should satisfy me.

"Thought?" I shoot back. "So you weren't sure?"

Kael's smirk returns, faint but infuriating. "Not until your mark flared. Until then, I was just watching some girl set a wagon ablaze to create her own cover." He pauses for a heartbeat, and I'm unsure if he'll continue, but he adds, "Wondering if what I felt was real."

I swallow thickly, the memory of the wagon burns at the edges of my mind, but I push it aside. My voice hardens. "And why were you in Virellin to begin with? What were you looking for? You're clearly not from here," I say, referencing his accent that I can't place.

Kael's expression grows guarded, his piercing gaze meeting mine without flinching. "I was there for Obsidian Shards. Therion needed them to conceal his magic," he explains simply. "And no, we're not from here."

His voice is clipped, so I don't push the latter. "Conceal it from *whom*?" I press. My curiosity—and irritation—deepens as I notice Therion stiffening at the mention of his magic.

Kael's answer comes slowly, as though he's weighing each word. "Therion is an Aetherstride. The most gifted tracker on the continent. His magic makes him an invaluable ally, but it also makes him... *noticeable*."

Seren, who has been silent until now, tilts her head. "Noticeable to *whom*?"

"To every Starborn in Dravara who can sense magic," Kael replies, his tone even. "We needed to track someone in Virellin, and we needed to do it without notice from the Royal Guard."

His words land heavily, the weight of what he's saying settling like a stone in my gut. I glance at Therion, whose jaw is tight, his sharp gaze locked on Kael. It's clear this isn't the whole story, but I decide to push forward with the more pressing question.

"And who were you looking for in Virellin?" My voice softens, but it's no less pointed. "Who were you tracking?"

Kael doesn't hesitate this time. His answer is simple, stark. "You, Lightborne."

CHAPTER TWELVE

"WHAT DO YOU WANT FROM ME?" I ASK, NARROWING MY EYES. "What could I possibly do for you?"

Though I suspected Kael had been looking for me, hearing him confirm it sends a sharp pang through my chest. His help in The Tannery wasn't selfless. He needs me alive—*for now*. And if he's anything like the men I've dealt with in the slums, he plans to use me for his own gain. I've been party to these kinds of deals since I was just five summers old. They never come without strings.

Kael's expression sharpens, heavy with meaning. "I have a feeling you could do plenty for me, Lightborne," he replies smoothly. "But what I want is to strike a mutually beneficial deal. Our goals align in this case, and I believe we can help each other."

Therion shifts uncomfortably, the distaste in his expression unmistakable. He seems to tolerate Kael's leadership, but there's an air of reluctance. Their dynamic intrigues me—a subtle but undeniable hierarchy. It's not familial; their contrasting appearances make that clear enough. Kael's ocean-blue eyes and broad, warrior's frame are as different from Therion's lean build, dirty-blonde hair, and sharp hazel gaze as night is from day. Yet Therion defers to him, even now. I file the observation away for later.

"A deal, you say?" I tilt my head, feigning casual interest. "And what exactly can you do for *me*? More importantly, what do you want in return?"

Kael steps closer, his tone even but commanding. "We will help you fulfill the prophecy. We'll accompany you to uncover the relics, protect you on the journey. In return, I need to use one of the relics."

I don't trust him. The deal sounds too clean, too convenient. As Gellesk once told me, *if it looks like gold, it's probably gilded.* I've lived by that truth ever since. Trust, in Virellin, is just another currency—rare, expensive, and easily faked.

"And which relic would that be?" I press, my voice cool. "And why?"

Kael's amusement flickers in his eyes. "Are you always this distrusting, Lightborne?"

"Yes," I reply curtly.

He doesn't miss a beat. "The compass."

"For?"

Therion's sharp intake of breath cuts through the air. He drags a hand down his face, clearly displeased. "Kael," he warns. "No. We'll find another way." His voice is tight with caution, his posture rigid with tension.

Kael ignores him, his focus locked on me. His gaze lingers—assessing, calculating. Finally, he speaks, his tone stripped of its earlier confidence, replaced by something rawer.

"King Maldrak of The Shadow Wastes is holding my sister captive." The words are steady, but there's grief in his eyes that can't be feigned. "We've tried to rescue her twice. Both times, we failed, and many good men died. We have failed to breach the inner walls of Kryntar Castle at all." He pauses for a heartbeat, exhaling deeply. "The compass is said to point to the user's truest desire. For me, that's my sister."

His admission catches me off guard. For a moment, I see him not as a Shadowweave or a potential enemy, but as a brother desperate to save his family. My chest tightens. I know that kind of longing—the ache of wanting to protect what little you have left. But I can't let sympathy cloud my judgment. The slums are full of soft stories and bleeding hearts. And every one of them ends in betrayal. I've learned the hard way—compassion doesn't keep you alive.

"Very altruistic," I say, forcing my voice to remain sharp. "But we don't need your help."

Kael's lips twitch as if suppressing a smile. "And how, exactly, will you navigate the forest? Or The Shadow Wastes? How will you slip past borders, outmaneuver guards, and survive the beasts waiting to devour you?"

His tone is infuriatingly calm, but Stars help me, he's right.

"We'll manage," I protest, though the words feel hollow even to me. I can practically feel Ronyn's incredulous gaze burning into the side of my head. He knows I'm fighting a losing battle, and worse, so does Kael.

So do I.

Kael steps closer, his voice dropping to a near whisper. "Elyssara, we both know you won't make it without us," he croons, almost teasing.

Surprise ripples through my body—*he knows my name. My true name.*

He notices my astonishment and that infuriating smirk kicks up his lips, "You really can't be that surprised we know who you are, Lightborne—the world has been looking for Elyssara, the Light-borne who escaped conscription, for twenty years."

I scowl in his direction, "No one knew my name—no one... until last night."

"We put two and two together, Elyssara. As soon as your magic flared, I knew who you were—just wanted to see if you'd admit it. Now, lay down your sword, so to speak, and accept some genuine help. A fair deal—for both of us."

"El," Ronyn pleads, his tone uncharacteristically serious. "He's right."

I glance at Ronyn, then at Seren, whose wide eyes are filled with worry but also quiet resolve. My heart clenches. For them—for the prophecy—I can't afford to let pride or mistrust get in the way. I take a steadying breath, my gaze locking with Kael's.

"What guarantees do I have that you won't betray me?"

Kael's expression softens with relief as if he's won—as if he can feel that I'm about to agree. "The same guarantees I have that you won't betray me. None."

CHAPTER THIRTEEN

As the light of day strengthens and the summer sun begins to blaze down, we clear a space on the outpost floor. The cracked stone beneath us becomes our makeshift table, where we spread out maps and the prophecy, preparing for the journey ahead. The dynamics of our newfound "team" are impossible to ignore—Ronyn seems far too pleased to have some other men on his side, Seren looks as though she might bolt at the slightest sound, Kael exudes infuriating smugness, and Therion... well, Therion seems pissed off. *Some team we make.*

"I've always assumed we'd just start from the first paragraph," I say, running my fingers over the delicate lines of my mother's handwriting. Her words feel alive under my touch, each stroke of ink a reminder of everything that's brought me to this moment. I clear my throat and recite:

> *"In the twenty-fifth summer beneath Lireal's Eye,*
> *The Lightborne shall rise where the Stars deny.*
> *Bound to the Sky, yet free from the flame,*
> *She carries the light—and an unspoken name."*

I glance around the group. "It was my Starday three days ago. So, I guess I'm officially in my twenty-fifth summer." I take a breath, willing confidence into my voice. "And I've reclaimed my name. Elyssara." My name on my lips feels like a rebellion against my past. I say it not in secret, not in defiance, but aloud, in the daylight, with them all watching.

I pause, glancing down at the parchment. "The next paragraph?"

Kael's eyes are already on me, steady and unyielding. "Bless the Stars for your birth, Elyssara," he says, his tone low but carrying the weight of sincerity. My name on his lips does something traitorous to my chest, heat blooming in my cheeks.

It's an ancient phrase—spoken only on a child's naming day among the Starborn. I blink. *Why does it feel like a vow?*

His hand lifts, brushing gently against my upper arm as he speaks.

Then, light flares.

It's not subtle. It crackles beneath his fingertips, sparking in the air around us in a golden burst that seems to ripple outward.

Kael jerks his hand back, inhaling sharply at the magic sparking under his touch. He tries to keep his features neutral, but I see the way his eyes flare almost imperceptibly. He's just as shocked as I am.

Everyone freezes.

Ronyn, of course, is the first to break the silence. "Wow. All that for *him* touching you? Should I be jealous—or taking notes?" His grin is almost gleeful.

My cheeks flare red again, and Therion huffs an almost imperceptible laugh, but I ignore it.

Kael doesn't look surprised. His gaze flickers between me and the fading glow around us, his brow furrowing in thought. "It's your magic," he says finally, his voice quieter now, as though the words carry a weight only he can feel. "It must be... *responding.*"

"To what?" I snap, though my voice is barely more than a whisper.

"To you... Your emotions," he says simply.

"And what were you feeling, El?" Ronyn snorts, wiggling his eyebrows up and down, nudging his chin toward Kael.

I shoot him a fierce glare, trying but failing to not rise to the bait. I turn back to the group, and Kael's eyes lock on mine, a mix of curiosity and something far more elusive—reverence, maybe, or familiarity. Whatever it is, it sends a shiver down my spine, and for a fleeting moment, I forget how to breathe.

"It's never done that before," I admit, trying to steady my voice, though I can't hide my unease. "Maybe it's just... getting more active now that I'm in my twenty-fifth summer? I don't know." My fingers fidget with the edge of the parchment, eager to move the conversation along. "Anyway, let's move to the next paragraph?"

I clear my throat, the words etched in my memory spilling out:

> *"Five keys await to unbind her light,*
> *Where shadow and star must share the night.*
> *Beneath the temple where fears take form,*
> *The blade ignites and the veil is torn."*

I glance around, trying to gauge their reactions.

"I think I know where to begin," Seren says softly, her voice barely cutting through the weight of the moment.

"What do you know, Little Star?" I prompt, my tone gentle but encouraging, hoping to bolster her confidence.

Seren hesitates, her eyes darting around self-consciously. But then she sits a little straighter, resolve flickering to life in her expression. "There are legends of a temple beyond the Frael Forest, near Mount Lyssar. It's said to be protected by an enchantment. Many think it's a myth, but some claim to have entered and returned... *different*. They speak of seeing loved ones long gone to the Stars and facing terrors they can't describe. It fits the prophecy's description."

The room goes still, Seren's words hanging heavy in the air.

Therion's constant gaze shifts, sharpening as it settles on Seren. His jaw tightens, and I brace for one of his cutting remarks. But when he speaks, his tone is softer, though still edged with curiosity.

"Not bad, little girl. Are you... Starborn?" His eyes narrow in scepticism.

Seren's eyes sharpen, her anger flaring brighter than I've ever seen. "No, I'm not Starborn—thanks for confirming I'm not 'blessed.' Just ordinary. Or would you prefer 'inferior'?"

Therion blinks, visibly taken aback by her sudden boldness. His voice softens, almost apologetic. "I mean no offence... I just thought I could sense magic—*something*—on you."

"Well, you don't. I'm ordinary," Seren snaps, her voice sharp as a blade. Then she stands, brushing imaginary dust off her linen skirt, and squares her shoulders. "Now, shall we get this blade or what?"

The silence that follows is deafening.

Ronyn, of course, is the first to break it. "Well, I guess we're going to Mount Lyssar," he says, slinging his bow over his shoulder with a grin. "Can't wait to meet these ghosts Seren was talking about. Sounds like a good time."

Kael nods once, his expression unreadable, though his eyes linger on Seren a moment longer. "Mount Lyssar, then," he says. "We leave immediately."

And so, the next verse of the prophecy begins—with us walking straight into it.

CHAPTER FOURTEEN

There is only one way to get to Lyssar Temple, and that is through the Frael Forest and over Mount Lyssar. Kael and Therion estimate it'll take at least two weeks on foot if we move fast and rest little. That path leaves us vulnerable and exposed to jagged terrain, unknown beasts, the Royal Guard, and the volatile temper of the elements.

We've barely eaten, have next to no supplies, and only one water skin between us—we need horses. Horses in the slums are a rarity—I've never ridden one, only seen the towering beasts that the Royal Guard trample through our streets.

We venture deeper into the outskirts of the Frael Forest to a place called Duskridge Hollow: a hidden trading post Kael knows. It's not a safe place, but it's our best chance to find horses.

Duskridge Hollow is a grimy, forgotten corner of the realm. It is nothing more than a cluster of crooked wooden structures and sagging tents pitched in a clearing. The air is thick with the tang of sweat, leather, and cheap alcohol. Traders and scavengers linger in doorways and around makeshift stalls, their eyes glinting with suspicion and thinly veiled hunger. The entire place smells like despera-

tion, and yet, as I step into its shadowy heart, a thrill pulses
through me.

I have been to plenty of places I shouldn't have, but never this
far from the slums. The realization that I am no longer in Virellin
unfurls in my chest like the first breath of clean air after a storm. It's
disconcerting but liberating. I shouldn't feel this way—not with eyes
watching our every move and hands resting too casually on
weapons, but I can't help it.

Kael strides ahead like he owns the place, his confidence carving
a path through the wary stares. He leads us to the far end of the
settlement, where a sagging stable leans precariously against a
cluster of trees. A surly man with a scar cleaved through his cheek
steps out of the shadows, one eye clouded and sightless. The other
gleams with a calculation that makes my skin crawl.

"Horses ain't cheap," the man growls, his voice as rough as
gravel. His gaze sweeps over us, lingering on our threadbare clothes
and empty hands. "And you don't look like you've got anything
worth trading."

Kael steps forward, his tone calm but firm. "We're not here to
waste your time. We need five horses strong enough to handle the
Frael Forest."

The man barks a laugh, a harsh sound that grates on my nerves.
"Five? You've got big dreams for people who can't even afford new
clothes." He gestures at Seren, Ronyn, and me with a sneer before
turning back to Kael. But when his gaze lands on Kael's well-fitted
leathers, polished and clearly of high quality, his expression flickers
with something like caution.

Kael's presence seems to expand, his posture unyielding.
Therion stands just behind him, a silent force that makes the man
take half a step back.

"We can pay," Kael says. "Or we can trade."

The man raises a sceptical eyebrow, his good eye narrowing.
"What've you got? Coin is no use around here. It holds no value.
Trade is our currency. So what is it? Food? Weapons? A fucking
miracle?"

We pool our belongings, placing them in a sad little pile at the man's feet—Ronyn's spare knife, a few arrows from his quiver, and some of our dried provisions. The man doesn't even try to hide his disdain as he kicks at the pile with the toe of his boot.

"This won't even get you a mule," he says, his voice dripping with scorn.

Kael's jaw tightens, the tension in his shoulders visible. "What do you want?"

The man's one good eye narrows as he points a gnarled finger at Kael's swords strapped across his back, the steel gleaming faintly in the murky light. "Those."

Kael's hand moves instinctively to the sword at his hip, his hands curling around the hilt as if he's about to cut down the man for simply asking. "They're not on offer," he says coldly, his voice a low growl.

"Then you've got nothing I want," the man snaps, turning away with a shrug. "Come back when you're worth my time."

Fuck. We need this trade. There is no way we'll make it without horses. I can sense that One Eye wants to deal—his greed is written all over his face. He's looking for something unique, something he can boast about. That's why he wants Kael's swords.

I hesitate, my fingers brushing the fabric of my tunic over my left biceps. My mother's marriage cuff—a delicate piece of beaten silver etched with intricate designs. It is the last remnant of a life I barely remember. I've worn it every day since I was a child, its weight a constant reminder of her love, her defiance. To give it up feels like cutting away the last tether to her memory.

My chest tightens as I unclasp it, its cool weight slipping from my arm. Giving it up feels like giving up *her*. But the living matter more than the dead.

I pull down the shoulder of my tunic, exposing bare skin, my mark mercifully lying dormant. For a moment, I feel Kael's gaze dart to my shoulder, lingering. It's subtle, but I catch it in the periphery of my vision—his eyes tracing the exposed curve of my skin before flicking to the cuff in my hand. Heat rises to my cheeks, but I don't lower my arm.

I hold the cuff out, my voice steady despite the ache in my chest. "Will this do?"

The man's good eye narrows as he takes the cuff, turning it over in his hands like it's a priceless treasure. His thumb drags across the intricate etchings, a spark of recognition flickers in his face. But it vanishes as quickly as it came, consumed by the cold greed that twists his features.

Out of the corner of my eye, I catch Kael's reaction. His jaw tightens, the muscles in his neck taut with restraint. His fists curl at his sides, and he takes a deliberate half-step forward, as if he's about to snatch the cuff back. His gaze locks on to me, burning with unspoken words—protest, frustration, or something else entirely.

"Elyssara—," he warns, but I cut him off.

"It's already done," I snap, dismissing him.

"For this... three horses. No more," One Eye says, his voice as casual as if we were bartering for scraps.

Ronyn stiffens beside me, his indignation palpable. "Three? There are five of us!"

The man shrugs, tucking the cuff into his pocket with infuriating ease. "It's all I've got. Take it or leave it."

Kael's voice cuts through the tension like a blade. "We'll take them."

We haggled longer than I thought possible, wringing two extra water skins and a small bundle of dried meat from One Eye in exchange for my mother's marriage cuff. It wasn't a fair trade— nothing about it was—but life isn't fair. I can't cling to the past at the cost of our future.

As we lead the horses away from Duskridge Hollow, I can't help but glance back at the trader's pocket where my cuff disappeared. A part of me feels like I've left a piece of myself behind.

"It's only silver," I lie to myself as we walk away.

The farther we walk the horses away from the settlement to regroup and plan for our first journey together, the more the shadows of the Frael Forest encroach. Its jagged canopy weaves a tangled web of darkness, cutting the sunlight to threads. A cold mist seeps from its depths, a sharp contrast to the blistering summer heat that clings to the outside world. The eerie calls of unseen creatures echo from within, each sound a reminder of what awaits us.

The oppressive silence is broken by Ronyn's familiar voice. "So, shall we address the obvious problem here? Has anyone thought about how exactly we're getting five people on three horses?"

I sigh heavily. *Yes, obviously.*

"No," I snap, my tone short.

Kael's lips twitch into a smirk, his expression thick with mischief. "You're a terrible liar, Lightborne."

Before I can retort, Therion cuts in, his voice as sharp and unyielding as ever. "I ride alone."

His tone leaves no room for discussion, not that anyone would particularly enjoy sharing a horse with the grumpy bastard, anyway.

"I'll ride with Seren," I say quickly, trying to defuse the tension.

But Ronyn, ever the thorn in my side, crosses his arms indignantly. "There's no fucking way I'll be sharing a horse with one of these beasts, thank you very much. And Seren's not going anywhere near them, either."

For the love of all the Stars in the sky. I would never let Seren ride with either of these men, both of whom look like they could kill someone with a single glance.

"Kael and Therion can share. I'll ride alone," I offer, though I already know how this is going to end.

"NO," the two men bark in unison, their voices firm and resolute.

"You're with me, Duskae," Kael purrs, his voice like velvet and smoke. His gaze pins me, heavy with meaning. "There's no way you're leaving my sight—I've waited years for you."

Something in his tone—a promise, a warning, or maybe both—makes my pulse race. His words are layered, and I crave to unravel them, to push and prod until I understand. But I swallow the urge and settle for incredulity. "Duskae?" I snap.

Therion's eyes dart to Kael in shock. His mouth presses into a thin line, and he shakes his head, as if in disbelief.

"Duskae," he echoes. "Suits you," he says, but doesn't elaborate.

I grunt in frustration. Every answer this man gives me only creates more questions.

"I'll make it entertaining," Kael promises, a teasing lilt in his voice as the corner of his mouth quirks upward.

"Let's just get it over with," I mutter, unable to hide my exasperation. The amusement on Kael's face deepens, but there's something else there too—a warmth in his gaze that sends heat spiraling through my chest. The way he looks at me is unnerving, as if he sees something no one else does.

The word pulses through my mind like a drumbeat.

Duskae.

Duskae.

Duskae.

I don't know why, but something about it feels familiar, warm, despite his teasing tone.

Duskae.

CHAPTER FIFTEEN

Kael swings onto the russet mare with a grace that borders on terrifying. His movements are fluid, effortless, like the horse is an extension of him. He reaches a hand down to me, his expression softening into something unexpectedly sincere.

I hesitate. The loss of my mother's cuff still weighs heavily, and now *this*—a forced closeness that feels too intimate, too exposing.

I place my foot in the stirrup, my heart pounding as Kael's hand wraps around mine. His grip is strong, steady, and for a moment, I feel anchored.

As our palms meet, something twists in my chest. Then it happens—a vibrant gold light flares, rippling through me, warm and alive. A traitorous response to his touch. My breath catches, and I squeeze my eyes shut, willing the sensation to fade.

This is the second time my power has flared at Kael's touch, and I can't ignore it anymore. My magic—wild yet bound—seems to recognize him, to respond to him in ways I can't explain.

Kael doesn't pull away. If anything, his grip tightens slightly, his gaze lingering on my glowing chest with an unreadable expression. For once, he doesn't smirk or tease.

"Are you all right?" he asks, his voice low, almost gentle.

"I'm fine," I reply quickly, though my voice wavers.

As he helps me settle in front of him, his arms brush against mine, and I can feel the heat radiating from him. It's infuriating and comforting all at once, and I hate the way my body seems to lean into his presence.

Behind us, Ronyn groans. "This is going to be a long ride."

Then, we cross the threshold.

We enter the Frael Forest.

CHAPTER SIXTEEN

THERION RIDES AT THE FRONT, HIS POSTURE STRAIGHT AND ALERT. Every movement of his horse is calculated and efficient. His sharp eyes dart to every sound or shadow that could signify danger, his focus unwavering.

Ronyn and Seren, sandwiched between us, are an entirely different story. They seem to inhabit a world of their own, their hushed conversation peppered with muffled snickers and not-so-subtle glances in our direction. Whatever they're whispering about, it's enough to make Seren bury her face in her hands, shoulders shaking with barely contained laughter.

Ronyn's voice carries just enough for me to catch snippets—teasing, exaggerated, and undoubtedly ridiculous. His dramatic gestures only make Seren laugh harder, her face flushed with joy.

Despite myself, I feel a smile tug at the corners of my lips. Ronyn is relentless in his role as her self-appointed big brother, and it's impossible to miss how fiercely protective he is of her. He's always been this way—brash and irreverent on the surface, but with a heart that beats for the people he loves.

"Honestly, how do you put up with him?" Kael murmurs from behind me, his voice laced with quiet amusement.

"Ronyn? He's harmless," I reply, my voice softer than intended. "He just wants to make Seren smile. It's... his thing."

Kael hums thoughtfully. "His thing?"

I glance over at Ronyn, who is now pretending to mimic Therion's stoic demeanor, puffing out his chest and narrowing his eyes in what he probably thinks is an intimidating glare. Seren giggles uncontrollably, nearly sliding off their horse in the process.

"Yeah," I say, shaking my head. "He's always been like this. A clown, sure, but he's also the one who shields her from the harsh realities of life in the slums or takes the heat when things go wrong. He's... family to her. *To us.*"

Kael is silent for a moment, his gaze following mine. "Family," he echoes, his tone softer now, contemplative.

Ahead of us, Ronyn has clearly decided to double down on his antics. He reaches over and plucks a leaf from a passing branch, placing it atop his head like a crown. "I dub thee, Lady Seren of the Hollow!" he declares, his voice mockingly regal.

Seren swats at him, her laughter unrestrained. "You're ridiculous, Ronyn!"

"And yet, I'm your favorite," he quips, his grin wide and shameless.

Seren rolls her eyes but doesn't deny it. Instead, she leans slightly toward him, her earlier nervousness about the journey momentarily forgotten.

It's a small moment, but it feels significant—a pocket of warmth in the midst of the unknown.

Kael's voice draws me back. "You're awfully quiet," he murmurs, low enough that the others can't hear.

"Maybe I just enjoy the silence," I reply, though the edge in my tone doesn't land as sharply as I'd like.

His chuckle is soft, almost amused. "Somehow, I doubt that. You don't strike me as the type of woman to stay silent unless you've got something on your mind."

I tense, and his grip on the reins adjusts, his hands steady but not intrusive. "I'm thinking about the temple," I say quickly, trying to steer the conversation elsewhere.

"Hmm," he hums, unconvinced. "The temple, or the cuff you just traded?"

The words hit harder than they should. I stiffen, and Kael must sense it because his tone softens slightly. "It's not easy, letting go of something like that."

"It's just a piece of silver," I lie.

"Is it?" he presses gently. "Because the way you hesitated... it seemed like it was more than that."

I don't respond. I can't. The lump in my throat is too big, and the weight of his words too heavy. My silence, apparently, is answer enough.

"You didn't have to do that," Kael says after a moment. His voice is quieter now, almost reluctant. "I would've given a sword if we couldn't find another trade."

I turn slightly, angling my head so I can glance back at him. His expression is unreadable, but there's something in his eyes—a mix of guilt and gratitude that I wasn't expecting.

"It's done," I say, more for myself than for him. "And we needed the horses."

His gaze lingers on me for a beat longer before he nods, the conversation dropping as quickly as it began.

Ahead of us, Ronyn lets out a loud laugh, and Seren swats at him playfully, her cheeks flushed with either embarrassment or joy —or both. The sound cuts through the tension between Kael and me, and for a fleeting moment, I envy their ease.

"Does he ever stop?" Kael mutters, a faint smirk tugging at the corner of his mouth.

"Not if he's awake," I reply drily. For the first time since we mounted the horse, I let myself smile.

Kael notices. I can feel it in the subtle shift of his posture, the faint loosening of his grip on the reins. It's as if my smile disarms him, even if just for a fleeting moment.

We ride in a silence that feels almost companionable, though I'm wildly aware of every slight movement of his hands. His left hand holds the reins loosely, while his right arm brackets my waist, his palm resting low and steady at my hip. The weight of it is steady, grounding, and maddeningly distracting.

Sometimes I think I feel his fingers brushing gently, almost imperceptibly, in small circles. My breath hitches, and I glance down quickly, only to find his hand still, resting where it has been since we started. My cheeks burn with a flush I'm grateful he can't see.

But when his hand shifts slightly, pressing against my lower stomach as the horse adjusts its stride, I startle out of my thoughts. It hits me like cold water—how much space he's taken up in my mind, how he's crept beneath my skin. I force myself to focus on my surroundings.

Kael shifts subtly behind me. Just enough to remind me he's still watching the world through a warrior's lens. Still watching me.

The forest around us grows darker, denser, the towering trees forming an oppressive shelter between us and the sky above. Their gnarled branches twist like bony hands clawing at the sky, blotting out the light. A damp, heavy mist clings to the forest floor, curling around the horses' hooves and muffling the sound of their steps. The air smells of damp earth and decaying leaves.

Then, suddenly, the atmosphere shifts.

The easy rhythm of hoofbeats falters as the eerie stillness takes hold. The distant calls of birds and the rustle of unseen creatures vanish, swallowed by an unnatural quiet that presses against my ears.

Therion reins in his horse sharply, his movements fluid and precise. His hand drifts to the haft of his axe, his voice low and commanding. "Listen."

Ronyn's playful grin is gone in an instant, replaced by the sharp focus of a hunter. His bow is already in his hands, an arrow nocked and ready. "Something's watching us."

My chest tightens, the sound of my own pulse suddenly deafening in the silence. Kael leans closer, his voice a steady anchor against the rising tension. "Stay alert, Lightborne."

Even the air feels wrong—too still, too silent.

My muscles coil tight, every nerve alive with anticipation. I scan the shifting shadows, but the forest offers no answers—only more questions, more unease. The golden light beneath my ribs flickers faintly, like a warning flare, pulsing against my skin in time with my racing heart.

And then I feel it—a presence, prominent yet unseen, the weight of its gaze pressing down on us.

We're not alone.

CHAPTER SEVENTEEN

THERION DISMOUNTS FIRST, HIS MOVEMENTS AS SMOOTH AND
purposeful as ever. He steps forward, his posture rigid, scanning the
darkened forest ahead with an intensity that's almost palpable. Seren
once told me that Aetherstride means "energy walker"—a gift that
lets its wielder move through the unseen, sensing what others can't.
They don't merely track footprints—they feel the pulse of life, the
lingering echoes of presence, the whisper of energy in every space
they pass. It's what makes them unparalleled trackers—not just
following trails but sensing them.

Kael dismounts with an ease that borders on predatory, landing
soundlessly on the forest floor. Before I can think to dismount
myself, his hands are on me, gripping my hips firmly. Without so
much as a word of warning, he hauls me off the horse, his strength
making the effort seem trivial. My feet hit the ground lightly, but his
hands linger for a fraction longer than necessary, their weight
steadying me—and sparking something else.

The warmth of his touch settles low in my belly, and my breath
catches before I force myself to focus. I can't let myself feel this—
not here, not now. *Not ever.*

"It's time to show me how you fight, Duskae," Kael says, his lips curling into a smirk that both infuriates and unsettles me.

I scowl at him, brushing my hands over my tunic to distract myself from the way his words settle over me like a challenge. "I thought *you* were meant to be protecting *me*, Shadow Boy," I bite. "I shouldn't have to fight at all." I snap the words like an insult, but we both know there's not a chance I'd let someone else fight my battles.

His gaze doesn't waver. It's sharp, unrelenting, and far too knowing. He unsheathes his twin swords in a smooth, deliberate motion, the steel catching the dim light as he holds them at his sides. "I'll protect you from what you can't defeat, Elyssara," he says, his voice low and steady. "But I know a warrior when I see one. And you're no helpless damsel. I've seen you set fire to things that stand in your way, and I know you won't sit idly by while others fight for you."

My flesh turns hot at his approval—something about how he says it makes me feel like he sees me. Truly sees me.

He takes a step closer, and the forest seems to fade into the edges of my awareness. His voice drops lower, softer, but no less commanding, rich with an unshakable confidence that wraps around me like a physical thing.

"I'll fight at your side and guard your back, Elyssara, like it's my own life on the line. You're mine to protect," his eyes bore into mine, "and I don't take that lightly."

His words punch straight through me—but it's the way he says *mine* that leaves me breathless. The possessiveness in his tone is undeniable, and though I should bristle, I don't. Instead, something in me responds, my breath catching as heat coils low in my belly. I know he's referring to the deal we made, but there's something in the way he claims me that feels like... *more.*

"I... understand," I manage, my voice strained.

He steps closer, the intensity in his gaze softening slightly, but the tension between us only deepens. "Good," he says, his lips curling into the faintest smirk. "Because no one touches what's mine."

The words linger in the air, heavier than the forest mist clinging to the ground. My throat tightens, but I force myself to look away, turning my focus to the dense shadows of the Frael Forest ahead.

Therion's voice cuts through the tension. "We're surrounded. We fight here. *Now.*"

Kael strengthens his grip on the hilt of his swords, his calm, predatory demeanor returning as if nothing had passed between us. But the weight of his words—and the heat of his touch—stay with me, burning beneath my skin.

"Seren, stay on the horse. Ronyn, nock an arrow and be ready. Therion, ready your axe. Elyssara..." Kael moves around, gaze searching for what he knows is present but cannot see, "your blades won't cut it—they're too short. You'll need more reach."

As if the weight of the unseen presses down on us, my chest tightens. Kael offers me the sword from his left hand—the one he refused to give away in Duskridge Hollow.

"Use this."

I notice Therion's eyes widen in disbelief, and he quickly shakes his head in disgust, his distaste for the gesture glaringly apparent. I don't know if it's the sword or the symbolism behind Kael offering it to me, but Therion looks like he's just watched a line get crossed. But now is not the time to debate the necessity of it.

"Thank you," I say with genuine sincerity. No warrior shares their weapon, especially not one made from whatever this is— blackened steel that looks like death incarnate.

Therion's voice cuts through the tension as he scans the shifting shadows. "Duskprowlers. Huge cats with fangs as long as your hand, and venom in their claws. They hunt by entrancing prey with their eyes. Fast, cunning, and relentless—once they've marked you, they don't stop." His tone is gruff but steady, the words carrying the weight of someone who's faced them before.

We form a tight circle, our backs to one another, the forest pressing in on us from all sides. The suffocating canopy overhead allows only faint trickles of light to break through, making the glowing amethyst eyes of the duskprowlers all the more menacing.

Seren's voice shakes as she speaks. "Don't make eye contact. They will lure you in. But I have an idea."

She fumbles in the saddlebag, her hands trembling as she pulls out flares. Lighting one, she tosses it to the ground. The sudden burst of light causes the prowlers to recoil, their shimmering coats catching the faint illumination.

"Ronyn!" she calls. "Grab a stick—light it from the flare!"

He does as she says, moving quickly and lighting a makeshift torch. He passes one to Therion, who swings it in a wide arc, forcing the creatures to keep their distance.

"Clever girl," Therion says approvingly.

"Keep them at bay!" Seren shouts, her voice firm now, as she lights another stick for Kael and one for me.

The fight begins in earnest.

Kael steps forward, sword glinting like a shard of darkness in the faint light. His stance is predatory, each movement deliberate, fluid. At his side, Therion wields his massive axe with a brutal efficiency that sends shards of bark flying as he readies himself for the duskprowlers' advance. They are a stark contrast—Kael's precision and lethal grace beside Therion's raw, unrelenting power. Together, they're a storm waiting to break.

Ronyn stands a little to the side, bow at the ready, his stance deceptively casual. He draws an arrow with practiced ease, his sharp gaze fixed on the shadows. His expression, usually filled with cheek, is now focused, calculating. He looses an arrow, and the whistle of the shaft slicing through the air is the only warning the first duskprowler gets before it collapses, the arrow embedded perfectly between its glowing eyes.

Another prowler leaps from the shadows, and Ronyn fires again without hesitation. This time, the arrow pierces the creature's open maw, silencing its guttural growl. "That's two," he mutters under his breath, his tone almost light, but his eyes remain razor sharp.

"Eyes up, Ronyn," Therion growls, swinging his axe in a devastating arc that cleaves through a prowler lunging toward his flank. The beast doesn't even hit the ground before he turns to the next, his movements swift despite the weapon's weight. He plants his feet, the sheer force of his strikes leaving gouges in the earth as he fights with a relentless warrior's precision. He turns before they move, as if their intent reaches him before their bodies do—Aetherstride in motion.

Kael moves like a shadow, silent and deadly, weaving between the advancing beasts. His sword and dagger flash in synchronized arcs, each strike precise and devastating. A duskprowler lunges for him, claws extended, but he ducks low, driving his swords upward into its chest and his dagger into the side of its neck in one fluid motion. He spins, using the momentum to slash at another beast, cutting it down before it can land a blow.

"Keep close!" Kael barks, his voice sharp and commanding as he throws his head toward me.

Seren, still lighting flares with trembling hands, shouts, "There's a weak spot! The base of their skulls—just below where the shimmer fades!" Her voice rises above the chaos, her intelligence cutting through the panic like a beacon.

Kael nods, adjusting his strikes to aim for the weak point Seren identified. His next kill is swift, his blade finding the spot with pinpoint accuracy. He casts her a brief glance of approval before returning to the fray.

I grip Kael's sword tightly, the weight no longer foreign in my hands. My small blades were perfect for the tight Virellin's streets, but here, in the open chaos of the forest, they feel like toys. Kael's sword feels different—alive, its weight pulling me into each move-ment, as though it's guiding me.

A duskprowler lunges for Seren, its claws slashing through the air. "Seren, down!" I shout, lunging forward to intercept. The blade in my hands moves instinctively, slicing across the creature's throat in a clean, upward arc. Blood sprays as it collapses, but there's no time to celebrate.

Another beast is already upon me, and I spin, ducking beneath its claws as I drive the blade into its side. My movements are clumsy compared to Kael's lethal grace or Therion's brute strength, but they're effective. I'm no warrior, but survival has always been my greatest skill, and I use every ounce of it now. Revryn's training urges my strikes to land with precision and my feet to move with practised skill.

Ronyn's voice rings out, cutting through the chaos. "El, left!"

I pivot just in time to see another cat-like beast with paws the size of Kael's boot lunging for me. Before I can react, Ronyn's arrow strikes true, embedding into the creature's neck. "You're welcome," he calls, his grin audible even in the chaos.

The flares Seren lit are starting to dim, their protective light fading. The duskprowlers press closer, their numbers overwhelming despite the kills we've racked up. My leg throbs, and I look down momentarily to see the left leg of my trousers ripped to shreds and crimson blood pooling in my boot. I've been clawed at some point in the fray, and the effects of the wound are slowing me down, but I force myself to keep moving.

Kael is suddenly there, his back pressed against mine as he cuts down another beast. "We need to finish this," he says, his voice a low growl. "Dig deep, Lightborne."

The words ignite something in me, a fire that burns through the pain and exhaustion. I tighten my grip on the sword and step forward, slashing at another prowler that dares to come close.

Therion's voice booms above the noise. "Hold the line!" He plants his axe in the ground, yanking a dagger from his belt and hurling it into the eye of a prowler creeping toward Seren. The beast drops instantly, and he's back to his axe in the blink of an eye, a feral growl escaping his throat as he swings.

The golden light beneath my ribs begins to flicker again, stronger this time, pulsing in time with my racing heart. My vision blurs, the world around me fading as the energy builds, demanding release.

Kael's voice snaps me back. "Elyssara, stay with me!"

"I can't—" The words catch in my throat as the light surges upward, searing through my veins.

"Everyone down!" Kael shouts, stepping aside and throwing himself to the ground just as the coiled magic bursts from me in a blinding wave.

The golden light surges from within me, rushing outward in waves. It's warm—scorchingly warm but not painful. The air hums with energy, crackling like a storm. My skin tingles as the power courses through me, and the faint scent of something sweet, like stardust, lingers in the air. The world blurs, consumed by the light, and for a moment, I feel weightless, infinite, untethered.

The light radiates outward, engulfing the duskprowlers. Their screeches echo through the forest as their bodies convulse, choke, collapse, and disintegrate into ash, the golden glow swallowing them whole.

The light fades. The forest stills. For a heartbeat, nothing moves —not even the wind. The air feels lighter, cleaner—*purified*—as if the darkness has been purged.

I drop to my knees, the sword slipping from my grasp as I clutch my chest. The pain in my leg returns with a vengeance, but it's drowned out by the sheer exhaustion weighing me down.

Kael kneels beside me, his strong arms scooping me up with a care that feels out of place in this brutal, bloodstained forest. His voice, so often commanding and sharp, softens to a murmur meant only for me. "Rest now, Elyssara," he says, his lips barely brushing my temple as he speaks. "You're safe. I've got you." The words settle over me like a promise, and as darkness begins to claim me, it's his warmth that lingers.

I begin to slip from consciousness, but I swear I hear Therion say, "You're making a mistake, brother. You're too close." But before I can press further, the world goes dark.

PART II
CHOICE

CHAPTER EIGHTEEN

ELYSSARA

Awareness creeps in slowly, like dawn through fog. The brittle snap of twigs, the musky blend of leather and oakmoss, and the uneven rhythm of a horse's gait pull me from the darkness. My eyelids feel like lead, my mouth as dry as sand, and my body aches as if I've been trampled by the beast beneath me. Then—*Stars above*—my leg.

I shift instinctively, trying to reach for my throbbing leg through the haze of my thoughts, but a strong arm wraps around me, steadying me. A low, gravelly voice rumbles near my ear, quiet but commanding.

"Easy there, El."

Kael.

The sound of his voice floods my senses, grounding and overwhelming all at once. I force my eyes open, blinking against the blurry haze until his face comes into view—broad and unyielding, framed by those waves of chocolate-brown hair. His scent—earthy and warm, oakmoss rich and heady—anchors me, even as warmth blooms in my core, betraying me entirely. *Traitorous fucking body.*

I realize I'm draped across his arms, cradled like a child, his firm grip keeping me steady in the saddle. My shoulder is pressed to his chest plate, and, Gods help me, my ass is planted squarely in his lap. I shouldn't feel this. But I'm not fucking blind—I can see all six feet four inches of his muscled warrior body. His gaze meets mine, vivid blue and entirely too aware, as if he can hear the riot of indecent thoughts clashing inside me. That smirk tugging at the corner of his mouth only makes it worse.

Mortification floods me, until it's swallowed by the memories.

Duskprowlers. Screams. Blades. Claws. Blinding light.

My blinding light.

"Wh—What did I do?" The words come out hoarse, barely more than a whisper. I'm not sure what I'm asking exactly—what I said, what I felt, or what the hell just happened—but the question feels like a reasonable catch-all for, well... *everything*.

Kael's voice is steady, quiet enough to be intimate but firm enough to make it clear he's not uncertain.

"Your magic won the battle against the binding spell. It broke free, momentarily... we think."

We.

Oh, flaming Stars.

I jolt upright, twisting awkwardly to take stock of the others. I'm perched sideways on the mare now, Kael's hand steadying me as my eyes dart across the group. Ronyn rides just ahead, his bow slung lazily across his back, Seren in front of him, her expression soft with relief, while Therion lingers further off, stoic as ever.

Ronyn catches my gaze, his grin widening in that maddeningly smug way of his. Innuendo practically oozes from the smirk. *Bastard.*

But they're okay. All of them. Relief crashes over me like a tidal wave, my chest loosening for the first time since I woke.

Kael interrupts my moment of reprieve, his tone clipped and leaving no room for argument.

"I need to check your wound."

"I'll do it," I start, lifting my chin, already trying to maneuver myself. "I just need to sit properly so I don't—"

Before I can finish, Kael moves. His hands slide beneath the backs of my thighs, lifting me with effortless strength. He shifts me in the saddle in one smooth motion, spreading my legs and guiding them to either side of the horse's neck.

"Happy to oblige," he says, his voice infuriatingly casual.

His hands linger on my thighs, firm and unyielding, the heat of his palms burning through the thin fabric of my trousers. The intimacy of the motion—the control, the precision—sends a fresh wave of heat rushing to my face. This man is impossible. Impossibly alluring. And he fucking knows it.

"Was that entirely necessary?" I bite out, breath catching as I scramble for composure.

Kael leans closer, his voice laced with intent. "It wasn't necessary, no. I just *wanted* to do it."

The words hit me like a spark, igniting something I don't dare name. I open my mouth to retort, but the words die on my tongue as his hands move to my injured leg, fingers brushing near the torn fabric with care I didn't expect.

Out of the corner of my eye, Ronyn shifts his weight, craning his neck back to look at me. "You good, El?" he asks, his grin softening slightly, though the teasing glint in his eye never quite fades. "Can't have the savior of the realms unable to do the saving, can we?"

"Keep your eyes forward, Ronyn," Kael snaps, his voice low and laced with warning.

Ronyn raises his hands in mock surrender, his grin only widening. "Touchy. Noted." He turns back to Seren, muttering something that makes her stifle a laugh.

Kael's focus, however, doesn't waver. His fingers brush the edges of my wound. The earlier teasing vanishes from his face, replaced by quiet concern.

"It's infected," he mutters, his jaw tightening. "We'll need to treat this before it gets much worse."

I jerk away from the wound. Yellow discharge seeps from it, the torn flesh is jagged and inflamed, and it is most definitely infected. Kael pokes at the outskirts of the wound, and the earlier teasing drains from his face, and is replaced with concern.

Kael whistles and Therion swiftly halts, as if it's some secret language between the two of them. "We need a healer, immediately." I'd argue, but after looking at it, I definitely need a healer.

"We're at least five days away from leaving the forest," Therion counters. "The horses won't make it—we've already been riding for two days without sleep," he snaps, the lack of sleep evident.

I've been unconscious for two days?

Seren's voice, a little more confident than when we first entered the forest, adds, "I saw some lunabark root at our last rest stop. I grabbed some," she rummages through her saddle bags. "It should get El through at least a few nights. Is there a healer anywhere near the fringe of the Frael Forest?"

"I know a place," Kael murmurs low.

"Oh fuckin' Stars, Kael. Not Mavyrn?" Therion drags a hand down his face, incredulous.

"Yes," Kael commands, no room for negotiation in his tone. "She's our best hope at healing this wound and continuing on to the relics."

"If she doesn't fucking hex us first," Therion bites back.

Kael ignores his reservations. "We'll push the horses hard and make it there in three days. Four at the most," he finishes, but swiftly observes the exhaustion marring the faces of our group. "We'll rest tonight."

"Thank the gods," Ronyn sighs, pumping his fists in the air.

"Bless the Stars themselves," Seren exhales. She looks bone-tired and drained, probably ravenous and most definitely in need of a bath. We all are. I'm certain we'd all settle for a stream. Ronyn and I have kept Seren shielded from many of the hardships of life in the Virellin slums—life on horseback is foreign for both Ronyn and me, but even more so for Seren. Ronyn and I have at least spent the majority of our lives physically training to endure hardship and fights with people bigger and stronger than us. But Seren has been sheltered from the violence, the lack.

"Fine," Therion acquiesces. "The girl will need the lunabark root if we plan to ride hard, then," he grunts, nudging his horse into a trot.

"Always a delight, that man," Ronyn quips.

Kael pulls our mare up alongside Ronyn and Seren, and she passes him a gnarled root.

"Lunabark root numbs the pain," Seren explains, rummaging through her satchel. "Mildly hallucinogenic. You'll either pass out and dream, or stay awake and... dream. Or both."

Fucking great.

"Oh, amazing, nothing to worry about then," I deadpan.

Kael fights a smile but loses, the corners of his mouth pulling up at my expense. "You'll be fine, Lightborne. I've got you."

"Go on," Seren urges.

I crunch down, and the taste of the lunabark root floods my mouth, sharp and jarring like biting into a bitter lemon. There's a fleeting sweetness, faint and deceptive, that vanishes almost instantly, leaving behind a sour tang that clings to my tongue. A subtle, numbing warmth begins to spread from my throat to my chest, dulling the sharper edges of the pain in my leg already. A strange coolness follows, almost minty, but not refreshing—like damp moss mixed with iron.

"Rest," Kael commands with just a hint of gentility, but before I can retort about rest not being possible due to the lack of comfort—as evidenced by the chafing between my thighs—my body gives out again, and the darkness takes me.

CHAPTER NINETEEN
KAEL

THERION'S ANGER ROLLS OFF HIM LIKE HEAT FROM A FORGE AS WE ride into the clearing he's deemed suitable for camp. He hasn't looked at me once since we left the last rest stop, and his silence is as sharp as his axe. We haven't spoken alone since the outpost. No chance to lay out a plan for the relic hunt. But Therion doesn't need words for me to read him. His anger simmers just below the surface, coiled tight and ready to strike.

Elyssara hasn't stirred since Seren gave her the lunabark root, and maybe that's a mercy. The wound festers, its edges raw and inflamed, though the root keeps her blissfully unaware of the pain. I slide her down from the horse and into Ronyn's waiting arms with a curt nod. "Let her rest somewhere. I'll prepare her bedroll."

Ronyn grins, the ever-present mischief in his expression dulled slightly by concern. "Don't worry, Captain. I'll guard her like she's my own flesh and blood."

I glare at him, but there's no real bite in it. "Just do it."

With her settled, I make my way toward Therion, who sits slouched against the trunk of a massive tree. He's tossing rocks at another trunk with deliberate, almost menacing precision. Each stone hits its mark with a dull, echoing thud.

I drop down beside him, the weight of the day pressing into my bones as I lean back and rest my head against the rough bark. For a moment, we sit in silence, the sounds of the forest filling the space between us—the faint rustle of leaves, the chirp of distant insects, the whisper of wind through the trees. But the quiet isn't peace. It's a pause, a held breath before the storm.

"Brother, what bothers you?" I finally ask, keeping my tone calm, though my patience is already thinning.

Therion turns, his gaze smoldering with barely leashed fury. He doesn't answer immediately, and when he does, his voice is low and measured, like a blade drawn with care. "This wasn't the plan."

I fucking knew this was coming.

I let out a sharp breath, my own frustration rising to meet his. "This was *exactly* the plan, Ther. Find the Lightborne. Get the compass. Rescue my sister. Take back what's mine. Free our people." My voice hardens with every word, and by the end, it's practically a growl. "We're fucking doing that."

"And where does flirting with the Lightborne fit into the plan, huh?" His words cut. "It won't end well, and you fucking know it. It can't."

I know he's right. It can't. She's starting to trust me, but that won't last. Not when she knows everything.

I meet his gaze, unflinching, the weight of everything I'm carrying pressing down on me like armor. "I haven't forgotten what we're here for, if that's your concern," I bite.

Therion scoffs, shaking his head. "No? Well, it seems like you're forgetting fucking everything," he spits the words, hurling another rock at the tree. "We agreed—no magic. No signals. No fucking risks. For all we know, Thalmyr's already sent legions after us. Maybe Maldrak, too." His chest rises and falls too quickly. "*Your* Lightborne," he snarls the words like an insult, "has just scorched the entire forest in a blinding fucking light that was the equivalent of a signal flare. It could be seen all the way to Kryntar, for fuck's sake. And if they didn't see it, any magic wielder on the continent *felt* it. And if Maldrak felt it, Thalmyr did too—and we don't want either of them coming!"

I know he's right. Stars help me—he's right. He pushes on, "I fear that you *have* forgotten what we're here for, *and* what the original plan was. Because this, sure as the fucking Stars, is not it," he pauses briefly, as if measuring his final words. "I see the way you look at her, Kael."

I rise to my feet, the tension crackling between us like a storm waiting to break. Not for a single heartbeat in ten fucking years have I forgotten my people. *So fuck him.*

I dust off my leathers, keeping my movements deliberate, and then fix him with a look I reserve for the battlefield—a silent warning that this conversation is over. I'm close to snapping. A single word from him, and I might. But no. Control is my armor. I won't lose it—to him or anyone.

"Remember your place, Therion," I say, my voice low and steady. "You're my brother in every way that counts, but don't think for a second I'll hesitate to remind you where you stand the next time you speak to me like a petulant fucking child." I shove myself up to stand. "You're on first watch."

He doesn't reply, his glare cutting through the dark, but I've said my piece. I stalk away, leaving his anger to smolder in the shadows behind me, an ember waiting for the right moment to catch fire.

CHAPTER TWENTY

ELYSSARA

I WAKE TO THE CRACKLE AND POP OF A SMALL FIRE, THE SOUND tugging me from a foggy dream. My eyes flutter open—or maybe they don't. The world feels distant, slippery, as if I'm caught in a half-formed thought. I try to sit up, but my body refuses to cooperate, tethered to the ground by some invisible force.

"You're awake," a low, gravelly voice says, somewhere just above me. "Good evening, Duskae."

Kael.

The sound of his voice tugs at something deep inside me, grounding and disorienting all at once. I force my head to roll toward him, my vision blurring, then sharpening just enough to make out his silhouette against the firelight.

"You..." My voice slurs, words tumbling out before I can catch them. "You're... really handsome. Like... unfairly handsome."

His lips quirk up in that infuriating smirk. "I'm glad you're finally being honest. Though I do wish it wasn't because you have duskprowler venom and lunabark root in your veins."

"Duskprowlers?" I echo, the word thick and clumsy on my tongue. I blink at him. "Is that what's happening? Or is it just you? You're... doing something to me."

Kael leans closer, his smirk softening, though his eyes stay sharp, watchful. "And what exactly am I doing to you, El?"

"You're... unfair," I murmur, flopping a limp hand in his direction. "With your face. And your shoulders. And your..." My eyes drift downward before I force them shut, heat rushing to my cheeks. "You're distracting. That's what you are."

Kael chuckles, low and deep, the sound vibrating through the space between us. "Distracting, am I? That's quite the accusation coming from you."

"I'm an unbathed girl from the slums," I say, my words tangling together. "Your eyes... they're like... the sky. No, waves. Big blue waves. Why are they so... blue?" I ramble nonsensically, half laughing, half groaning. "You're too much, Kael. Too... symmetrical."

His brow arches, and he leans back slightly, clearly amused. "Symmetrical?"

"Dangerously so," I mumble. "It's not fair. It's just not..." I trail off, my head lolling to the side again. "I like your face. A lot. Even though you're really bossy... and... arrogant."

His smirk falters, just for a moment, and his gaze softens. "You're beautiful too, you know," he says, his voice quieter than before, almost hesitant, as if admitting it aloud shifts something neither of us can take back. "Even if you *are* high on that unholy combination, Duskae."

The words hit me like a warm rush, but my brain is too foggy to process them fully. Instead, I let out a soft laugh, the sound strange even to my own ears. "I knew it. You like me," I giggle, my tone tender.

"Maybe," he says, his voice low, teasing. "But you're impossible to deal with when you're like this."

"I think I would really like to kiss you... Your lips look very soft. You've been with hundreds of women, haven't you?" I ramble, and I cannot for the fucking life of me stop the words from falling from my mouth. "You probably have a really big—"

Kael splutters a cough, cutting me off.

"Alright, alright—time for sleep," he laughs, reaching for me. He leans in, smirking. "And yes—it's huge." He smiles, completely unrestrained. It's the first time I've seen him smile like this, and I like being the cause of it.

"Hold me," I blurt, the words spilling out before I can stop them. "I'm... so cold." My hand wipes at my brow, slick with sweat, trembling as I shiver against the heat burning in my veins.

Kael's expression shifts, the teasing glimmer in his eyes replaced by something deeper, more serious. He hesitates for a heartbeat before moving closer, his arms sliding around me with a careful strength that makes my chest tighten.

"I've got you," he murmurs, his voice impossibly gentle. His breath is warm against my temple, steady and grounding, yet it sends a shiver racing down my spine. *How could someone feel so safe and so dangerous all at once?*

The warmth of his embrace seeps into me, chasing away the chill in my veins. My head rests against his chest plate, the rhythmic thud of his heartbeat steadying the chaos in my mind. For a moment, the world feels safe.

"Here," he says softly, reaching for something at his side. "Chew this. It'll dull the pain and help you sleep."

He presses a piece of lunabark root to my lips, and I obediently take it.

"Kael..." I mumble, my voice trailing off as the root takes hold. "You smell nice. Like how I'd imagine a rainforest. Warm, earthy... safe."

His arms tighten around me, just slightly, as he murmurs, "Rest, El. I'll keep you safe." His warmth is overwhelming, like a raging fire in the dead of winter, and yet the chill clinging to my skin refuses to release me.

The weight of his words settles over me, heavy and comforting. My eyelids flutter closed, the heat and the ache in my body softening as darkness pulls me under once more. Somewhere in the fading edges of my awareness, I swear I feel his lips brush the top of my head, feather-light, before everything fades to black once more.

CHAPTER TWENTY-ONE
ELYSSARA

WE PACK UP IN TENSE SILENCE, SMOKE STILL CLINGING TO THE AIR. My thighs ache from nonstop riding, the leather saddle rubbing them raw. The lunabark has nearly worn off, leaving only sharper pain behind.

Therion leads the way, as always. *Grumpy bastard.* Ronyn and Seren follow, their voices a soft hum of conversation ahead, and Kael and I bring up the rear.

It's quiet at first, save for the rhythmic plodding of the horses' hooves. But I can feel him. Smirking. Watching. Even without turning around, I know his insufferable grin is etched across his smug face.

I spin around in the saddle, my irritation bubbling over. "What is it?"

"Why so agitated, Lightborne?" he smirks. "Is it my symmetrical face? Or my big shoulders?"

The blood rushes to my cheeks so fast it's dizzying. *Fucking Stars.* It wasn't a dream.

I scramble for composure, praying the heat on my face isn't as obvious as it feels. I opt for feigned ignorance as my tactic, "I have no idea what you're talking about."

"Well," he drawls, leaning forward slightly as if to share some great secret, "if it wasn't my symmetrical face, or my big shoulders, or my soft lips," he starts gesturing towards his groin, pressed into my ass in the saddle, and punctuates the gesture by raising his eyebrows, "Perhaps it was my really big—"

"Oh my Stars, enough!" I cut him off, my voice louder than I intend, as I throw my hands up to cover my face. My fingers dig into my temples as if I can erase the memory of whatever ridiculous nonsense I spewed at him last night.

Behind me, Kael laughs, deep and rich, the sound rolling through the forest like a rumble of thunder. It's the sort of laugh that demands attention, that feels both infuriatingly smug and impossibly warm.

"Don't worry, El," he says, his voice softer now, though the teasing edge remains. "I found it... endearing."

I groan, pulling my hands from my face to glare at him over my shoulder. "I was... delirious," I scoff. "Obviously."

He grins, his gaze locked on mine, and for a moment, something flickers there—something that makes my heart stutter. But then it's gone, replaced by his usual playful arrogance.

Ahead, I hear Ronyn snicker. "Having fun back there?"

I narrow my eyes, ready to retort, but Seren's quiet voice interrupts, her tone equal parts teasing and concerned. "Your cheeks are quite flushed, El. Are you okay?"

"I'm fine!" I snap, a little too quickly, and both of them exchange a knowing glance. Ronyn's grin widens, and I swear I hear him whisper, *"Symmetrical."*

Kael chuckles again, and I curse the Stars under my breath as we continue on.

The days and nights blur, melded together only by flickers of half-formed memories—Seren's soft voice urging me to drink, the creak of leather saddles, the low murmur of Kael's voice in the dark. I drift between restless sleep and fleeting moments of sharp clarity, the world around me reduced to a haze of movement, sound, and heat.

I have lost all sense of time. It could be days, weeks, or even heartbeats since the duskprowler attack.

When we finally reach the forest's edge, I am drenched in sweat, my skin burning as though set aflame, and shaking so violently it's a wonder I haven't fallen from the saddle. My leg, oozing and swollen, has darkened to an ominous shade of black, veins creeping outward like vines of decay. Each breath feels like dragging shards of glass through my lungs.

Kael keeps me upright, his arms steady even as mine falter. We've stopped countless times for me to wretch, my body rebelling against the poison in my veins. My foot is numb, the flesh gangrenous. The ache is distant now, replaced by a gnawing cold that creeps up my spine.

If it weren't for Morrathys, God of Death, looming over me, I'd celebrate crossing the threshold of the Frael Forest. Instead, the thought of an additional half-day ride to the healer feels a cruel joke from Morrathys himself.

"You're not dying," Kael says, his voice calm, as though my impending demise is nothing but a figment of my imagination.

Did I say that out loud, or are my thoughts simply written across my face?

"I am. And we both know it," I rasp, my voice barely audible between gulps of air.

"Elyssara," Kael says, his tone sharp and severe. "You will be one of the most powerful magic wielders the realms have ever seen. It won't be a scratch that ends your existence. You will not die today." His voice drops, almost reverent. "Morrathys can't have you."

The words land somewhere between a prayer and a command. I want to believe him, but the cold in my veins whispers otherwise.

"Okay then," I manage, my voice weak, barely a whisper.

For the next few hours, I offer silent prayers to Morrathys, begging him to spare me. Promising vengeance against Dravara's King, a rebellion for the Starborn, freedom for the forsaken. Promising a better world, if only he lets me live. Promising not to waste what the Stars marked in my blood.

The world blurs and sharpens in fragments as we ride, the cold creeping deeper into my bones. I hear the others' voices—Kael's commanding, Therion's gruff, Seren's soft and soothing—but they feel like echoes in a dream. The rhythmic clop of hooves and the distant hum of the wind become my only companions.

Then, the air changes. It feels lighter, crisper, as though we've crossed some invisible boundary into a different world. The trees thin, and the canopy opens up to let the sun drench us in light.

I force my heavy eyelids open, just barely, to see a cottage nestled in the shadow of what I assume must be Mount Lyssar.

We're here. And I whisper one last prayer—not for peace, but for vengeance. For the chance to burn down the king who tried to erase me.

CHAPTER TWENTY-TWO
ELYSSARA

Mavyrn's home is nestled at the foot of Mount Lyssar, where lush green ranges climb through the clouds like a living wall. I can barely reconcile the barren, cracked earth of the Virellin slums with the fertile, dense range before me.

We approach the tiny home, a home unlike anything I've seen before. It's quaint and wild all at once, with moss creeping up the stone walls and vines curling around the crooked shutters. The roof is uneven, thatched with dark reeds, and a thin trail of smoke rises from the chimney, curling into the dusk sky.

Odd trinkets hang from the eaves—wind chimes made of bones, dried herbs tied with twine, and what looks like a glass jar filled with something glowing faintly. The scent of earth and spice drifts on the breeze, mingling with the distant sound of water trickling over stone.

Kael dismounts first, his movements swift and controlled, and then he's lifting me from the saddle like I weigh nothing at all. I try to protest, to insist I can walk, but the moment my feet touch the ground, my legs buckle, and Kael catches me before I collapse.

"Don't be stubborn, Lightborne," he murmurs, his voice low but firm.

The door to the cottage creaks open, and an older woman steps out, her presence as commanding as the mountain looming behind her. Mavyrn's long, gray hair flows like a wild river down her back, streaked with silver that glimmers in the fading light. Her piercing, storm-gray eyes scan the group before settling on me. She's dressed in layers of dark fabric, adorned with belts and pouches that clink softly with every step. Around her neck hangs a pendant—a crescent moon encircling a small, glowing orb.

Mavyrn's gaze narrows as she takes me in, her lips pressing into a thin line. "What in the flaming Stars have you foolish men done to this girl?" she snaps, her voice sharp enough to cut through the haze in my mind.

"She was attacked by duskprowlers," Kael begins, his tone calm but tight. "The venom—"

"I can see the venom, boy," Mavyrn interrupts, striding forward with surprising speed. "And the infection. And the complete lack of common sense. *Typical of you*," She points a bony finger at Kael, her eyes blazing, telling a story that I'm not privy to. "Get her inside. *Now*."

Kael carries me over the threshold, and the air inside the cottage is warm, filled with the scents of dried herbs, wood smoke, and something faintly metallic. The interior is as eclectic as the outside —shelves crammed with books, jars of powders and liquids, bundles of dried flowers hanging from the rafters. A large wooden table dominates the center of the room, its surface cluttered with an assortment of tools and trinkets. A cauldron simmers in the hearth, its contents bubbling faintly.

Mavyrn points to a worn cot near the fire. "Lay her there. And don't touch anything unless you want to end up cursed."

I'm reminded of Therion's comment about her hexing us, but I shake it from my mind.

Kael sets me down gently, his touch lingering for a moment longer than necessary before he steps back. Mavyrn approaches, her hands surprisingly gentle as she examines the wound on my leg. Her stormy eyes soften, just slightly, as she mutters under her breath.

"This will not be easy," she says, more to herself than to anyone else. "The venom is deep, and the infection worse. She'll need more than salves and stitches."

"Can you save her?" Seren asks, her voice trembling.

Mavyrn doesn't answer immediately. Instead, she stands, moving to one of the shelves and grabbing a handful of dried leaves, a small vial of silvery liquid, and a stone pestle. "I can try. But she'll need to fight, too. The Starborn blood in her is strong, and might just be stubborn enough to pull through."

Kael steps forward, his tone low and urgent. "What do you need from us?"

Mavyrn glances at him, her expression unreadable. "Stay out of my way, boy. And pray to whatever gods you hold dear."

The room hums with tension as Mavyrn begins her work. She moves with purpose, gathering ingredients from her crowded shelves, muttering under her breath in a language I don't recognize. The flickering firelight casts long shadows across the walls, making the strange trinkets and jars appear alive, watching. Without looking up at the others, eyes firmly on my wound as she meticulously cleans away the evidence of my infection, the brusque yet warm woman says, "So I'm assuming she is the culprit for the dazzling light performance five nights ago, hm?"

"Yep, that's our girl!" Ronyn puffs his chest out proudly.

She kneels beside me, her sharp eyes scanning my face before drifting to my leg. Her expression remains unreadable, but I sense the weight of her thoughts—calculations, plans, decisions made in moments.

"This will hurt," she says simply. "And it will take more than my hands alone."

Kael steps forward instinctively, his presence a steady force. "What do you need?"

Mavyrn doesn't look at him, her focus fixed on a bundle of herbs she's crushing with practiced precision. "Your magic. And his," she says, nodding toward Therion, who stiffens visibly. "And hers." Her gaze flicks to Seren, who looks startled.

"Me?" Seren's voice trembles slightly. "I don't have magic. I'm not Starborn."

Mavyrn's lips twitch, almost a smirk. "Not yet, perhaps. But there's something in you—latent, hidden. You'll do."

"What about me? Need my help?" Ronyn chimes in.

"Not you, boy," Mavyrn answers, and Ronyn folds his arms petulantly.

Seren looks to Ronyn, panic flickering in her wide eyes, but he nods, his humor replaced with quiet reassurance. "You've got this, Seren."

Mavyrn's attention shifts to Kael and Therion. "Your magic will provide the foundation, the raw energy. I'll act as the conduit, transforming it into something that can heal. The girl's body will have to do the rest."

Therion crosses his arms, his jaw tight. "You want us to pour our magic into you? Do you have any idea how dangerous that is?"

"Of course I do," Mavyrn snaps, the storm in her eyes flashing. "But the poison in her veins won't wait for safer methods. If you're too afraid, step aside."

Kael places a hand on Therion's shoulder, his touch firm but steady. "What exactly do you need us to do?"

Therion exhales sharply, his displeasure clear, but he doesn't argue further. Instead, he moves to stand beside Kael, their postures mirroring each other—two warriors bracing for battle.

Mavyrn places a hand on my forehead, her touch surprisingly gentle. "Stay with me, Lightborne," she says softly. "This will take all the strength you have."

I nod weakly, the edges of the world blurring as the pain pulls me under.

She spreads her arms, her voice rising in a chant that feels both ancient and otherworldly. The air in the room thickens, charged with an energy that makes the hairs on my arms stand on end. The fire dims, its light replaced by a silvery glow emanating from Mavyrn's hands.

"Place your hands on me," Mavyrn commands, her voice resonant with authority. Kael and Therion hesitate for only a moment before doing as she says, their hands resting lightly on her arms.

Seren approaches reluctantly, her small hand trembling as she places it on Mavyrn's shoulder.

"Now—give me your magic," she commands.

Kael and Therion summon their gifts with practiced ease and pass them smoothly through their hands. Seren concentrates with measured focus, trying to do something, *anything*.

"Relax, child. Breathe," Mavyrn instructs. "Reach for the place in your body where your energy lives. It will feel like a gentle hum or buzz... *a tingling*. Reach for it and imagine drawing it to your finger tips." She pauses for a moment, closing her eyes. "Yes. Like that."

The glow from Mavyrn's hands intensifies, spreading like liquid light. It seeps into my skin, traveling toward the wound on my leg. A soft hum fills the air, growing louder, resonating like a distant chorus of voices.

Kael's grip on Mavyrn tightens slightly, his magic flowing through him like a current. Somehow, I recognize it in my body as it travels through my veins. It's warm, steady, grounding. Therion's magic feels different—sharp and electric, a crackling force that makes my body feel charged. Whatever Seren is able to share with me is hesitant. Uncertain. Curious. A faint pulse of energy, a spark waiting to ignite.

Mavyrn's body trembles, her voice breaking for the first time as she channels their magic through her. Sweat beads on her brow, and the glow around her grows almost blinding. "Hold steady," she commands, her voice strained. "We're almost there."

The light converges on my leg, sinking into the infected flesh. Pain erupts—sharp, searing, all-consuming—and I unleash a guttural scream in agony. If this is the end, I want to rage against it. For the first time, I'm not ready to go.

But then, it shifts. The cold venom in my veins burns away, replaced by a warmth so intense it feels like fire and sunlight combined. I gasp, my body arching off the cot as the energy surges through me.

The glow fades slowly, leaving the room in hushed stillness. My chest heaves as I collapse back onto the cot, my skin slick with sweat but the pain in my leg... *gone*. I look down to find the black veins and infection gone, leaving only a cut that could be easily remedied with stitches, herbs and bandages.

Mavyrn staggers, catching herself on the edge of the table. Her hands tremble as she wipes her brow, her expression weary but triumphant. "You're okay."

Kael's relief is palpable, though he masks it quickly, his gaze flicking to Mavyrn. "How long until she recovers?"

"That depends on her," Mavyrn replies, her voice rasping with exhaustion. "The wound needs to be closed, but the venom is purged. Though the body remembers, so she'll need rest."

Her eyes linger on Kael for a moment, something unspoken passing between them. "You've inherited more than your father's arrogance," she murmurs, trying to keep it low so only he can hear, but failing.

Kael's expression hardens, but behind his eyes, I see a flicker of something else—grief, or guilt, or both. He says nothing, just looks at me.

The world softens at the edges, like ink bleeding through parchment. I would question what in the Stars Mavyrn means, but consciousness evades me. The magnitude of escaping Morrathys' grip drowning me under a blanket of exhaustion.

CHAPTER TWENTY-THREE
ELYSSARA

I wake to the sound of the wind whispering through the trees, the cool night air brushing over my skin. The fire has burned down to embers, the remnants of a shared dinner are strewn across the table, and the subtle aroma of cooked meats drifts from the hearth. My body feels heavy, thick with a bone-deep exhaustion that comes after surviving something I probably shouldn't have. The others are curled up on the floor—Seren under Ronyn's cloak, Therion on the floor using his own as a pillow. I'm grateful they're getting some respite after our arduous journey through the forest, not to mention duskprowlers and leaving everything they knew in the Virellin slums.

The ache in my leg is dull now, more of a throb from the stitches than the searing agony from before. I shift slightly, wincing at the stiffness, and that's when I feel him.

He's seated next to the cot, his broad shoulders hunched forward, elbows resting on his knees. His face is turned toward the fire, the faint light catching the sharp lines of his jaw and the unruly waves of his hair. The steady rise and fall of his chest is the only indication that he's relaxed, though his posture is rigid. Vigilant.

A slight flicker of surprise chases up my spine at his presence. "You're still here," I murmur, my voice hoarse from disuse.

He turns immediately, his piercing blue eyes locking on to mine. There's a softness there that catches me off guard—concern, relief, something unspoken.

"I am. Where else would I be?" he replies, his voice low, grounding.

I offer a weak smile, shifting slightly to sit up. "I thought you might've gotten bored. Sitting around, babysitting the slum girl."

His lips twitch, but the smirk doesn't quite form. "You're not so boring, Lightborne. You've got a habit of keeping things... interesting."

I huff a quiet laugh, though it takes more effort than I'd like to admit. My gaze drifts to the shelves lined with vials and trinkets, the faint scent of herbs lingering in the air. "Mavyrn. She's... something else."

Kael nods, his expression thoughtful. "She's an Arcanist," he says, watching the embers. "It's... rare. Part inherited, part learned. Some sort of blend between magic and science." He pauses, breath catching in his throat like he's hesitating. "She was close to my father," he says eventually.

There's a weight to his words, something guarded, but I press gently. "Your father?"

His jaw tightens, just slightly, before he speaks. "He died. A long time ago." His eyes flicker toward the fire, the light reflecting a storm of emotion he doesn't voice.

"I'm sorry," I say softly, my chest tightening at the heaviness in his tone.

He shrugs, but it's not dismissive. "It's part of life. Loss. Death. It shapes us."

For a moment, I consider telling him about my parents, about their sacrifice for me, about the simmering vengeance that drives me forward. But the words lodge in my throat. Trust doesn't come easily, not when survival has always hinged on keeping parts of myself hidden.

"They're gone too," I say instead, my voice barely above a whisper. "My parents."

Kael's gaze snaps back to mine, his expression softening. "I'm sorry."

I nod, swallowing hard. "It was a long time ago, as well." The words slip out before I can stop them, though I don't give much away. I can't. Their names have vanished from the lips of everyone in Virellin—as if they never existed. Ghosts of the past that live on crumpled parchment in my pocket. No. I won't say more—this is safer.

His hand moves slightly, as if he's about to reach for mine, my breath hitches, but he stops himself. Instead, he leans closer, his voice quieter now. "That's why I need to find my sister. She's all I have left."

His words settle over me like a weight, heavy and raw. For the first time, I see the cracks in the armor he wears so well—the pain, the determination, the desperation that drives him.

"You'll find her," I say, and for once, I mean it. "If anyone can, it's you."

Kael's lips press into a thin line, but he nods, the faintest flicker of hope sparking in his eyes. "I have to."

Silence stretches between us, but it's not uncomfortable. It's a shared understanding, a fragile connection forged in the quiet of the night.

I lean back against the cot, exhaustion tugging at the edges of my consciousness. "You should sleep. You can't protect me if you're dead on your feet."

Kael smirks faintly, his expression softening. "I'll rest when you're strong enough to keep yourself out of trouble."

I roll my eyes, the faintest smile tugging at my lips. "Bossy."

"Always," he replies, and there's a warmth in his tone that makes my chest ache in a way that has nothing to do with pain.

As my eyes drift closed, I let myself believe, just for a moment, that maybe, just maybe, I can trust him. But the secrets I keep remain locked away, their weight a reminder that trust is a luxury I can't afford—not yet.

CHAPTER TWENTY-FOUR
ELYSSARA

THE MORNING AIR IN MAVYRN'S COTTAGE FEELS HEAVY, CHARGED with an energy that prickles against my skin. I rouse to the scent of herbs. Something faintly metallic fills my lungs as I watch Mavyrn work, her long fingers moving with precision as she arranges vials and stones on the worn table. Every now and then, she mutters under her breath, words I can't catch but that seem to carry weight, nonetheless.

Therion, of course, is pacing. His boots thud softly against the wooden floor, his frustration practically vibrating off him. "Are you sure this thing won't send us into the side of a mountain?" he grumbles.

Mavyrn doesn't even glance at him, her sharp gray eyes fixed on the glowing circle she's been crafting in the center of the room. "If it does, it'll be because you're too sour for the Gateway to tolerate."

Kael snorts quietly from his place against the wall, arms crossed, his lips twitching as though fighting back a smile. "Careful, Therion. She's known to curse people for less," he croons.

Therion growls, muttering something I can't hear, but Mavyrn cuts him off with a wave of her hand. "Oh, hush, you grump. You act like I've never met someone with a guarded heart before. Let it go, or the Gateway might just spit you back out."

I stifle a laugh and glance at the shimmering circle etched into the floor. I've never seen—or heard of—anything like this in my lifetime. This is magic that goes beyond the constellations. This is sorcery of legend—something I'd hear whispered in fever dreams or half-burned books. Threads of light twist and weave through the air above it, glowing faintly with a rainbow hue that shifts as I move closer. The magic pulses softly, the hum low and melodic, like the strings of an unseen instrument. It's mesmerizing and a little unnerving, as if the threads have a mind of their own.

"What... is it?" I ask, my voice quieter than I intended.

Mavyrn finally looks up, her expression softening just slightly. "This," she says, gesturing to the circle, "is a Gateway of Threads. A passage spun from the fabric of magic itself. Gateways can take you anywhere, so long as you have a piece of the place with you. This one will take you to the foot of Lyssar Temple—I had a little something in my jars from there. But be warned, it's not without its risks."

Her words hang in the air, and I can't tear my eyes away from the Gateway. The threads seem to shimmer more brightly as I stare, drawing me in. I almost cannot believe that I am looking at the very essence of magic.

"Risks?" Ronyn asks, his tone light, though his eyes are sharp.

"The Gateway is bound to only take you to the temple. It listens to intention. If you think of anywhere else, even for a heartbeat, it'll spit you out—or worse. The Gateway demands your trust and focus. Think solely of Lyssar Temple, step clearly into its center, and free fall," Mavyrn explains.

"Great," Therion mutters, crossing his arms. "A magic doorway with a fucking attitude."

Mavyrn shoots him a sharp look. "Be glad I can sense the purity of your heart, Therion. I'd have cursed that scowl off your face years ago."

Ronyn chuckles, and even Kael allows himself a small smile. I can't help but feel a flicker of warmth toward the older woman.

She might be jarring, but there's an undeniable care in her sharp words.

Then her gaze shifts to Kael, and her expression softens further, though a shadow passes over her face. "And you," she says, her voice quieter now. "You carry too much. You always have. Be careful, Kael. You can't have it both ways."

Kael stiffens, his jaw tightening, but he doesn't respond. The silence feels heavy, weighted by something unsaid.

What does that mean?

Finally, Mavyrn turns to me. Her eyes seem to pierce right through me, seeing more than I want to reveal. "Elyssara, you are more than the Lightborne—do not forget that," she says, stepping closer. "Your path is not an easy one, and betrayal often comes from the places we trust most. Be vigilant."

The words send a shiver down my spine, but I nod, swallowing hard. I don't know what to say, so I simply stay quiet.

"Now," Mavyrn says, clapping her hands once, breaking the tension. "Gather yourselves. The Gateway won't hold forever."

Kael steps forward first, his movements confident and purposeful. The threads of the Gateway ripple as he approaches, almost like they're alive, responding to him. He pauses just before stepping in and turns to me, his blue eyes steady.

"Ready yourselves on the other side—we don't know what's waiting for us," he says. And then he's gone, the threads swallowing him in a burst of light.

Therion follows, his steps grudging but firm. The threads seem to tighten around him, and I catch the faintest flicker of unease on his face before he disappears.

Ronyn winks at me as he steps forward. "See you on the other side, El." He vanishes into the light, the hum of the Gateway shifting faintly as he passes through.

Seren hesitates, her eyes wide as she looks from me to Mavyrn. "Are you sure it's safe?"

Mavyrn places a hand on her shoulder. "You'll be fine, child. The Gateway knows who you are, even if you don't."

Seren eyes her warily, but nods, her movements stiff, and steps into the circle. The threads shimmer around her before she vanishes like the others.

I'm the last. I rise slowly, my leg still weak, but my determination steady. I glance at Mavyrn, searching her face for the softness beneath her thorns. Needing the assurance of someone who stands to gain nothing from me.

"Thank you," I say quietly, and I mean it.

Mavyrn smiles, the warmth in it unexpected but genuine. "You'll do great things, Elyssara. But remember—greatness always comes at a price."

I step into the circle, the threads shifting around me like silk brushing against my skin. The hum grows louder, the air thick with energy. For a moment, I feel weightless, untethered. And then the light swallows me whole, and the world falls away.

CHAPTER TWENTY-FIVE
ELYSSARA

I FEEL SICK. TRAVELING BY A GATEWAY OF THREADS IS AKIN TO being far too deep in my cups at the tavern, and my stomach lurches with every phantom twist and turn. I'm certain Mavyrn would disapprove of my conduct, as I've cursed the infernal thing more times than I can count.

The Gateway spits me out without warning, tossing me unceremoniously onto the ground with a force that rattles my teeth.

Not overly graceful, Elyssara.

Ronyn's goofy, lopsided grin greets me as I scramble to my feet. It's the same grin that stole my heart all those summers ago in that Virellin alley, the one that promises everything will somehow be okay. Seren almost knocks me over with a fierce embrace, her wild blonde hair obscuring my vision as she clings to me for dear life.

Therion and Kael, however, are ready for anything. Weapons drawn, they've already turned their backs to us, their movements deliberate and silent. Therion edges forward, his body taut as a bowstring, his Aetherstride magic rolling off him in waves. Small, precise hand signals pass between him and Kael, a secret language honed over years of fighting side by side. They're completely at ease in this moment, two predators moving as one.

I tuck Seren behind me and bring my fingers to my lips, signaling her to stay silent. As I fall into step behind Therion and Kael, I unsheathe my daggers, the well-worn hilts steadying my hands. Every step feels heavier than it should. It's not the first time I've walked into the unknown, but this is different. This is the prophecy's first test. *My test.* The air hums with an unspoken weight, and the sharp edge of inevitability presses against my skin.

Therion halts, signaling for us to stay put, and directs Ronyn to a higher point. Ronyn climbs to the nearby rocky outcrop, taking a vantage point with his bow, his movements swift and practiced. Therion seems to trust him with this, and I appreciate the strategy and the small sign that perhaps Therion isn't always a giant asshole.

Seren and I crouch behind a jagged boulder, the cold stone pressing against my back as I glance at her. Her spine is straight, brows furrowed in determination, but her trembling hands are unmistakable.

For the first time since tumbling out of the Gateway, I take in our surroundings.

Lyssar Temple rises from the rugged cliffs of Mount Lyssar like an ancient guardian, its spires piercing the sky. The temple appears to be carved directly from the mountain, its walls textured with intricate etchings that shimmer faintly in the dim light. Symbols of long-forgotten lore intertwine with constellations, their meanings a mystery I'm not yet privy to.

The air here feels alive, charged with an energy that prickles against my skin. Stone steps, worn smooth by time, wind upward toward a massive archway framed by twisted columns. Statues of mythical beasts flank the entrance, their eyes sharp and other-worldly, as though they see through to the marrow of my soul. I can't decide if this place feels divine or terrifying.

A tug in my chest pulls my gaze toward the temple. It's faint at first, a gentle nudge, but it grows stronger with each passing moment. It's not just the temple calling to me—it's something inside it. The blade, I realize, my breath catching in my throat. The blade is here, and it knows me. It calls to me. The pull is magnetic, undeniable, as though an invisible thread has tethered us together.

Beneath the temple where fears take form,
The blade ignites and the veil is torn.

The prophecy rattles through my mind—a reminder that this is my blade. My prophecy. My destiny.

Kael and Therion return, their weapons still drawn. Kael's presence steadies me somehow, though his sharp ocean eyes give nothing away. I often feel as though there is a connection growing between us—something inexplicable, magnetic—but on the other side of our moments of connection, there is a wall. A guard that he pulls up and wraps around himself, as if shielding himself from... *me*.

"The perimeter is clear," Therion says, his voice low. "But inside... there's *something*. The enchantment isn't on this level, but I can feel it below. The air shifts, like a ripple through the threads." Aetherstride magic in action is a marvel—sensing that which cannot be seen is both eerie and mesmerizing.

"I feel it, too," Seren says quietly, her gaze fixed on the temple's looming archway.

She can feel it, too?

I nod warily, gripping my daggers. The hum in the air presses against my skin, heavier now, and I glance toward Kael. His smirk is already forming, and the infuriating curve of his lips is a familiar taunt.

"What approach are we going for?" I ask. "Stealth? Confrontation?"

"Stealth isn't exactly your strong suit, Lightborne," Kael teases, the smirk deepening.

"My stealth was fine, thank you. It was the magicked lock," I remind him.

"Yes, well, stabbing it certainly disrupted the stealth, didn't it, El?" Ronyn chimes in from above, his grin audible even from his perch.

I roll my eyes, refusing to take the bait.

"The plan," Kael says, cutting through the banter, "is to approach with stealth. Once we're inside, anything could happen.

Therion believes the enchantment is below the temple, which aligns with the prophecy. No magic unless absolutely necessary. The last thing we need is to alert the entire realm to our presence here."

His gaze sweeps over us, lingering on me for a fraction longer than necessary. "Stay close. Watch each other's backs. And remember: if it moves and it isn't us, stab it."

I swallow hard, the weight of the prophecy pressing against my chest as I glance toward the temple. The tug grows stronger, pulling me forward, and I can't help but wonder what awaits us inside. Whatever it is, it feels personal, like the temple knows who I am—and what I'm here for.

"Ready?" Kael asks, his voice steady but charged.

I nod, stepping forward as the others fall into place behind me. The temple looms ahead, its spires piercing the heavens, and I can't shake the feeling that whatever lies within will change everything.

We climb the winding stairs and push through the oak door. Lyssar Temple is vast and cavernous, its ceilings stretching high above, adorned with murals that depict battles, rituals, and cosmic phenomena. The colors are impossibly vivid, as though painted only yesterday, yet there is an unmistakable sense of age. Columns line the walls, their bases carved with depictions of mortals and gods united, their tops disappearing into shadow.

The central chamber is dominated by a circular pool of water, its surface so still it resembles glass. The water glows faintly with an other-worldly light, as though reflecting Stars that do not exist in the sky above. Around the pool, an array of stone pedestals hold relics encased in crystal, their forms just barely discernible through the shimmer.

The acoustics of the temple amplify every sound—a whisper becomes a murmur, and a footsteps echo like a drumbeat. It's as though the temple listens, every noise a conversation with the divine. At its heart, Lyssar Temple feels alive, a place that has seen the rise and fall of empires, the forging of oaths, and the unraveling of fates.

The air carries a faint scent of stone, metal, and something indefinable—perhaps magic itself. There is a weight here, as though the temple bears the collective history of all who have come before.

It is not merely a structure; it is a testament, a memory, and a warning, all at once.

The pull in my chest grows stronger with each step, like a tether tightening, guiding me deeper into the temple's embrace.

Seren moves beside me, her steps light but purposeful. Her wide eyes scan the intricate etchings carved into the walls, her hand brushing against them as if to steady herself. The golden light filtering through the crystalline fragments embedded in the walls makes her hair glow like a halo, but her expression is far from angelic—it's intense, focused, as though the temple is speaking directly to her.

"It sings," Seren whispers, her voice barely audible over the steady hum of magic in the air.

I glance at her, frowning. "What sings?"

She doesn't answer immediately, her fingers tracing the patterns of constellations and symbols. When she speaks again, her voice is distant, as if she's caught in a trance. "The walls. The etchings. They're telling a story."

"Have you read about them?" I ask.

Seren shakes her head, seemingly unable to speak.

Therion pauses ahead of us, his broad shoulders blocking part of my view as he turns back, his brow furrowed. "What do you mean, a story?"

Seren looks up at him, her eyes wide and shimmering with something between wonder and fear. "It's a memory. A song. They were cursed by Eltheira, the Goddess of Balance and Harmony. These people—the ones on the walls—are forgotten. Lost. They sealed their blade here, hidden and enchanted, to be reclaimed only by their bloodline—or someone worthy who can restore balance and remember them. Find them."

I keep my eyes locked on her, unable to reconcile the fragile girl from the slums with the woman before me.

Kael's gaze sharpens, his voice low and commanding. "How do you know that?"

"I just... do," Seren replies, her voice trembling slightly. "I can feel it. It's like a whisper in my mind, like I've always known. You can't feel it? Hear it?"

Ronyn leans against a nearby pillar, his bow slung casually over his shoulder, though his eyes are anything but casual. "You're saying the walls are talking to you?"

"They're not talking," Seren says quickly, almost defensive. "It's more like... they're singing. And I understand the melody."

"Who? Who are the people? The lost ones?" I question, confused.

"I don't know. But they feel familiar," Seren offers, working it all out in real time.

Her words send a shiver down my spine, and I grip my daggers tighter. The air feels heavier now, charged with an energy I can't explain, and the pull in my chest becomes almost unbearable.

"We need to move," Kael says, his voice cutting through the tension like a blade. "If Seren can feel the etchings, they might lead us to what we're looking for. Seren, does it say anything about how to access the chamber below the temple?"

Seren nods, stepping forward with a confidence that feels out of place in this eerie, sacred space. She leads us deeper into the temple, her hand brushing the walls as though guiding herself by touch alone. The patterns on the stone seem to shift as we move, the constellations twisting and weaving into new forms. It's mesmerizing and unsettling all at once.

Then, she stops abruptly, her gaze fixed on a section of the wall where the etchings form a spiral, their golden lines glowing faintly. "Here," she says, her voice barely above a whisper. "There's a passage they would like us to enter."

Ronyn steps forward, inspecting the wall with a critical eye. "I don't see—"

Before he can finish, Seren presses her palm against the center of the spiral. The stone shudders, the sound reverberating through the temple like a low growl, and then the wall begins to shift. The stones pull apart, revealing a narrow staircase that descends into darkness.

"Of course," Ronyn mutters, rolling his eyes. "Because nothing bad ever happens in dark, hidden staircases."

Kael shoots him a sharp look, and Ronyn falls silent, though his grin doesn't fade.

We descend slowly, the air growing colder with each step. The pull in my chest is almost painful now, a constant tug that makes it hard to focus on anything else. The staircase opens into a vast chamber, its walls lined with more etchings that seem to shimmer and pulse in the dim light. In the center of the room stands a pedestal, and on it rests a blade. *My blade.*

It's beautiful, its hilt encrusted with gemstones that catch the faint light and cast fractured rainbows across the chamber. The blade itself seems to hum with power, its edge sharp enough to split the air, and runes are carved into the blade. *And it's calling to me.*

But as I step forward, the air splits apart with a roar. Shadows erupt from the walls, and the illusions begin.

CHAPTER TWENTY-SIX
ELYSSARA

My heart hammers in my chest as I watch Seren clutching her head, her eyes wide and glassy, as if staring into the void. She staggers backward, her muttering incoherent, her trembling hands clawing at the air as though warding off invisible monsters. Her breaths come in ragged, shallow gasps, the sound mingling with the pounding of my own blood in my ears.

"Stay together!" Therion growls, his voice low and guttural, his axe primed in his hands. His movements, normally deliberate and calculated, are jerky and unsteady, his sharp eyes darting to every shadow. "It's a trick! They're inside our minds!" His voice cracks on the last word, uncharacteristically unhinged.

Kael stiffens at my side, his hands gripping the hilts of his twin swords so tightly his knuckles blanch. His breath is harsh, uneven, and when I glance up at him, I see a flicker of something I never thought I'd see—fear. His face is ashen, his jaw locked, but his eyes betray him, wide and haunted, as if he's already lost the battle within.

And then it crashes over me.

The chamber dissolves in an instant, the walls replaced by the crooked, suffocating alleyways of the Virellin slums. The stench of rot and desperation chokes me, filling my lungs with bile. My heart stutters as I hear the familiar cries of the slums—the shuffle of starving bodies, the wails of children, and above it all, the muffled screams of my parents.

"No, no, no," I whisper, shaking my head violently, my vision blurring. "This isn't real," I murmur to myself.

But it feels real. It smells real. The dirt-covered cobblestones are gritty beneath my feet, the air hot and humid with the rankness of the streets. I whirl around, and there they are—my mother and father, their faces twisted in agony as the King's guards drag them away, leaving a trail of blood wiped across the ground in their wake. My mother's screams are broken, guttural cries that pierce through me, and my father's voice, usually so strong, cracks as he shouts my name.

I stagger forward, my legs barely functioning, my chest heaving with sobs I didn't know I had in me. "Stop!" I scream, my voice raw. "Stop, please!" But they don't. They can't. My hands pass through the guards like smoke, the weight of my powerlessness pressing down on me like the world itself is collapsing.

My mother's eyes meet mine for a fleeting moment, wide with terror and something worse—resignation. She knows what's coming. She knows there's nothing I can do. And then she's gone, her cries fading as they vanish into the endless, dark alleys of Virellin.

I crumple to my knees, the blood-smeared ground soaking into my trousers. "No," I whisper, my voice a broken plea. "Please, no..."

"Elyssara!" Kael's voice cuts through the haze, dragging me back to the present. My head jerks up, the image of my parents fading in fractured pieces, but the weight of the memory still claws at my chest.

Around me, the others are locked in their own battles against the illusions. Therion's axe swings wildly, his breaths coming in ragged gasps, while Seren has collapsed to her knees, her trembling hands clutching at her temples. Ronyn is the only one who seems unshaken, his bow drawn, his sharp gaze scanning the chamber.

And then, the air shifts. It thickens, grows colder, like the breath of something ancient brushing against the back of my neck.

A low growl echoes through the chamber, guttural and resonant, making the stone walls tremble. Shadows, once clinging to the edges of the room, begin to coalesce. They twist and churn like ink spilled in water, pooling together into vague, shifting shapes. At first, they are formless, their edges rippling and unstable. But then they solidify.

Figures step out of the darkness, human but wrong. Their faces are blank voids, smooth and featureless, yet they exude a menace that sends a chill down my spine. Their limbs are elongated, their movements unnervingly fluid as they advance. Some wield weapons—swords, spears, axes—while others simply flex clawed hands, their sharp tips glinting in the faint light of the runes.

"They're forming! Strike!" Therion growls, his voice edged with fury. He spins, his axe cleaving through one of the shapes. It shatters like glass, dark shards scattering before evaporating into nothing. But for every one he destroys, two more seem to rise from the shadows in its place.

Kael is already moving, his twin swords a blur of silver as they slice through the encroaching figures. His movements are deadly and precise, his strikes surgical. One of the figures lunges at him with a spear, but Kael sidesteps with predatory grace, his sword slashing through its torso in one smooth arc. The figure dissolves into shadow, but Kael doesn't pause, already pivoting to face the next threat.

"Stay close to me!" he shouts, his voice cutting through the chaos.

Seren lets out a strangled cry as one of the figures closes in on her. Her wide, tear-streaked eyes dart around frantically, her breath shallow and panicked. The creature lunges, claws outstretched, slicing into Seren's flesh above her knee but Ronyn's arrow finds its mark immediately, piercing through its head. The shadowy form collapses, writhing for a moment before shattering.

"Get up, Seren!" Ronyn calls, his tone sharp but not unkind. "Keep moving!"

Seren, clutching at her leg, stands on shaky feet and seeks safety behind Ronyn.

Therion is surrounded now, three of the figures circling him like wolves around wounded prey. He swings his axe in a broad arc, keeping them at bay, but one manages to slip through his defense. Its clawed hand rakes across his arm, drawing a thin line of blood. Therion snarls, turning on it with a vicious strike that obliterates the creature, but the effort leaves him open.

Another figure lunges, its jagged blade aimed directly at his chest.

Ronyn moves before I can even shout a warning. He leaps into the fray, his dagger flashing as it intercepts the shadow's blade mere inches from Therion's chest. With a deft twist, Ronyn plunges his dagger into the creature's neck, and it collapses into smoke.

Therion stumbles back, his breathing heavy, his eyes wide with a mixture of shock and something softer—gratitude. He nods at Ronyn, a silent acknowledgment, before turning back to the fight.

I barely register the moment as another figure barrels toward me, its clawed hand swiping for my throat. I duck, my daggers flashing as I drive them upward into its midsection. The creature lets out a piercing screech before disintegrating, but I don't have time to catch my breath. More are coming, their movements relentless and unyielding.

Kael is a whirlwind of destruction, his swords carving through the shadows like they're nothing more than mist. Yet even he begins to falter, the endless tide of enemies wearing him down. His chest heaves with exertion, sweat slicking his brow, but his movements remain precise, calculated. He's fighting for all of us, and he knows it.

The blade's pull grows stronger, a burning urgency in my chest that drives me forward despite the chaos. I dodge another swipe, my heart pounding as the tug leads me toward the center of the chamber. The shadows press in from all sides, their guttural growls filling the air, but I don't stop. I can't stop.

"Elyssara!" Kael shouts again, his voice raw with desperation. He's fighting to reach me, cutting down everything in his path, but the creatures are relentless.

"I'm going for the blade!" I yell back, my voice barely audible over the cacophony. The blade's presence is undeniable now, a beacon of light in the overwhelming darkness. It's close. So close.

The shadows seem to understand my intent, their movements growing more frenzied, more violent. They're trying to stop me, to keep me from the blade. *My blade.* But their desperation only fuels my resolve. Vengeance is my battle cry.

The blade calls to me, its song resonating through my very bones, and I know—this is my destiny.

The pull only grows stronger with every step, an unrelenting force that feels as though it's tugging at my very soul. The illusions press harder, the shadowed forms converging like a tide determined to drown me before I can reach it. My breaths come fast and shallow, my arms trembling from the endless swings of my daggers, but I keep moving.

I'm so close.

Kael's voice cuts through the chaos again, raw and desperate. "Elyssara, move!" He's still cutting through the shadowed forms with relentless precision, but even he looks like he's beginning to tire.

The blade's call strengthens, drowning out everything else. My vision narrows, the chamber blurring at the edges as I lock on to the pedestal. It's there. Gleaming. Perfect. *Mine.*

A figure lunges at me, its jagged blade glinting in the eerie light, but I sidestep at the last second, driving my dagger into its side. The shadow screeches, its form shattering into shards, but another takes its place almost instantly.

I'm enveloped in ink-black shadows, surrounding me without touching me—there is a clear tunnel void of shadows between me and my blade. A clear path. *Kael's magic.* I start moving forward and realize the otherworldly howls and screeches of the overwhelming number of attackers in the underground chamber go completely silent.

"Go, El!" Ronyn yells. "We've got this!"

"Touch the blade, El—everything will stop," Seren shouts to me through the shadow magic blocking my view of the others.

I grit my teeth, forcing my legs to keep moving even as my still-healing leg threatens to drag me down. The pedestal looms closer, the blade glowing faintly with an ethereal light that seems to reach out to me. With one final lunge, I reach the pedestal. My trembling hand closes around the blade's hilt, and the world stills, the blade instantly soothing me and the world around me.

For a moment, there's nothing but silence. Kael's shadow magic dissipates around me, the shadow attackers evaporate back into the walls, their forms no longer visible. Then, the hilt warms beneath my grip, a perfect fit, as though it were crafted for me and me alone.

Light erupts from the blade, a radiant burst that floods the chamber. I stagger back, the intensity of the light overwhelming, but I don't let go. The warmth spreads from the blade to my arm, then to my chest, igniting something deep within me.

Pain and exhilaration crash over me as the Lightborne marking on my chest flares to life. Slowly, the glowing mark begins to fade, save for the Stars at the edge of my chest near my collarbones—they stay. Imprinted—glowing with a luminous brilliance.

As the light fades, I press trembling fingers against the glowing Stars spattered like luminous paint at the edge of my chest. The mark is permanent now, etched into my flesh as a promise—or perhaps a curse. My magic thrums beneath the surface of my skin, wild and unrelenting, fighting its bindings as if it's been imprisoned for too long.

A blaze of light shoots from my fingertips, spearing into the ground beneath me, and leaving a jagged hole in the chamber's floor. The others leap back, a flash of panic in their eyes, as if I might hurt them. I feel a tingling heat rushing through my veins, and a frenzied urge to expel it from my body.

"Elyssara, breathe. Your magic is trying to unleash. Breathe. Command it into submission. You control *it*, not the other way around." Kael's soothing tone is the most unsettling part. I can hear the concern lacing his words.

"I don't know how!" I yell back, my voice breaking on the last word—I can feel myself losing control, my magic threatening to take me over. I feel as if I'm going to combust.

"I want you to find the place in your body where your magic

lives—start with your chest, where your mark is," he instructs, tone measured.

I close my eyes, turning my gaze inward.

"Yes, I feel it," I whimper, placing my hands over my chest.

"Imagine your magic is contained within a small ball of light. Now search for any magic within your body that is not held within that ball. Find it, call it back. Command it to return to its rightful place," his tone serious.

"Okay. Okay. I'm trying. It's not listening!" I sob.

"Breathe. Do not ask it, Elyssara. Tell it. Command it. *Make it.*"

I breathe deeply into my belly, the way my mother taught me to do when I was having nightmares, and I attempt to leash my magic.

Return home.

Come back to me.

You are not needed.

I am safe.

Come home.

The heat in my skin begins to dissipate, and I can feel the tingling in my veins retreat, slowly but definitively, my magic is receding into its home inside my chest.

"Good girl. That's it," Kael encourages.

My cheeks warm at his approval, and a hot pulse pools in low in my centre. *Get a fucking grip, Elyssara. Not the time for this!*

I take one more deep breath and lift my eyes to glance around the group, everyone seeming to exhale properly for the first time since we flung out of The Gateway.

But it's short-lived.

A roar fills my ears—not from within the chamber but from the world outside. The ground trembles beneath my feet, and the air grows heavy with an ominous charge. Thunder rumbles in the distance, deep and menacing, and a flicker of lightning illuminates the chamber for a brief moment.

"What the fuck was that?" Ronyn mutters, lowering his bow as he stares at the trembling walls.

Kael steps toward me, his gaze sharp and wary as he eyes the blade. "Elyssara, are you doing that?"

"I'm not doing anything, I swear it. I'm calm. My magic is contained," I try to temper my voice, but I cannot keep the panic out of it.

But the storm outside grows louder, the thunder rolling closer, and a deep unease settles over me. From the small glimpse of sky I can see through the chamber entrance, the clouds above churn like a cauldron, black and furious, streaked with veins of lightning that tear through the heavens. It isn't a natural storm; it feels... deliberate.

"What's happening?" I whisper, my voice barely audible over the rumble, but there is no mistaking how out of control I feel.

Therion steps beside me, his expression attuned to the energy and elements as he stares toward the chamber's entrance. "This storm is not born of the elements. It's made of The Shadow Wastes."

The blade hums softly in my hand, its glow flickering like a heartbeat.

Realization of the prophecy slams into me, demanding attention.

The blade ignites and the veil is torn.

I don't know what it means, but I know for certain the veil is torn. And whatever has been set into motion—there's no going back now.

CHAPTER TWENTY-SEVEN
ELYSSARA

WE CLIMB THE CHAMBER STAIRS AND MOVE BACK INTO THE MAIN
area of the temple, the air feeling clear and settled, the temple
returning to the tranquil and sacred state it is meant to be.

The clear blue sky beams into the temple, the storm—*the tear*—
having passed in little more than a few heartbeats, and reminding us
that it is likely still before the sun's peak.

"Well, I have *a lot* of questions," Ronyn states, always the one to
break the silence.

Therion approaches Ronyn and throws his right hand up.
Ronyn catches it just in time, before Therion pulls him in for an
embrace and claps him twice on the back. "Thank you... brother,"
he seems a little awkward, but there is something about this gesture
that feels significant. A connection and bond between our group
that goes beyond a mutually beneficial alliance to get what we want.

"Ahh, it was nothing. Really. Any time," Ronyn states casually, as
if he didn't just save his life.

"It *was* something. I understand how you've all stayed alive for as
long as you have. It is... commendable, what you have been able to
get through together." Therion clears his throat, compliments
clearly not natural for him at all.

Ronyn shrugs before adding, "We're family. That's what we do for each other."

"I will not forget this," Therion says, like a prayer and a promise.

I feel as if I've just witnessed something special, and for the first time since we started this insane hunt across the realms, I'm beginning to wonder if we might actually pull this off.

"May I see the blade? It has something on it, and I'd love to research it when we're near a library." Seren's excitement and curiosity shift the energy of the room.

"You were... brilliant in there, Seren. You're very clever," Therion gives her a curt nod as he finishes the last word.

"Th—Thank you... Therion. That's very kind of you," Seren responds, surprised by the compliment.

"See—he's not always an asshole," Kael quips.

"Fuck off, Kael," Therion snaps, cheeks flushing.

I can't fight the chuckle that's been building in my throat, and I let it out freely. Laughing throatily and with abandon for the first time in a very long time.

Kael's eyes settle on me, his smirk turning softer, and I swear he looks at me with fondness, his gaze lingering for far longer than necessary.

I clear my throat and place the blade on the marble altar to our right. Everyone gathers around and stares at it, awed by its beauty.

The blade is forged from a metal that seems otherworldly—dark and iridescent, shifting between shades of silver, deep blue, and obsidian as it catches the light. Faint, swirling runes are etched into its surface, pulsating with a warm, golden radiance, twin to the Lightborne mark on my chest.

The runes appear almost alive, their intricate patterns forming constellations and celestial swirls that shift subtly when the blade is moved, whispering an ancient song only the chosen can hear. Tiny sparks of light flicker and dance along its edge, giving the impression of Stars being born and fading in an endless cosmic rhythm.

The hilt of the blade is equally captivating, wrapped in dark, supple leather. The pommel is shaped like a crescent moon, its edges embedded with fragments of glowing crystals that pulse faintly, as if mirroring my heartbeat when I hold it. The crossguard sweeps outward like wings in mid-flight, delicate yet unyielding, etched with more flowing patterns that mirror the blade's celestial artistry.

This weapon is not merely forged, it is crafted by the cosmos itself—a harmony of raw power and intricate beauty. It feels alive, a tangible connection to something far greater than myself—and pulsating with the promise of both creation and destruction.

We're all mesmerized, unable to break the ethereal silence the blade has commanded from us.

Seren hones in on the blade, bending down at different angles to see the runes, her honey-brown eyes noticing everything. She is whispering to herself, brow furrowed in confusion or concentration, I'm not sure.

"What do you see, Little Star?" I prompt.

"I... know what these runes say," she says, confused.

"Have you read about them?"

"No. I just... feel it... like before." Seren looks unsettled by this knowledge she holds without understanding how. Her bottom lip begins to tremble, and she looks up at me, fear in her eyes, "What am I? *Who* am I? Mavyrn told me I didn't yet know who I was."

She's unraveling, losing her grip on reality. On herself. I squeeze her arms gently. "Breathe, Little Star," I soothe.

"How do I know *this*? What is wrong with me? What—"

"Mavyrn is a crazy old bat, little one. She's full of shit. Tell us what you know," Therion cuts in. For once, I agree with him.

"Exactly. Now, what do you know?" I keep my tone gentle.

Seren's brow furrows as her hand rests against the blade. Her lips move silently, as though reciting words only she can hear. When she speaks, her voice is low, distant. "These runes—they're more than words. They're stories. Memories. A history that's... *forgotten*." She hesitates, then adds in a whisper, almost to herself, "But not to me." She pauses for several heartbeats before continuing, "They're an... introduction of sorts."

"An introduction? Of who?"

"Of the blade itself," Seren says with trepidation, but she grabs the hilt with conviction, moving it closer to her, and begins to read the runes.

> *"I am the Starforged Blade, born of fire and celestial song.*
> *Bound to the one who wields both light and shadow,*
> *I strike for balance, I sing for harmony.*
> *In my edge lies the power to sever veils,*
> *To unite what has been torn, and to awaken what lies*
>   *dormant.*
> *Only the worthy shall command the Stars."*

"Incredible," Kael says, and I'm not sure if he's talking about Seren, the blade or both, but, regardless, I agree. He reaches out to the blade, moving to pick it up, but as he gets nearer, it begins to wobble and shake, as if agitated or unsettled by him. He wraps his hand around the hilt, only to recoil instantly, a hiss escaping through his teeth. His palm is red and raw, as though burned.

"Fuck!" He hisses. "It doesn't want me to touch it," he mutters, his voice laced with both awe and confusion.

"It's hers," Seren says softly, her voice trembling but certain. Her gaze is fixed on me, wide with both fear and wonder. "The blade chose her."

"And what about you? Why does it let you touch it?" Kael's question is soft, no accusation in his tone.

"I have absolutely no idea," Seren answers honestly. "It's as if it recognizes me... it feels *familiar*."

"Well, that makes absolutely no fucking sense. But let's be honest, it's a celestial blade with personality preferences—that's enough for me to steer clear," Ronyn chimes in.

The room fills with laughter. I rearrange my daggers, making way for the Starforged Blade to sheathe at my thigh.

Kael slides his eyes up my body from the dagger, slow and unhurried, tracing the lines of my body with deliberate intensity.

I feel exposed under his gaze, his stare taking me aback and prickling my skin.

"Beautiful," he whispers.

A flood of warmth spreads through me, and I can't seem to look away from him.

Ronyn clears his throat, loudly, bless him. "On that note, I could use a drink, a bath and big fucking meal, anyone else?"

Thank all the gods for Ronyn's impeccable timing for once.

"Let's go to Galreth. I know a place," Therion states.

The promise of a full belly and a crisp ale is enough to make me move my sore and still-healing body. I nod eagerly, "Gods yes, let's go."

Kael's heated gaze is still lingering on me, a muscle in his jaw ticking, as if he's holding back the words dying to spill from his lips, and although I know I should not let this—*him*—distract me, I cannot deny that I like his attention. A lot. And gods, it *is* fucking distracting.

CHAPTER TWENTY-EIGHT
KAEL

THE MOUNTAIN AIR IS THIN BUT CRISP, CARRYING WITH IT THE strong scent of pine and stone. The path away from the temple winds sharply along the edge of Mount Lyssar, the cliffs plunging into a chasm of mist far below. Sunlight spills across the trail, glinting off the jagged rocks, the warmth on my back at odds with the cold shadow still lodged in my chest.

The others are quiet, their exhaustion palpable. Therion leads the way, his axe slung across his back, every step deliberate. Ronyn lingers near the middle, his bow strung and ready, his sharp eyes scanning the horizon. Seren walks beside him, her wide gaze flitting over every detail of the trail as if the mountain itself might whisper secrets. Elyssara brings up the rear, her pace steady but guarded, as though the temple's weight still clings to her.

I hold to the back, my steps purposeful. Or so I tell myself. In truth, I'm here because of her. Not because of her magic or the prophecy, but because of the way she pulls at me. The way she fills the spaces I've spent years trying to keep empty.

We walk in light conversation for several hours, the group weaving between banter and silence as the trail shifts from rugged mountain paths to softer, forested terrain. The valley below comes into clearer view, Galreth nestled within like a secret the mountain keeps close. Smoke curls from chimneys, promising warmth, and the faint scent of earth after the storm lingers in the air.

But my thoughts remain here. *With her.*

Elyssara walks just ahead of me, her auburn hair catching the sunlight, the loose waves ripped free from her braid cascading over her shoulders like molten fire. Dirt streaks her face, a smudge just beneath her sharp cheekbone, but it doesn't diminish her beauty. If anything, it sharpens it. She's stunning—strong and lethal, with a presence that commands attention. Her jade-green eyes flicker between wariness and resolve, and there's a faint glow to her Light-borne marking that peeks out from her tunic. Every step she takes is measured, every movement purposeful, but there's an unconscious grace to her, a natural magnetism that I can't ignore.

And gods help me, I've tried.

The Starforged Blade is strapped to her thigh, its hilt glinting faintly in the sunlight. My gaze lingers there too long, the blade a poor distraction from the thigh it's bound to. *Gods those thighs. Those fucking thighs.* The sheer volume of debased thoughts I've had about those pretty little thighs, about what it would feel like to be buried between them, is nothing short of indecent. She's the most dangerous thing I've ever encountered—not because of her power, but because of the way she makes me want. I am hungry for her, and I want to *feast.*

I catch myself staring again as she brushes a strand of hair from her face, her fingers grazing her lips. My breath hitches. Those lips —sensuous and inviting despite being chapped and stained with the faintest trace of blood—are a distraction I don't need. The way they curve when she smiles, the way they part when she's lost in thought, the way she sucks on her bottom lip when she's ready to fight. The way they'd look wrapped around my cock. I want to taste those beautiful lips. I want to taste all of her—her lips, her neck, whatever she'll let me have.

I'm so fucked.

I curse under my breath, dragging my focus to the trail. I'm a fool. A godsdamned fool. And yet, even as I force my gaze forward,

I feel her pulling me back. It's not her magic—not yet, anyway—but something far older, far more dangerous. It's a tether I can't see, but I feel it tightening and tugging at my chest with every step.

The path dips, leveling out as the rugged peaks of the mountain give way to gentler slopes. The village grows nearer, its stone buildings nestled together as though sharing warmth. The sun is high now, its light catching on the cobbled streets of Galreth, but even as the promise of food and rest draws the others forward, I feel stuck in the shadows of my own mind.

Elyssara slows her pace, and my steps falter in response. She doesn't notice me watching, focusing on the trail ahead, but her presence fills the silence between us. She tucks a strand of auburn hair behind her ear, her lips parting slightly as though tasting the air, and my chest tightens in response.

I don't know what it is about her that does this to me. Maybe it's the way she carries herself, like she's lived a thousand battles and is still ready for more. Or maybe it's the way she makes me feel seen— too seen. As though she can peel away the layers I've spent years building.

I can't afford to feel this way. Not now. Not ever.

The temple had dragged me back to that night in The Shadow Wastes, to the moment the guards tore my sister from my arms. The illusion of Nalya haunts me—the way her screams twisted into Elyssara's. Her face, her fear, all bleeding together until I couldn't tell who I was trying to save. I'd clawed at reality, trying to reach for her. *For them.* To save them.

But I couldn't. I never could.

The vision wasn't real, but its echo is. It claws at me, threatening to unravel the control I've fought so hard to maintain. Control I can't lose—not now, not with her.

The others' voices drift back to us, lighter now as they banter about the warmth of the tavern ahead. Elyssara glances over her shoulder, her green eyes catching mine, and for a moment, I forget how to breathe. There's something raw in her gaze, something unspoken. It's not an invitation, but it's close enough to break me.

Her lips twitch, as though she's about to say something, but she turns away, her pace quickening. The moment passes, but it leaves me reeling.

I don't know if she feels this pull between us, but I know I can't let her see how it's unraveling me. Whatever this is, it's too dangerous. For her. For me. For all of us.

The prophecy may bind us together on this journey, but I can't let it control me. Not when I still have a choice. Not when the plan is already in place.

The others move ahead, the promise of Galreth pulling them forward, but Elyssara lingers behind. My steps fall in sync with hers, the tension between us stretching taut, and I feel the weight of every unsaid word pressing against my chest.

I'll fight it. Whatever this pull is, whatever it means, I'll fight it. Because giving in to her would mean giving up everything else. Everything I've fought for, everything I've sacrificed. Even if it kills me.

CHAPTER TWENTY-NINE
ELYSSARA

THE LIMITED EDUCATION WE RECEIVED ON THE STREETS OF THE
Virellin slums spoke nothing of what lived beyond the Frael Forest
and Mount Lyssar. Only the Starborn received true learning behind
The Lightborne Barrier. For the rest of us—the Earthbound, and
me—knowledge was stolen, overheard, or wrestled from forbidden
books. That's how I became a frequent visitor to The Underbelly—
smuggling texts that hinted at a wider world but spoke little of its
thriving heart beyond the mountains.

The people of Virellin know very little about life before King
Thalmyr usurped the throne—fragmented snippets, moments of
lucidity punctuated by hazy details, but nothing solid. Nothing
certain. Even those old enough to remember life before his reign
seem to have forgotten exactly what it was like. *Were we a happy
people? Did we laugh? Were we always this hungry? Were the Earthbound and
Starborn always so at odds?* We already know that Thalmyr keeps a
tight leash on knowledge, but it's truly as if *he* is our history. Pages
torn from our books, stories stolen from our lips, memories taken
from our minds—all of it selective, and all of it hidden. How, I've
not a clue. Where, I do not know.

But I do know.

Revryn told me of Galreth once, of its artisans and villages, but his words were dull compared to the colorful life that greets me now. Perhaps he wanted me to see it with my own eyes. Or perhaps no words could ever do it justice.

Nestled on the northern outskirts of Mount Lyssar, where the rugged cliffs give way to rolling hills, lies the peaceful village of Galreth. The town is a vibrant tapestry of life, its terracotta-roofed buildings clustered together—neighbors within arm's reach. The air is tinged with the sweet aroma of wildflowers that grow along the pathways. Sunlight bathes the cobblestone streets, casting soft, golden light on to the bustling market stalls and quaint artisan shops.

The market square, the heart of Galreth, is a lively hub of activity. Merchants peddle their wares from wooden carts laden with handwoven textiles, polished trinkets, and fresh produce. The scent of baked bread wafts from a small bakery tucked into the corner of the square, its chimney releasing thin wisps of smoke into the clear blue sky.

A merchant's deep voice booms as he haggles with a customer over the price of handwoven blankets. Nearby, a woman laughs brightly, holding up a necklace that catches the sunlight. The clinking of coins and the rustle of fabric blend into a symphony of life that feels foreign to me.

Children dart between the stalls, laughing and playing, their carefree joy a stark contrast to the tense, purposeful energy of our group. More poignantly, it is a stark contrast to the streets of the slums, where children could be heard crying of hunger, the heat, or the absence of a parent. It's strange, unsettling even, to see so many carefree children. Their laughter is light and easy, unburdened by hunger or fear. I don't think I've ever heard a sound like it in the slums. For a moment, I'm gripped by an unfamiliar ache—jealousy, perhaps? Or grief for something I never had and never will.

A well-trodden path lined with flower boxes leads us to a modest tavern near the edge of the village center, its weathered sign swinging gently with the wind; *The Twilight Hearth*. The sound of distant laughter and the clinking of mugs creates an inviting warmth, a stark reprieve from the chaos of the temple.

The peace here feels almost unnatural, as though the storm we left behind at the temple might find its way to us again. I try to shake the thought, but it lingers like a shadow in the back of my mind.

Here, I realize, there is no magic—or at least, none that I can see or sense. The people are unmarked by the burdens of power or prophecy, their lives defined by simple rhythms and shared moments. There's a tranquility to Galreth, a fleeting sense of safety that wraps around me like a fragile shield.

The Twilight Hearth seems to be the pride of the village, with locals crowded around the entrance, spilling in and out in a rhythm. Inside, it's warm and inviting, with low timber ceilings, a roaring fireplace, and long tables where villagers and travelers have gathered to share stories. Handwoven tapestries depicting ancient myths hang on the walls, the scent of roasted meat and spiced cider wraps around me, and for the first time in years, I feel my body relax. It's strange, this warmth, this sense of belonging that isn't mine. I've spent so long surviving on the edges of existence that I'm not sure how to let myself sink into it.

Young suitors sit at a table near the window, their heads bent close together as they share a bowl of stew. The man brushes a strand of hair from the woman's face, and she laughs softly, the sound warm and free. I glance away, a strange pang twisting in my chest. *What would it be like, I wonder, to laugh like that? To belong like that?* The barkeep approaches us with a broad smile, but his eyes linger on Ronyn's weapon. His grin falters, just for a moment, before he places a tray of full-to-the-brim mugs on the table. "Welcome to Galreth," he says, his voice even but cautious. "It's rare to see new faces this time of year."

Therion gives the barkeep a curt nod, and turns back towards us, cutting short any further conversation with the burly man behind the bar.

"I don't know who's paying, but I want one of everything!"

Ronyn pierces the heaviness of my thoughts with his usual levity, and I huff a laugh.

Therion strides towards Ronyn and places gold coins into his hand. "It's the least I can do. Fill your bellies, we'll be back soon—we have some things to take care of."

Even as warmth seeps into my muscles, my mind refuses to follow. Years of surviving the streets have taught me that peace this complete rarely lasts, and the mention of 'things to take care of' is all it takes for my guard to snap back into place.

The spell of Galreth is broken. I'm watching for the blade behind the smile. Always looking for ways I will be crossed or stabbed in the back—literally or metaphorically. Gellesk has taught me to always be sceptical of those offering help—usually because he was the one fucking me over.

"What things?" My gaze flicks between Therion and Kael, searching their faces for deception. "Therion? Kael? What are you doing?" I try to school my voice into cool indifference, but the rising octave of my voice betrays me.

Kael chuckles gently, "We're just going to acquire rooms for the evening—we all need a good night's rest. And, Therion and I have a couple of friends here—we just need to check in with them. Let them know we're okay."

Kael brushes his hand down my arm, leaning close enough that his breath is a caress against my skin. "Will you miss me, Duskae?" he whispers, his voice rough and low, curling down my spine. Heat blooms in my chest, unwanted and unrelenting, and I force my gaze to the hearth, to the flames licking at the charred logs. Even they fail to chase away the smirk I can feel etched into my skin.

Gods help me, I hate him. And gods help me, I'm a fucking liar.

Something about Kael's tone feels too casual, too easy. My instincts bristle, a sharp tug at the back of my mind, as though the air here carries more than just baked goods and wildflowers. The peace of Galreth is fragile. Like glass, it waits for the first crack to shatter, and so does this alliance, I realize. A small part of me—quiet, buried—wants to believe him. Wants to lean into the warmth he exudes so carelessly. But the streets taught me that warmth is often the prelude to a blade in the back.

"Ugh. No, I will not miss you, Kael," I snarl, imbuing my words with more bite than I feel. "But don't fuck us over. Or you'll realize that what I did to those duskprowlers was childplay."

Kael chuckles again, "So mouthy when you're hungry, El. You should eat. I hear this tavern has the best ale in town—it's brewed with local honey. And the roasted pork is god-sent."

"I, for one, *love* roasted pork... and ale! Right, gents, go get us a room. We'll order!" Ronyn has always had a one-track mind, especially when it comes to food.

Kael winks at me. He fucking *winks* at me. The audacity and arrogance he wears like a mask snaps firmly back in place, and I'm not sure if I'm grateful for the distraction from everything—the prophecy, the flirting, or the unsettling sense of foreboding—or if I miss the small parts of him he's started to reveal to me. Kael's charm is a weapon, honed and precise. I tell myself it's no different from the daggers at my side—sharp and dangerous. But the version of me that hasn't been hardened by years of distrust wonders if it's something else entirely.

"If you're finished bickering like children, we'll see you back here shortly," Therion says, his tone as dry as the wind brushing through the tavern door. He claps Ronyn on the shoulder, his nod conveying far more than words ever could.

The tavern door swings shut behind them, and I turn back to our group, and throw an arm around their shoulders, "Well, I guess it's just us again. Let's eat!"

"And I *really* need a drink," Seren says, a bashful smile tugging at her lips.

Seren's admission earns a mock gasp from Ronyn, who clutches his chest like she's confessed to treason. "Our little Seren, taking her first steps into debauchery!" he teases, and her blush deepens. I laugh, the sound startling even me. For a moment, the weight of the prophecy feels lighter.

We've never seen her have a drink in all our years together, and Seren hastily adds, "I mean, it's not like I've ever had one, but I feel like this is the perfect chain of events where one *would* start drinking... right?"

"Right!" Ronyn and I say, laughing bubbling up, in unison.

We make our way back to the barkeep, and order enough food to keep us full for days, and enough honey-brewed ale to forget the weight of the realms that feel like it's sitting firmly on my shoulders.

As we settle at the table, mugs in hand, the warmth of the tavern seeps into my bones. For a moment, I let myself forget the prophecy, the temple, and the storm. I allow myself the luxury of laughter, the rare comfort of Ronyn's teasing, and Seren's bashful grin. But peace like this is fragile, I remind myself—easily shattered. The cracks are there, waiting to break. And when they do, I wonder which side of them I'll find myself on.

CHAPTER THIRTY

ELYSSARA

We are deep in our cups, having laughed, danced, and filled our bellies for hours. I can't remember a time when I've felt this... full. Rich with the sort of happiness that doesn't come with a catch. For once, I'm not bracing for the next blow or measuring every word to survive another day. It feels fragile, fleeting. But gods, do I want to hold on to it for just a little longer. The ale cloaks me in a layer of warmth, its golden haze softening the edges of the world.

"So, El... Kael is a mighty fine-looking lad, is he not?" Ronyn's face is already split into that lopsided grin. "Very symmetrical," he adds, his voice dripping with mock innocence.

I groan, covering my face with my hands. "Oh gods, I'm never going to be allowed to forget that, am I?"

"Nope," Ronyn quips, his laugh spilling out with reckless abandon.

"Definitely not," Seren confirms, her grin stretching wide enough to light up the room.

"Can I at least get a free pass, considering I had both Lunabark root and duskprowler venom in my veins?" I grimace, already knowing there's no chance of escape.

"I'd allow it—if you hadn't also guessed he had a really big cock," Seren blurts. Then freezes. Her hands slap over her mouth, her eyes wide with horror. "Oh gods, I just said that out loud, didn't I?"

We all explode into laughter, the kind that shakes your ribs and makes your cheeks ache. I can barely breathe, tears forming at the corners of my eyes. For once, there's nothing else—no prophecy, no fear, just us.

The warmth of the room tilts suddenly, a chill slipping down my spine even as laughter spills from my lips. Kael's shadow falls over the table, broad and imposing, before he slides in beside me with a casual grace that makes my pulse quicken. He doesn't ask for permission; he never does. Instead, he picks up my mug, takes a sip, and looks around the table, his smirk firmly in place.

"So, what are we laughing at?" His voice is low, smooth, and entirely too self-assured.

I bury my head in my hands, wishing I could disappear into the floorboards. The heat in my cheeks spreads to my neck, and I'm certain Kael's smirk is aimed directly at me. He leans closer, his shoulder brushing mine, and the warmth I'd been reveling in turns into a blaze I can't escape. "Something you wanna tell me, Duskae?" Kael asks, his voice rich with teasing, his eyes gleaming with far too much satisfaction.

All I can manage is a vehement shake of my head, my hands still plastered over my face as if that will stop the inferno that's erupted under my skin.

Our laughter rises again, louder and more chaotic, but my heart pounds in my chest, a frantic beat that has nothing to do with the ale.

Between bursts of laughter, Seren asks, "Where's Therion? He's been gone a while."

Kael leans back, the corner of his mouth twitching upward in that infuriating way of his. "He's coming in a moment, with a couple of our... friends." The pause in his sentence alerts my instincts, but he doesn't give me time to question it. "We've secured a couple of rooms that should suffice for a night or two, depending on when we're ready to leave for the next relic."

Friends? The word sinks in slowly. I've spent too many years looking for hidden meanings in the simplest words, and Kael's casual delivery only sharpens my suspicion. I force a sip of my drink, letting the warmth spread through me as I fight to settle the gnawing feeling that something—or someone—is about to disrupt the fragile peace we've found here.

And then, as if summoned by my thoughts, the tavern door creaks open. The warmth of the hearth spills out to greet three shadowed figures who step into the room with an ease that makes my pulse spike.

The first is a woman—tall, confident, and strikingly beautiful. She removes her hood with a flourish, revealing long, raven-black hair that falls in a smooth cascade over her shoulders. Her deep brown eyes gleam with intelligence and a hint of mischief, and her lips curve into a knowing smile as she spots Kael. Everything about her exudes power and familiarity, as if she belongs here in a way I never will.

The second figure is an older man, his grizzled beard streaked with silver and his eyes as sharp as a blade. He carries himself like a warrior, his movements steady and deliberate, yet there's a warmth to the way he surveys the room, as if taking stock of every detail but judging none.

Kael stands, the smirk on his face softening into something warmer, something... *personal.* He clasps the man's forearm in a warrior's greeting, then turns to the woman, who pulls him into a tight embrace. Too tight, if you ask me.

"Well, if it isn't Jax and Merrik," Kael says, his voice tinged with a rare affection that makes my chest tighten. "Took you long enough."

Jax arches a brow, her smile widening as she swats his arm. "Firstly, as if you've ever waited patiently for anything in your fucking life. Secondly, it is *us* who have been waiting for *you.*"

Their camaraderie is immediate, seamless, and it sets me on edge. Kael's walls—those carefully constructed barriers that keep everyone else at bay—don't seem to exist with her. And I hate that I notice. I hate that it matters.

Merrik's gaze sweeps over the rest of us, and when it lands on me, there's a kindness in his eyes that I didn't expect. He nods once, the gesture warm and deliberate. "You must be Elyssara," he says, his voice deep and gravelly but full of quiet reassurance. "Kael's told us about you."

Has he?

My curiosity bristles against my better judgment, and I force a polite smile. "All good things, I hope."

Merrik chuckles, his laughter like the rumble of distant thunder. "Mostly," he winks at me conspiratorially, and my heart aches at the gesture because it is akin to one Revryn offered me regularly. Merrik's gaze swings to Kael before adding, "You didn't tell me she is absolutely stunning, though." He quickly brings his eyes back to me, dipping closer to my ear and whispers, "He did, I just want to see him get in trouble. He told me you have quite the mouth on you."

I like him already, and I cannot help the wide smile that stretches across my face at his cheek. "Did he now?" I say, looking to Kael in mock admonishment.

"I would never downplay Elyssara's beauty. It is obvious for everyone in this tavern to see," the sincerity in his words stun me, and I can feel my cheeks heating under his stare. "And she really does have quite the mouth," he adds, the phrase loaded and heady.

Jax's gaze flicks to me then, her dark eyes sharp but unreadable. Her smile doesn't falter, but there's something in the way she looks at me—an assessment, a calculation—that sets my nerves humming. Her smile is pleasant but her tone is razor-edged. "And you've been keeping Kael in line, I take it?"

Her words are light, but there's a warning curled beneath them, like the edge of a blade concealed under pretty skirts.

My smile doesn't falter, though I feel the prickle of irritation warming my skin. "I wasn't aware he needed managing," I say coolly. "He seems capable enough of looking after himself."

"Capable is one way to put it." Jax leans back in her chair, her eyes never leaving mine. "But Kael has always thrived under the right kind of... influence."

The words are a challenge, her intent as clear as the smirk tugging at her lips. I force a sip of my ale, letting the warmth coat my tongue as I consider my response. "Funny," I say after a moment, letting my voice turn mockingly sweet, "he seems to do just fine when left to his own devices. Almost... untouchable."

Kael's laugh cuts through the rising tension, rich and full of amusement. "Now, now," he says, his gaze bouncing between us, "Play nice. Jax has claws, El—though I'm confident that wouldn't deter you."

"I don't need confidence, Kael," I say, turning to him with a slow smile. "I have blades."

Jax raises a brow, her smile unwavering but her eyes narrowing ever so slightly. "Confidence and blades are important," she says, tapping at the sword belted at her waist, her tone deceptively kind. "But trust? That's earned."

"Then I guess we'll see how that works out, won't we?" I reply, letting the edge in my voice match hers.

Kael looks between us, his smirk widening as though he's enjoying the show far too much. "Well, this is going to be fun," he murmurs into his honeyed ale, low enough that I'm sure only I hear it.

"I'm gettin' a round for everyone," Merrik says to no one in particular, trying to get out of this conversation as quickly as possible, no doubt.

Jax's attention finally shifts, but her unspoken warning lingers in the air like smoke. And though I meet her smile with one of my own, I feel the weight of her claim. This is her territory, her familiarity with Kael a fortress I've yet to breach. But if she thinks I'll back down, she doesn't know me. Not yet.

The drinks flow freely, and the food never stops coming. Jax has kept one eye on the patrons inside the tavern and one on me for the entirety of the night. She clearly distrusts me, but I can't say I'm overly trusting of her, either. My greatest weapon has always been my keen perception, and I've applied it thoroughly to Jax. She is dressed in fighting leathers that are well worn and carries a fine blade, bejeweled at the hilt, and despite her imposing beauty, she looks tired. The kind of tired that wears on you from a life without comforts, and inherent safety. Jax mentioned having waited for Kael, which makes me think she's been here, or somewhere nearby, holed up with little of life's luxuries for a while. But the way she is churning through her ale with little effect on her senses and speech, she seems to be no stranger to a drink. Jax is built like a warrior, and she moves, speaks and watches like one, too. Never missing a thing.

Whenever she does steal her eyes away from the tavern, and settles into the steady rhythm of conversation amongst our group, she seems at home. She has an obvious lighthearted and mutually respectful relationship with Merrik, and she has a somewhat *personal*, or dare I say, *intimate* relationship with Kael, which makes me grind my teeth. I am aware that I have absolutely no claim on this man whatsoever, and in fact, it would be incredibly irresponsible to act on any desire I feel for him. Still, I can't help the simmering fury that bubbles away in my chest at the sight of her grazing his chest plate and resting her hand on his knee.

I watch him. His dark hair tousled by travel and rain hangs across his forehead, shadowing the sharp lines of his face. His eyes flick up to me as Jax drifts her hand down his arm, *again*, and his eyebrow quirks up in silent amusement at whatever he must see written all over my face or in my body language.

I huff at him and roll my eyes, crossing my arms—*very mature*—and turn towards Merrik for what he has proven will be a fun, engaging and cheeky conversation. Merrik begins to regale me with tales of past battles and tells me of those he fought by Kael's father's side. I prompt him for details and specifics, but he is masterful in his evasion, so I settle for what he *is* willing to tell me. He waxes lyrical of pranks and jokes the warriors played on each other, and that he has taken it upon himself to uphold this wherever he goes and whoever he fights alongside. "Nothing bonds people together like laughter and shared memories," he says. My gaze drifts up as I listen and I catch the eye of a handsome gentleman at the bar. He nods at me and throws me an unfairly charming smile. I look over to Kael, and he is engrossed in a conversation with Jax, their eyes locked on one another. In a fit of frustration, I make a decision.

I interrupt Merrik's tales, "Merrik, excuse me. I'm so sorry to interject, but I need to use the privy. Can we pick this conversation back up in a moment?"

"Of course, darlin'. I've been waffling all night! It's out the back past the bar, love."

I get up from our table, and make my way towards the bar and the handsome man who smiled at me.

"Good evening," I say in my most sensuous tone, before realizing that I am absolutely filthy and haven't bathed in days, and I'm also quite drunk, as evidenced by the way the room tilts in my vision. *Fucking Stars, Elyssara.* Well, I'm here now, so I guess I'll have to keep going.

The man at the bar turns toward me, his smile widening as his eyes rake over my face and down my body, lingering too long in a way that feels invasive—just enough to make my skin prickle. "Good evening, indeed," he replies, his voice smooth and confident. "You're not from around here, are you?"

"Is it that obvious?" I ask, letting my lips curve into a sly smile, even as my pulse quickens. *Stars, Elyssara, what are you doing?* But just as I move to turn, acknowledging that this was a bad idea, I feel Kael's eyes on me from across the room, burning into my back, and something reckless inside me takes over.

"Obvious? No," the man says, leaning slightly closer. "Intriguing? Definitely."

I tilt my head, playing into the moment despite the gnawing voice in the back of my mind telling me that this man is all pretty smiles and dark motives. "Intriguing can be dangerous."

"Danger can be thrilling," he replies, his grin widening. The easy charm in his tone feels forced now, like he's trying too hard to impress. But it doesn't matter—this isn't about him. "Where is a pretty woman like you staying tonight?"

"A gentleman never asks a question like that without offering to solve the problem, now does he?" *Oh my gods, why am I still speaking?*

Before he can reply, the warmth at my back shifts, a shadow falling over me. My heart stutters, and I don't need to turn around to know it's Kael. His presence is unmistakable—solid, command-ing, and suddenly, terrifyingly and thrillingly close.

"El," Kael's voice is low and quiet, but there's a steel edge to it that sends a shiver down my spine. "I think you've had enough fun for tonight, don't you?"

I glance back at him, my expression carefully neutral despite the way my blood hums in my veins. "You are not in charge of my *fun*, Kael. Go have some of your own—Jax is waiting." I wave him off with a dismissive flick of my wrist.

"Let the lady have a little fun, my friend," the man remarks, and I instantly know that he has made a grave error.

Kael's eyes are dark, his jaw tight as his gaze flicks briefly to the man at the bar before settling back on me. "You are mine to keep safe," he grits out.

"Oh?" I ask, my tone light but biting. "And when did I become yours? Before or after Jax was basically sitting in your lap?"

His lips twitch into a smirk, suddenly becoming amused. "Jeal-ousy looks good on you, Duskae." Without taking his eyes off me, he adds, "He can't give you what you're looking for. We're leaving."

Before I can respond, Kael steps closer, his muscled body brushing against mine as he places a gold coin on the bar. His pres-ence is a wall between me and the man now, and the air around us crackles with unspoken tension. "Her drink's done," he says flatly to the man, who blinks in surprise. He looks like he's about to argue, but he leaves and returns to his comrades.

Kael turns back to me, his voice low and for my ears only. "I am the only man that will solve the problem of where you are sleeping tonight and any night, do you understand?"

"I am not yours to command," I counter, my tone clipped. I furrow my brow in annoyance as my chest tightens at the possessive-ness in his gaze. "I was perfectly fine here." *No I wasn't.*

"I don't share," he says, his hand brushing my arm as if to guide me away from the bar.

The words hit me like a blow, sharp and deliberate, and yet they ignite something dark and exhilarating in me. I don't fight him as he leads me toward the stairs at the back of the tavern, his grip firm but not rough.

As Kael's hand brushes my arm, the weight of his words lingers in the air: *I don't share.* My heart pounds against my ribs, an intoxicating mix of anger, defiance, lust, hunger, and something darker I don't dare name. His grip is firm but steady as he leads me toward the stairs, but before we can reach them, the man from the bar reappears, flanked by two companions.

"Taking off already?" the man sneers, his earlier charm now replaced with something far more sinister. He steps into our path, his smile a taunt. "We were just starting to get acquainted."

Kael's body shifts subtly, his stance broadening as he steps partially in front of me. His hand releases my arm, but the weight of his presence wraps around me like a shield. "You're making a mistake," Kael says, his voice low and calm, like the first rumble of thunder.

The man chuckles, his companions flanking him. "Are you always this possessive of your whores? Look at her filthy body, Galreth's finest lady of the night." He says it with grandeur, and looks around at his companions, who snicker at his taunts.

Kael's smirk is cold, lethal. "Wrong answer."

The man's grin falters, and Kael's hand moves so fast I barely see it, gripping the man by the collar and slamming him against the nearest wall. The impact reverberates through the alley, and the man's cocky demeanor vanishes, replaced by wide-eyed panic. "Do not touch what is mine," Kael growls, his voice edged with something primal.

The man's companions step forward, drawing daggers, but Kael is faster. In a fluid motion, he spins, using the first man's body as a shield as he deflects a clumsy slash. The alley erupts into chaos, and I'm shoved back against the wall, my breath catching as I watch Kael move with terrifying precision.

His blade flashes in the dim light, a streak of glinting onyx cutting through the shadows. He disarms one of the men with a brutal twist of his wrist, the dagger clattering to the ground. The other lunges at him, but Kael sidesteps easily, driving an elbow into the attacker's ribs with a sickening crack.

The Starforged Blade sings at my side, begging me to draw and use it, so I don't hesitate. I unsheathe the blade, its bejeweled hilt glinting from the Stars in the night sky. The man with the obviously broken ribs moves towards me with wild rage in his eyes, but I am nothing if not at home in alleyway fights for survival. I stalk towards him, my blade yearning to slice through flesh.

The man lunges, his movements wild and unrefined—predictable, even. I drop low beneath his haymaker, the Starforged Blade singing as it slices through the back of his leg. He crumples, screaming, but I don't hesitate. The streets taught me better—hesitation gets you killed. Revryn's voice echoes in my mind: *Incapacitate first, then go for the kill.* My knee drives into his chest as I drag the blade across his cheek. Control the fight. End it before it begins.

For the first time, I see the singe marks left in the blade's wake. He screams in agony, so I lean close to his ear before spitting the words at him, "You should keep better company." I get off him, a blood-curdling scream ripping from his throat as his hands search his face for the damage, and I'm satisfied that he won't fuck with me again.

I look up in time to see one of the men slump to the ground, groaning, while Kael turns his attention back to the leader. He's still pinned against the wall, Kael's forearm pressed against his throat. "Now that she's available to give you her full attention, *apologize,*" Kael demands, his tone ice-cold.

The man gasps for air, clawing at Kael's arm. "I— I'm sorry! I didn't mean anything by it!"

Kael's smirk returns, a shadowed expression that sends a chill through me. "Didn't mean anything by it?" His voice is a low rasp, thick with contempt. "That's the best you can muster? After touching what doesn't belong to you? After disrespecting her?" His forearm presses harder against the man's throat, eliciting a strangled gasp.

"Kael," I say softly, the sound of my voice surprising me. The fire in his gaze flicks to mine for the briefest moment, and I can see the battle raging in him—control versus destruction. It's raw, dangerous, and devastatingly alluring. His honed body, all muscle and vein, arrest my attention. He looks to be carved by the gods themselves.

He exhales sharply through his nose, turning back to the man. "You should thank her. She's the only reason you're still breathing." His arm releases, and the man crumples to the ground, coughing and choking as he scrambles backward, away from Kael.

Kael doesn't look at him again. Instead, his eyes find mine, and the intensity in them is almost unbearable. The chaos around us fades—the groaning bodies, the bloodied ground, the smoldering magic from my blade—all of it seems to vanish under the weight of his ocean-blue gaze.

He steps toward me, slow and deliberate, and my breath hitches as the distance between us disappears. "Are you hurt?" he asks, his voice quieter now but no less commanding.

I shake my head, still clutching the Starforged Blade in my hand. "No, I—" My voice catches, and I force myself to steady it. "I'm fine. I can handle myself."

His eyes flick down to the blade in my hand, then back to my face. There's a glint of approval there, but also something darker, more possessive. "I don't doubt that," he says, his voice rough. "But you shouldn't have to."

"And yet, here I am," I bite back, forcing steel into my voice. "I don't need you to fight my battles, Kael." But even as I say the words, the memory of his blade flashing through the shadows—his rage, his precision—makes my breath hitch.

His lips curl into a smirk, but it's softer this time, less taunting and more... something else. "I know you don't," he murmurs, reaching out to brush a thumb along my jawline, smearing a streak of blood I hadn't realized was there. "But I told you—I don't share." His thumb brushes over my jaw again, slower this time, as if to emphasize his words. "And what's mine doesn't bleed for scum." His gaze holds mine, the storm in his eyes daring me to argue.

I swallow hard, my chest tightening at the weight of his words.

His. The air between us crackles with unspoken tension, thick and suffocating, but I can't bring myself to look away from him.

"Come," he says, his voice softer now, though the edge of command still lingers. "I have something for you," he says, his tone gentle, though the edge in his eyes remains. "Something I've been waiting to give you."

"Shouldn't you go back to Jax?" I can't believe it's still at the forefront of my mind, but it's out before I can catch it. *Jealousy isn't a virtue, Elyssara. But Stars, it's burning through me, anyway.*

An amused quirk kicks up one side of his mouth, "No, Duskae. It's not like that." Without another word of explanation, he nudges my elbow to lead me away from the tavern. I hesitate, just for a breath—a life in the slums will do that to a person—before following him. My legs move before my mind catches up, drawn by the quiet command in his touch.

I sheathe the Starforged Blade, the heat of the fight still coursing through my veins. My pulse thunders, not just from the violence but from the way Kael looked at me—like the chaos didn't unsettle him, like he saw the darkness in me and welcomed it.

"Let's go," I say finally, my voice steadier than I feel.

As he leads me away, I glance back at the carnage we're leaving in our wake. It should horrify me, but it doesn't. Instead, I feel... alive. And Kael, with all his unrelenting fury, feels like the only person who might truly understand that.

This darkness, this violence—it terrifies me, but gods, it draws me to him like a moth to a flame.

CHAPTER THIRTY-ONE
KAEL

The warmth of the tavern buzzed around me—the low hum of chatter, the crackle of the hearth, the scent of spiced cider and roasted meat. Yet none of it touched me.

My senses were attuned elsewhere.

Drawn inevitably to her.

Elyssara.

Even across the room, laughing and leaning into her companions, she commanded my attention in a way no battlefield or blade ever had. I told myself it was strategy—necessary. She was unpredictable, volatile—the wayward point of a sword. If I didn't keep my eyes on her, she might slip through my fingers entirely.

But Stars help me, it wasn't just strategy.

There was something about her I couldn't define.

I'd known fierce women. Soft women. Cunning women.

None of them had ever sunk under my skin like this.

It wasn't her sharp tongue or fire, though those drew me like nothing else. It was the way she carried the weight of a world on her shoulders—and refused to let anyone see it. The way she kept her walls up, only to let them slip when she thought no one was watching.

It was maddening.

It was magnetic.

And I couldn't fucking look away.

"She's watching you," Jax murmured, her voice pulling me back to the present.

I didn't turn my head, but I felt the weight of Elyssara's gaze even from across the room. "She watches everything," I replied, my tone deliberately nonchalant.

"She's watching *you*," Jax said again, her lips curving into a faint smirk. "And if looks could kill, I'd already be halfway to the grave."

I chuckled, low and under my breath. "You'd survive. You always do."

Jax arched a brow, her gaze sharp despite the teasing lilt in her voice. "You're playing a dangerous game, Kael."

"I like dangerous games," I said, leaning back in my chair and letting my eyes drift briefly to Elyssara. She was tense, her laughter slightly too loud, her glances sharper than they needed to be. She was trying too hard not to look at me.

"Do you?" Jax's tone shifted, turning softer, almost pitying. "Or are you just trying to lose yourself in something that doesn't matter?"

I didn't answer. Jax had always been good at cutting to the bone, at seeing the things I didn't want anyone to see.

"You know how many people are relying on you, right?" she pressed, her voice dropping low enough that no one else could hear. "Merrik and I included. And whatever this is," she nodded toward Elyssara, "it's a distraction you can't afford."

Her words were a gut punch, but I kept my expression neutral. "It's nothing," I lied.

Jax laughed softly, bitterly. "You don't look at her like it's nothing."

Before I could respond, Merrik appeared, sliding into the seat beside me with a casual grace that belied his age. "What's this? Jax lecturing you again, Kael?" he asked, his voice warm and teasing.

"Someone has to," Jax muttered, though her lips twitched upward.

Merrik grinned, leaning back in his chair and crossing his arms. "Leave the boy alone, Jaxxy. He's got enough to worry about without you adding to it."

"Exactly," Jax said, her sharp gaze cutting back to me. "He's got enough to worry about. And *she's* not helping."

I clenched my jaw, forcing myself to keep my tone even. "I'm perfectly capable of managing my priorities."

Merrik chuckled, the sound like distant thunder. "Sure you are. Just remember, priorities don't mean much if you're dead—or if the rest of us end up buried because you weren't paying attention."

"Noted," I said flatly, though the words twisted in my chest. They were both right, and I hated them for it.

Elyssara rose from the table, her head held high, shoulders squared as though she were walking into a battle rather than to the bar. Her steps were deliberate, purposeful, every movement carrying a defiance that seemed etched into her bones. She hadn't bathed in days, her clothes still marked with the dust and grime of the temple and the journey that followed. But it didn't matter.

She was beautiful, regardless.

I'd felt desire before, countless times. I'd bedded more women that I cared to admit purely because I could. But this wasn't desire—not *just* desire. My mind had always been sharp. Unyielding. Focused. But this pull to her unraveled me—and I hated how powerless it made me feel. Almost as much as I craved it.

There was something raw about her. It wasn't the polished beauty of court women—their beauty crafted in gilded mirrors and false smiles, with their carefully arranged hair and embroidered gowns. Elyssara wasn't just a force of nature—she was the storm itself. Untamed. Fierce. And breathtaking in a way that didn't allow for pretense.

Jax's voice cut into my thoughts, low and laced with warning. "She's trouble, Kael. And you don't have the luxury of trouble right now."

I met her gaze evenly, forcing calm into my voice. "She's an asset," I said flatly. "If we're going to succeed, I need to know I can trust her. That requires observation."

"Observation?" Jax echoed, her lips quirking into a sardonic smile. "Is that what you're calling it now?"

I didn't respond, letting my silence speak for itself. But inwardly, the lie churned in my gut. Elyssara wasn't just an asset, no matter how much I tried to convince myself otherwise. I watched her because she fascinated me. Because her fire and defiance compelled me. Because, Stars help me, I didn't *want* to look away.

Jax sighed, her sharp edges softening for a fleeting moment. "I'm not saying this to be cruel, Kael. I just... don't want to see you lose sight of our goals."

Jax, damn her, was right. Elyssara was trouble I couldn't afford. She was a distraction—a dangerous, maddening, irresistible distraction. And yet, when she reached the bar and leaned against the counter, her hair catching the warm light of the hearth, I felt that pull again. It was primal, undeniable, and it terrified me.

I forced myself to lean back in my chair, dragging a hand through my hair in a futile attempt to shake off the tension coiling in my chest. Merrik chuckled from beside me, his gaze following mine. "Let her breathe, lad. She's not going anywhere."

"She's going to regret talking to him," I muttered, my tone sharper than I intended.

"She's not talking to him to talk to him," Merrik said, his grin widening. "She's talking to him to get a rise out of you."

The bastard wasn't wrong.

I hated how easily she got under my skin. *Hated more that she knew it.*

When she turned toward the man at the bar, I felt my patience snap.

It was one thing to let her needle me with her sharp tongue and defiance. It was another to watch her give someone else that fiery attention, even if I knew it wasn't genuine. He was smiling too much, leaning too close. His gaze lingered in ways that made my blood simmer, and Elyssara... she let him.

The air in the room shifted, the hum of the tavern fading beneath the steady thrum of my pulse.

It wasn't just the way she let him lean too close or the way his smile lingered—it was the flicker of her gaze, daring me, challenging me to act. Before I could stop myself, I was on my feet, crossing the room in long, deliberate strides. I didn't think. I didn't plan. I just *moved.* And when I stopped behind her, close enough to feel the heat radiating from her, my voice was low, a growl edged with something I didn't want to name.

"You've had enough fun for tonight."

She tensed before she turned to face me, her gaze sharp enough to cut. I saw the flash of surprise in her eyes, quickly buried beneath a mask of irritation. Her retort was quick, biting, and full of the fire I'd come to expect from her. But beneath it, I caught a flicker of something else. Uncertainty, maybe. Or something deeper.

The man at the bar—fool that he was—decided to speak. His words were a mistake, his tone dripping with false bravado, and I shifted closer to Elyssara without thinking, my body a wall between her and whatever threat he posed. I glanced down at her fierce green eyes full of defiance, her slender neck, and her collarbones that promised a path straight to sin and seduction. *That's when I knew I was gone for her.*

When she fired back at me, her voice laced with jealousy, it took everything in me not to smile. She could deny it all she wanted, but the way her gaze flicked to Jax, the way her tone sharpened, told me everything I needed to know. She didn't like it. Didn't like *her.*

The man's laugh grated against my nerves, and I turned to him, my voice colder now. "Her drink's done."

The look in his eyes shifted, unease replacing his earlier confidence. He muttered something under his breath before stepping back, his retreat doing nothing to cool the fire simmering in my chest.

I turned back to Elyssara, leaning close enough that my voice was for her ears alone. "I am the only man that will solve the problem of where you are sleeping tonight and any night. Do you understand?"

Her response was defiant, of course. Her clipped tone and furrowed brow only made me want to pull her closer, to shake her until she admitted what we both knew—that she wanted this as much as I did. But instead, I brushed my hand against her arm, guiding her away from the bar.

As we left the tavern, I felt the weight of their gazes lingering too long. The scrape of boots behind us was quiet but deliberate, setting my nerves on edge before the first words were spoken, and I knew the night wasn't over.

The alley fight didn't happen all at once. It built, like the tension in the tavern. The man from the bar and his companions followed us outside, their laughter low and mocking.

"Leaving so soon?" the leader sneered, stepping into our path.

Elyssara stiffened beside me, her hand instinctively brushing the hilt of her blade. I moved first, stepping in front of her, my stance broadening as I faced the man.

"You're making a mistake," I said, my voice low and steady.

The man didn't back down. His grin widened, and when he called her a whore, every muscle in my body coiled tight. The words weren't just an insult—they were a challenge, a provocation—and I answered without hesitation. My hand shot out, gripping his collar as I slammed him against the nearest wall.

The fight that followed was chaos.

Elyssara moved like a storm, her blade flashing in the dim light. She didn't just wield that blade—she danced with it, her movements fluid and unrelenting. Watching her was like watching a storm: breathtaking, wild, and impossible to control. And I didn't want to.

Every movement was deliberate, every strike calculated. She wasn't just defending—she was dominating. And it was the most mesmerizing thing I'd ever seen.

When it was over, and the bodies were groaning at our feet, I turned to her. The fire in her eyes hadn't dimmed, and the sight of her, bloodied and unyielding, hit me like a blow.

"You shouldn't have to fight like that," I said, my voice quieter now, though the edge hadn't entirely left.

Her retort was as sharp as I expected, but even as she snapped at me, I saw the way her breath hitched, the faint tremor in her hands.

I stepped closer, brushing a streak of blood from her jaw. "I told you—I don't share."

The air between us crackled, heavy with tension and something darker, something I didn't dare name.

"Come," I said, my voice rough. "I have something for you."

Her eyes were full of both trepidation and hunger, a mirror of my own. Because whilst I know that I am playing a dangerous game, I can't help but keep playing.

I had spent the last few hours arranging things she would never ask for.

A soft bed.

Fresh linens.

Warm water.

Clothes that actually fit.

Not because she needed them.

Because she deserved them.

And maybe—just maybe—because I wanted to be the one to give her something good.

Even if only for a moment, before duty tore it all away.

From both of us.

But as her footsteps fall in line with mine, and her mounting trust—fragile, reluctant—lingers between us, I know this truth like a blade at my throat: she will cost me everything.

And I'll bleed for her anyway.

CHAPTER THIRTY-TWO

ELYSSARA

THE STREETS ARE QUIETER NOW, THE DIN OF THE TAVERN FADING behind us. The scent of damp stone and smoke hangs in the air, mingling with the faint metallic tang of blood from the fight. My legs wobble slightly, the effects of the ale and the fight coursing through me now that the alley is far behind.

Kael walks just ahead, his stride unbothered, his presence as steady as the stones beneath us. I hate how easy it seems for him, how he can slip from blood-soaked brawls to calm silence without a trace of effort.

I, on the other hand, am unraveling. I always am after a fight. I'm not sure if it's my recklessness, stupidity or love for my family that makes me impulsively enter into situations that constantly have me outnumbered and under-armed—perhaps it's all three—but I am *always* drawn to the fight.

But now is different, because I'm not alone.

Kael's presence changes things. The weight of his steadiness presses against my chaos, unsettling in a way I can't explain. Usually, I'd drown myself in a pint or two, light up a drag of shadeleaf, or lose myself in someone else's touch. Anything to forget the blood, the fight, the gnawing hollowness that comes after.

I've become quite good at tracking down all three, to be honest. *Too good.* The pints of ale blur the edges of my mind until I can barely remember the blood under my nails. Shadeleaf dulls the sharpness of a life lived purely for survival, and lets me drift somewhere softer, to places where the faces of those I stopped from returning home to their families don't linger. And the third—well, the third is easiest.

I remember one night back in The Barrier District. My hands still shook from a skirmish with raiders, my pulse too wild to let me sleep. I'd found someone—*what was his name? Does it even matter?* He'd been kind enough, his touch eager and clumsy, unskilled and hurried, simply chasing his own release. Regardless, for a moment I'd almost felt whole, almost forgotten. But when it was over, and he'd smiled at me like he knew me, I'd felt nothing but emptiness. No, not emptiness. *Shame.*

I shove the memory down, burying it beneath the numbness I've carefully cultivated over years of fighting and killing and fucking and smoking my way through my pain. But I remind myself often; *this is survival.* And survival doesn't leave room for regret.

And, I can't do any of that now, anyway.

I glance at his back, the line of his shoulders too straight, his stride too sure. He doesn't feel the same ache I do. Or maybe he does, and he's just better at hiding it. Either way, he's a reminder of everything I hate about myself right now—the dirt under my nails, the ache in my bones, the way I'm barely holding it together while he seems untouched.

The night air bites at my skin, seeping through the thin fabric of my tunic and the dampness clinging to me. My body hums with tension, and my thoughts won't quiet. Every step feels like it stretches the space between us, even though I could reach out and grab the edge of his cloak if I wanted.

Not that I would. I don't need him. I don't need anyone.

"Ronyn and Seren," I say, breaking the silence before my thoughts have the chance to swallow me whole. "Will they be okay?"

Kael slows his pace, just enough for me to catch up. "Therion's with them. He would cut down an army of men before he'd let harm come to them."

The way he says it, so confident, so sure, makes something inside me twist. I want to believe him. I want to let that calm assurance seep into me, to ease the tightness in my chest. But I can't. I don't trust certainty. Certainty is fragile, and the moment you rely on it, it shatters.

"Ronyn doesn't think," I mutter. "He just acts."

Kael's lips curve into a faint smile, though he doesn't look at me. "Therion does. They balance each other." He pauses, his eyes finally sliding to mine, his gaze heavy with something I can't quite place. "Like all great partnerships."

The words hit harder than they should, and I look away, letting my hair fall over my face. "This isn't a partnership," I say, my tone sharper than intended. "It's a means to an end."

Liar.

Kael doesn't argue. He doesn't need to. His smirk portrays everything he thinks, and he starts to surge ahead of me again. Just as I think the conversation is over, he looks back at me and adds, "If you say so, Lightborne."

He doesn't look back, doesn't check to see if I'm keeping pace. Of course he doesn't. Kael is always sure of himself, sure of the world around him, as if it bends to his will. I envy that certainty. Envy it, hate it, crave it all at once.

My gaze drifts to the cobblestones beneath my feet, damp with lingering mist. *How far have I come from the life I knew?* The streets of Virellin aren't so different from these, but they hold none of the hope this place seems to breathe. Back home, the stones are always crusted with blood and despair, not damp with harmless dew that glisten peacefully under the Stars. And yet, I'm not sure which feels heavier—those streets, or the weight of everything I'm trying to carry now.

A fight. A drink. A vice to forget. That has always been my answer before. But the weight didn't lift, not really. It clung to me, tangled in my thoughts no matter how hard I tried to shake it free.

And now, with Kael just a step ahead, his silence pressing down on me, my usual methods of coping feel out of reach.

Kael stops, turning to lock eyes with me and gestures towards a building. It doesn't seem like a typical place Kael would lead me to, but then again, I've stopped trying to predict his moves.

The building we approach looks unassuming, tucked into the shadows of the street with nothing to set it apart from the rest of the village. But when Kael pushes open the heavy wooden door, the difference is immediate.

Warm air envelopes me, a stark contrast to the biting chill outside, and I pause in the doorway, overwhelmed by the subtle richness of the space. The scent of vanilla and polished wood is unexpected, almost cloying in its gentleness, and the soft light from the lanterns bathes everything in a golden glow. For a moment, I feel like I've stepped into a dream—or someone else's life.

The grand staircase catches my eye first, its handrails gleaming like something out of a fairy tale. I catch my breath, glancing down at my own dirt-streaked hands, the grime of the road caked beneath my nails.

I don't belong here.

Behind a modest desk sits a young man, no older than twenty, his sandy hair falling into his eyes as he straightens at the sight of Kael. Something changes in his posture, a sharpness that wasn't there a moment ago. He raises his hands, his fingers forming a deliberate symbol—an upside-down triangle, I think, though the motion is so fluid it almost doesn't register.

Kael's response is just as quick, though not quick enough to escape my notice. His eyes flicker toward me, then back to the boy as he shakes his head subtly. The boy freezes, dropping his hands as though nothing had happened, but the tension in the room lingers like smoke.

"What was that?" I ask, narrowing my eyes at Kael.

He doesn't miss a beat. "I've stayed here before," he says, his tone so calm and steady that it almost sounds rehearsed. "It's a symbol we share amongst brothers. He knows me well."

Too well, I think, but I bite back the comment. Something about the exchange gnaws at me, the edges of my instincts bristling. The boy's deference, the practiced symbol, Kael's sharp reaction—it doesn't add up.

As we move toward the stairs, I glance back, catching the boy's eyes. He looks away too quickly, and my stomach tightens with unease. My fingers curl into fists, itching to find Ronyn and Seren later. I'll ask them what they saw.

Something isn't right.

After taking the keys off the desk from the young man, Kael ushers me up the stairs, and along a quaint and understated hallway —the intentional and thoughtful decor, art and furnishings far from ostentatious, though still beautiful. The doors are closed, and I suspiciously walk beside Kael, alert and on edge. The Starforged Blade at my thigh hums in preparation for a fight, as if it's connected to my own senses. *Maybe it is?*

"It's okay. You're safe here," Kael says, his posture stoic.

"Saying it doesn't make it so," I counter, breaths quickening, the sound of my blood pumping in my ears.

"Perhaps I can show you then?"

"Show me what, exactly?"

"That you will always be safe when I am with you, and that I would never put you at risk. I thought I proved that to you tonight?" He ventures, before adding, "But if you need extra... *convincing*, allow me to show you *this*."

Kael opens the door to the room in a sweeping arc, and I immediately freeze. Warm light spills from lanterns mounted on the walls, their soft glow reflecting off polished wooden floors. The air smells of sandalwood and vanilla, a stark contrast to the stench of sweat and dirt that clings to me. A steaming bath sits in the corner, the water clear and inviting, with rose petals floating idly on top of the water, and a large, ornate, four-poster bed with clean linens waits against the far wall.

I can't move. My boots rooted to the floor, and my chest tightens with a mix of emotions I can't name. It's too much. Too clean. Too warm. Too... *everything*.

Kael's eyes narrow slightly, tracking every frantic breath I take.

His eyes pin me in place and his voice breaks through the haze. "Safe, Elyssara. You are safe. Go ahead," he says, gesturing to the bath. "It's yours."

I look away from him, confronted and suddenly embarrassed by the state of my clothes, my hair, my nails, my... Everything.

I do not belong.

I am nothing more than a thieving street rat.

I don't move into the room, my arms folding over my chest as if to shield myself from the decadence that awaits me. "I don't need this," I mutter. The words taste bitter on my tongue, even as I say them. "I don't deserve this."

"Whatever you think you've done doesn't change the fact that you deserve to be treated like you matter, Elyssara. Stop punishing yourself," Kael replies, his tone even.

My chest tightens, my breaths becoming frenzied. I squeeze shut my eyes, hoping that it will somehow make the feelings, the memories and the realities go away. My hand clutches at my chest, and I slide down the door jamb, burying my face in my palms before looking up at Kael, tears prickling in my eyes. *Do not fucking cry, Elyssara. Not in front of him. Hold it together.*

Through gritted teeth, I seethe, "I have killed people, Kael. People who most likely didn't deserve it. I have taken fathers from their children and wives. I've stolen from others to feed myself. I have chosen violence, damage and chaos over everything." I pull at my clothes—my rags—and screech at him, "Look at me! I am disgusting! I am nothing but an orphan who ran from the fight while her parents were fucking murdered. I don't belong here! I don't deserve to enjoy any such luxuries!" My voice breaks on the last word, and so does the dam that was keeping my tears contained. They streak down my face now, making a trail through the dirt, blood and grime from the days past.

Kael's jaw tightens, a flicker of something like pain crossing his face. He doesn't speak right away, and the weight of his silence presses down on me harder than his words ever could.

He looks at me. *Truly* looks at me, but his gaze is not laced with pity or disgust or fear, or anything that I assume I'll see. He bends down, and grabs my chin, forcing me to look directly into his eyes, and not hang my head in self loathing like I am itching to do.

"You think we all haven't done horrific things to survive? You think we all haven't taken lives to save our own in this fucked up world? Elyssara, you didn't run. I'd bet that you've never run from a fight in your entire fucking life. You are a fighter. You have a warrior's spirit," his face moves closer to mine, and I feel like he can see into me, hear every thought, sense every emotion. "People like us don't wait for things to be handed to us—we take them. We create our own fucking destiny." His words are like a punch to the gut. Loaded with understanding, laced with resolve.

But I can't help myself—I laugh, the sound harsh and hollow. "What destiny? I am a monster beholden to the fucking Stars, Kael!"

He moves even closer, his presence overwhelming without even touching me, aside from his thumb and forefinger still holding my chin. "I've seen monsters, and you're not that, Elyssara. I'm not scared of who you are. I can handle you—every part of you."

The lump in my throat threatens to choke me. I want to shout at him, to push him away, to tell him he doesn't know me, doesn't understand. But the words won't come, because I know they're bullshit. Instead, I stare at him, my eyes swollen and stinging. Kael's arms slide under my legs, and the other around my shoulders, and he picks me up off the floor, kicking the door shut with his boot.

My body stiffens instinctively as his arms slide beneath me. Every muscle screams at me to pull away.

But when he holds me—solid, unwavering—something in me breaks. The fight drains from my limbs. I sag into his chest.

I hate how safe I feel in his arms. "I've got you," he murmurs, and despite myself, I lean deeper into his chest.

Kael gently unravels me from his arms and places me in a chair near the bath. I lean back into it, exhausted from my still healing wound, the alertness that I wear like armor every single day, and the pressure that threatens to break me. Kael drops to one knee, lifting my foot onto his other knee, and begins untying the laces of my boot.

I sit bolt upright, "What in the fucking Stars are you doing?"

"I'm taking off your boots, Duskae. One usually removes their clothing before bathing," he teases gently, a ghost of a smirk curving his mouth.

"I can do that myself. I don't need your charity," I snap, rushing to snatch back my foot and place it on the ground. But before I've managed to remove it from his knee, Kael's hand is on my shoulder, and his other hand is clasped around my ankle.

"I know you can, but just because you *can* doesn't mean you should have to. Now, I don't get on my knees for just anyone, Elyssara, so sit back and let me take care of you."

The promise in his voice snakes its way down my spine and ignites heat in my core.

Kael's fingers are careful, almost reverent, working the laces free —steady, practiced, natural.

I want to fight, but there's something about Kael on his knees before me that threatens to crumble the walls I've built. "Okay," I say tentatively.

Kael finishes removing my boots, and once again, commands me, "Now stand up and turn around."

I have no idea why in the Stars I am complying with his commands, but my body moves of its own accord and I turn around, my back to him.

Kael's hands smooth down the wild auburn strands of hair that have come loose from my braid, and he gently removes the leather band holding the remainder in, before unraveling the braid and combing his fingers through my hair.

I've fought men twice my size without hesitation, but this—this gentle, unguarded moment—feels like the most dangerous thing I've ever faced. My instinct is to pull away, to retreat behind the walls I've spent years fortifying. But Kael's touch... it makes me want to stay.

Despite desperately needing to keep him at arm's length, I find myself closing my eyes. Leaning into his touch and taking comfort from this small act of tenderness and care. "You're quite good at that, you know," I breathe, filling the silence.

"I have a sister, remember. And two very overbearing female cousins who made me join in their games when we were children. Of course, that involved braiding, applying kohl to our eyes and stains to our lips," fond nostalgia woven through his tone. "Don't you fucking dare tell Therion."

And despite myself, I laugh. A genuine laugh. The sound surprises me as much as it seems to surprise him. A real laugh. Not the bitter bark I've perfected over the years, but something lighter, freer. "Well, it certainly paid off. And I wouldn't dare."

He chuckles, and says, "Bathe, Elyssara, and I'll be back soon. I have something for you."

"I thought this *was the* 'something'," I say, gesturing vaguely to the room.

"There's one more thing. Bathe." And with that, he exits the room, and I look at the bath again. It gleams, its surface rippling gently with rose petals. My breath catches. I've washed in shared basins all my life. This kind of luxury belongs to someone else— someone softer, cleaner, *better*.

The water scalds at first, but I don't care. I sink into it, the heat searing away blood, grime, tension—everything. My body aches, but it's nothing compared to the ache in my chest.

I've spent years scraping by, stealing what I could, giving what I had to in order to survive. Comfort isn't something I've earned; it is something I've forgotten how to even want.

But Kael... he makes me *want*.

My thoughts spiral back to the symbol the boy had made. Something about it tugs at the edge of my mind, but I can't place it. The way Kael shut it down so quickly only adds to my unease. He is hiding something. *Of course he is.*

I close my eyes, letting the heat of the bath pull me under, but no amount of water can drown the questions swirling in my head— or the way his voice lingers in my ears.

I don't get on my knees for anyone, Elyssara. Sit back and let me take care of you.

Oh Stars. *I am so fucked.*

CHAPTER THIRTY-THREE

ELYSSARA

I soak until my skin starts to wrinkle.

A gentle knock at the door sounds, and I sit up again, grabbing the Starforged Blade from the stool next to the bath.

"It's me," Kael's voice is slightly muffled through the door.

"I'm still in the bath. Hold on, I'll put my clothes on," I shout back, scrambling to get out of the deliciously deep bath.

"Don't," he quickly replies. *What?* "Wrap yourself in a towel... it'll make sense in a moment."

My muscles tighten in anticipation, and I can't keep the butterflies from fluttering in my belly.

I wrap the towel around myself, tucking a corner into the space between my breasts and securing it. "Come in."

As soon as he walks into the room, the air shifts. As if my body knows he's near and responds instantly. He's had a bath of his own, and is dressed in fresh linen pants and a sky-blue tunic that matches the hue of his eyes. He carries a bundle of clothing—I can see linen pieces the color of rust and stone, and black leathers piled atop each other, and some... rather scant underthings sitting on top.

"These are for you," he says, his voice calm but firm.

He places them on the bed, unfolding each piece, and showing me the leathers that appear expertly crafted and tailored. The smell of new leather fills the room, mixing with the sandalwood and vanilla from the bath, as he fingers through the pieces.

I stare at them, my chest tightening with awe and anger and something else I can't name. "I don't need your pity," I try to say it with bite, but it comes out as a whisper.

"It's not pity," he replies, his tone even. "It's basic decency, and necessary for our travels ahead."

"I don't need you to save me, Kael," I shoot back.

Kael's lips twitched into a faint smile. "I know you are quite capable of keeping yourself alive. But being alive and truly living are not the same thing, Duskae. You don't have to do it all alone. Let me help you."

His calmness—and the accuracy of his words—infuriates me, and the heat in my chest spills over. "How did you even know my size?" I snap, my voice trembling with the cascade of emotions spilling over.

His smile deepens, slow and deliberate. "Elyssara, I've been studying every dip and curve of your body for days," he says, slowly raking his eyes over my body.

Heat flares in my cheeks, and I hate the way my body reacts to his words, his presence, his gaze. I hate the way he can unravel me with a single look. I hate the way I feel so much when he's around.

I'm not sure if it's the ale, the bath, the tenderness, or the way his gaze clings to me, heavy-lidded and searing, but my hands move to the corner of the towel tucked between my breasts. My fingers hesitate, trembling slightly. I don't look away from him, watching instead for any flicker of doubt, any sign that I should stop.

"Elyssara, no. Don't do that," Kael's voice is low, strained, but firm. The sting of rejection washes over me, sending heat to my cheeks and making my stomach clench.

He must see it in my expression because he quickly adds, softer this time, "Not because I don't want to, Duskae. You've had ale. You've fought for your life tonight. I can't—not like this."

His restraint should irritate me. It should make me push harder. Instead, it leaves me reeling, caught somewhere between frustration and yearning. "You won't fuck me, Kael?" The bitterness in my voice coats every syllable.

His jaw tightens, and his gaze drops to the floor for a moment as if grounding himself. When he looks at me again, his eyes are smoldering, a storm of need and control warring within him. "Oh, Elyssara, I'll fuck you," he says, the words dripping with raw honesty. "But when I do, it won't be because you're running from something. It'll be because you're so hungry for me that you beg."

The breath catches in my throat. His words are a blow to my chest, knocking the air out of me and setting every nerve alight. Before I can stop myself, my fingers flick the edge of the towel free, and it falls to the floor in a whisper of fabric, pooling around my feet.

Kael's reaction is immediate, visceral. His eyes sweep over me, lingering on my breasts, my hips, and the place between my thighs where my need for him is unashamedly obvious. He groans, low and guttural, raking a hand through his hair, his head tipping back as though he's pleading with the Stars themselves. "Fuck," he growls, his voice rough. "You're going to destroy me, woman."

I take a step closer, emboldened by his reaction. "I want you to fuck me, Kael. *Now*."

His eyes snap to mine, his body taut with tension. "I'm trying to be a gentleman," he mutters, but the way his gaze roams over me betrays him.

"I don't want a gentleman. I want *you*," the words tumble out before I can stop them. They hang in the air, raw and unguarded.

For a moment, he doesn't move. His chest rises and falls heavily, his hands curling into fists at his sides as if trying to hold himself back. Then, with a growl, he closes the distance between us in two strides. His mouth claims mine, hungry and frenzied, branding me with his taste. It's not soft, not gentle. It's heat and fire, the brand of kiss that steals thought and leaves only feeling.

His hands roam my body, warm and firm as they trace the outline of me like I'm a map. His hands linger at my waist before sliding lower. My skin ignites beneath his touch, and when his thumb finds my clit, brushing light circles over it, I moan against his lips, pressing closer, needing more.

"You're so wet for me," he murmurs, his voice a husky rasp that sends a shiver down my spine.

"I always am," I admit, breathless and unguarded.

His growl is deep, primal, and the sound sends a jolt of pleasure straight to my core. He dips down, his hands sliding around my hips, slow and deliberate, before grabbing the backs of my thighs and lifting me effortlessly. My legs wrap around his waist, and the hard line of his cock presses against me through his linen pants. The friction draws a whimper from my throat, and I grind against him, desperate for more.

He pauses, his gaze locking on to mine, his voice heavy with restraint. "I won't fuck you tonight, Elyssara. But I will bring you pleasure that will make you see the Stars themselves. Is that what you want? To drown in it?"

I nod, unable to form words.

"I need your words, Duskae," he says, his tone soft but commanding.

"Yes," I whisper, my voice trembling.

Something in his expression softens, even as his desire deepens. "I want you, too," he whispers into the crook of my neck, the words like a promise.

He carries me to the bed, laying me gently on my back. The cool sheets are a stark contrast to the heat of my body, and I shiver as his hands trail down my arms, coaxing them away from where they've folded protectively over my chest.

"Let me see you," he commands, his voice low and rough.

I take a breath, steadying myself, before slowly dragging my legs across the bed, parting them just enough for him to look. His gaze rakes over me, dark and heavy, as though committing every inch of me to memory. "This is what you do to me," I murmur, running a finger through my wet center.

His breath hitches, and he closes his eyes for a moment as if the sight of me is too much to bear. "You're stunning," he says, his voice reverent. He leans forward, his brown hair just shy of black, falls across his brow and brushes his collarbones, and gods it makes me mad with lust. His massive frame towers over me, and he grabs my hand, bringing my fingers to his mouth. He licks them clean, his eyes closing as though savoring the taste. "Addictive," he whispers. "I've wanted to taste you since the moment I met you."

Kael drops to his knees at the edge of the bed, his hands sliding up my thighs to hook them over his shoulders. My hips jerk up in response. "So needy, El," he murmurs, his breath hot against my skin. "So perfect."

Kael's breath fans over my center, sending a shiver through me as anticipation coils low in my belly. He pauses, his eyes fixed on me as if waiting for permission, though he doesn't ask outright. The weight of his gaze sends heat rushing to my cheeks, but I nod, the smallest gesture, and that's all he needs.

His lips press against my inner thigh first, soft and deliberate, the scrape of his stubble sending a delicious jolt through me. He kisses a path up my skin, each touch of his mouth igniting a spark until he reaches my core. The first sweep of his tongue is slow, exploratory, and it pulls a gasp from my throat.

"Oh, Stars," I breathe, my hands fisting the sheets at my sides.

Kael hums against me, the sound vibrating through my body. "Relax, Duskae," he murmurs between strokes. "Let me take care of you. Let me help you forget."

His tongue moves with purpose now, alternating between broad, slow licks and focused, teasing circles over my clit. My hips buck of their own accord, seeking more of the exquisite pressure he offers, but his hands grip my thighs, holding me in place.

"So impatient," he chuckles, his voice thick with amusement and something darker. "You'll get what you need. I promise."

His fingers join the fray, one sliding into me with a precision that makes my back arch off the bed. He curls it just so, brushing against a spot inside me that I didn't know existed. A moan escapes me, unbidden and raw, and Kael's responding growl sends another wave of heat crashing over me.

"You like that?" he asks, his lips brushing against my clit as he speaks.

"Yes," I gasp, my voice breaking on the word. "Stars, yes."

"Tell me what you want, Elyssara," he demands, his tone soft but firm, like an irresistible command.

My breath comes in short, ragged bursts, and I force my mind to form words through the haze of pleasure. "I... I want you to keep going. Don't stop. *Please*." I plead the words, almost begging.

"Good girl," he purrs, and the praise sends a new rush of heat coursing through me.

I've never let anyone this close before, not really. It terrifies me, but somehow, with Kael, it doesn't feel like losing something—it feels like being found. Every touch, every word, peels away another layer of the armor I've spent years building. And yet, I don't want him to stop. Stars, he can't stop.

He adds a second finger, the stretch sending a sharp edge of pleasure through my building tension. His tongue and fingers work in tandem, coaxing my body higher and higher until the pressure becomes unbearable. My breaths quicken, my hands reaching out to grab at him, at the sheets, at anything to ground me.

"I can't... I don't know if I can—" The words tumble out of me, frantic and breathless.

"You can," Kael interrupts, his voice steady even as his movements quicken. "Come for me, beautiful," he purrs, before my pleasure surges and my back arches off the bed, my hips grinding to add more pressure to my clit. My breathing is ragged and intense, my moans getting louder, and my pussy clenches around his fingers.

"Good girl," he encourages again.

His words are the final push I need. The tension inside me snaps, and my body shatters under the weight of the pleasure. My back arches off the bed again, a cry ripping from my throat as wave after wave crashes through me. My hands grip the sheets so tightly my knuckles ache, but I don't care. In this moment, there is nothing but Kael and the Stars bursting behind my closed eyes.

Every nerve in my body is on fire, but it isn't just the physical sensation. It is the way he looks at me, like I'm not broken, like I'm not running from something. Like he sees all of me and doesn't flinch. I've given pieces of myself away before, but never like this.

This isn't taking or giving—it's being seen, and Stars help me, it terrifies me.

As I come down, my body trembling with aftershocks, Kael doesn't stop. His tongue laps at me gently now, soothing, drawing out every last flicker of sensation until I can't take any more.

He pulls back, his lips glistening as he looks up at me. The hunger in his eyes is still there, but it's tempered by something softer, something almost reverent.

Kael removes his fingers, once again, licking and sucking them until there is nothing left but the afterglow from his mouth.

I stare at him, my chest still rising and falling quickly, and ask, "What... what was that?"

His gaze snaps to my eyes. "No one's ever made you come like that?"

I'm silent. Still reeling.

"That's how every lover should make you feel, El. You deserve that every time."

"Oh," I whisper.

He presses a kiss to the inside of my thigh, his voice low and rough, "You took me so well, El." He brushes another kiss to my thigh, "I loved watching you fuck my mouth, Duskae. And my fingers."

My cheeks flush, words catching in my throat. I let out a breathless laugh, the sound shaky but real. "That was... you were..."

Kael smiles, a rare, genuine smile that softens the sharp edges of his face. He grabs a blanket from the foot of the bed and drapes it over me, tucking it around my body with a care that feels almost out of place after what we've just shared.

Kael lingers on his knees, his chest rising and falling with controlled breaths. His fingers trembling slightly as he fidgets with the blanket, and for the first time, I realize that his restraint isn't effortless. He is fighting his own battles, just as I am.

Kael pushes to stand, making his way to the top of the bed, and lies back, one arm tucked behind his head. "Come here," he invites, motioning for me to lie with him.

I drift up, resting my head on his chest, curling into him in the afterglow of new found pleasure. "Thank you," I murmur, as my eyelids start to get heavy. I don't even try to fight it, I simply let myself enjoy the safety of his embrace, even if it's just for now.

"Rest, El," he says, his voice quieter now. "I'll stay until you fall asleep."

I want to argue, to tell him that I don't need him to stay, but the weight of my exhaustion and the comfort of his presence are too much to fight against.

I want to stay here, in this quiet moment where I'm just a woman in the arms of a man who doesn't see me as broken. But I've learned that nothing in this world lasts—not warmth, not safety, not people. As Kael's arms tighten around me and his steady breaths lull me toward sleep, I let myself imagine, just for tonight, that this could be different.

Even as sleep pulls me under, a voice inside whispers: nothing this tender ever lasts.

CHAPTER THIRTY-FOUR

ELYSSARA

My eyelids creak open after the most peaceful slumber I can remember having in my lifetime. The room is awash with a golden glow, sunlight spilling through the crack between the heavy curtains. For a moment, I'm disoriented, unsure of where I am but certain I must surely be lying on a cloud. The memory of the previous night dawns on me like the rising sun—the warmth of his embrace, the searing intensity of his gaze, his fingers, his glistening mouth, the vulnerability that followed. My cheeks heat with both desire and the glaring reality that habitually hits after nights like that—regret, shame. Though in honesty, there have not quite been *any* nights like *that*, and the glaring reality feels tender this time.

I sit up slowly, the cool air brushing against my skin, and I notice the tray of food on the small table by the bed. Smoked meats, soft rounds of tangy cheese, and bread flecked with herbs. A pot of mint tea sits steaming beside the tray, its aroma sharper and fresher than any herb I'd ever known in Virellin. The food is simple by the standards of Galreth, I suppose, but to me, it feels like decadence beyond imagining. This amount of food would have fed Ronyn, Seren and me for a week in the Virellin slums—what feels like gluttony is a daily norm here. A note, folded neatly, rests beside the toppling tray. Picking it up, the handwriting is bold and precise:

> *Duskae,*
> *Turn left out the front door, walk down the hallway to the last door on the right.*
> *We'll be waiting for you.*
> *—K*

I set the note down, glancing around the room. A sense of gratitude wells up in me, mingling with the ever-present unease. This luxury isn't mine and it doesn't feel like it ever could be, yet here I am.

I coax myself out of bed, biting into the last scraps of food on the tray, and stretch my arms out wide and over my head, shaking the sleep—and the memories of Kael—from my body. A strange pressure builds in my chest, sharp and insistent, before it rushes down my arm like lightning seeking release. It's white-hot and searing, like the Stars themselves are surging through my veins.

My fingers tingle. Burn. Before I can pull back, a burst of silvery-white light erupts from my hand—a force both divine and feral, too big for bone or skin to contain.

The lamp beside me shatters in an instant, splintering into a thousand glittering fragments that disintegrate into fine, powdery dust. The dust lingers in the air, catching the sunlight like glittering flecks before settling silently on the floor. My breath hitches as I stare at the remnants, my chest tightening with a cocktail of fear and frustration.

The magic feels alive, untamed, and it frightens me more than I'm willing to admit. I press my hand to my chest, trying to steady my breathing, but the echoes of that wild power linger, a reminder of just how little control I have. *What if this happened around Ronyn or Seren? What if I hurt someone?* The thought twists my stomach tighter than any physical wound ever could.

This has been happening more and more frequently. Since unbinding the first part of my magic with the Starforged Blade, my Lightborne magic has been... *temperamental.* I have no control over it —it's unstable, as if growing restless at still being bound. A caged animal, desperate to be released. I can't afford this chaos—not when every step forward feels more treacherous than the last. If I don't master it soon, it won't just be lamps that I destroy.

The prophecy sings through my mind;

> *Her destiny looms, unknown and untamed,*
> *To balance the world or shatter the frame.*

Balance. Or shatter the frame. The words haunt me. Balance feels impossible when every breath threatens chaos. Shattering feels inevitable, as though the Stars themselves expect me to set the world ablaze.

The panic coursing through me threatens to take hold, as I feel my heartbeat quicken and my breathing comes quicker. Louder. More ragged. Revryn always helped me when I started to panic. He would hold me tight and say the exact same words:

Tell me something you can smell, see and feel, little one.
One heartbeat at a time.
One foot in front of the other.
One moment is all you have.

I wrap my arms around myself, holding myself in a tight embrace, and force myself to notice. *Sandalwood. A giant bed. Fresh linen clothing. Breathe. Breathe. Breathe.*

As my heart and breath begin to calm, I slowly unfurl my arms and feel my awareness expand. Taking a moment to settle my nerves and shove the thoughts of the prophecy aside, I decide to focus on putting one foot in front of the other. *The note. The others.*

After dressing quickly in my rust-hued linens—scant, lacy underthings, too—I follow Kael's instructions, my footsteps echoing softly in the quiet hallway. When I reach the door, I hesitate, the sound of voices drifting through the cracks. Discussions of the next relic, the next binding, the next step in fulfilling the prophecy that threatens to swallow me whole.

Steeling myself, I push the door open and step into a whirlwind of activity. The room is alive with energy, the quiet tension of my thoughts giving way to the buzz of voices and rustling paper.

The first thing I notice are the fresh linen tunics and trousers that Seren and Ronyn are wearing. Seren, a dark forest green and Ronyn, in all black. *He did this for them, too.* Tears threaten to spill from my eyes at the significance of seeing my family well-rested, fed, bathed and clothed, but I manage to contain them to a well that sits behind my lashes, and swallow down the emotion.

Maps and books are strewn across the large table dominating the room. Seren and Therion are bent over a particularly large map, deep in discussion. *I suppose it's nice to see them not verbally sparring with one another for a change.* Merrik and Ronyn are thumbing through worn books, folding pages and jotting down notes. Kael, ever composed, stands at the head of the table, his presence commanding even in the midst of the clutter. And then there's Jax. *Fucking Jax. Of course she's here.* She leans against the wall, arms crossed, her sharp gaze flicking between the group.

Kael looks up first, his lips curving into a sly smile. "Good morning, Duskae. I was just telling everyone about the night we had."

My heart stutters, and I freeze in the doorway, horror coursing through me. "You *what?*"

He raises a brow, clearly enjoying my discomfort. "The alley fight," he clarifies, his voice teasing. "Remember? You were brilliant."

Relief floods me, though it's quickly replaced by irritation, especially as I notice the small half-smirk on his face. "Of course," I mutter, stepping fully into the room, and throw him a look that could kill. "What else would you be talking about?"

Therion chuckles, obviously not fooled by Kael's loaded statements, and Seren shoots Kael a look that's equal parts exasperated and amused.

My irritation quickly gives way to overwhelming discomfort as I look around the simple yet elegant room filled with people I consider to be family, and those that are becoming more significant in my life the further we press on.

Seren notices the change in my expression, and mirrors it back to me with her own. "What is it, El? Where did you just go?"

I swallow down the pride and self-preservation that wants to build walls around me, but I fight it, and offer a truly honest answer. "I just... none of you need to do this. It's an unnecessary risk. And it's not even your fight. I can't walk away from this but *you* can," my voice rises an octave, belying my composure that's hanging by a thread.

It's Ronyn who steps forward, gaze penetrating into my soul. He shoves the book aside, pacing. His fists clench. When he speaks, his voice is hoarse with something deeper than anger—grief.

"El, fuck that. And fuck the King and his merry band of dim-witted nobles and his Royal Guard without minds of their own. They've cast out an entire population of great people because of how the Stars were shaped when they were born. Fuck *that*," he spits the words with a venom I've never heard from him.

Of course I know he cloaks his vulnerability in humor, but hearing his seething rage in front of everyone hits me differently. "You are an essential part of restoring balance, however the Stars see fit to actually do that. I may not be Starborn, but I know injustice when I see it. I'm sick of starving, fighting and stealing my way through life," his voice cracks on the last word, and it almost snaps the tight leash I'm keeping on my tears. "I'm sick of not wanting to get attached to anyone for fear of them fucking dying. I'm sick of watching children fend for themselves in the streets. There is no way I'm leaving this fight... or *you*," Ronyn seethes, his breathing ragged.

"Yeah, El. Fuck that!" Seren agrees, and all eyes in the room turn to her, yet again surprised by her boldness.

Seren's voice is steadier than I've ever heard it. Fierce. Loyal to the bone. "You are my family. You could not keep me away from this for all the coin in the realms." Her expression shifts, some cheek appearing in the wake of her intensity, "Plus, you need me. I'm the most well-read person in this room, and I can hear the walls talking, remember?" I huff a laugh, sniffing. Hearing her conviction warms me—Seren has always doubted her contribution and skill, and has thought herself nothing more than a burden.

"We've all made our choice, Elyssara, and we all have different reasons for being here. We're not going anywhere," Therion's stable presence and directness cut through my doubts and hesitations. Somehow having him committed to this cause—the least likely and the most disagreeable of everyone in the room, save perhaps, for Jax —strengthens my resolve, a tenderness flooding through me at his unmistakable confidence in this. In *me*.

It was not long ago that Therion thought all of us useless, burdensome weights that he would begrudgingly have to save. His conviction now shows me that something has changed. Something has shifted in Therion's commitment, in his stake in this—and I can't help but feel relieved by that.

"Come on, El," Seren wraps her arm around my shoulder and directs me to the table she's been working at. "We've been trying to narrow down the location of the next relic, based on the next part of the prophecy," Seren says, gesturing to the old parchment with my mother's handwriting and a map.

> *"On starlit peaks where the heavens sigh,*
> *The compass rests 'neath the watcher's eye."*

Seren recites the words. "The Watcher's Eye is key," she adds.

"The constellation?" I ask, moving closer.

Seren nods, her excitement palpable. "It's more than that. It's not *just* a constellation. The Watcher's Eye represents truth, and it can only be seen from the highest peak in Aevryn. Legend says the sighing winds that sweep the peak carry truths for those brave enough to listen."

Her words hang in the air, heavy with meaning. *Truth*. It's a concept I've spent my life avoiding, and the idea of facing it—of it being unavoidable—makes my chest tighten.

"That sounds truly daunting, to be honest," I murmur.

"Says the soon-to-be-strongest magical wielder in all of Aevryn and the prophesied savior of the realms," Ronyn barks a laugh.

I wave a dismissive hand at him, unwilling to share about the lamp I just accidentally turned to dust while trying to stretch my arms. *If only they knew I could be undone by a lamp.*

"The sighing winds?" Kael's voice penetrates the levity, it's calm, but I don't miss the flicker of intensity in his expression.

"Yes," Seren continues. "They're said to reveal the deepest truths to those who climb the peak. It's why the compass resides there. Only those willing to face their truth can claim it," Seren speaks with authority, before adding, "Or at least, that's my running theory based on pulling information from these books." Seren taps a pile of books that towers from the floor to her waist. "I just need to pinpoint the highest peak and the precise location we can see The Watcher's Eye *from* that peak. According to this book," she taps the book Ronyn is thumbing through, "there is only one ridge on one mountain where we can meet that criteria." Seren counts it out on her fingers, "We can see the constellation, we can hear the sighing winds, and we are also standing at the highest peak in Aevryn... oh! And we also will have to see it at night—starlit peaks and all, you know?"

Oh, only a few small requirements, then.

"Where in the Stars did you get all of these books, anyway?" Looking around at the guest room that appears to be in the throes of transforming into a library.

"Oh, it was easy actually. Therion and I broke into Galreth's library last night," Seren states matter-of-factly.

My eyes flick to Ronyn in question—he's usually her loyal protector—and he shrugs with nonchalance. "Our little girl is growing up, El. She's drinking ale, speaking of cocks and now she breaks into libraries. Sacred libraries of all things!" He feigns shock with the last words, before breaking out into laughter he has quite obviously been trying to contain.

The whole room tries to stifle their own laughs before giving in to raucous laughter that warms my heart, despite the stakes on the line in front of us. Seren's face burns bright red, clearly mortified by the crass—and entirely honest—teasing from Ronyn.

"Ronie!" she gasps in admonishment.

Therion's brow rises. "Well, I knew about the ale and the library, but the other part... you are quite the intriguing woman, aren't you?" His comment is intended in jest, but something about him referring to Seren as a woman, rather than a girl, hangs in the air. It's the first time he's done so, and we all notice it. And obviously so does Seren, as a small smile breaks free on her face.

"Yes. I would say that I *am* a very intriguing woman," she stands a little taller, accepting the compliment in earnest.

Therion clears his throat, trying to dismiss the loaded moment. "Anyway, that's all well and good about the theory for the compass, but we'll need to get to the peak. There's a storm rolling in. We can't leave Galreth until it passes, no matter which direction we're going."

"We'll use the time to prepare," Kael says decisively. "We'll secure the plan and the route, acquire horses, food, supplies. And..." His gaze shifts to me. "Elyssara needs training."

I stiffen. "Training?"

Kael moves closer to me, leaning into my ear. In a hushed voice meant only for me, "Your magic responds to your emotions, Elyssara. Your skin glowed bright enough to light up the entire room when you came last night, beautiful. We need you to be able to control it."

Mortification floods me. *Oh my fucking Stars.*

"Your magic is unstable, and it responds to... heightened emotions," he says so the room can hear. "You need control, or it will control you."

Well, that was a diplomatic way to say it.

"And you know someone who can help, I'm assuming?" I ask, though I already know the answer.

Jax steps forward, her boots echoing softly against the wooden floor. The room stills as if her presence alone demands it. Her voice is cool and measured, but it cuts through the air like a blade. "I'm a Luminaar. Controlling chaos is my thing."

Great. She's fluent in chaos.

A Luminaar. I've heard whispers of them from the past—rare, dangerous, and almost mythical in their power. My stomach twists, unsure if I'm about to gain an ally or face a new kind of chaos.

The tension in the air could be cut with a blade.

I have a feeling this will not be fun.

CHAPTER THIRTY-FIVE
ELYSSARA

Apparently, I'm going training with Jax... *right now*. Kael escorts me back to my room, where he instructs me to change into my fighting leathers and the new boots he left in place of my barely held together ones. The memory of him delicately removing those boots last night flashes through my mind, stirring something I can't quite name—desire? Trust? Warmth? Perhaps all of those?

Now that we're alone, an intensity crackles between us. The playfulness of the group fades, replaced by something raw and focused. Our eyes meet briefly, then dart away, as though pretending we both don't feel this. Whatever *this* is.

Kael breaks the silence with that infuriating half-smirk. "Did you have a fight with the lamp this morning, El?"

I sigh, already regretting the confession. "Unexpectedly, yes. I was... thinking about last night. Probably a result of that whole heightened emotions thing." I look away, heat creeping into my cheeks.

"Every Starborn has been there, El. Controlling magic as strong as yours isn't simple, nor is it easy. Jax will help a lot with that." His words are meant to reassure me, but the mention of Jax only tightens the knot of unease in my stomach.

I slip behind the changing partition, my heart pounding as I pick up the leathers. The soft, supple material feels inviting and unyielding under my fingers, a perfect blend of elegance and resilience. "So," I call over my shoulder, "what exactly *is* a Luminaar? I've heard stories of their power but don't know the specifics. I actually thought they were a myth."

Kael clears his throat. "Luminaars don't have magic of their own. They alchemize what they borrow—reshape it, bend it. They're not the strongest in any one kind, but they're fluent in them all. That's what makes Jax a brilliant trainer—she understands magic better than anyone alive."

I tug on the pants, their tailored fit hugging my legs as though made for me alone. "How does that even happen? What constellation was Jax born under?" My voice carries more irritation than curiosity.

"Luminaars are born from bloodlines, not constellations, Duskae. There's more to magic than what you were taught in Virellin. Jax is the last known Luminaar. She knows how to control the chaos of every constellation."

The weight of his words stuns me. "So, her parents...?"

"Her mother was a Luminaar. And no, they're no longer with us." His tone hardens, but after a pause, he adds, "They were advisors to the true King—King Aurius—before he was usurped by Maldrak. He killed anyone who wouldn't bend the knee to his rule."

I step out from behind the partition, my new leathers molding to my body like a second skin. "I'm sorry for Jax," I say softly. "This world is unjust. It might be foolish, but I hope to correct that—for all of us who've lost too much."

Kael doesn't answer. His gaze rakes over me, lingering in a way that sends heat prickling across my skin. He drags a hand through his hair and exhales slowly. "There is nothing sexier than a beautiful woman who fights for a cause she believes in."

The directness of his words steals my breath. Before I can respond, he steps back, his smirk returning. "Jax will be here in a moment. She'll take you out of the village to start training."

Kael leads me to the rear of the inn where Jax awaits. Without a word, she leads me to a clearing just outside the village. The air is crisp, the storm's approach evident in the way the wind carries a sharp edge. Dark clouds roll in the distance, their slow churn mirroring the turmoil inside me. She doesn't waste time with pleasantries, diving straight into explanations of magic and its volatile nature.

"Magic is chaos," she begins, pacing in front of me with a deliberate intensity. "It's raw, unbridled energy. Each constellation's chaos expresses itself in a different way, but it all starts out as chaos. If you try to suppress it, it will find a way to escape. You have to guide it, shape it, or it will destroy you."

I swallow hard, the memory of the Frael Forest flashing through my mind—the way my magic had surged uncontrollably, leaving ash and devastation in its wake. My throat tightens. "And can you teach me to control it?"

Jax stops pacing and looks at me, her piercing gaze pinning me in place. "I can show you how to turn things to ash when you actually mean it, yes." There's a glint of amusement in her eyes, like she knows I'm one wrong word away from wanting to turn *her* to ash.

Before we begin, Jax places her hands firmly on the ground, her expression shifting to one of deep concentration. A faint ripple spreads outward from her fingers, like the surface of a pond disturbed by a single drop. The air around us thickens, humming with an unseen energy. Slowly, a translucent dome shimmers to life, enclosing the clearing in a faint, silvery glow. It sparkles like Lightborne magic caught in a glass sphere, but its presence feels heavy, anchoring us to the earth.

"This is a Nullveil," Jax says, standing and brushing the dirt from her hands. Her voice is even, but there's a flicker of pride beneath the surface. "A Luminaar technique. It insulates magic—no detection, no eavesdropping. Whatever happens here stays here." She narrows her eyes at me, her tone sharpening. "It's not easy to maintain, so don't waste my effort by holding back. If you lose control, the Nullveil will protect us, so I expect your best. Understood?"

She crouches again, this time picking up a handful of dirt and letting it sift through her fingers. "The first lesson is this: magic is like this soil. It has potential. You can let it run loose, blown away by the wind, or you can compress it, give it form." She clenches her fist, and the loose soil transforms into a compact stone in her palm. "The key is to connect with it, feel it, and shape it into what *you* want—not what it wants to become."

I glance at the stone in her hand, then back at her. "And if I can't shape it?"

Her smirk sharpens. "Then you'll *be* chaos, and all of us will have done this for nothing. So, let's not, hm?"

The training is grueling. Jax starts by having me close my eyes and focus on the sensation of my magic—the pulse of it, buried deep beneath the surface. "Stop trying to control it outright," she commands. "Feel where it's pulling you. Magic isn't a slave to be whipped into submission. It's an ally you negotiate with."

I take a deep breath, tuning in to the sensation. It's like trying to grasp a whirlwind. It flares and spirals, shifting direction faster than I can follow. My hands tremble as I try to channel it into something steady, but all I can manage is a flicker of light in my palm before it fizzles out. Frustration gnaws at me.

"Not bad for a beginner," Jax says, though her tone is far from reassuring. "Again."

Hours pass. Each time I try, the magic resists, pushing against me like a river raging against its banks. Jax doesn't let up, forcing me to keep going, even when I'm on the verge of collapse. "Feel the chaos. Let it move through you. Then, *shape it.* It's like a wave in the ocean—you don't force it to stop; you flow *with* it."

Eventually, she steps behind me, her hands firm on my shoulders. "Your breath controls everything," she says, her voice low and steady. "Inhale, feel the magic rise. Exhale, guide it where you want it to go. Don't think. Just feel."

I close my eyes, tuning out everything but her words and the rhythm of my breath. The magic stirs, wild and hot, but instead of panicking, I let it flow. My pulse races as I guide it, tentatively shaping it into something tangible. A faint shimmer of Lightborne magic dances in my palm, steady and beautiful.

"Good," Jax murmurs. "Now, hold it. Don't let it collapse."

The moment I let doubt creep in, the light explodes into sparks, sending a burst of energy outward. I stumble back, but Jax doesn't flinch. "Not bad. You held it longer than I expected. But don't get cocky—you're nowhere near ready."

During a break, I gather the courage to ask her about Kael. Her expression softens slightly, a rare crack in her usual stoicism. "We grew up together. Our parents were... close. We have mutual goals. That's all."

"Mutual goals?" I press, sensing more to the story.

"You'll understand in time," she says, her tone sharp enough to end the conversation. *Well that sounds fucking ominous.* She stands, brushing off her hands. "Break's over. Back to work."

I swear I'm about to collapse into the soil and not get back up, when the young man from the inn barrels into the clearing, heaving and panting in exhaustion. Before I can stand, Jax creates a shield around us, instincts taking over, before she realizes it's the young boy. Recognition hits her, and she brings down her shield.

"Kael sent me," he says, leaning his palms on his knees, breath ragged. "The weeping eye blood sigil is on the door of the inn. We've been marked."

Panic flares in Jax's eyes, and I have absolutely no idea what's going on, only that it's not good.

"I hope you've been taking note today, Lightborne. You're about to use it," Jax tugs me up off the ground and gestures to follow her. She takes off at breakneck speed, and I try desperately to keep up after hours spent exhausting myself. My mind is reeling and my thighs are burning.

What the fuck is the weeping eye? What does being marked mean? And why have we been marked in the first place? And who is this boy that keeps popping up? Fuck. Fuck. Fuck.

Jax slows when we've almost returned to the inn, eyes keenly observant, as if she's looking for something specific. Her gaze fixes on a door to our right, one door back from the corner building positioned diagonally from the inn. A small upside-down triangle is etched into the wooden door, and I would've missed it had Jax's gaze not clung to it.

She withdraws a blade from her thigh and nods at me to do the same. The Starforged Blade sings in my hand, sharp and ready.

Taking a deep, preparatory inhale, Jax steels herself, nods to me, and rushes through the door. She instantly presses into a body and lands an elbow into the attacker's face. I don't know what happens with her next, because I am accosted by a solid body. I swing my elbows before lashing out with my blade, piercing skin, and the sharp intake of breath and a hushed "fuck" comes next. Seren's voice cuts through the air, "El, stop! Stop. It's us!"

The rush of a fight quickly fades before I realize that I've nicked Kael, the skin on his side bleeding and sizzling. I look around and find Jax with her blade at Therion's throat, before seeing Ronyn, Seren and Merrik watching on in this dimly lit storage room that reeks of damp wood and rusting tools.

"Oh my Stars, I'm so sorry," I gasp, scrambling to reach him. "Kael, I didn't mean—"

He catches my wrist. "It's fine, Duskae. Just a scratch. I'm more impressed than wounded."

But I see the grimace he tries to hide.

Without dwelling on whatever just happened, I say, "Okay is someone going to explain what in the fucking Stars is going on?" I ask, looking around for an explanation, the air thick with tension.

Seren clears her throat, a book clutched to her chest like a shield. "We've been found," she says quietly. "Marked by The Aegis Covenant."

"The Aegis what?" I blink, because that wasn't an explanation at all.

"The Aegis Covenant are a rogue faction of anti-prophetic rebels that want to shield the realms from destruction. They believe that if the Lightborne rises, the world shall fall." Seren states it without emotion, trying to shield me from the weight of her words.

"They believe I will be the end of the realms," I murmur quietly. I knew there would be people who were sceptical of the prophecy, so I'm not sure why hearing this stings so much.

"Elyssara, these people are trying to play the role of the gods. They're nothing but a nuisance," Merrik adds. "If it's not this prophecy, it's something else they're making a big noise about."

"Regardless, they're a threat and they've marked us. Their symbol is a weeping eye—it represents the Stars weeping when the balance is tipped—and they've smeared it over the inn's door. It was our safe house, and none of us have left since we arrived. Someone's been watching us. These people see themselves as vigilantes—protectors of the realms. They may be a big noise, but their blades are still sharp," Therion chimes in with common sense as usual.

"They'll be coming and they'll be out for Elyssara's blood. We haven't got long, so it's time to make a plan," Kael's no fuss approach is a balm to my nerves.

"I still have a lot of questions," I murmur.

"Later. I'll answer them *all* later. But for now, we prepare to fight."

CHAPTER THIRTY-SIX
ELYSSARA

THE NEXT HOUR IS A BALANCE BETWEEN A WAITING GAME, AND thorough strategy from all angles. I keep one eye on the group huddled in a tight circle around an old crate, running through possible scenarios for the impending fight, and the boy from the inn, who is keeping watch through a crack in the wooden door.

I don't trust him. I don't trust any of this.

So many questions are running through my mind about The Aegis Covenant, the triangle symbol, the role of this boy, the weeping eye blood sigil, Kael and his true motives and everything else that has happened since I left the Virellin slums. So many questions, so few answers.

I am so fucking tired of being left in the dark.

I know Kael is keeping secrets, but that knowledge becomes more and more ominous as the hours pass by. I also can't deny the pull to him. It's infuriating, almost as if something within me is drawn to him like a magnet, despite the stark awareness in my mind that he can't be trusted.

Kael's steady steps penetrate my thoughts and he moves around me to the boy at the door. "Finn, I need you to do what you do best and stay out of sight. Find Torvyn. Tell him *it's time.*"

Finn. Torvyn. I store the information away for later.

Questions.

Questions.

Questions.

I hold on to the thought that Kael will answer all of my questions later in the way a child clings to a soft toy. That knowledge is the only thing quelling my urgency... and my magic. I can feel it swelling and dissipating at my fingertips, the lesson with Jax having already paid off in this small way of being able to soothe my magic into submission.

The boy that I now know as Finn slips out through the door, thankfully covered by the darkness that has settled over us after the setting sun made her descent.

"Come, let's discuss the plan," Kael ushers me back to the group, and leans over the dusty crate that is serving as our table for the battle plan.

"The Aegis will be gathering strength, and they'll use the cover of darkness to their advantage," Kael says, his voice steady but laced with urgency. He crouches over the crate, carving lines into its worn surface with the tip of his blade, sketching out a crude but functional map. "We need to hold this intersection. Ronyn, you'll take the highest vantage point." He taps the edge of the makeshift map, indicating the building adjacent to ours. "You'll be our eyes—pick off anyone who slips into our blind spots."

Ronyn nods, his usual smirk absent for once, replaced by a focused determination.

"Therion," Kael continues, his sharp gaze shifting to the hulking warrior, "you'll be on the ground. Use your senses to detect their movements before they reach us. Hold the line and do what you always do." Kael's subtle nod is met with a grunt of acknowledgment from Therion, his grip tightening on the haft of his axe.

"Seren," Kael says, his tone softening just slightly as his attention moves to her, "you'll stay with Ronyn. Keep working on the route to the compass. We need it nailed down by dawn." He straightens, pointing his blade toward Jax and Merrik. "You two will be with me. We'll cut through their ranks and keep them from over-whelming the rest. No mercy."

"And what about me?" I say, my voice sharp with indignation. "I suppose you want me to hole up and hide?" The words are bitter, but they're born of a deeper fear—that I'll be sidelined, treated as a liability instead of an asset.

Kael's piercing eyes lock on to mine, fierce and unyielding. "I know better than to tell a warrior to walk away from a fight," he says, his voice low but brimming with intensity. "You'll fight at my side."

I swallow hard, his words sinking in. "Okay then," I manage, my voice steadier than I feel. The trust he's placing in me sends a ripple of something I can't quite name through my chest. Gratitude? Pride? Respect? Whatever it is, it feels like a small victory in a sea of uncertainty.

Merrik strides to the back of the dusty storage room, muscles bunching as he drags a heavy chest out of the way. Behind it, a hidden compartment is revealed. He pries the cover loose with prac-ticed ease, revealing an array of weapons and armor neatly stashed within. Blades glint in the dim light—throwing knives, razor-edged chakrams, war axes, swords, a small crossbow, a broad blade, and a bow with its quiver of arrows.

They knew this was coming. They've prepared for this moment.

"I'd like the crossbow... please," Seren says, the last word sweet-ened with characteristic politeness. She looks up, meeting the incredulous stares from the group. "What? I'm part of this as much as any of you. If I'm going to be with Ronyn, I might as well help. I already have the route mapped to the compass, anyway," she adds, her chin lifting slightly in defiance.

Merrik lets out a low chuckle, his cheer a stark contrast to the tension hanging in the air. "Well, the crossbow is yours, little lady," he says, handing it to her with a small flourish. Seren takes it with surprising confidence, inspecting the weapon as though she's been wielding one her entire life.

The moment is a brief reprieve, but it doesn't last long. The air grows heavy again as Kael finishes marking the map, his gaze sweeping across the group. The plan is clear, but the unspoken weight of what's coming presses down on all of us.

We're ready—but are we ready enough?

Jax reaches for the chakrams, the razor-edged rings glinting with lethal precision as she secures them to her belt. I take the throwing knives, their weight familiar and reassuring in my hands, and strap them to my belt above the Starforged Blade and Revryn's dagger. Each weapon feels like a promise of death—one I'm determined to keep.

Therion hefts the war axe, its heavy, brutal head gleaming with a dull menace as it joins the arsenal strapped to his broad back. Kael takes the broad blade, sliding it into the sheathe at his side. No doubt a backup—he's never without his dark, menacing twin swords strapped in an X across his back, their hilts peeking over his shoulders like silent sentinels. Ronyn grabs the extra bow and quiver of arrows, his expression calm but focused. He's the one who will keep us covered from above, and he knows it.

We move silently, a shadowy procession slipping through the tight confines of the storage room. The air feels thick, heavy with unspoken words and the weight of what lies ahead. Outside, the world is cloaked in darkness, the dim light of the moon barely illuminating the labyrinth of alleys and streets. We split off to our assigned positions, each of us dissolving into the shadows like ghosts, taking cover in the empty buildings and crumbling structures that line the intersection.

Kael and I slip into an abandoned building, the wood creaking softly underfoot as we weave through the remnants of a forgotten life. Dust clings to the air, and the faint scent of mildew lingers. We crouch behind old crates and barrels, their rough surfaces digging into my palms as I settle into position.

"I don't see anyone else arriving to help, Kael," I whisper, the edge of panic creeping into my voice despite my best efforts to suppress it. My heart pounds, the rhythm uneven, as if my body is betraying my attempt at calm.

"They'll be here, Duskae," Kael murmurs, his voice low and

steady, like the hum of a distant storm. "Just breathe. It's just you and me for now. That's all you need to focus on."

His words, paired with the quiet confidence in his tone, are enough to anchor me—for now. I force myself to take a deep breath, then another, the cool air filling my lungs. I focus on grounding myself, on finding three things I can see, hear, and feel, just as Revryn taught me.

The peeling paint on the wall across from us catches my eye, the edges curling like brittle parchment. I notice the faint sound of Kael's breathing beside me, steady and even, a stark contrast to my own. I press my hand against the rough surface of the barrel, the splinters biting into my skin grounding me.

The air before a fight always feels the same—heavy, tense, brimming with the unspoken promise of violence. It presses against my skin, tangling with my nerves. Even the nocturnal world holds its breath. The croak and chirp of nearby insects and birds have stilled, leaving behind a silence so absolute it feels alive.

The predators are closing in.

We don't wait long before the shadows begin to stir. Dark figures emerge from all directions, their movements deliberate and predatory. They're cloaked in black armor that absorbs the faint moonlight, their faces obscured by half-masks that make them seem less human, more specter. Strapped across their backs are weapons I've only ever heard of in whispers: whistle swords.

Revryn's stories come rushing back with chilling clarity. Curved blades, almost like bows, designed to be held with twin handles. Their true terror lies in their sound—the eerie whistle that cuts through the air before the blade strikes, a haunting harbinger of death. A weapon as much psychological as it is physical. They haven't been seen on the battlefield in decades, maybe longer, and yet here they are, wielded by this group of zealots. The sight alone sets my stomach churning, the dread coiling tight and cold.

"Come out, come out, wherever you are, little Lightborne," a voice taunts, slithering through the stillness like a predator's hiss. The tone is mocking, sinister, and disturbingly playful, its familiarity sending a cold shiver down my spine. My breath catches as I scramble through my memory, desperate to place it.

"It's the man from the bar," Kael says, his voice dropping into a low, lethal register. His features sharpen, his gaze like a blade drawn and ready. The air around him seems to shift, his mask of control replaced by something fierce and primal—a warrior's instinct taking over.

Fuck.

"Did you think I didn't know what that blade was strapped to those pretty little thighs?" The voice continues, dripping with lascivious amusement. "Did you think I wouldn't notice the marks you left on my comrade's face?" Though I can't see his full expression through the mask and shadows, I can hear the sneer curling his words, oozing smug superiority. "Naughty little Lightborne, straying from your cage."

My chest tightens as my magic stirs, unbidden. It rushes to the surface, igniting in my veins with a heat that burns hotter than my fear. It surges down my arms and into my fingertips, desperate to lash out and silence this dogmatic, pontifical moron once and for all.

My magic is rising—too fast, too hot.

Before I can stop it, a faint silvery-white glow flares to life along the tips of my Lightborne mark, betraying our position in an instant. The light reflects off the surrounding walls, shimmering like liquid starlight, as if to mock my lack of control. Panic claws at me as I wrestle the light back into submission, forcing it to retreat before it spills over completely.

But the damage is done.

Shit.

"Don't miss, Duskae," Kael says, his voice far too casual as he stands, twin swords sliding from the scabbards across his back with an ominous hiss. The movement is smooth, practiced, as if we aren't about to engage in a fight where we're unambiguously outnumbered and out-armed.

Right. Well, here we go.

Figures converge on the intersection like shadows bleeding into the light, their numbers swelling until the streets feel suffocating. At least fifty, their black uniforms blending with the darkness, their whistle swords glinting faintly in the dim light. The masks obscure their faces, but not the menace in their movements. And then there's us—barely more than a handful against fifty. Maybe more, if Finn has done his part.

My fingers brush the hilt of the Starforged Blade, the familiar weight grounding me as I draw it from its strap at my thigh. I shift into a fighting stance, the blade catching a stray beam of moonlight as I tilt it slightly. My voice, sharp with mockery and dripping with saccharine sweetness, cuts through the tension. "I look forward to using this blade from my pretty little thighs to slice open your neck."

The man from the bar steps forward, his sneer audible in his voice. "Look around, sweetheart. How do you think that's going to happen?" He gestures to the sea of his allies, their whistle swords poised to sing death.

"Do you need reminding of how we deal with being outnumbered by overconfident assholes with poor swordsmanship?" I reply, my tone sharp as a blade. I can see it in his stance—the tightening of his grip, the slight twitch of his shoulders. His control is slipping, the leash on his emotions fraying. *Good*. I want him wild with rage, careless with his strikes. "How about I show you?"

And with that, I move.

The intersection erupts into chaos, the clash of steel reverberating through the night. Kael charges forward, his twin blades a blur of deadly precision. He moves like a storm, each strike deliberate, each motion calculated to end a life. The air is thick with the sounds of battle—grunts, cries, and the harsh scrape of metal against metal.

I force myself to block out the noise, to drown the chaos in the razor sharp focus I've honed over years of survival. My breath steadies, my body moving instinctively as I sink into the warrior's stillness—a place where fear, doubt, and rage dissolve into a singular, icy clarity. My vision narrows, locking on to my targets. Their movements become predictable, as though the chaos itself has whispered its secrets to me. My blade cuts through the dark, unerring and precise, and for a fleeting moment, I feel nothing. No fear. No sorrow. Just the killing calm.

Beside Kael, Jax becomes a whirlwind of destruction, her chakrams spinning in elegant, deadly arcs. One whistles through the air, ricocheting off a lamppost with a metallic ping before embedding itself in the neck of a Covenant soldier. She yanks it back with a flick of her wrist, her expression as cold and unforgiving as the blade she wields.

A sudden flurry of arrows rains down from above, each one striking its mark with uncanny precision. My head snaps upward, and there's Ronyn, perched on a rooftop like a shadowy sentinel, his bow an extension of his body. His movements are fluid, almost effortless, as if he were born to this. Beside him, Seren clutches her crossbow, her knuckles white around the grip. Her pale face betrays her fear, but determination burns in her eyes. She looses a bolt, and when it finds its target—a soldier's shoulder—her expression shifts from surprise to fierce resolve as she quickly reloads.

The rhythm of the battle shifts. The sound of boots pounding against cobblestones grows louder, closer. My stomach twists as more soldiers pour into the fray, their dark armor glinting in the moonlight. They move with swift, purposeful strides, their weapons raised and ready. Panic gnaws at the edges of my focus as I realize just how many more are coming.

We are the prey now.

I glance at Kael, trying to catch his eye to signal a plan, but his focus remains unshaken, his movements as precise as ever. He's lost to the killing calm, utterly consumed by it, unaware that the tide is turning. My pulse quickens, and for the first time in the fight, doubt creeps in.

Then something catches my eye.

The soldiers flooding the intersection move differently—not the reckless aggression of the Covenant, but with practiced precision and controlled ferocity. They crash into the Covenant's ranks like a wave, their blades cutting through the enemy with brutal efficiency.

I blink, my mind struggling to reconcile the scene. Are they fighting... for us?

One of the newcomers—a tall, broad man wielding a massive blade—locks eyes with me for a brief moment, his gaze sharp and assessing. Before I can fully process his presence, he shifts seamlessly to deflect a strike meant for my back, the sheer force of his counter sending the Covenant soldier sprawling. He moves with a grace that belies his size, guarding my flank as though we've fought side by side for years. My eyes catch the small, upside-down triangle etched into the hilt of his weapon, and the realization hits me like a gust of cold wind.

They're allies.

The shock roots me to the spot for a split second, my mind scrambling to catch up. My gaze darts through the fray until I spot Finn, darting like a shadow between legs and strikes. He's too small, too quick for anyone to grab, and with a mischievous grin, he yanks the legs out from under a Covenant soldier, who topples with a crash. Finn flashes a glance my way before disappearing again into the chaos.

Relief and confusion swirl inside me, threatening to drown me. I barely have time to process the shift in the fight before a blade sings past my shoulder, jolting me back to reality. The rebels may have turned the tide, but the battle is far from over.

The broad man—Torvyn, I assume—cuts through the Covenant ranks like a force of nature. His massive blade cleaves the air, each swing calculated to devastate. Amid the chaos, he shouts orders in short, sharp bursts, his voice carrying over the clash of steel. His hand signals and curt commands weave the rebels into a deadly, coordinated machine. Every move he makes exudes authority, a quiet but undeniable proof that this is his battlefield.

He turns briefly to Kael, and their gazes meet for a fleeting second. A silent exchange passes between them, speaking volumes in the space of a heartbeat. Warrior to warrior. Leader to leader. The ease with which Torvyn commands the rebels, his force and presence, all make sense now. He's not just a fighter; he's a symbol.

"Duskae," Kael's voice cuts through the noise, sharp but steady. The strike meant for me never lands—his twin blades are already there, intercepting it with precision. His eyes lock on to mine for a moment, flickering with an intensity that roots me back in place. "Focus."

I nod sharply, forcing my mind to steady and my body to follow suit. The two men flanking me—Kael and Torvyn—move with fluid precision, their motions so practiced and deliberate, as if they've done this countless times before. *They probably have.*

I tighten my grip on the Starforged Blade, the hilt warm in my hand, and settle back into the rhythm of the fight. Whatever questions I have about these rebels, about Torvyn's presence or Kael's connection to him, will have to wait. Right now, survival is all that matters.

CHAPTER THIRTY-SEVEN
ELYSSARA

THE BODIES OF COVENANT SOLDIERS LITTER THE GROUND, BLOOD pooling in the dirt and staining the cobblestones like a grim tapestry. The air is thick with the metallic scent of death. The rebels move efficiently among the fallen, binding the hands of the survivors with rough rope. Only one is left conscious and unbound, kneeling in front of Torvyn, Therion, Kael, and me. His mask has been torn away, revealing a face bloodied and swollen, but his eyes burn with undiminished defiance. It's him—the man from the bar.

Torvyn steps forward, towering over the captive. His broad blade rests casually against his shoulder, but there's nothing casual about his presence. His shadow looms over the man, who sways under its weight. "Talk," Torvyn says, his voice low, dangerous—a predator circling wounded prey. "Who sent you?"

The man spits blood onto the dirt, his sneer curling back over bloodied teeth. "Do you think I fear you?" His voice is sharp and brittle, like glass ready to shatter. "You're rebels, clinging to a lost cause. The Lightborne will fall, and balance will be restored."

Torvyn doesn't flinch, his silence more menacing than any threat. He leans down, grabs the man by his chest plate, and yanks him forward with a jerk that forces him to meet his eyes. "Who the fuck sent you?" Torvyn repeats, his voice cutting like a blade through the cold night air.

The captive laughs—a hollow, grating sound that grinds against my nerves. "You're already dead," he says, his tone dripping with malice. "Thalmyr will see to that. He sent us ahead of the Royal Guard to bring her back." His gaze shifts to me, and the sneer widens, filled with cruel satisfaction. "The Lightborne escaped conscription. That's treason, punishable by death. Or maybe he'll use her for breeding first."

Beside me, Kael stiffens, his presence coiled like a predator about to strike. But it's my magic that reacts first. It rises like a storm, crackling at my fingertips and lighting the air with an angry hum. "You don't get to decide my fate," I snap, my voice trembling with fury as the faint glow of my Lightborne mark illuminates the man's face.

For the first time, his bravado cracks, fear flickering in his eyes like a candle caught in the wind.

Torvyn doesn't release him. His grip tightens on the chest plate, his knuckles white with tension. "Keep talking," he growls, the words like gravel in his throat. "What does the Covenant want with her?"

The man's opposition resurfaces, twisting his bloodied face into a grotesque mask of defiance. His voice takes on an eerie, incorporeal quality, rising in fervor as if possessed. His smile stretches wide, unhinged and maniacal, as he recites:

> *"When the Lightborne rises, the Stars shall mourn,*
> *Balance shall break, and the realms be torn.*
> *To preserve Aevryn, sacrifice is our shield,*
> *Order demands blood, and fate must yield."*

The words hang in the air, thick with fanaticism, as if the very ground trembles beneath their weight. Before anyone can react, Kael steps forward, his blade slicing across the man's throat in a single, fluid motion. The Covenant soldier collapses with a gurgling gasp, blood spilling from his neck as the final echoes of his mantra linger like a curse.

The battlefield falls silent. The man's body is still, but his words—those dark, twisted words—replay in my mind, relentless and unyielding.

Balance shall break, and the realms be torn.

I barely register Torvyn turning toward me. His gaze softens, a surprising warmth breaking through the hardened steel of his demeanor. "They're a bunch of fundamentalist twats, love. Better to be fuckin' rid of 'em." His voice is steady, grounding. "Don't let their horseshit sink in too deep."

But the fear in the man's voice when he spoke of me, the conviction in his creed—it lingers. Even as Torvyn's words wash over me, their fanaticism clings to me like a second skin. And no matter how many times I try to tear it away, I know it's already sunk too deep.

CHAPTER THIRTY-EIGHT
KAEL

"She's going to demand answers, you know," Therion says, his voice slicing through the heavy quiet of the room. He leans back in his chair, legs stretched out, boots crossed at the ankles, eyes fixed on the amber liquid swirling in his glass. It's a familiar scene: the aftermath of a battle, a bottle between us, and more unspoken truths than either of us is willing to count.

"I know," I reply, the words dragging out like a sigh. The weight of the bottle feels lighter than the conversation ahead. I take a slow drink, savoring the burn as it slides down my throat. I could use more of it, but no amount of liquor will dull this ache.

"If you still plan on seeing this through, you'll need to tell her something solid," Therion says, his tone sharper now, slicing straight to the heart of my hesitation.

"I fucking know, Ther. I know," I snap, the edge in my voice cutting more than I intend. The words grind against my chest, frustration aimed as much at myself as at him. "And what do you mean 'if I still plan on seeing this through'? Of course I fucking do. These are my people. My sister. Justice for all of us."

He watches me, silent, his expression impassive save for the faint twitch of his jaw. Then he leans forward, resting his elbows on his

239

knees. "I know you believe that, brother. But I think we both know it's not that simple. Not anymore."

My fingers curl tighter around the glass, but I force myself to meet his gaze. "What the fuck does that mean? Nothing's changed. The goal is still the goal." My tone is cold, a reminder of who leads this.

Therion doesn't flinch. His scepticism is obvious in the arch of his brow, his expression utterly unshaken. "I can scent you on each other," he says evenly. "There's a connection here, Kael—one that goes beyond mere alliance. You've not been this... protective," he says the word carefully, deliberately, "since Nalya."

The name lands like a punch to the gut, but I don't let it show. I bury the reaction, mask it behind cold pragmatism. "She's essential to our plan, Therion. Without her, we have no plan. I'm protecting an asset."

Therion's lips twitch, the faintest trace of amusement breaking through his usually impassive demeanor. "I've never protected an asset like that," he quips, his tone light but laced with a deeper meaning.

"Fuck," I mutter, unable to hold back the begrudging smile tugging at the corner of my mouth. It fades as quickly as it comes, sobered by the weight of what's to come.

"We'll figure it out," Therion says after a moment, the words offered more as solidarity than assurance. He's always been my confidant, my anchor—the one person who tempers my darker impulses. The one who never stops fighting by my side.

I rake my hands through my hair, gripping the roots as if the pressure might hold me together. He's right, of course. He always is. But admitting it out loud would crack open something I'm not ready to face. "I still need to tell her something."

Therion raises his glass, studying me over the rim before taking a slow sip. "Then tell her half-truths," he says, his voice calm, almost casual, though the weight of his words presses down like iron. "The smallest ones—but truths, nonetheless. Give her enough to placate her, to keep her from digging too deep. At least until after the compass."

The compass. The word alone sets my teeth on edge, a reminder of how precarious this plan truly is. My knuckles tighten around the glass. "Any trust we've built will be eviscerated by anything I tell her," I say, my voice low, strained. "She could just as easily burn us to ash."

"And if you don't tell her anything, the same is also true," Therion counters smoothly. His tone remains steady, but his eyes are sharp, cutting through my defenses. "She's not stupid, Kael. You've felt her magic. You've seen her light. Do you really think she'll let this go unanswered? Keep her in the dark too long, and you'll lose her entirely."

"Fuck." The curse slips out in a whisper, the weight of it settling in my chest like lead. No drink can drown the nausea clawing at my gut, and Stars know I've tried.

Therion doesn't press further, letting the silence stretch between us. It's his way—letting me wrestle with my own thoughts until I unravel. He's maddeningly good at it.

"She's going to hate me," I say finally, the admission cutting raw and jagged through the fragile calm I've tried to maintain. "When she finds out—when she learns even the smallest truths—I'll lose whatever part of her trusts me. Whatever part of her—" I stop short, shaking my head. I can't say it. Won't say it.

Therion's gaze softens, just slightly. "Maybe she will. Maybe she won't. But if you don't tell her anything, you'll never know."

I glance at him, my throat tightening. "And after the compass? What then?"

"That's a question for another bottle," Therion says, lifting his glass in a mock toast before draining it. His casual demeanor doesn't fool me. I see the tension in his shoulders, the way his fingers tap idly against the table. He's as uneasy as I am, though he hides it better. "We both know what's coming after the compass. That's when everything changes."

The silence between us stretches, heavy with truths neither of us is willing to voice. I swirl the amber liquid in my glass, its surface rippling like my thoughts. *Half-truths.* They sound like a solution, but they feel like betrayal. Of her. Of the fragile trust we've built. Of something deeper I can't bring myself to name.

But Therion is right. He usually is. I don't have a choice. Not if I want to keep her close. Not if I want to protect what little balance we still have.

With a long, slow breath, I set my glass down and meet his gaze. "What would you tell her?"

Therion leans back, folding his arms across his chest. "What you want her to believe."

His words sink into me like a blade, sharp and deliberate. I know what he means. I know what I have to do. But the weight of it threatens to crush whatever part of me still hopes this might end differently.

Because deep down, I know it won't. Regardless of what's stirring in me—what she's awakened—nothing will stop me from what I have to do. No matter the cost.

CHAPTER THIRTY-NINE
ELYSSARA

THE GROUP, EXCEPT FOR KAEL AND THERION, MAKE THEIR WAY BACK
to the room at the end of the hallway of the inn, which I've been
informed belongs to Seren and Ronyn. It's serving as a headquarters
for our plans, due to the inordinate amount of books and maps that
are lining every inch of the space. *Typical Seren.*

My body hums with the aftermath of the fight, every nerve
vibrating with something dark and primal. I'm not afraid or
remorseful—I'm angry. Furious, even. I'm done being the hunted,
the one who hides while others dictate my life. The rage burns
hotter than the magic in my veins, and before I realize it, light
sparks at my fingertips, casting flickering light across the room.

"Easy, El. Let's not light the whole joint up, eh?" Ronyn's voice
is soft, his hand brushing my arm with a familiarity that cuts
through the chaos in my chest. His touch anchors me, pulling me
back before the light can consume me—or anyone else.

I force a breath, then another, shoving the light down until it
settles into a glowing spark in my chest. My hands tremble as I press
them to my sides, the heat fading. Around the room, everyone
stares. Ronyn's gaze is steady, full of belief. Seren smiles, awe

lighting her face. But Jax and Merrik exchange wary glances, and Finn looks ready to bolt, his hand hovering near the door.

"I'm fine, I'm fine. I'm under control," I try to assure them, but my tone is shrill and laced with intensity. Jax raises her hands in submission, and backs away until she is, again, leaning against the wall.

Seren rustles through one of the countless papers on her dining table—-clearly never used for its intended purpose—until she finds the one she was looking for. "Ah! Here it is! Okay," she flashes an excited smile, her mass of golden curls shrouding her face, but she shoves them back and over one shoulder before continuing. "I made a plan. I'm certain this is the exact spot we need to go to for the Astral Compass."

Kael and Therion stroll in—liquor and glasses in hand, cutting through the room's tension like a blade.

"Finally decided to join us," I say, leveling a glare at Kael. My tone drips with venom, but the truth—that I was worried—lurks just beneath the surface. I bury it with a scoff.

"Miss me, El?" Kael's smirk is sharp, almost cutting. There's something darker beneath it, something that tightens the air around us. He pours himself a glass with a casualness that feels deliberate, almost like he's hiding behind it.

"Go on, Little Star," I say, turning to Seren with forced indifference. "Where are we going?"

Whenever Seren is excited about a new discovery, she speaks at a cadence that I can barely decipher. She is a flurry of words and theories and lore that all weave together to create a tapestry of unmatched knowledge.

"Skaedor's Crest," Seren says with a barely contained squeal, as if the name alone is enough explanation. When we all stare blankly at her, she rolls her eyes. "Oh come on. It's only one of the most legendary peaks in Aevryn!"

"Seren, I'm going to need a little more than that," I deadpan.

She exhales, looking exasperated that we don't know what in the Stars she's talking about.

"Skaedor's Crest is a jagged, snow-capped mountain that rises high above the surrounding peaks of the Nyvaryn Range, located a day's hard ride from Galreth. So, if we leave at first light, we'll arrive at the perfect time to view The Watcher's Eye. I am certain of it!" Her enthusiasm is infectious, and I find myself smiling back.

"You are truly brilliant," I offer, and kiss her forehead affectionately.

"What can we expect in the ranges—and at the peak? What's waiting for us?" Therion sinks into an arm chair in the corner, a fresh glass of liquor poured, and leaning on his thighs, hands raking through his clipped, sandy blonde hair still speckled with the blood of The Aegis Covenant. He says the words like a sigh, exhaustion pulling at his features.

"I'm so happy you asked!" Her tone is still high-pitched and giggly. I watch the ever-serious Therion from where I'm standing, and notice an almost imperceptible smile tugging at his lips. He doesn't let it turn into anything overt, but it was there.

"From what I can find, Skaedor's Crest is... well, it's place of myth and legend," Seren begins, her voice trembling with excitement. She shuffles through a pile of papers before pulling out a faded map, her fingers tracing the jagged peaks. "It's the highest peak in the Nyvaryn Range, always snow-covered, always treacherous. Skaedor was a Starborn warrior—a myth, really—who hid the compass there to keep it from unworthy hands. It's said that kings have sent armies to claim it, and every one of them failed."

She pauses, looking at each of us in turn. "The mountain doesn't just test your strength. It tests your truth. The sighing winds... they reveal what you're hiding, even from yourself. To take the compass, you have to offer something real—your deepest truth. And it's not optional."

I don't miss the fleeting exchange of weighted glances between Kael and Therion, and something about it sets my instincts on edge.

"And on the way? Do tribes still inhabit the ranges? What of animal life?" Kael's directness is all command.

Seren clears her throat, trying not to shrink under the weight of Kael's authority. "I have read nothing of tribes in that region since Skaedor's time, due mostly to weather. The ranges are covered in snow, making it almost impossible to climb, let alone live there. However, I read of shadow lynxes and frost drakes occupying the area."

"And what is their method of attack?" Therion asks. He'll be our best weapon out there, sensing their presence before the rest of us.

"Shadow lynxes move like living shadows, silent and invisible until they strike. They're said to hunt in pairs, their glowing red eyes the only warning before an attack. Frost drakes are worse—massive, wingless beasts with icy breath that can freeze a man where he stands. Or at least, that's what the books say."

Kael moves forward, drink in hand, all unflinching command and authority. "We leave at first light. Finn, Torv—reset after the attack, rally the rebels and do a full sweep through the village. I want no trace of The Aegis here when we return," Finn and Torvyn nod efficiently at their orders. "Jax, Merrik—I need you to gather horses and supplies, and then I need you to resume your duties at The Joining before suspicion arises. We need to be able to access the tunnels after the compass."

"Alright, lad," Merrik agrees, slapping him on the shoulder affectionately. The scowl on Jax's face speaks volumes for how she feels about the order, but she nods indignantly, not trusting herself to speak.

"Ronyn, Seren, Elyssara, get some sleep. We leave in a few hours," with that, Kael spins on his heel and makes for the door. Apparently he thinks this is over, but I'm only just getting started.

"And who the fuck put you in charge?" I lace my words with menace, my earlier fury returning with a vengeance.

I can hear the mutters and murmurs of the group around us. "We'll give you some space, love," Merrik's pained expression, and the hand he drags down his face belie his soothing tone. He makes for the door, but before he gets there, I harness my growing rage.

"No one fucking move," I pronounce each word explicitly. "I have quite a few questions, and you will all answer me." I lean closer to Kael, and drop my voice an octave, "There's no battle to silence my questions now—so sit the fuck down. We're going to have a little chat." My venomous words are punctuated by a bright flare from my Lightborne marking.

Good. I let the glow linger—a reminder of what I could unleash.

Kael's jaw clenches once, like he's biting down on something that wants to escape. His dark expression falters—traces of guilt or hesitation mar his face, though he takes a seat at the table. "I promised you answers."

And I promised him questions.

Lots of questions.

CHAPTER FORTY
KAEL

Elyssara's fiery rage should frustrate me, or at the very least, make me nervous. But for some fucked up reason, it turns me on. There is nothing more beautiful than a woman who isn't afraid to show her dark side. Even more so when she is covered in the blood of her enemies who dared to stand in her way.

Therion clears his throat and gives me a pointed look as if to say *focus, you fool.* I sit up straighter, making eye contact with Elyssara. "Where would you like to start?"

She all but snarls at me, and says, "Let's start simply, seeing as even simple truths have proven to be difficult for you."

Ronyn snorts a small laugh before covering his mouth and forcing his features into submission. Elyssara shoots him a look that I'm glad to evade for once, and he says, "What? I'm just glad you're not directing it at me!" For all his jokes and playfulness, I like him. She spins back around, eyes searing into me.

"Who is Torvyn?"

I make a silent promise to tell her the truth for as long as I can.

"He is the Galreth leader of the rebellion. He is also Finnick's father, and a long-term friend of mine."

She seems to mull the answer over, deciding if she's content with it. "Okay. And who is Finnick to this rebellion? What does he do?" Some of the bite—but not much—has come out of her tone, seemingly soothed by my honesty.

"Finn acts as the Innkeeper at The Broken Stag—here, where we're staying. He's also a messenger between The Shadow Wastes and Dravara. I'm sure you noticed that he can move without notice quite easily." I keep my answers stripped back and raw, hoping that the more honesty I offer her, the sooner her curiosity will be satisfied.

She huffs a sigh, expression unreadable. The air is thick with tension, heavy and loaded with meaning. This moment feels like a tipping point. "And The Broken Stag? It's not a regular inn, is it?"

Clever girl.

"No. It's a safe house and meeting point for the rebellion."

"And you? Who are you in all of this?"

Fuck. I let out a shaky exhale. She's starting to ask more of the right questions, and I know everything is about to change. "I am the leader of the rebellion."

She presses on, taking what I've just revealed—no doubt for later—and pushes on, hungry for answers. "And Merrik? Jax?"

Her questions come in a flurry, desperate, adamant.

"Merrik and Jax have been with the rebellion since it began ten years ago, and I've known them both since I was a child. They've infiltrated the Dravari Guard at The Joining, and they transport goods to The Shadow Wastes, spy, that sort of thing."

For whatever reason, this seems to hit Elyssara harder. *I'm such a fucking bastard.* I can feel the trust we've built dissolving between us every moment this conversation continues.

"Why? Why do they need to infiltrate The Joining? Are you resourcing *The Shadow Wastes*? Arming their soldiers?" she spits the words as if they repulse her. Whatever she thinks she knows about The Wastes is likely wildly inaccurate fallacies and indoctrinations. Everything she knows about the realms will be obliterated when she finally knows the truth.

"There is so much you don't know, Elyssara—"

"Then fucking tell me! Stop treating me like a vacuous little child and tell me the godsdamned truth!" She cuts me off, screaming the words. Years of living in the dark have taken a toll— and it's unfurling out of her in real time. Her skin glows a bright, golden yellow. *Beautiful.*

"Duskae," I stand to soothe her, her breathing now ragged and fast.

"Don't fucking patronize me, Kael. Just tell me," she sobs the words, and clenches at her chest, as if that will somehow soften the pain she's feeling. All I want to do is go to her.

"No passage is granted across the continent unless sanctioned by both kings. We need to be able to move around without notice, build up our numbers for the rebellion. We have good people who have given up everything to fight with us, and we need to feed them, arm them, care for their families."

She's nodding, as if starting to piece some of this together.

I continue, "We're also piecing together trade routes between the realms. Dravara has been resourcing The Wastes with food and medicine for decades." I pause, breathing heavily—I know I'm about to crack the foundations of her reality.

Therion is looking at me with hesitant eyes, as if begging me to just *tell her what I want her to know.* But I can't. I have to keep going.

"But what does Dravara get in return? Why are tensions building between the realms?" I ask, urging her to figure it out.

"I've wondered this for a long time," Seren whispers, eyes focussed on the floor, piecing it together.

"Well, I haven't. I've been too busy thieving scraps from others that are starving to be worrying about greedy kings and their fight for control," Elyssara bites, and I can feel her rage about to snap.

But I can't stop now. I've come this far. Therion sucks in a breath, already aware of what I'm about to say.

"Threvenar," I say.

Here eyes snap to mine. "Threvenar?"

"It's a plant. Native to The Wastes. It's used in a complicated memory suppressant," I say.

Her breath hitches, realization beginning to strike.

"Have you ever wondered why no one can remember who came

before Thalmyr? What Dravara was like before his tyranny?" I press, my voice strong and unyielding.

"We can't remember," she breathes, eyes wide.

"No one in Dravara can remember, Elyssara. All it would take is a single withheld shipment of threvenar. And the entire kingdom would remember what it was forced to forget," the heavy implication falls from my lips. I know I've said too much, but I don't regret it.

"What the fuck?" Ronyn asks, and for once, he's serious.

"It's in the water supply," Therion clarifies.

"Our memories are being stolen? Our history rewritten?" Elyssara clenches her fists, knuckles turning white.

"We don't know how it works. Not entirely. We know it's selective to specific time periods and memories, but nothing more. It's complex magic. Old magic. That's what we're trying to figure out," Therion explains.

Elyssara is reeling. Pacing, panting, unstable.

"So, why do *you* care about Dravara?" She spits the words like accusation.

I pause, selecting my words carefully. "The true King of The Wastes—Aurius, the King usurped by Maldrak—was on peaceful terms with Dravara. We want to get back to that. Return Aevryn to peace."

Truth. That's the truth.

She stares off into nothingness, piecing information together, joining dots, making sense of it all.

Her eyes snap to mine. Her voice is low, breathless. "You want the throne."

I swallow thickly—there is no coming back from this.

"The Shadow Wastes are not what you've been led to believe. There is more to the story. To its history. King Maldrak killed King Aurius and usurped the throne ten years ago. He has murdered, captured, and raped his way to power," my voice rises in volume, stronger and more vicious. "He has plunged The Shadow Wastes into further decay and degradation. *He* is the man who has my sister.

He is the man that took everything we all love," I throw my arms out, gesturing to the people—*my people*—around the room.

"The Shadow Wastes are your home," Elyssara whispers again, and I can sense the thoughts rushing through her mind, trying to make sense of everything.

"Yes, we are from The Shadow Wastes. But our rebellion is continent-wide. Every single town and village has our rebels in it. We are growing, and we are becoming powerful, and we *will* get what we want," menace slips into my tone, and I can feel Therion's stare burning into me.

"I thought everyone in The Wastes was deranged. Distorted and cursed," Elyssara shakes her head, trying to reconcile what she has always known with the new information.

"The Wastes have been cursed for as long as anyone can remember. Our capital, Kryntar, and all its surroundings are shrouded in The Decay—a blighted barrier that has cast it into death and darkness. Morrathys cursed our lands after the century-long war between Starborn and Earthbound. Our mission is to take the throne from King Maldrak, and restore The Wastes to what they once were."

"Kael," Therion warns in a low growl. "*Enough.*"

Elyssara's face is blank, devoid of emotion and expression. "So, what do you want with me? I'm assuming it's more than the compass?"

I clench my jaw. Steeling myself. What I'm about to say will make or break this alliance... or whatever this is.

"Yes," I say with more confidence than I feel. My gut roils, and I can hear my pulse pumping in my ears. "We *do* need the compass. And… we want you to help us take down The Decay," I pause briefly, weighing my words. "The Shadow Wastes is my home. *Our* home. The Decay keeps our people cursed, and the entire continent locked in the trade agreement that's killing us."

"Hmm," Elyssara's non-committal response sets me on edge, like a predator about to strike. "When were you going to tell me this?"

"When you started to trust us... perhaps even started believing in our mission." The words feel empty and feeble on my tongue.

"How would I do that, Kael? You don't fucking tell me anything! You just use me!" Her rage returns with force. "I am nothing more than a pawn in a game between powerful men who seek to use me. I am nothing but a vessel for power to be taken and exploited. A body to be fucked and used. A human to be cast out and starved. You are no different to these kings, Kael. At least Maldrak doesn't hide who he is!"

Her words slice through me in a way that no blade ever could. *She's right.* I *have* used her. I *am* using her.

"Elyssara, please. There is so much more that you don't know." *What sort of response is that?* I can't think of anything else to say that will salvage this conversation.

"Oh I fucking believe that," Elyssara's words are dripping with sarcasm. I think she's going to continue handing me my ass, but she wheels around, eyes locking on Therion. "And *you*," she stabs her finger in his direction, "don't think I've forgotten about you." Fury has taken her over now, and all any of us can do is hold on for it to pass, as we watch magic crackling at her fingertips. I resist the urge to snuff it out with my shadows, and let her release some anger. "What is it that you do for our King of Rebels here?" She mockingly sweeps an arm out, as if addressing someone royal.

Therion, for the first time in our lives, looks genuinely stunned by the entire turn of events. "I'm Kael's General of War," his tone even and clipped.

"Oh, just a General of War," her eyes roll indignantly, "Of course you are. Another puppet master pulling strings while I dance to your tune. You are fucking complicit in all of this, too. Another power hungry man who is completely okay with using and abusing me, no matter the cost!"

"None of us are okay with this, Elyssara," Therion's expression is sincere and almost downcast.

"*Lies!* I have been nothing but a pawn to fucking everyone my entire life! I was starting to believe that *this* was different." Everything about her changes in an instant. Her rage, her fury, her anger, all acquiesce to what is living underneath—betrayal. Agony. Heart-break. Her body slackens and she drops to her knees, sobs tearing from her throat as her head falls into her palms.

Despite my better judgement to let Ronyn take her, I can't help myself. *I'm a bastard.* I know I shouldn't be the one to pick her up when I'm the one who put her there, but I'm selfish and I want to be there for her. I want it for myself. I scoop her into my arms, and to my surprise, she melts into my chest, braids hanging over my arms, tears running in rivers down her blood-speckled cheeks. *Beautiful.*

"I'll take her to her room," I murmur to no one in particular on the way out, blocking out the sound of Seren's sobs, Jax and Merrik conferring about being right, and Therion not saying anything at all, which is quite possibly the loudest.

Yes. Trust is definitely broken.

CHAPTER FORTY-ONE
KAEL

I call for a maid to draw a bath as I carry Elyssara back to her room, kicking the door open with a sharp crack of my boot against the wood. The room is dim, the lingering scent of rose water clinging to the air, but my focus is solely on her. I place her down gently, the bloodied and battered leather of her armor stark against the soft, untouched blankets.

Her head rests against my chest, and for a moment, I let her stay there. Let her take whatever comfort she can find in the heat of my body against hers. My hand brushes her tangled braid, and I tuck her closer, as though shielding her from the world might make the truth we've uncovered less cruel. "I'm sorry," I murmur, my voice low, rough with the weight of everything I've done. "You were just an idea to me—a prophecy. A name. But now..." My words trail off.

How do I even begin to apologize for what I've turned her life into?

She doesn't answer, but she leans into me, nestling her head beneath my chin. It's a silent truce, and for now, I'll take it. For now, it's enough.

We stay like that for a while, her weight pressed into me, her breathing steady but hollow. I let myself imagine, just briefly, a life where this is all there is. No rebellion. No prophecy. Just us. A ridiculous fantasy, but the thought lingers longer than it should. The scent of her—sandalwood, vanilla, steel, and sweat—floods my senses. It's intoxicating, dangerous. Her scent reminds me that she's both a weapon and something infinitely more fragile.

The maid returns, announcing the bath is ready, and I feel her stir slightly, but she doesn't move. The fierce warrior I saw in battle, the one who fought with relentless fire and grit, sits here like a shadow of herself, broken and quiet. My jaw clenches. That fire is still there—it has to be. I won't let it die.

"Your bath is ready," I say carefully. "I'll leave you to undress and clean up. If you need me, I'll be with Therion."

Nothing. She doesn't so much as flinch.

I let out a breath and walk back to her, resting my hand lightly on her shoulder. "Would you like help?" I ask, my tone softer than I thought myself capable of. When she doesn't pull away, I take that as my answer.

Lifting her into my arms, I carry her toward the bath. She doesn't resist. It's almost unsettling how still she is. I sit down on the chair beside the tub, settling her on my lap, and start undoing her armor.

The buckles on her leather pauldrons are stiff with dried blood, and they creak as I work them loose. The plates fall away, revealing the curve of her shoulders, smooth and lightly sun-kissed with the faint lines of scars. She doesn't make a sound, just lets me strip away the hardened pieces of her protection. One by one, I unfasten the vambraces from her forearms, my thumbs grazing the tender skin beneath.

When I reach her chest plate, my hands falter for a moment. This is her armor—what keeps the world out, what keeps her invincible. Undoing it feels almost sacrilegious, like I'm peeling back layers of who she is. But I press on, unbuckling the straps that hold it tight to her frame. The leather is heavier than I expect—or perhaps that's just me—as it slides free, clattering softly to the floor. Beneath it, her tunic clings to her skin, damp with sweat and streaked with dirt and blood.

Her breath catches as I work my fingers down to the belts and thigh guards of her fighting leathers. The laces are stiff, resistant, but I take my time, careful not to tug too hard or hurt her. When the last strap is loosened, the leather drops away, leaving her in nothing but her undergarments.

I should stop here. I know I should. But then she moves, slowly shifting her braid over her shoulder, baring her back to me. The gesture is deliberate, an unspoken invitation that makes my throat tighten. I stare at the laces of her corset, my hands trembling faintly as I reach for them. The laces come undone, one by one, until the fabric loosens and slips down her body.

She turns slightly, and the sight of her steals the breath from my lungs. She is... radiant. The faint light of the room glows against her bare skin, highlighting every curve, every scar, every mark that tells the story of her strength. Her body is a battlefield, but it's also a masterpiece. She is untamed, powerful, and utterly mesmerizing.

For a moment, I can't look away. She is more than the prophecy, more than the warrior who wields a blade of Stars. She is a woman, raw and unguarded, and the weight of that realization threatens to crush me.

"You're... exquisite," I whisper before I can stop myself. My voice comes out rough, betraying the storm inside me. She doesn't respond, her eyes distant as she stares into the steam rising from the bath.

Gently, I lift her from my lap, sliding her undergarments from her hips, and lowering her into the water. The warmth engulfs her, the rose petals clinging to her skin as she leans back against the tub's edge. For a moment, she looks peaceful, her eyes fluttering closed, the tension in her body easing.

I stand, my fists clenched at my sides, forcing myself to look away. "I'll leave you to it," I murmur, stepping back toward the door. She doesn't say anything, but I linger for a moment longer, watching her in the stillness of the bath.

I stand at the door, one hand on the handle, intending to leave and give her privacy. But something holds me back. The sight of her, sunk low in the steaming bath, the rose petals clinging to her skin, makes it impossible to walk away. Her head rests against the edge of the tub, her braid—a cascade of intricate weaving—draped over her shoulder in the style ancient female warriors favored. It's not just a hairstyle. It's her identity as a warrior, and a reflection of her resolve.

I hesitate before speaking, my voice soft. "Do you want help with your hair?"

Her eyes flicker open, weary but curious, and after a long moment, she nods.

Crossing the room, I kneel beside the tub, my movements deliberate and measured, as if I might scare her off if I move too quickly. The braid is beautiful, a lattice of twists and knots intertwined with thin leather cords and stray strands of gold that glimmer faintly in the light. It's a work of art, but it's also matted with blood, sweat, and dirt from the battle. My hands hover over it for a moment, unsure where to begin. Then, gently, I start to untangle it.

The leather cords come first, unwrapping easily from the strands they hold together. I set them aside, my fingers moving through her hair with an intimacy that feels both foreign and natural. As the braid unravels, her hair falls free, cascading down her back in waves. It's longer than I expected, the weight of it heavy and silken in my hands, despite the grime.

She doesn't say anything, but I catch the faintest sigh as my fingers work through the knots. Slowly, methodically, I untangle each section, careful not to pull too hard. The silence between us is thick but not uncomfortable. It feels... significant, like this moment means more than either of us is willing to admit.

When the last knot is undone, her hair spills into the water like liquid gold. It glimmers even in the low light, strands of dark caramel, russet and honey mingling with the steam. My hands linger in it for a moment, feeling its softness, before I reach for the soap.

"Lean back," I murmur, my voice gravelly. She obeys, her head tipping back as I scoop water into my hands and let it pour over her hair. The dirt and blood run away in rivulets, streaking the water with faint crimson swirls. I work the soap into her hair, massaging it into her scalp. She closes her eyes, her breathing evening out, her body relaxing for the first time since the fight.

It's a strangely tender act, washing her hair. Something I've never done for anyone before, and yet, it feels like the most natural thing in the world. The warrior in her is stripped away, leaving the woman beneath—a woman who is vulnerable, resilient, and breathtakingly beautiful.

As I rinse the soap from her hair, the strands gleam anew, free of the grime that had dulled them. My fingers linger one last time, smoothing the length of her hair as it fans out across the water.

"All done," I say softly, rising to my feet. She doesn't open her eyes, but I catch the faintest ghost of a smile on her lips. It's enough to carve a space in my chest where my resolve used to be.

Without another word, I leave the room, shutting the door behind me with a quiet click. Duty is the only thing that can pull me away from her, and I hate that *I* am the reason she is hurting. *I betrayed her trust.* My stomach is in a knot, but I have no time to give it any credence. The realms hang in the balance.

My heart pounds as I walk down the hall to Therion's room— we need a new plan.

I knock quietly before entering. Therion's in his usual chair, his posture deceptively relaxed, a glass of amber liquor cradled in his hand. His face is unreadable, but the liquor is a tell—it's how he unwinds when things have gone to all hells. A second glass waits beside the chair I usually take, and without a word, I grab it and sit.

Our eyes meet, and we exchange a thousand unspoken words in a single glance. That's the way it's always been between us. Neither of us is particularly good at talking, but we've never needed to be.

"How is she?" Therion asks, his demeanor solemn and genuine.

"Hurting." That's all I can think to say.

Therion hums in acknowledgement, then adds, "It did not go well."

"No, it didn't," I say, confirming the obvious.

"She still doesn't know who you really are, the plan for Nalya, or anything about The Sky in the prophecy. You did what you needed to do and told her the truth, without telling her everything. It could've been worse." Therion always has a way of rationalizing the existential.

"Barely," I say, which is the truth. My plan was to slowly introduce her to the truths and realities of the realms—and my plans to right some of its wrongs—but The Aegis Covenant really fucked that plan up tonight. I didn't want to bombard her with talk of rebellions, and political games and plans everyone knew of except her. I wanted her to slowly piece it together with some well-placed conversations. Maybe even some books that Seren may just so happen to have stumbled across. I hoped that she'd become sympathetic to our mission, willing to help take down Thalmyr, The Decay and Maldrak.

Fucking idiot.

That opportunity is gone now.

Now, we'd do it the hard way.

"Now we just have to retrieve a magical relic that makes us face hidden truths. Shouldn't be too hard to keep it all a secret," Therion states drily.

I can't fight the smile that breaks free on my face, but it doesn't last long. He's right.

Even if we get to Skaedor's Crest, what truths will we have to face?

Will they unravel everything we've worked so hard to build?

The silence between us stretches thin, taut with things neither of us is willing to say. We settle into a rhythm of drinking, refilling, and staring at nothing in particular. The sound of the liquor sloshing in the bottle and the occasional scrape of glass on wood are the only noises in the room.

Therion breaks the silence first. "Will she be ready to go in the morning?"

His voice is quiet, but there's a tension beneath the words, a hesitation that's unlike him. He's usually the steady one, the one with the plan. But everything is riding on this, and we both know it.

I down the last of my drink, letting the burn chase away the knot in my throat. "I have absolutely no fucking idea."

Therion doesn't press. He just nods, his expression grim, and pours another round.

CHAPTER FORTY-TWO
ELYSSARA

THE MORNING AIR IS BITING, CRISP ENOUGH TO STEAL THE BREATH from my lungs if I'm not prepared. Evidence of last night's storm—broken branches, stray belonging strewn everywhere—is thick. It's all a stark contrast to the cloying heat of Virellin. I wrap my cloak tighter around me as the group gathers in the small courtyard of the inn. Our breath plumes in the cold, the faint clinking of bridles and the low snorts of restless horses filling the silence.

Therion is methodical as always, ensuring every saddlebag is secured and loaded with food and water canteens, and every weapon easily accessible. Jax and Merrik stand near the packhorses, adjusting straps and tying down supplies. I can see their hushed exchanges and their displeasure at not coming along. Torvyn, no fuss and stoic, sharpens his blade, the steady scrape of steel on whet-stone a sound I've grown too familiar with. Finn, on the other hand, busies himself with checking the horses' hooves, muttering under his breath about the terrain ahead.

"El, are you alright? You haven't said a word," Seren's expression is fraught with worry, her tone tense, and I can't blame her—I've been silent and passive, save for the shivering.

I nod, unable to squeeze a single word from my body. Ronyn

throws his arm around my shoulder, pulling me in tight. His affection warms me. *I need this.* I melt into him, nestling my face into the crook of his underarm.

"Please know that *we*," he wags a finger emphatically between himself and Seren, "haven't forgotten *our* goals. Just because they have theirs, doesn't mean we have to deviate from ours." King Thalmyr. Vengeance. Unbinding my power. "We're family, El."

The sting of impending tears threatens to overcome me, but there is not a chance in the Stars that I'll let that happen in front of these people. Moisture rims my eyes and my throat aches with the effort to hold back the flurry of emotions swirling inside my chest. "Okay," I concede, barely above a whisper.

The three of us. It's *always* been the three of us. No matter what, I have them. They have me. We are in this together.

We huddle together, fogging our warm breath into the palms of our hands intermittently to keep the chill at bay. I watch as the stableboy rushes around the horses, double and triple checking frantically. Of course, it doesn't help that Kael is looming over his shoulder, correcting and instructing him with brusque command.

I watch Kael—he's quiet, his expression unreadable, but his hands are precise as he adjusts the straps on the saddle for the fourth time. There's a tension in his movements, a tightness in his jaw that betrays whatever storm brews beneath his calm exterior.

As if he feels the weight of my stare, he turns towards me, eyes locking on mine. *Is that remorse lining his features? Or am I just hoping that's what I see?* I break his gaze first, choosing instead to take in the towering black stallion with eyes like polished obsidian standing next to him. He is magnificent.

Kael starts moving towards us, his smooth gait unfaltering and dominant. "Lightborne, you're with me." *Lightborne.* Devoid of emotion, he calls me the name that makes me feel like nothing more than a prophecy. Not a woman, not a friend, not a daughter. *A thing.* Or maybe even *nothing.*

Or perhaps my name is too intimate. *Too real.*

I nod, knowing that resisting this would be futile. Kael holds out an arm for me, ushering me towards the intimidating black stallion.

As I move past him, a ghost of warmth brushes against my lower back—a sensation as fleeting as a whisper. My breath catches, and I glance down instinctively, only to find his arms at his sides. The air around me feels charged, as though I've walked through the static of a storm. *What in the Stars was that?*

The horse tosses his head, dark mane rippling like liquid shadow. His silver-ringed eyes lock on me, unblinking, as though he can see something beyond what is visible. His hooves shift uneasily, stamping against the frozen earth, but he doesn't retreat. It is almost as if he can't decide whether to challenge me or bow. Kael shushes him, gliding his strong calloused hands underneath his mane and along his neck. The horse instantly soothes and settles, as if Kael's very presence comforts him.

"He's beautiful." I breathe the words in awe, not realizing they've escaped me until Kael's eyes flash towards me.

"This is Nyx," he states simply, though I notice the fondness in his tone.

"He's yours?"

Kael nods. "My little sister begged me to name him Moonpie," he gives a light huff of laughter, but there's no mistaking the nostalgia and sadness woven in his words. He looks at me then, eyes brimming with guilt, "Elyssara—" His voice cracks, softer than I've ever heard it. "I never wanted to hurt you. But you have to know—"

"Don't. Please don't." I swallow down that still-present lump in my throat. "I understand why you did it." And I do. I understand the lengths I'd go to for my family. The people I'd take down to free them. "It's bigger than me. I am unimportant in the grand plan of saving your people. I'm disposable. I understand." I swallow hard, my voice barely holding. "I just... don't trust you anymore."

Whatever was building between us is gone, and our fragile alliance is all that remains.

Kael's expression looks raw and pained, but he nods tightly, acquiescing to my wishes. He spins on his heel and gives a short farewell to Finn and Torvyn. He turns to Jax and Merrik, clasping their forearms in a warrior's embrace. "Be ready for us in two days at the latest. If we're not back, get word to Daelen and proceed as usual."

Daelen. Word. Two days. The way Kael said the name—certain, matter-of-fact—pricks at the edges of my thoughts. I may have been blind to his motives before, but not anymore. My trust is shattered, but my perception? Sharper than ever.

Ronyn and Seren sit atop their bay mare, Ronyn's bow slung over his shoulder, and Seren clutching a historical text in one hand and, surprisingly, her small crossbow in the other. Therion, unyielding and alert, sits atop a gleaming white mare, her tail shimmering and rippling in the sunlight like a waterfall. She is mythical, regal, otherworldly, and the perfect steed for an Aetherstride who needs to track and blend into the snow. He looks almost ethereal astride this horse. "She's *his*, isn't she?" I murmur to Kael, awestruck by their almost synergistic and palpable connection.

"Yes. That's Aura. Therion and I both received our horses as gifts from our fathers at the solstice ten years ago." The look in his eyes is wistful and warm.

"How long have they been here in Galreth?" I probe, trying to glean as much information as I can about how their entire operation works.

"A couple of months. We leave them here when we cross The Joining. Galreth is close, so it makes sense. Plus, they'd kind of stand out if we were to take them further."

I smile despite myself, and silently reprimand myself for the way Kael can distract me from... well, *everything*.

We mount Nyx, setting off towards the Astral Compass, and settle into a comfortable tempo behind the others.

The rhythm of Nyx's hooves against the frozen earth is almost hypnotic, steady and reassuring despite the tension that coils tightly between us. The Nyvaryn Ranges rise ahead like jagged teeth against the pale sky, their peaks shrouded in mist. Snow clings stubbornly to the cliffs, even as the sun struggles to burn through the haze.

Therion leads the group with quiet precision, Aura's white coat blending almost seamlessly with the frost-dusted ground. It's almost eerie how perfectly horse and rider match. Behind him, Ronyn rides with Seren perched behind him, her nose buried in her book while Ronyn scans the terrain with sharp, calculating eyes.

I try to focus on the path ahead, but the silence between Kael and me is deafening. The steady sway of Nyx's gait pulls my back closer to Kael's chest, his warmth bleeding through the layers of my cloak. It's both comforting and maddening, a reminder of just how close we are despite the chasm that's forged between us.

The terrain shifts as we enter the heart of the Nyvaryn Ranges. The air grows thinner, sharper, and every breath feels like it scrapes against my lungs. The once-clear trail narrows into a rocky path, bordered by steep cliffs on one side and a drop into fog-shrouded oblivion on the other.

Nyx moves with care, his steps deliberate as he navigates the uneven ground. I can feel Kael's tension through his rigid posture, and I wonder if he feels the same pull I do—the sense that we're being watched.

"Does it always feel like this here?" I murmur, breaking the silence.

Kael doesn't turn, but his voice is low when he responds. "The Nyvaryn Ranges don't like trespassers. The land has a way of reminding you that you don't belong."

A shiver runs down my spine, and I clutch the saddle tighter as a gust of icy wind whips through the pass.

The wind sharpens as we push further into the Ranges, threading between towering cliffs of slate and ice. The cold seeps deeper now, slicing through layers of fabric and biting against exposed skin.

Therion tightens his cloak against the chill, his keen eyes scanning the ridgeline above. I've watched him enough now to know when he is wielding his Aetherstride magic. Something preternatural takes over him, his eyes move with animalistic precision and alertness—always tracking, always seeing the unseen. Aetherstrides are born under The Sapphire Lynx constellation and are imbued with *Hunter's Focus* and *Swiftstep*. They track targets with unerring accuracy, and their speed and reaction time is uncanny, embodying traits of the lynx they are born under.

There is something here, something watching. I can see it in Therion's stillness.

I feel it too.

Nyx's ears flick back, his muscles bunching beneath me as he senses something beyond my comprehension. A presence, silent and vast.

A sudden gust howls through the pass, carrying with it a sound so low, so deep, it takes me a moment to register it.

Not the wind.

A chant.

It is distant at first, a steady hum like the echo of thunder rolling across the peaks. The sound is not human, not entirely, but it carries the weight of voices—layered, ancient, reverberating through the stone like something buried and waiting.

Kael's hand instinctively shifts to the hilt of his sword. We all feel it.

Ronyn mutters a curse under his breath whilst he nocks an arrow with haste. "I don't fucking like this."

Seren stiffens behind him, her book nearly slipping from her grasp. Her pupils dilate as she tilts her head, as if listening to something beyond our world.

Then, they appear.

Emerging from the mist and stone, cloaked figures descend from the cliffs, their movements eerily fluid, as if the mountain itself has released them from its grasp.

They move in perfect silence, except for the chant—a resonance so deep it rattles inside my bones.

Their skin is deep bronze, and on their skin between their furs and brown leathers, they are marked with inked symbols that coil like constellations across their hands, chests, and throats. Their hair is jet black, woven into thick braids interlaced with strips of dark iron.

And their masks—carved from pale bone, smoothed by time, each one marked with the same sigil: a crescent moon pierced by three stars.

They do not raise weapons.

But they do not need to.

They *are* weapons.

Each one carries a long, blackened wooden staff, the ends wrapped in strips of silver and adorned with carved symbols that match the ink on their skin. *Runes.* When they move, the staffs barely make a sound, but the air around them hums as if the mountain itself acknowledges their presence.

They stop before us, their masked leader standing at the center.

And then, in one unified motion, they slam the staffs into the ground.

A deep, resonant boom echoes through the valley.

A declaration.

A summons.

We're in their territory now.

One of them steps forward—a woman, though there is something ageless about her presence. Her mask is different, more intricate, carved with runes that seem to shimmer faintly as she moves.

She does not speak. Instead, she pulls something from beneath her cloak—a small, flat stone tablet, etched with precise markings.

And then, she kneels. *Why in the fucking Stars is she kneeling?*

The others follow, tapping their staffs against the earth in perfect unison.

The sound thrums through me, deeper than a command—an acknowledgment, a vow.

The air shifts. My breath catches.

I barely register Seren's sharp inhale as she leans forward, trying to see the markings more clearly. Before Ronyn can do anything about it, she slides off their mare and approaches the woman. The woman almost imperceptibly nods and holds out the tablet—an invitation. Seren's fingers brush over the symbols. Her breathing hitches, her pupils blown wide.

When she finally speaks, her voice trembles.

"They've been waiting for you."

The leader slowly lifts her head, her dark eyes locking on to mine through the carved bone mask. She speaks in a language of the ancients, her words smooth and deliberate, filled with a weight I do not yet understand.

Seren translates, her voice steady but tinged with something like awe.

"I am Syphra, keeper of Skaedor's Crest, leader of the Vaythari."

Another tap of staffs against the earth. A reaffirmation. A name spoken into the air, carrying with it a history older than I can grasp.

Syphra's voice deepens, her next words firm, unyielding.

Seren listens, swallows, then continues.

"We are the last of Skaedor's people, those who guard his legacy. We have lived in these mountains, unseen, waiting. We have waited for the one who would bear his mark."

A shiver rakes down my spine. I do not need to ask who they mean.

Syphra steps closer, gesturing to me to make my way to her. Kael's firm hands squeeze around me, and he's not breathing. "Trust me," I whisper before I fully comprehend the weight of my words. *Trust me.* As if it's not the most difficult thing in the world to trust another with your life. Your safety. *Your heart.*

He releases his hold on me, his breath still lingering on my neck. "I'll be right here if you need me." It's fleeting, but there is weight to his words. As if he meant that he would be here for me, beyond simply wielding his sword, or to protect an asset.

I dismount from Nyx, much to his obvious trepidation, and step tentatively towards Syphra.

She raises the stone tablet in my direction and I reach out my hands. She presses it into my palms, cupping them between her own. She drops her head in a way that feels a lot like a bow of deference.

Seren's voice barely rises above the wind.

"You bear the mark of Skaedor. His burden is now yours."

The Vaythari warriors watch silently, their staffs still planted firmly into the ground. I look down at the stone, tracing the carved words with my fingers.

Seren translates, her voice barely above a whisper.

"The fallen are scattered. They must be guided home. That is your task."

Fallen. Home. Task. *Holy Stars.* My hands tighten around the stone as the weight of it settles into my bones.

The words linger, heavy with unspoken meaning.

My hands tighten around the stone. It does not say who they are, nor where they have fallen from. Or at least, not to my eyes.

A sharp gust cuts through the pass, lifting the edges of the warriors' furs. Kael's jaw tightens, but he remains silent, waiting.

Seren glances at me. Her eyes hold something—concern, maybe fear.

Still, she speaks. "Skaedor sought to unite them. He failed."

My heart pounds. "What happened?"

Syphra does not answer immediately.

Instead, she lifts her staff and taps it against the frozen ground once.

The warriors do the same.

The sound reverberates through the mountain like an exhale, a sigh from something greater than all of us.

Seren hesitates before translating.

"The cost of unity is always blood."

I force my voice to remain steady. "Skaedor was betrayed."

Syphra nods, slow and deliberate.

"And you will face the same test."

The wind howls through the pass. I feel it curl around me like a whisper, like a warning.

The Vaythari leader pulls something from a pouch at her side— a vial filled with an ink-like substance, thick and gleaming like blackened Lightborne magic.

Syphra rises and stands before me. Her frame is small but muscular. Honed and carved by a lifetime in these mountains.

The others tap their staffs once, twice.

A steady rhythm, a promise.

Seren exhales softly. "She is marking you."

The woman dips her fingers into the ink, tracing an ancient mark onto my palm.

It burns—not painfully, but with a radiance I cannot describe. Almost akin to a surge of my own power.

The mountains hum with something unseen.

The sky above us shifts, responding to this mark being bestowed upon me.

The leader finally lifts her gaze, and when she speaks, I already know what she will say. Seren gasps, but steadies herself before breathing, "You are Skaedor's heir."

CHAPTER FORTY-THREE
ELYSSARA

SYPHRA AND I STARE AT EACH OTHER, GAZES LOCKED. HER HONEY-
brown eyes bore into mine, steady, assessing—not as a challenge, but
as something older, weightier. I should feel intimidated. Instead, I
feel seen. Respected. *Awed.*

I force myself to break her stare, turning instead to Seren.
"What does that mean? What do I do with that?" I aim for curiosity,
but my voice betrays me, coming out high, frayed at the edges—
raw.

Syphra doesn't hesitate. She reaches once more for the stone
tablet and ink, her fingers moving with purpose. Symbols flow from
her hand in swift, confident strokes, ancient runes forming at a
cadence I can barely track.

Seren watches, eyes flicking rapidly over the symbols, lips
parting as understanding dawns. "We were separated from our kin
when The Shadow Wastes were cursed and The Joining was formed
—it fractured the continent." Her voice is softer now, reverent. "We
must be reunited with our sister tribe. You must bring them home—
to the mountains."

Her breath hitches. "It is your duty to the Vaythari."

The words land like a physical blow.

I stagger under the weight of them, shaking my head. "How? How am I supposed to do that? Why me?"

Why me? Why do the prophecies keep calling my name? The mountains? These people? This duty that does not belong to me?

Seren swallows, a flicker of uncertainty flashing across her face before she continues. Her voice is soft, almost hesitant, as she translates more of Syphra's words.

"Ravira and Halun, goddesses of war and peace, gifted us the compass to find our people—to bring the fallen home."

The moment stretches, thick with meaning.

Seren's next words shatter something in me.

"But the compass only activates for Skaedor's heir—the paragon for war and peace, just as he was."

She swallows. "It is you. The compass will take you where you need to go—even when you don't know where that is."

The air is suddenly too thin.

I am not who they think I am.

I am no one.

My breath comes fast and shallow, my fingers curling tightly into my cloak. The weight of expectation is suffocating, pressing against my chest, threatening to fold my knees.

Syphra shakes her head firmly, rejecting my resistance without needing translation. Her grip tightens on her staff.

And then—she lifts it high and strikes it against the frigid earth.

The sound is like thunder.

"Zhari!"

The word booms through the mountains, resonating off the peaks like a drumbeat.

I flinch, the vibration crawling along my skin.

"Zhari!"

More voices join her.

The warriors slam their staffs against the earth, sending shockwaves of sound through the air.

"Zhari! Zhari! Zhari!"

The chant.

The same one that traveled on the wind before we arrived.

The same one that had settled into my bones, wrapped around my skin like a calling.

I feel it now—a hum beneath my ribs, a pulse that does not belong to me.

My mind fights it.

But my body—

My body *responds* to it.

A force older than my own will sings inside me, resonating with the deep, rhythmic chant. It knows what I refuse to accept.

That it is mine.

That it is for me.

I don't realize my hands are trembling until Seren turns to me, her eyes wide with something between awe and certainty.

Slowly, she presses a hand over her heart, and when she speaks, it is barely above a whisper.

"Queen."

CHAPTER FORTY-FOUR

ELYSSARA

Syphra and a handful of her most trusted warriors lead us towards Skaedor's Crest with evident knowledge of every inch of the ascent. They're sure-footed and powerful, never tiring despite the steep and arduous terrain. I allow myself the respite of leaning back into Kael's sturdy chest—despite knowing that every time I acquiesce to my desire for his embrace, I make my own path harder —and stare blankly into the vast distance.

My mind is racing with thoughts of the Vaythari, their kin, my role, the prophecy, not to mention the Astral Compass that is mere hours ahead of us. I cannot even begin to imagine that there is a secret left within me that I have not yet faced. I shudder to think of what the heavens will whisper to me.

The Vaythari appear unfazed by the thick snow that coats the narrow, undulating track. Their heavy, snow-hardened boots slosh through the inches-deep icy mush that would see anyone else fall face-first.

Syphra's gaze drifts to me frequently, but she bows quickly in deference every time I meet her gaze. It's unnerving and dense, but we manage to settle into a steady rhythm, and I take the moment to admire the beauty of this gleaming white land.

Skaedor's Ascent is a treacherous, unforgiving climb that carves through the heart of the mountains separating Dravara from The Shadow Wastes. A jagged spine of ancient stone, it rises in tiers of sheer cliffs and ice-laden ridges, each step a battle against nature's cruelty. The path is scarcely more than a crumbling ledge, winding upward along cliffs that plunge into mist-filled chasms below. Winds howl through the ravines, carrying the cries of distant predators and the eerie whistle of air funneled through unseen fissures in the rock.

The ascent itself is a gauntlet of elements and endurance. At lower altitudes, skeletal trees claw at the sky, their twisted branches blackened by perpetual frost bite. Higher still, the air turns razor-thin, biting with an unforgiving chill that sinks into bone and flesh. Ice sheets coat the rock, forcing the sheer faces to become a certain merciless fall for anyone who would dare risk the climb. Kael tells me that the mountain itself resents those who dare its slopes, shifting stone and summoning storms to repel the unworthy. The fact we are still here is somewhat comforting, I suppose.

The howls move closer, echoing off the sheer faces and reverberating through my body.

Okay, not the wind then.

Syphra and her warriors appear calm despite the howls sounding as if they are only a handful of heartbeats away, coming from every direction, and descending on us quickly. I look at her repeatedly, as if expecting her to realize the imminent arrival of a mighty snow beast and taking up a fighting stance. Syphra does no such thing and simply raises her hand. Her eyes close, and her warriors stop, following her silent command. "Velmara," she breathes the words with reverence, eyes softening into something akin to tenderness.

Our eyes dart between each other looking for an explanation. "Velmara?" I ask Seren, hoping she can elucidate whatever is taking place.

"The Shadow Lynx," Seren's voice is enchanted, and her eyes widen in awe as the silken night-black fur of a pair of shadow lynxes ripples under the setting sun as they gracefully prowl toward the warriors, a staggering contrast to the pristine white of the mountains.

In unison, Syphra and her warriors drop to one knee in the snow, and place one hand over their hearts. With her other hand, Syphra reaches down to grab a stick, quickly scribbling a series of symbols in the snow.

"We thought they had abandoned us. We have not seen the shadow lynx since the separation of our kin," Seren swallows audibly, pausing for a moment whilst Syphra continues. "We hear their howls often, phantoms of a past long forgotten. They are our astral wardens. Sent from the Stars to protect us." Her gaze pins me in place, stealing the breath from my lungs, "This is an omen for our reunion."

Goosebumps ripple across my skin, as if my body recognizes Syphra's words as the truth.

The Shadow Lynxes move closer to Kael and me, one of them crossing the narrow track in front of Nyx, who stomps and throws his head, uncertain about these feline creatures. Kael soothes him yet again with a slow stroke to his neck. The shadow lynxes stop moving then, flanking Nyx, as if protecting us. *Protecting me.*

Syphra approaches us, holding the stone tablet out for me to see. "I— I'm not sure what that means," I offer.

"We will meet you on your descent for the ceremony. Velmara will lead you to the compass now," Seren explains.

The ceremony?

I nod, unable to find words for... well, everything in my life at present.

Syphra and her warriors turn to descend back down the mountain without another word, and we urge our horses to continue.

"Are you alright?" Kael's voice has a rich, deep timbre that vibrates against my back as it ripples up his body.

"Fine." The word snaps out, clipped, hollow. I refuse to be anything else. I refuse to let myself be anything else. But the lie lingers, curling around my ribs like mist.

"You've just been declared Queen of a lost people, your best friend is casually deciphering ancient runes like a bedtime story, and

we're about to walk into a place most people don't return from...
and you're *'fine'?"* He pauses. Then, with mock consideration,
"Truly, I must learn your ways."

I spin around in the saddle to admonish Kael for his complete
lack of tact, but he quirks an eyebrow and his smirk tips up on one
side, and I find my rage from one heartbeat ago suddenly lacking.
Stars, this man.

"Well, I'm not *fine*, I suppose," I concede with a huff of meagre
irritation. "I'm... processing." A soft chuckle escapes him, but before
he can say anything, I add, "I just don't understand why the Stars
chose me. My entire life has been about this prophecy, but I am just
a girl born under the Stars like anyone else." I sigh, shoulders
slumping back against him, and I comb my fingers through the
strands of hair that have wrestled free of my braid.

"No," unfettered fury laces his voice, and he spins me around to
lock eyes with me. "You are unlike anyone I've ever met, Duskae.
When are you going to believe that you are already someone?" His
tone is stoic, direct and penetrating. "Regardless of the prophecy,
your magic, some ancient tribe. You are already someone, Elyssara."

I hold his stare. One heartbeat. Two. And for a flickering
moment, I almost let myself fall—into him, into the safety of his
arms, into the illusion that I could be something more than what
fate has carved into my bones.

But the moment snaps. Hardens.

"When men like you stop trying to use me," I say, my voice like
cold steel. "For my magic. For this prophecy. For your own fucking
gain." His name is a dagger between my teeth. "Then, Kael, maybe
I'll start believing my value exists beyond those things."

He flinches. Barely. But I see it. *Feel it.* Kael, who stands unshaken
in the face of war and death, looks as if I've cracked something inside
him. His jaw tightens. His gaze drops—just for a fraction of a second.

Then, his voice comes, rough, quiet. "I deserved that." A pause.
A breath. "And you're right. I have no fucking right to ask that of
you." For someone who commands every room and everyone he
comes across, I'm shocked that he gives me this concession. "And I

won't. I won't ask anything of you again, if you grant me one thing," his expression is staunch as always, but the fragility bubbling underneath doesn't evade me.

Therion, Ronyn and Seren are obviously eavesdropping, their horses slowing to allow us to catch up. Therion can probably hear with his Aetherstride abilities, but the other two are just fucking nosey.

"So, let me get this straight; you wish to ask me for one more thing, and then you will never ask another thing of me? That sounds really fucking counterintuitive, Kael," I roll my eyes indignantly.

He fights the smirk that tries to make an appearance again, "Yes, Your Highness. I wish to ask you for one more favor. Do I have permission to make my request?"

I huff a breath of frustration and nod once.

"Stay with me for the rest of the relics," he pleads.

I whirl on him, ready to tear into his hidden agendas, but he speaks before I can.

"I want to show you something."

There's something in his voice. Not just hope. Something heavier. Something closer to desperation. The faintest crack in the armor.

"Promise me, Elyssara." A beat. "Promise me you'll let me show you."

"What is it that you wish to show me?" Fury makes way for intrigue.

"My home. My people. I want you to understand... *why.*"

Why he lied. Why he hid important information. Why he needs me to take down The Decay so desperately. Why he is doing all of this in the first place. Why. Why. Why.

I consider the alternative of making this journey on our own. Of returning to it just being Ronyn, Seren and me, but something about that feels lonely. *Wrong.* Despite myself, I want Kael with me, and dare I say it, Therion, too.

"Fine." The word is quiet. Heavy.

He nods, the tension bleeding from his shoulders. But something inside me stays wound tight.

I spin back around, letting my gaze stretch far up the mountain.

The Velmara continue leading us up the merciless terrain, their dark forms cutting through the snow like phantoms. None of us speak. We don't need to. We've settled into an unspoken rhythm, a shared understanding that the air is too thin, the climb too brutal, and whatever waits for us at the summit demands our silence.

But the stillness doesn't last.

The altitude has stolen the warmth from my body, and now it feels like the cold is burrowing into my bones, pressing into my ribs with bony fingers. The sun has long given way to the moon, and the first Stars have begun their slow emergence across the sky. It can't be much farther.

Anticipation knots tight in my stomach, a visceral unease that I can't shake. Kael shifts behind me, subtly inching closer, pressing his thighs more firmly around my own, his arms settling against my sides like a shield against the cold.

I pretend not to notice.

I pretend I don't feel the sturdy wall of his chest, the impossible warmth of his body. I pretend I don't feel safe in his presence, even though I shouldn't. Even though I can still taste the betrayal on my tongue. Desire and fury coil together, inseparable.

The final stretch of the ascent is brutal—more ice than stone, the incline near-vertical. My legs ache from clenching around Nyx's massive frame, but the tightness in my chest is worse. Something waits at the top.

And the Velmara know it.

They break ahead of us in unison, their movements fluid, effortless, untouched by exhaustion. They reach the summit before we do, their dark forms shifting against the pale backdrop of the mountains.

But instead of continuing forward, they stop.

This is it.

A rocky outcropping splits down the middle, a narrow path leading toward a snow-covered plateau. The magic in my chest thrums, a steady pulsing beat, as if whatever lies ahead is calling to me. *Waiting.*

We dismount in silence. The first thing I notice is the stillness. No wind. No sound. As if the mountain itself is holding its breath.

Then—the growl.

It rumbles through the cliffs, deep and unearthly, a sound that vibrates through the ice and stone beneath our feet. The Velmara move as one, stepping forward to block the path.

Massive paws press into the snow, tails lashing once before curling back. Their silver eyes glow, fixed on us.

No one moves.

No one breathes.

Then, Ronyn—of course it's Ronyn—raises his hands in mock surrender and takes a slow step forward.

"We don't want to hurt you. We just need to get to the compass, okay, little fellas?" He croons.

The answer is immediate.

A snarl rips through the night as one of the Velmara lashes out, a single, casual swipe of its paw nearly knocking Ronyn on his ass.

"Woah. Woah. Okay. I guess I'm not passing."

Therion's laughter is sharp and unexpected. He claps Ronyn on the back, grinning. "It's okay, bud. Being scared of a kitty cat is nothing to be ashamed of."

Ronyn shoves him off, but the lopsided smirk on his face remains.

But I don't laugh.

The Velmara aren't just blocking the way.

They are guarding it.

I step forward.

The cold burns my skin, my pulse hammering against my ribs. Testing them. Testing myself.

Zhari. Zhari. Zhari.

The ancient Vaythari chant beats against the inside of my skull. I don't know why I think of it now. But I let it settle there, let it guide my next step.

Seren inhales sharply behind me. I hear the whisper of her hands clasping over her mouth.

I ignore the fear pressing in from all sides. Instead, I let my magic pulse outward—not an attack, not a command, but an offering. A promise.

"I mean no harm," I murmur, voice barely more than a whisper. A prayer. "I wish to help your people."

The Velmara do not move.

Not at first.

But their silver eyes remain locked on to mine, watching, waiting, deciding.

A sharp exhale leaves my lips as I take one more step.

And then—one of them lowers itself.

Slowly, deliberately, it settles onto its haunches, then shifts onto its belly, paws stretching out in the snow. A posture of submission.

My breath catches.

"They are submitting to you." Kael's voice is steady, unreadable. But I hear what he isn't saying.

They are submitting to you because they know what you are. *Who* you are.

The second Velmara follows, bowing before me, their massive forms unmoving.

The way forward is open.

"I'll go with you." Seren's voice is hesitant but determined. She swallows, shoulders squaring. "There might be runes or symbols—it needs to be me."

"I'll go." Therion and Ronyn speak at the same time. I turn, glancing between them. Before I can decide, Kael speaks, "I don't think it's our choice."

His voice is quiet but firm, eyes never leaving mine. "It can't be Ronyn. They'll never let him pass. Seren, it makes the most sense if you go. Will you try?"

Seren hesitates. But she nods, stepping forward, her breath unsteady.

The Velmara rise instantly.

Their hackles lift. Their lips curl over dagger-sharp teeth.

Seren stops short.

I don't need to tell her to step back. She already knows.

Kael's gaze shifts. "Ther?"

Therion steps forward. Same reaction.

A warning growl rolls through the mountains. The Velmara's message is clear.

We permit who may pass.

Kael steps forward.

No hesitation. No fear.

His towering frame moves with the unshaken confidence of a man who has never bowed to anything in his life. Dark waves spill over his cerulean eyes, half-masked by the falling snow. He moves like a warrior.

And the Velmara—they do not move.

Kael stops just before them, looking down at them, dominant and unyielding, and they lower their heads. *Submitting.*

I exhale, something inside me uncoiling, something shattering and reforging itself in the same breath. "I guess it's you, then."

Kael lifts his gaze to mine.

"It's me," he says simply, but the words mean something more.

It's always him.

CHAPTER FORTY-FIVE

ELYSSARA

The air is razor-thin here, carrying a sharpness that cuts through breath, through thought. Skaedor's Crest is less a mountain peak and more a plateau where the world dares to brush against the sky. Bare stone stretches wide and open, cracked and weathered by winds that have never known rest. The silence is profound—not the peaceful kind, but the kind that feels watchful. *Expectant.*

Above us, the Watcher's Eye looms—not a sun, not a moon, but a constellation carved into the night like an ancient sentinel. Its stars burn in an unnatural formation, eerie in their precision. They do not flicker. They do not waver. They only watch.

All around me, Aevryn unfurls like a map drawn by unseen hands. Forests coil like dark veins. Rivers glint like slivers of silver. Towns and villages pulse with firelight. From this height, the land looks smaller. Contained.

Until I turn east.

And I see it.

The Shadow Wastes.

The rest of Aevryn is a dance of light and shadow, beauty and ruin. But The Shadow Wastes? They are a wound.

A vast, blackened scar swallowing the land whole. Nothing

moves. Nothing breathes. Even from here, I can tell—it is dead. Decayed. No rivers cut through its scorched earth. No trees break its cracked, barren surface. It is not land. *It is absence.*

A sickness unfurls in my gut. A slow, crawling nausea. This place should not exist. It is a festering, burdensome wound, and yet— somewhere deep inside me, I know it. Not in memory. Not in understanding. But in my bones.

I feel Kael's eyes on me—penetrating, watchful, omnipresent, just like the Watcher's Eye above. He said there is more to this place —his home—but I can't see how that's possible.

The wind shifts.

And then, the Stars press closer.

From the eerie silence, a sound begins to rise.

The Watcher's Eye does not blink. Does not shift.

But it moves.

Not like the Stars, slow and inevitable, bound to the pull of time. This is different. Deliberate. Aware.

A vibration shudders beneath my feet, a low hum that isn't sound but something deeper—a feeling, a force. The air tightens, drawing inward as if the world is holding its breath.

Then, the stillness shatters.

The sky exhales.

A gust of wind tears from the heavens, cold as death, sharp as a blade, swirling into a tunnel of churning turquoise light. It comes for us—not with violence, but with purpose, rippling with something ancient, something alive.

Magic.

I stagger as the wind wraps around me, pressing against me like a second skin. The world beyond disappears—no sound, no movement, just Kael and me, suspended in the tunnel of light.

And then, the sighing begins.

Not words. Not music. Something else. Something that crawls into the spaces between thought, between breath.

It is not heard—it is felt.

It moves through my ribs, my spine, my skull, shifting and curling, as though a thousand voices speak over one another, tangled in an ancient, haunting chorus.

And then, the heavens speak.

The sighing twists, shifts, and makes itself known. The whispers do not speak, yet they fill me, surround me, weave through me like threads of silver light.

The words are not my own. They are not spoken.

They simply *are*.

> *"Before the fall, before the flame,*
> *The gods walked where mortals reign.*
> *Light unbroken, power untamed,*
> *Until the world is bound in chains."*

A pulse of magic rushes through my veins, burning like fire, like memory. I stagger, the truth curling around me, seeping into the marrow of my bones.

> *"The gods did not fade. They were taken.*
> *Torn from this realm by hands unclean.*
> *Bound, broken, cast aside.*
> *Not by time, nor fate, but greed."*

A flicker of something—a face, a hand raised in power, a shadow swallowing the sky.

King Thalmyr.

A sorceress cloaked in darkness.

A sudden weight crushes my chest.

It was him. He did this.

> *"A ruler's hunger, a sorceress's hand,*
> *Banished the gods, unmade the land.*
> *But power cannot be cast away,*
> *And light will rise on judgment's day."*

The wind tightens, curling around me, pressing against my ribs like a vice.

> *"The light sleeps in mortal skin,*
> *The gods' last breath lies deep within.*
> *A vessel forged, a fate unmade,*
> *A power caged—a debt unpaid."*

A vessel.

My breath locks in my throat.

I lurch back as if struck, but there is nowhere to run. The words tighten around me, latch on to something deeper than bone.

They left their power in *me.*

Not as a gift. Not as a blessing.

But as a final act of desperation.

I am the last fragment of what was stolen.

The Stars whisper their final truth.

> *"Rise, Lightborne, bearer of flame.*
> *The world is shifting, the Stars have named.*
> *The chains will fall, the past undone,*
> *And fate will bow before its sun."*

The wind shatters. The sighing vanishes.

The world slams back into place. My ears ring with the absence of sound, as though the gods' voices carved themselves into the marrow of my bones, leaving a hollow where they once were. The silence is too sharp, too sudden. I can still feel the echo of their whispers, still feel them clawing at the edges of my mind.

I turn to him, breathless, something burning in my chest that was not there before.

I am not just Starborn.

I have the magic of the gods in my veins.

For the first time, I understand—I am more than the prophecy. I am the one who can rewrite it.

CHAPTER FORTY-SIX
KAEL

THE WIND TIGHTENS AROUND ME, THE PRESSURE SINKING INTO MY chest like an invisible weight. The world outside the tunnel of turquoise light is gone—nothing but silence, nothing but this.

Elyssara stands beside me, breath shallow, eyes wide, lost in whatever truth the heavens are whispering to her. But I don't hear what she hears. I hear something else entirely.

A slow hum grows, deep and resonant, a vibration that isn't sound but feels like it's pulling me apart thread by thread. My body locks against it, every instinct urging me to resist, but it doesn't matter—the heavens have already decided.

The sighing shifts, curling through my mind, pressing into my chest like something alive, something searching.

And then, it speaks.

Not with words. Not with sound. But with haunting certainty.

"You were sent to destroy her."

A cold stillness settles into my spine. *No. It can't be right. The heavens are wrong. They have to be fucking wrong.* But the words press deeper, slicing like steel between my ribs.

"You are the balance. The blade at the throat of power unchecked.
If she's destroyed, the world is saved. If she isn't, all is lost."

I don't breathe. I don't move.

The air feels thinner, sharper, pressing into my skull until it might split open.

"She is not salvation, unless destroyed. She is ruin. And you are the one that must destroy her before the fire spreads."

My fists clench at my sides, nails digging into my palms, but the pressure in my chest won't ease. The weight of the words coils in my gut like a slow-turning dagger.

Elyssara is shifting beside me now—her face soft with wonder, or hope, or with relief perhaps. She doesn't look at me, doesn't see the way my breath comes sharp and uneven, like something inside me is fracturing.

She doesn't know what I've heard.

The wind around us begins to fracture, the tunnel of light flickering, fading. Reality is rushing back in, the Stars overhead returning to their watchful stillness, but the words remain.

Heavy. Unyielding. A command. A fate.

Destroy her.

The silence that follows is absolute. The mountain air bites against my skin, sharp and cold, but I barely feel it.

Elyssara exhales, steadying herself. And smiles. *She fucking smiles.* The sight of it almost cripples me.

I force my face into something unreadable. Something she won't question.

She doesn't know what I've been told.

And Stars help me, I don't know if I can do it.

And Stars help us all if I can't.

CHAPTER FORTY-SEVEN
ELYSSARA

THE SILENCE IN THE AIR LINGERS, AND SO DOES THE EYE CONTACT between Kael and me. His expression is stoic and unreadable, hardened over years of keeping a careful mask in place and solid walls around his heart. *But I know better.* I saw the way he fought the truth from the heavens. The way he flinched. And the way he slipped his mask and walls back in place before meeting my gaze.

He pauses, as if figuring out what to say. "So, you heard it then?" He asks in a voice that's far too even and calculated.

"The compass first," I say, clipped, in lieu of an answer. "And then I'm assuming you'll hear my truth, anyway."

Something in his eyes belies his calm exterior—a moment of panic, or realization dawns on him as I get the words out.

He gives me a brief, emotionless nod and sets off to locate the compass.

"Ah, Kael?" He spins around to face me once again, "I can feel it calling to me. Just like the blade." I don't wait for his response, before saying, "This way, come on."

Across the star-drenched stone where ancient memories float on the wind, I lead Kael to the jagged edge of the plateau. *It's here.* There, resting atop a raised slab of stone—like an altar abandoned by time—is the Astral Compass. It makes sense now, why the Vaythari and Velmara made themselves known as we approached; they guard Skaedor's Crest with their lives, leaving the compass untouched for the rightful heir. *For me.* And cutting down anyone who isn't.

We both slow our approach, as if we might spook it if we make any sudden movements.

"It's here," Kael whispers, awe lacing his words, as we come up to it, eyes beaming.

The Astral Compass is not merely an object—it is a remnant of something beyond time, beyond mortal understanding. It does not sit passively upon the slab; it feels placed with purpose, as if waiting for the right hands to claim it.

It is large enough to demand reverence—crafted from a metal that is neither gold nor silver, but something older, something celestial, shimmering with an iridescence that shifts with the light. The surface is etched with constellations, some familiar, others long forgotten, their lines carved so finely they seem to glow from within.

At its center, a floating core of shifting metallic liquid pulses with slow, rhythmic light—like the heartbeat of the heavens themselves.

Without further thought, I reach for it, hand outstretched. I wrap my hands gently around the outside of it, and hiss—the pain sears through my palm like molten fire, and I jerk back with a sharp gasp. My breath stutters, the raw sting latching on to my nerves like claws. I pull my hand back and see scorch marks on my palm—the same kind Kael had on his after touching the Starforged Blade. "Fuck," I grit out, blowing on it to ease the sting.

Kael reaches for my hand, tenderly stroking around the burn. "You can heal this, you know."

"How the fuck can I do that?" I bite.

"You were born under The Eye of Lireal constellation. You are imbued with the magic of shielding, destruction," he pauses then, blowing on the burn for me, "and healing, Duskae."

"Well, I don't know how to do that, obviously," sarcasm turning my words into something bitter.

He chuckles, and I'm not sure that I've heard anything as sweet.

"I'll teach you. Close your eyes," he prompts with a gentility that comforts me. "Find that place inside you where your magic resides," he gives me a moment. "Got it?" I nod, "Now, imagine a small thread of your magic—Lightborne magic—unweaves from the center, and makes its way down your arm." He traces a faint line down my arm towards the burn, and my skin turns into gooseflesh under his touch. I hear his breathing shift, barely, but it's there. "Now, you want to slowly, patiently, pull your magic to the surface of your skin. Not like when you push magic outward towards something—or someone," he says with levity in his tone, "but delicately. As if you want the magic to just kiss your skin."

It takes great effort and concentration to not let the magic shoot out from my hands, and for the first time since we left the inn in Galreth, I feel warm.

"Good," he encourages, and I'm embarrassed by how much his approval turns my insides molten. "Now that it's on the surface, let it ripple across the palm of your hand where the burn is." I do as he bids and drag my Lightborne magic bit by bit across my palm.

"Open your eyes, Elyssara," he says, approving.

I glance down to see a faint shimmer of my magic still lingering on my palm, and underneath it, healed, fresh skin.

Awed, I shake my head in disbelief. "It's— It's gone!"

A genuine smile of warmth spread across his face, "You healed yourself."

"Holy fucking Stars!" A laugh bursts out of me, and for a moment, I forget what's at stake as we stand here.

He watches me, eyes lingering for a moment too long.

I snap myself back to the task at hand, "Okay, so obviously the compass doesn't want me to touch it. The Velmara let *you* pass, maybe the compass wants you—maybe it knows our deal for you to use the compass, anyway."

"I don't think so, El. I think it wants your truth first," his expression now back to cool indifference.

"What do I do? Just... speak to it?" *This feels fucking ridiculous.*

"I guess we'll find out. Go on, then. Make your royal decree," he says with mock regality.

I shoot him a withering stare, but turn back to the compass, exhaling the weight of this moment.

The truth rests in my throat like a stone. The moment I speak it aloud, there is no turning back. But the compass will accept nothing less. So I exhale and let the words carve my fate into the Stars.

"I... would like to offer you a truth in exchange for use of the compass... please," I tack on. "I have magic of the gods in my blood," Kael startles, his eyes boring into me, and the compass itself begins to faintly glow, as if I've awakened it. "I am to find a way to bring the gods back to the realms after being sent away, somehow, by King Thalmyr," the glow illuminates further. "I am to change the fate of the realms—restore the gods, reunite the Vaythari, and bring Aevryn back to peace."

I think that's what I'm meant to do, anyway.

I hear a gentle click, as if the compass itself is unbound from its own restraints. I don't make the same mistake twice, so this time, I place the pad of one finger on the side of the compass to test it.

"Fuck! Again!" I hiss, as the compass brands me with its heat yet again. "Can you offer the Starsdamned thing a truth? I think it has enough of mine."

Kael nods tightly, as if he was expecting this, and steps forward. He hesitates for a moment, holding his breath. He looks unsettled. "My truth is that I will keep Elyssara safe and protected, no matter who tries to stop me, or how many people get in my way. My blade is her blade," he directs his words at the compass, but his eyes never stray from mine, as if he is making an oath.

For a long moment, nothing happens. The air between us holds still, heavy with expectation. And then—click. Click. Click. A sound so soft, yet final.

I know I can't trust him. I know he will always keep secrets. But the compass recognizing his words as a truth worthy of unlocking it, does something to me. It makes me want to reach for him, to bury my face in his neck, to let him wrap his arms around me. But I slip on my own mask, and go for indifference instead.

I reach for the compass again and the metal is cool in my palm, soothing the burn on my index finger.

"We have it," I breathe, wonder coating my words.

"We did it—" but before he can continue, my magic surges, searing through me like lightning through a storm cloud. Shimmering white-gold light sprays from my fingers, reaching to the Stars themselves, as if it recognizes its kin. My Lightborne marking illuminates with phosphorescence, etching another portion of the marking permanently into my skin. As if an unseen hand is branding me, the lines of my skin marking continue in from the edges. Stars etched with permanency, the mark encroaching on the center of my chest, beginning to form The Eye of Lireal. The constellation of the Lightborne.

My magic explodes out of my hands once again, coursing through me with such ferocity that I can do nothing but let myself burn. My skin is on fire, or at least, it feels like it. It surges, seeking, devouring, searching for something to burn. It twists through my veins like a storm with no anchor—until I feel it. A ripple of something cool, something steady, curling up my spine like a tether to the world. Not a command, not a restraint, but a question. Asking if I will let it in.

I acquiesce, allowing the coolness to balance my heat, and free fall into the whim of whatever is taking over me.

It feels like cool silk rippling up my body—rapturous. I tip my head back and lift my face to the Stars, reveling in the crisp ripples. For a moment I think it is the winds of Skaedor's Crest, but I can feel *him*. This sensation of soothing, comforting, unwavering presence is Kael. I bring my eyes back down, and see him through the chaos, shadowed mist seeping out, controlled, from his hands. He pins me in place, and I see him direct his shadows around my magic, as if our magic is dancing, tangled in each other, playing. He is not trying to drown me out, or suppress my magic, he is... *complimenting it*. Shaping it from wildfire into a weapon of both destruction and healing.

I can't hear him over the roar of our magic moving together, but I make out the words he mouths to me, "Breathe, Duskae." I breathe a deep inhale and let it fall gently from my mouth. "Find one thing to focus on."

Stars save me, but he's the only thing I want to focus on.

I stare at him, then. His ocean eyes, his unruly hair that falls into his eyes when he's concentrating, his sharp jaw, his sun-warmed skin, the mouth that speaks words that threaten to be both my ruin and salvation.

Kael makes his way towards me, "I love seeing you become more unbound. More powerful. You're beautiful when you let go."

I look around to the calm, peaceful plateau—no trace of the turquoise channel, no trace of our magic. Just us. I almost don't say anything, wanting to hold on to my anger over his secrets and omissions, but there is something about this man that draws me in, makes me want to give him everything.

"You're beautiful, too."

It's the first real compliment I've given him, and somehow, it doesn't even begin to convey how I feel.

CHAPTER FORTY-EIGHT
KAEL

THE VELMARA RISE THE MOMENT THEY SEE US. THEIR EARS TWITCH, bodies poised, waiting—suspicious. For a breath, they don't move. Then, as we step through the gap in the rocky outcropping, they relax. We're in one piece.

"Well?" Ronyn asks eagerly, Therion and Seren flanking him with urgent expressions. "What in the Stars happened up there?"

"You couldn't see?" Elyssara asked, intrigued.

"We couldn't hear or see anything other than complete silence," Seren's voice is stern, as if concern has woven its way through her very being.

"We got the compass," I answer simply, pointing to the iridescent compass hanging weightily from Elyssara's neck.

"Fucking obviously, Kael. I mean *what else* happened?" Ronyn scoffs and waves a hand in my direction, immediately fixing his eyes on Elyssara and staring at her impatiently. I can't help but fight a smile at his obvious comfort around me now, seeing as he shot an arrow at my head only ten days ago.

"The heavens spoke, and we... definitely heard some interesting *truths*," Elyssara says the last word as if those truths are still in question. As if they're not absolute in the eyes of the compass.

"For fuck's sake, you two, just spit it out," Therion's tone is impatient and clipped. *Typical.*

"I have magic of the gods in my veins. Apparently they left it within me as a last attempt to keep their magic here in the realms, because King Thalmyr and a sorceress have somehow... banished them? I think," her words are a little uncertain.

"Ahhhh... okay? So you're basically a god then. Do we bow?" Ronyn quips.

Elyssara shoves him in the chest with a giggle and I fucking relish the sound, "Oh my Stars! No, you idiot," she chides. "I'm a *vessel* for their magic... or at least, that's how the voice described it."

"And you?" Ronyn's eyes land on me. "Are you a god or a king or something too?"

"My truth," I say, too smoothly, too easily, "is that I must protect Elyssara at all costs."

A traitorous fucking lie.

Stars help me, but I won't destroy her. I *can't. I won't.*

And the worst part? I don't know if I just defied fate, picked a fight with it, or doomed us all. Therion barely keeps his rage on a leash, his hands balling into fists that turn his knuckles white, clearly livid at how this will affect our plans. This has been his greatest fear all along—that I'll fall for her and it'll change everything.

He's fucking right. Looks like I'll be having that conversation later.

"Not quite as fun, but I guess it works," Ronyn says flippantly.

Seren exhales in relief. "Okay, that's a lot to take in. All of it." She inhales, expression terse, "We should go—the Vaythari will be waiting."

We all mount our horses, Nyx seems to have relaxed slightly around the Velmara now, and we settle into a rhythm at the back of the group, the Velmara now leading Therion at the front.

We ride in relative silence for a few hours, the weight of everything settling into our bones—Elyssara's role with the Vaythari, the reunion with their kin, the god magic in her veins, her role in their fate. Elyssara hasn't spoken, and I respect her need to process it all.

The first sign of the Vaythari camp is not the firelight—but the music.

A deep, steady drumming pulses through the night, low and insistent, like the earth itself is speaking. The air hums with it, a resonance I can feel beneath my ribs, in my blood. It's not the formal cadence of a military march, nor the orderly rhythm of temple bells. This is raw, untamed, older than discipline, older than kingdoms. *Primal.*

Then comes the whistle of skyflutes, threading through the percussion in sharp, breathy notes—haunting, dissonant, beautiful. They weave through the air like wind over ruins, like voices calling from the past.

The scent reaches us next. Charred meat. Spiced smoke. Something sharp and herbal, almost metallic. Not just from the fire—from the land, from the people themselves.

A plume of silver-gray smoke curls skyward in the near distance, rising in soft, spiraling tendrils against the blackened sky. And beneath it, flickering in the dark like embers scattered by the wind, golden glows of torchlight pulse and sway.

The Velmara see it first. Their ears flick, their bodies tensing for half a heartbeat—then, just as suddenly, they run.

They know this place. They know their kin.

I feel Elyssara straighten slightly in the saddle, a subtle shift, but enough to tell me she's alert. Her breath is steady, but I don't miss the faint hitch in it.

Anticipation. Wariness. The weight of expectation on her shoulders.

"Are you alright?" I ask, my voice low enough that it doesn't carry.

"Yes." A pause. "And no. It's just..." She exhales, then nods once, more to herself than to me. "Yes. I'm alright."

She's not. Not fully.

I smile to myself, but I don't let her see it.

"I can feel your stupid face and your smug smirk behind me, Kael. Even if I can't see it."

My smile deepens. "My blade is your blade, your majesty," I say it with sarcasm, but the truth in it bleeds through, regardless. Then, quieter—meant only for her—I add, "I won't leave your side. If you want to leave, say the word and we're gone."

She doesn't answer. She just breathes, and we fall into silence, the only sound is the distant music of the Vaythari, our breath and the horses treading through the snow.

The camp emerges from the dark, sprawled in the natural basin between ancient, jagged stones, as if the land itself carved out a space for them.

The fire at the center roars with life, fed by something unnatural, burning higher than any ordinary kindling should allow. It casts shifting shadows against the rock, distorting figures as they move, dancing wildly, their bodies twisting in a fevered rhythm.

The Vaythari move like both predators and spirits. Some are bare-chested, their skin streaked with ash and shimmering gold dust, muscles flexing as they beat at the ashdrums. Others move with sharp grace, wielding knives mid-dance, the steel flashing with each flicker of firelight.

And then, there is the sound.

It is laughter and song, sharp bursts of it woven between the music—not careful, not restrained, but full, open, alive, completely uninhibited. It doesn't belong to the halls of kings or the courts of lords. It does not ask permission to exist.

It simply *is*.

And for the first time in a long, long while, I see something in these warriors that we've forgotten—freedom, belonging.

Not just caution, or strategy, or winning, or dominion. But a true sense of belonging to something bigger than war and battle and kings and queens. *Kin*.

The firelight flickers against the rough stone and animal pelts, the night air even thicker now with the scent of spiced meat, the faint metallic tang of strong spirits, and something richer—a heady anticipation, a current humming beneath the revelry.

The Vaythari are celebrating *her*. Their *Zhari*.

The drumming grows louder as we dismount, the air vibrating with the thrum of anticipation for what this means. What *she* means.

They break into cheers when they see us, voices rising in a

primal, exultant cry. They do not bow to her. No, bowing is for kings, for rulers of blood and conquest. This is different. This is acknowledgment. This is acceptance.

Syphra emerges from the crowd, moving with a warrior's grace, her dark eyes gleaming like polished onyx. She doesn't speak at first—she simply gestures for Elyssara to follow.

Elyssara hesitates, a flicker of uncertainty crossing her face as she glances toward me.

I tilt my chin slightly—not a command, not reassurance, just encouragement to trust her instincts. If I've learned anything, it's that she needs to make her own choices.

She follows.

The Vaythari part as she moves through them, some raising curved hunting knives in silent tribute, others slapping their chests in a rhythmic pattern. They do not question her right to be here. *They already know.*

We pass the smoking carcasses of freshly hunted beasts, the air thick with the scent of them. The Vaythari feast like warriors—they hunt their land, they cook over open flame, they eat with their hands. This is no pristine courtly gathering. This is raw, alive, untamed.

At the center of it all, carved into the natural rock, rests the throne. Or at least, their version of one.

Made of polished stone and layered with thick furs, it is not ostentatious, but ancient. A place where warriors sit, where battle-leaders command.

Syphra gestures to it. A silent invitation.

Elyssara looks back at me again, her fingers flexing at her sides, almost as if readying herself to fight.

I arch a brow, amusement curling in my chest. She may be Star-born with magic of the gods, but she's still an on-edge street girl at heart.

I give her the smallest nod. *Sit, Duskae.*

She does, and I take up the position on her right, and Therion, Ronyn and Seren form a line next to me.

Immediately, a drink is pressed into her hands—a dark, glimmering liquid swirling with silver flecks. It catches the firelight, almost as if the Stars themselves have been dissolved into the drink.

She eyes it warily. Syphra makes a symbol with her hands and directs it towards Seren.

"It's Silverwake," Seren murmurs hesitantly. "It's a celebratory drink. Said to be made of the dust Stars leave in their wake."

Her brows lift. "Well, that's poetic."

Syphra's face contorts into something sly, and she makes another symbol to Seren, her slender finger flicking emphatically between Elyssara and me.

"It's also an aphrodisiac," Seren says, amusement coating her tongue, and she winks at Elyssara. *Seren is definitely growing on me, and by the glint in Therion's eye, she's growing on him, too.*

Ronyn slaps his thigh and barks a riotous laugh. "I fuckin' love what this journey has done to you, Little Star."

Elyssara chokes, coughing on the first sip, her eyes watering as the liquid burns its way down her throat.

I smirk. Stars, she's beautiful when she's flustered.

The fire crackles and rises against the mountain, enveloping the space in warmth that belies the icy wind.

The drumming shifts into something slower, deeper. The Vaythari begin to dance—bare feet kicking up dust, bodies twisting in fluid, hypnotic movements, losing themselves to the celebration. Their skin glistens in the glow of the fire, sweat forming droplets on their brows as they let the beat of the drum command them.

Two women approach Elyssara, their hands streaked in shimmering golden ink. They gesture to Elyssara to stand and remove her leather vest.

"What—What do you mean? Take off my clothing?" She exclaims, voice laced with horror, though she still stands.

She looks over at Seren for solidarity on the matter, but she's also been approached by other women, and she's already undoing the laces on her leather bodice, and losing the ties on her billowing sleeves.

"You can't be serious, Seren!" Elyssara exclaims in shock.

"What?" Seren says indignantly, though her smile is all mischief.

"We're here to celebrate, El. I want to dance for once in my Stars-forsaken life!"

"Oh fucking Stars," Elyssara mutters, and submits to the women in front of her. They grab at her arms, unbuckling her bracers, and immediately move to her vest. I know I shouldn't look but Stars help me, I can't look away. That one taste of her wasn't enough.

My hands twitch at my sides, half a breath away from reaching for her, from stopping them from touching my—

I have no right.

Not after everything I've put her through.

But Stars help me, I want to tear them away from her. I want to be the only one who sees her like this.

I steel myself, knowing that what she does with her body is not my decision, but my hands curl into fists at my side, nonetheless.

The women begin untying the laces on the front of her tunic. She pulls it over her head, flustered and flushed, and presses it on top of the pile one of the Vaythari women is holding for her.

In front of me, stripped bare, save for the undergarment covering her breasts, and the luminous auburn hair framing her face and falling over her shoulders.

Holy fucking Stars. She's stunning. Regal, like a deity. She has no idea of her own beauty, and that only adds to it.

I drink her in, unwilling to give up the moment I have to take her in like this. Her eyes don't move from mine, locked in a silent conversation that says a thousand words, and nothing at all. I can't help but roam her body, tracing every dip and curve with my eyes, locking it away in my mind.

Without a word, the Vaythari dip their fingers into the mixture and begin making swirls, symbols and shapes on her slightly sun-kissed skin from years on rooftops in the Virellin slums.

The symbols glow faintly before sinking into her flesh.

"Runes, El!" Seren's excited voice cutting through the weight of the moment. "They mean prosperity, love, and protection," Seren calls over the heads of the women painting her body, too. "Aren't they beautiful?" She giggles with an innocence that I know Elyssara has protected with her life.

The runes shimmer golden against her skin, catching the fire-light in flickers of movement. It makes her look almost otherworldly —like something out of legend. Something untouchable.

And yet, my hands itch to touch anyway.

Elyssara watches in awe as the women mark her body with precise and intentional shapes from the waist up, moving gently around her Lightborne marking, over the soft skin of her stomach, around the swells of her breasts. A smile tugs at her lips, and despite herself and her obvious uncertainty, she is enjoying this.

This is their rite of passage. Their way of marking her as one of their own.

Then, Syphra approaches, and the Vaythari fall silent.

The silence is more deafening than the music had been. The weight of it presses into my ribs, thick with meaning.

Then—

"Zhari!"

The ground trembles beneath the weight of a hundred stomping feet.

With command and certainty, Syphra's booming voice projects across her people. Though the language is unknown to us, there is no mistaking the power and conviction in her statements, nor the weight of the moment.

Seren's hushed voice reaches Elyssara and me, "They are proclaiming you as Skaedor's rightful heir, and the savior of their people." Elyssara nods in agreement, as if for the first time, she is accepting that this is... *right*. That she accepts the role and the duty that comes with it.

Syphra's voice booms again, her people respond with primal cries and cheers, feet, staphs and drums reverberating and mingling in agreement.

"They bow to you, serve you, honor you as the leader of the Vaythari," Seren translates.

The Vaythari ball their fists into a ball then, and hold it across their chests, beating it three times, and no matter what language you speak or where you come from, this is a sign of a warrior's allegiance.

Syphra is the only one to move then, moving closer to Elyssara, before reaching to a golden chained belt around her own waist, that, until now, has been obscured by the heavy furs she wears.

The belt is intricate, ancient, its center adorned with a single black opal that seems to devour the firelight, and a single rune carved into its center.

"Sovereign," Seren breathes, awe-inspired again. "It is a warrior's belt that denotes the ruler of the tribe."

Syphra unclasps the belt and holds it out to Elyssara.

She looks momentarily stunned. Not uncertain, just... still.

Like she is feeling the weight of this moment press into her bones. *Into her blood.*

She exhales, slow and steady, like she's letting go of the girl she was.

Then, she straightens, like she's stepping into the woman she's becoming.

As if deciding she *is* a ruler, a leader, *a queen.* Her bare shoulders gleam in the firelight, the golden ink shimmering across her collarbones and down her arms.

She takes the belt and secures it around her waist, the opal sitting in the center. She lifts her eyes to the tribe of Vaythari staring back at her, and with more conviction than I've ever heard from her, she casts her voice far and strong, forging it with power, meaning and acceptance of her role.

"Zhari!" She bellows, emotion cracking through her voice.

They erupt in acknowledgement, chants and screams and hollers of joyous acceptance written through the camp, and the ashdrum and skyflutes pick back up with vigor.

She is one of them now.

A Queen.

And I can't stop staring.

She is stunning, standing beneath the Stars, wild and untamed in a way that makes something tighten low in my gut. Her hair whipping in the night air, bare skin with the glint of golden paint and belt adorning it, dirt marring her face from the journey here— she is a vision.

Ronyn lets out a low whistle. "Well, your majesty. May I have this dance?" bowing low with mock formality and gesturing towards the uninhibited Vaythari dancing around the fire.

Elyssara laughs, throws her arms around his neck, "Oh shut it, Ronyn. Let's fucking dance!" Ronyn's movements are exaggerated and ridiculous, making Elyssara shriek with laughter that makes me tip my head back for the beauty of the sound. *Gods, I'm so fucked.*

Therion is still as stone at first, watching, but Seren grabs his wrist and tugs him into the circle and pulls him into a spinning dance, ignoring his grumbling. He lets her, and just like that, the tension breaks into joy.

And then there's me. Watching these people who were meant to be an alliance that I could bend to my own will. To be manipulated for the gain of my own people. To be used in the war again King Maldrak and the curse on The Shadow Wastes. But the further we go into this, the more I realize they have become something more, and I find myself in a war of my own—my people or my conscience. My sister, or whatever this is between Elyssara and me.

Elyssara turns, smiling, her face flushed from the heat of the fire and the Silverwake. She approaches me, cheeks flushed, chest rising and falling with the effort from dancing and laughing with her friends, and I can't bring myself to do anything to interrupt her feeling this way.

"You look like the entire realms are on your shoulders, Kael," she says between breaths.

I huff a laugh, "Sometimes it feels like it." *Sometimes, it is.* I exhale, "But tonight, we celebrate—regardless of everything."

"That sounds like an expert way to evade a real conversation, but I suppose you're pretty good at that by now," she quips. Then, she holds out a hand. "If you're not going to give me your honesty and trust, Kael, the least you can do is give me a dance."

I arch a brow. "No."

She huffs. "Come on, Kael. Give me a night to forget."

I take a slow sip from the Silverwake flask, watching her wait with obvious anticipation. *At least I'm not the only one riddled with desire and tension.*

I let the silence stretch between us, let her anticipation simmer.

Then, slow and deliberate, I lean in just enough to make her breath hitch.

"If you had a night with me, Duskae, you wouldn't forget."

Her breath catches, her pupils blown wide. She bites her lip.

And then, the challenge flickers in her eyes. Dangerous. Reckless. Tempting.

She steps closer.

"Well then, Kael," she murmurs, tilting her chin just slightly. "Give me a night to remember."

Then, without waiting for a response, she turns—walking straight into the firelight, leaving me standing in the dark.

CHAPTER FORTY-NINE

ELYSSARA

I feel his gaze like a brand on my skin.

I roll my hips under the Stars, the golden belt cinching my waist, drawing his eyes exactly where I want them.

I don't know if it's the runes on my skin or the Silverwake in my veins, but I move like a woman possessed. The ashdrum thrums in my bones, a pulse that is no longer separate from my own. I twist under Ronyn's arms, spin with Seren, and even manage to sway with Therion, but the entire time, I feel him watching.

Kael is a presence—solid, unyielding, inevitable.

The weight of his stare settles between my shoulder blades, heavy, intoxicating. I close my eyes, lifting my arms over my head to drag them through the thick night sky, feeling the moment slip between my fingers like silk.

I feel him approaching a breath before his hands snake around my stomach, and move lower over the curve of my hip. Not tentative. Not questioning. Possessive. Claiming. As if he's lost a battle with his restraint.

His hard chest pushes against my back, enveloping and intoxicating, the scent of oakmoss and leather wrapping around me like a snare. He lowers his mouth to my ear. His voice is all smoke and sin.

"Let me give you that night to remember, Elyssara."

My breath hitches.

There's no more pretending.

His mouth brushes against the long column of my neck, hovering just close enough that I feel the heat of his breath but not the press of his lips. Teasing. Holding me in place with nothing but anticipation. A heavy, torturously seductive sensation pools low in my belly. A sensation I am utterly helpless against.

I've lived my life without pleasures, without the power to choose what I desire. But this?

This, I want.

I swallow thickly. "Dance with me first, and then... I'm yours."

Kael's growl is pure satisfaction. His arm tightens around my waist, pressing me against the length of him. "You've always been mine, Elyssara—even before you knew it." He pauses, his breath hot against my temple. "You always will be."

Oh, Stars.

I turn toward him, pressing my hands to the solid expanse of the leathers pulled taught across his broad chest. His pulse is steady, but his breathing is not. My fingers drift over the tops of his broad shoulders, trailing down his arms, committing every inch of him to memory.

He grips my chin gently, tilting it up so I'm looking into his eyes.

Without breaking my gaze, Kael's voice comes out like a low, reverent rumble. "I want you."

The world tilts.

The bindings around my heart unravel. The weight of the past, of restraint, of denial—it all ceases to exist.

Because Stars save me, but I want him too.

I give in.

"I want you, too."

Kael moves then. Not with hesitation. Not with uncertainty. He spins me—a controlled, effortless motion, like a warrior handling a blade he knows too well. He moves me across the dirt, guiding, leading, commanding, as if we are in a grand ballroom, skirts billowing.

We glide around the fire, the world dimming into nothingness around us. There is only him and me. Only the way our bodies move as one, the way our hearts beat in time to the same unrelenting drum.

The music begins to slow.

And so does he.

His hands skim down my spine, the touch light, reverent.

My arms wrap around his neck, my forehead pressing to his chest. His scent, his warmth, the solid weight of him—it drowns out everything.

We stay like this for a while, rocking gently to the drums and skyflutes that make this night feel outside of time, outside of fate itself.

My arms tighten around his neck, my forehead pressing against his chest. He is solid. Unshaken. A steady anchor while the rest of the world spins.

We sway in time with the final beats of the drums, the skyflutes weaving haunting, lingering notes through the air. My breath slows. His does too.

Neither of us speaks. Neither of us moves.

The fire crackles behind us. The sounds of the Vaythari—distant laughter, the rhythmic stomp of feet, the clatter of drinking horns—all of it fades into a soft hum at the edges of my awareness.

But Kael is still here. Still holding me.

Still waiting.

For me to make the choice.

I exhale, a slow, shaky breath.

His hand slides up my back, fingers tangling into my hair, tipping my head back just enough to meet his eyes.

"Come," he murmurs. Not a command. Not a request. An inevitability.

And gods, I go.

He doesn't let go of my hand as he leads me away from the fire. Doesn't pull. Doesn't rush. Just walks—slow, steady, deliberate.

I follow.

The night air wraps around us, cool against my skin where the warmth of the fire still lingers. The distant rhythm of the revelry fades with each step, replaced by something heavier. More intimate.

I don't have to look to know that Ronyn is smirking, that Seren is biting back a grin.

That Therion looks like he's swallowing knives.

Kael doesn't acknowledge them. Doesn't break stride.

Neither do I.

I barely notice the gold symbols shimmering along the worn path, leading us forward—until we're standing before it.

The tent.

Ours.

And this time, I don't hesitate.

The tent rises before us, standing taller and more regal than the others, its heavy fabric shimmering in the firelight like woven stardust.

Thick, dark hides stitched with golden thread stretch across the wooden beams, reinforced with carved bone. The entrance flap is embroidered with the same symbol that gleams on my belt—a mark of belonging, of sovereignty, of something more.

Low-burning lanterns dangle from the outer posts, casting flickering patterns across the fabric, their glow dancing like captured fireflies. The air is thick with sandalwood and spice, curling tendrils of incense weaving through the space like a quiet invocation, a silent acknowledgment of the night's purpose.

Inside, the air is warmer, quieter, the pulse of the music outside muffled to a steady, rhythmic hum. The walls are draped with heavy tapestries, embroidered in ancient patterns—stories of warriors, gods, and Stars stitched in silver and gold thread. Furs and thick woven blankets line the floor, soft and decadent, a stark contrast to the raw, primal energy of the Vaythari revelry beyond the canvas.

At the center, a low wooden table holds a decanter of Silverwake, two ornate drinking vessels carved from onyx, and a delicate plate of honeyed figs and spiced nuts—a quiet offering, a final indulgence before the night unfolds.

The bed is no mere cot, but a nest of thick pelts and layered silks, the kind meant for a queen—or for ruin.

I swallow hard. My fingers tighten around Kael's.

He says nothing, but I feel the shift in his stance, the way his breath deepens just slightly.

He feels it too.

The weight of this. The inevitability. The choice.

And this time, for the first time in my life—I choose.

I choose *him*.

I release his fingers then, and begin loosening the laces on my leather pants, boots long since forgotten around the fire.

"Stop," he commands. "Let me do that. Lie down."

I do as he bids, liquefying under his instruction.

My body melts into the silks, smooth and decadent against my skin. Kael's hands smooth back my hair, brush down my cheek— deliberate, reverent.

"A fucking goddess." The words are thick, dark, and worshipful. Before I can respond, his mouth claims mine, a slow, languid stroking of his tongue against mine, taking his time with me. I don't know whether I relish it or want to combust.

He shifts lower, removing the lacy straps of my undergarments, exposing my breasts to the cool air. A shiver cascades down my spine—but then his mouth is there, warm and wet, sucking, biting, claiming.

A small moan escapes me, and his grip on my thigh tightens.

"I dream of that sound every night, Elyssara." His voice is breathy, rough with hunger.

His tongue circles my nipple, his mouth devouring me like a man who's suffered too long without this.

"It's enough to bring any man to his knees."

Another moan rips from my throat, my back arching, and something in his restraint snaps.

He pauses, breathing heavy. The room thickens with something unspoken.

"I don't want any man," I pant. "I want *you*."

His entire body stills.

And then, his voice drops to something lethal, something edged in pure, brutal possession. "Well, allow me to get on my knees, then."

Holy fucking Stars.

He makes quick work of my laces, dragging my leathers down, taking my undergarments with them, peeling them from my body like he's unwrapping something forbidden. Something he intends to keep.

Kael kneels before me, grips my thighs, and spreads them open—wide enough that my breath catches.

His tongue drags along his bottom lip, eyes darkening as he takes me in.

"The sight of your legs spread for me and the taste of your wet pussy is what I think of every time I touch my cock."

I let out a desperate, ragged moan, but he only smirks.

"What do you think of when you're fucking your hand, Elyssara?"

My stomach clenches, pleasure tightening inside me. My head swims, my pulse thundering.

I should be embarrassed. But I'm not.

"You," I whisper, voice breaking. "It's always you."

Kael growls. "Good girl. I'm the only one you think of, understand?"

And then, his mouth is on me.

He licks into me like he's starving, like he needs this, needs *me*.

My fingers twist into his hair as I cry out, arching into his mouth, chasing his tongue.

"Don't forget that, Elyssara. Who do you think of?"

He slides a finger into me, slow, deliberate.

"Who do you belong to?"

"You," I whimper. "I'm yours."

He groans, slipping another finger inside, curling them just so, pressing against that spot that sends pleasure crackling through me like a spark.

"Do you like the sight of me bowing before you, Duskae?" His voice is a dark, hushed promise. "Does the sight of me on my knees for you make your pussy wet?"

I let out a whimper, but that's not enough.

He stops. Pauses.

"Use your words, or I stop," he threatens.

I gasp, my body desperate for him, for more.

"Yes," I pant. "Yes. I am wet for you."

His fingers thrust deep.

"That's my girl," he croons seductively.

Kael flips me onto my stomach in one fluid motion, his hands firm on my hips, his breath hot against the back of my neck.

"Hands and knees, Elyssara," he commands.

I obey without thought, arching my back, offering myself to him. A slow, satisfied hum rumbles from his chest.

"Fucking perfect," he purrs.

His fingers slide into me again, two this time, pressing deep, working me open with unhurried precision. He's watching me, I can feel it, and the thought of his gaze locked on my pussy makes me wetter.

"You're soaking for me," he murmurs, dragging his tongue up my spine, teeth grazing the sensitive spot at my nape.

"You want my cock, don't you?" His fingers curl inside me, hitting that devastating spot again, and I gasp, nodding frantically.

He stills.

"Use your words, Duskae," he demands.

I whimper, rolling my hips against his hand, desperate for more friction, more of him.

"I want your cock, Kael. I need it. Please—"

He lets out a low, vicious groan. "Beg me again."

He withdraws his fingers, leaving me empty, aching.

"Kael," I gasp, turning my head to look at him over my shoulder. "I need you. *Now.*"

His restraint snaps. Quickly removing his pants, and leaving his vest in place, urgent, hungry for me.

Kael stands before me, his cock hard, dripping with moisture already, broad shoulders rising and falling with measured breaths.

I swallow thickly at the enormous sight of him. I rise onto my knees, my hands move to his leathers, fingers skimming the edges of his vest, ready to strip him bare. But before I can pull the ties loose, he catches my wrists, stilling me.

There's a shadow in his eyes when he catches my wrists. A ripple of something unspoken, something caged. But he buries it, and I let him.

His breath is heavy. Controlled. Too controlled.

"Not now," he murmurs, his grip firm but gentle.

I blink up at him, my lips parting—but there's something in his stance, something fleeting in his eyes. A hesitation. A line he won't let me cross.

His thumb brushes over my pulse. A silent plea. *A distraction.*

"I want to focus on *you*." His voice is pure certainty, but something in my chest tightens.

My stomach clenches, but I let it go. Because right now, I don't care.

"Then do it," I say with conviction.

Kael growls low in his throat—and then he's kissing me deep enough to wipe out every last thought. He pulls back for a moment, drinking me in, and for the life of me, I can't help but do the same.

I should be moving. I should be reaching for him, pulling him down to me.

But *I can't.*

My gaze drags over the deep cut of muscle along his hips, the trail of dark hair leading lower. *Stars help me.* Every part of him is carved from war, from battle, from years of training.

And every part of him is *mine.*

Heat coils low in my stomach. My mouth goes dry. My pulse thrums in my ears, a traitorous, unrelenting drumbeat.

He watches me watching him. A smirk edges the corner of his mouth, dark and knowing.

"You like what you see, Duskae?" His voice is hoarse, like he's barely holding himself together.

I wet my lips. "Yes."

His restraint shatters. He's on me in a breath.

A strangled sound slips from my lips, more breath than voice, before I gasp, "Oh gods—"

He stills.

For a single, aching heartbeat, I feel the shift in the air between us—the sudden stillness, the sharp edge of possession that darkens his gaze before his hand slides to my throat.

Not rough. Not cruel. Just enough. Enough to make my pulse hammer beneath his grip. Enough to make my breath catch as he leans in, his lips grazing my ear.

"There are no gods here, darling." His voice is a growl, low and dark, filled with something I feel more than hear. His thumb brushes over my racing pulse, his grip tightening just enough to hold me exactly where he wants me. "If you say anyone's name, it's mine," he commands.

A shiver runs through me—not fear, never fear, only need. It curls deep, hot and relentless, unfurling through me as his words settle like a brand against my skin.

He spins me, lowering me to my hands and knees again, as he drops to his own behind me, nudging my knees out wider for better access. He grips my hips so hard I'll have bruises tomorrow—bruises I want him to leave.

I feel the full, thick warmth of him against my pussy, and then he thrusts deep, burying himself inside me in one possessive, primal stroke.

A sharp, shattered gasp rips from my throat.

Stars fucking save me.

He fills me so completely, so perfectly, it's devastating. I breathe deeply, acclimating to the stretch his cock demands. He gives me a moment to adjust, but I don't need it. I push back into him, grinding against his cock, desperate for the friction and the full length of him.

"Look at you," he grits out, his voice raw. "You take me so well, darling." He pulls out almost entirely, then thrusts back in, deeper this time, making me feel every inch. "So tight. So fucking perfect. You're made for me, Elyssara."

Kael fucks me like he's claiming me. Like this is the only way he'll let himself have me.

His fingers dig into my waist, his thrusts deep, slow, dragging pleasure from me with every snap of his hips.

"Say it," he demands, his voice breaking. "Say you're mine."

My moan is wordless, breathless, but that's not enough for him.

He fists my hair, yanking my head back just enough to arch my spine even further.

"Say it, Elyssara."

"I'm yours, Kael," I pant.

He growls, thrusting harder, like my words unhinged something in him.

I can barely breathe, barely think, caught between the primal, ruthless possession in his movements and the way my body yields to him completely.

The sound of him—his groans, the filthy and intoxicating words coming from his mouth—is almost too much.

His grip tightens. "You feel that? You take me so fucking well, my perfect girl."

His arms brackets my sides, one hand reaching around, fingers find my clit, circling, stroking—shocking pleasure through me, white-hot and all-consuming.

The pleasure builds—a slow, relentless tightening, a climb with no end, no escape. My muscles coil, my body bowing, stretching between overwhelming fullness and the ruthless precision of his touch.

"That's it," his voice is wrecked. "Come for me, Elyssara."

And *I shatter.*

Ecstasy ripples through me, ripping me apart, rebuilding me at the same time. My vision bursts white-hot behind my eyelids, pleasure crashing in waves so deep, so *endless,* I can't tell where I begin or end.

I wail his name, my hands clawing at the furs, at anything to anchor me against the sheer force of my climax.

But Kael isn't done.

He doesn't stop.

His fingers keep working me, his cock still thrusting deep,

prolonging my pleasure until my body is shaking, too much, too good, I can't, I can't—

A second wave crashes through me—violent, devastating, leaving me wrecked and undone beneath him. My thighs tremble, my nails curving under from my grip on the furs, my voice breaking on the ruins of his name.

"Fuck—Elyssara—"

"I'm going to fill your pussy," his voice is pure torment, his thrusts losing rhythm, going wild, desperate, on the edge of breaking.

And then he does—

One. Two. Three brutal, perfect thrusts—and he's gone.

Kael follows me into oblivion.

His groan is animalistic, almost tortured, as he pulses inside me, claiming me, wrecking me.

He collapses against me, his weight pressing me into the furs, his breath ragged against my skin.

My body still trembles. Still wrung out. Still ruined.

I can't think. Can't move.

I feel like I've been undone at the seams.

He rolls to the side, pulling me with him, holding me close.

His hands tremble slightly.

He buries his face in my hair, and when he speaks, his voice is quiet, almost reverent.

"Mine," he murmurs against my skin.

A breath. A kiss. "Always."

CHAPTER FIFTY
KAEL

I kiss Elyssara on the forehead as she sleeps, sinking deep into the furs, naked but warm under blankets that make her seem so fragile, so small.

I should stay. Should keep my arms around her, bury my face in her hair, lose myself in her warmth.

But duty pulls me away. *I need to talk to Therion.*

An ache sits heavy in my chest, deep and dull—like a second heartbeat that doesn't belong to me. A sensation so foreign that I press my palm against my sternum, as if I can physically quiet it. It's not pain. It's not desire. It's awareness. *A tether.*

Even as I slide my boots on and step out into the night, I still feel her.

The fire burns low, embers crackling softly. Most of the camp sleeps, but Therion remains, seated by the flames, staring into them as if they hold the answers he's looking for. Smoke curls through the air, thick with charred wood and distant rain.

He doesn't look up, but he knows I'm here.

He tosses a flask in my direction. *Silverwake.*

I take a swig, letting the burn chase away the tension curling in my gut. But I don't hand it back. Not yet.

Therion exhales through his nose, "So… are we still using her?"

My fingers tighten around the flask.

Therion finally looks at me, gaze cutting and calculating. "Or have you decided to choose a girl over this entire fucking war we've been planning for ten years?"

I clench my jaw, restraining myself from punching him in the throat.

Before I can get a word out, he keeps going.

"You've had plenty of women before, Kael. It's never made you reckless." His tone sharpens. "Or fucking stupid."

A growl rises in my throat. *I will rip him apart for this.*

"This isn't about fucking her, Therion," I bite out, the words like sharpened steel. "It's… more than that."

He studies me, realization flickering over his face like a blade catching moonlight.

His posture shifts. His anger dims just enough to let something else creep in.

"Then what is it?"

I swallow thickly. My fingers flex. The words feel dangerous, like speaking them aloud will make them permanent.

But I say them anyway.

"I can feel her."

Therion stills. But not in the way he does before a fight—not the slow, assessing stillness of a warrior calculating his next move. No, this is something else. Something closer to disbelief.

His brow furrows. His fingers tighten around the flask. "What?"

"Even when I'm not with her. I can… *sense* her."

The words settle in the space between us, heavy and irrevocable.

And Stars help me, but it's the first time I've let myself acknowledge it.

"It's like a thread between us I never meant to pull."

Therion flinches. Not visibly—never visibly—but I see it in the way his fingers tense around the flask, the brief, fractional shift of his shoulders.

"No," he says flatly, but his voice isn't as sharp as before. "No, that's not—" He shakes his head once, as if trying to shake off the words. "That's not possible. It can't be."

But the way his breathing turns shallow, the way his gaze flicks over me like he's searching for a crack—it tells me he knows I'm not lying.

It tells me he's afraid I might be right.

I drag a hand over my chest again, pressing against the ache. "It's like she's within me. Entwined. Mine somehow."

Therion's jaw clenches. His breathing turns shallow. "Fuck," he mutters, his entire posture rigid. "That's not... possible. I can't sense anything within her other than her magic." But I already know this goes beyond his Aetherstride abilities. This is something... *other*.

Therion exhales through his nose, eyes locked on the fire, and says nothing.

Silence falls heavy between us.

Therion's stare sharpens, his mind calculating in real-time.

I force myself to breathe through the tension in my ribs. Through the absolute certainty settling into my bones.

Therion leans back on his hands, inhaling deeply. Then—his voice softer, but no less edged, "So what now? What does this mean?"

I don't hesitate.

"It means we'll find another way."

Therion exhales sharply, shaking his head. "Kael—"

"No." There is nothing uncertain in my tone. Nothing to argue against. "She is not a pawn. We'll find another way."

Therion leans forward, dragging his hands through his hair—exhaustion and frustration settling into his posture. He braces his arms on his knees, flask dangling from his fingers. "We don't have another way, brother." He exhales audibly. "We've been trying for years. This—*she*—was our last hope." He steels himself then, knowing that whatever he's about to say will toe a line I won't like, "And," his eyes penetrating, "she *is* a pawn."

My patience snaps.

I turn to face him fully, my voice like shattered stone.

"So if it were Seren? If we were meant to use *her*—would you be fine with *that?*"

The words hit him like a strike to the ribs. His head whips toward me so fast I think he might actually throw the flask at my head.

Silence.

Not even the fire cracks between us.

Therion swallows once. Twice. His jaw flexes. "That's not the same."

I let the silence stretch until he meets my stare again.

"Isn't it?" My tone is even. Controlled. "I see the way you look at her. Would you throw her to the monsters and let them destroy her?" I seethe.

He shakes his head vehemently, words not forthcoming. His throat bobs. I've clearly struck a nerve. "This is different, Kael." His voice is quieter. But we both know it's a lie.

I lean in, resting my elbows on my knees. "No, it's not."

Therion exhales hard, frustration twisting his features. "And you think Maldrak will just give us another way? That he'll just let us rewrite the game because your heart—or worse, your cock—is dictating strategy?"

"I will not say it again without drawing my blade—this isn't about fucking her."

Therion scoffs, but there's an edge to it. "Then what? What is it, Kael? Because whatever this is, it's irrational—"

I turn to him fully, teeth bared in a snarl, voice like a war drum. "I would burn down the fucking realms for her."

The words hang between us like a blade.

Therion's breath stutters. A rare slip.

He looks at me then, truly looks at me, and whatever he sees in my face makes his expression go blank.

No anger. No calculation. Just understanding.

Because he finally knows.

Finally fucking knows.

I'm lost in this. And there's no pulling me back.

The fire crackles in the silence.

A long moment passes.

Then, he exhales, shaking his head. His tone is dry, but the weight of his words is heavy. "Stars save you."

I let the silence stretch between us, thick and unyielding. Therion prays to the Stars, but I already know—

"They won't."

Therion drags a hand down his face. "You're really fucking doing this, aren't you?"

I don't even hesitate, "I am."

He swears under his breath, his whole body going slack as he shakes his head again. Another long silence.

"Fuck," Therion mutters, dragging a hand down his face. "You really are lost to this, brother?"

He stares at the fire for a long moment, jaw clenched, shaking his head like he's trying to find another argument—another way to change my mind.

But there isn't one.

"Fine," he finally exhales, voice gruff. Begrudging. Defeated.

"We'll figure something else out. But if we die because of this, I'm haunting you in the afterlife."

I smirk, the first ghost of amusement in this entire conversation. "I'd expect nothing less."

Therion groans, tipping his head back to the Stars. "Stars save me, I fucking hate you."

"You don't."

"No, I don't," he mutters. Then, cutting me a glare, "But if you ever tell her how soft you've gone, I will personally slit your throat."

I laugh. A real fucking laugh.

The tension shifts. The decision is made.

We are not using Elyssara.

We will find another way.

And no matter what's already been written in the Stars—I'll have her. I'll keep her.

And I'll win my godsdamned war.

CHAPTER FIFTY-ONE

ELYSSARA

"Good morning, Duskae," Kael's tender words reach me behind closed eyes and the heaviness of sleep.

I pry them open to see his ruggedly beautiful face—which is still infuriatingly symmetrical—staring at me from the tent's entrance. "Good morning," I say heavily, voice thick with sleep and memories of last night.

He huffs a laugh at my sleep-addled demeanor, "As much as I would love to crawl back under those furs with you, we have to go."

I pull the blankets up and bury a groan along with my face, but still, he continues, "We need to get back to Jax and Merrik." Reality comes crashing down at his reminder, "We need access to those books and maps to plan the next part of the journey, before the Royal Guard hit Galreth." *Fuck.* "Oh," he adds flippantly, "and everyone is already waiting for you, including the entire tribe of Vaythari."

I leap out of bed, instantly alert at the thought of everyone awaiting me—their Zhari—before realizing that I am completely and utterly bare. I move to cover myself, when Kael interjects, "Darling, you could cover yourself for the next one hundred years, but I will never forget the shape of that beautiful body." He bites his lip then, "And I regret having to say this, but, if you don't get dressed quickly, I will make everyone listen while I lick your sweet—"

"Okay! Okay!" I cut in. "Gods, Kael," I laugh at his terribly effective strategy at getting me up and dressed, and begin moving for my leathers.

I promise the Vaythari I will find their sister tribe, reunite what was broken. Then we ride—down the mountain, away from Skaedor's Crest and all it awakened.

The chilling winds have calmed, as if they, too, have sighed with relief at our leaving. Despite having countless things to discuss—like Seren translating the language of the Vaythari, the gods magic, my being Skaedor's heir, and the fact that my magic thrums through my veins with frightening tenacity—we let our horses tread carefully down the rocky, snowy descent and settle into a comfortable silence.

I'm grateful for the silence, because it gives me a moment to reorder the thoughts that whip like a tornado through my mind.

Everything has changed.

I began the ascent to Skaedor's Crest with vengeance in one hand and uncertainty in the other. Doubt whispered in my bones. I had never feared the fight—I feared not being enough for it. Not strong enough. Not trusting enough. Not the type of powerful that bends kingdoms.

Being ruthless in the slums is different—it is survival. It is instinct. A sharpened edge that keeps you alive.

But out here? In the wide-open air of the realms, where birds still sing and people live in peace?

It is far easier to forget that the world needs changing.

But the winds did not forget.

The heavens chose me.

The Stars named me.

The skies whispered my fate.

And now, for the first time, I do not just accept it—I hunger for it.

For the first time, I do not fear what I am becoming—I crave it.

Vengeance is no longer a weight in my palm.

It is the fire in my blood, the breath in my lungs, the blade in my hand.

The echoes of the Vaythari chanting my name still reverberate across the valley as we ride, but it is Kael's steady heartbeat and breath at my back that anchors me to reality.

This is real.

This is mine.

And finally, I am not afraid.

Ronyn bellows, "So... are we gonna talk about Seren suddenly speaking mountain-tongue, or are we all just gonna pretend that's normal?"

Seren flushes, but before she can speak, Therion exhales sharply, as if he's been holding this in for a while.

"I don't sense magic on you," he says, looking at Seren. "Not the kind I know. But that doesn't mean it's not there."

Her brow furrows. "Then what does it mean?"

Therion's jaw ticks. He weighs his words, careful, calculating. "I don't know yet." He looks at her then, sharp and assessing. "But when I first met you, I thought I felt something. Like... you were reading me. Testing me. Probing."

A beat of silence.

"Maybe it was me?" I offer, though even as I say it, I know I'm wrong. "My magic was still there, even if I couldn't use it."

Therion shakes his head. "No. Yours was thrashing, wild. Hers was... quieter." His gaze flickers to Seren. "Like a shadow that doesn't want to be seen."

Seren swallows hard.

Ronyn claps his hands together, breaking the tension. "Well, it sure as shit wasn't me—unless my supernatural gift is my charm with the ladies." He grins and bounces his brows.

Kael snorts, shaking his head as he reins Nyx closer to the group. "Ronyn," he drawls, voice rich with amusement. "If that's a gift, it's one the gods forgot to bestow."

Laughter ripples through the group, easing the weight in Seren's face.

And yet... something lingers beneath Therion's words. A question none of us are quite ready to answer.

There is a connection between us all that didn't exist before we began our journey up the mountain.

A softening.

A melding together.

As if we are no longer five fractured souls, but rather, whole.

I have never belonged to anyone.

I have never *let* myself belong.

And yet... I do.

We all have something to lose, yet we have all chosen to let each other in, to open ourselves up and belong to something greater than ourselves.

It is beautiful.

And terrifying.

Kael senses the shift in me then, because he leans forward, pressing firmly against my back, the scent of leather and oakmoss enveloping me.

"You are so godsdamned beautiful when you laugh, Elyssara."

My breath catches on his words, the reality of this—of him—settling into my bones.

"Are we really doing this?" I say, the words loaded with meaning and heavy with context.

Without hesitation, he speaks like the unflinching warrior he is. "I told you last night that you're mine," he pauses for a moment, looping an arm around my waist. "And I meant it. *Always*."

And this time, I do not hesitate either.

I lean into him, his heartbeat steady against my spine.

"And you are mine."

CHAPTER FIFTY-TWO
KAEL

THOUGH GALRETH LIES AHEAD, I STAY SHARP AS WE MOVE THROUGH the Nyvaryn Ranges—a perfect place for an ambush. I know Therion feels it, too. His back is straight as an arrow, and his grip on Aura's reins is so tight his knuckles are white. I can see the almost imperceptible swivel of his head from behind, indicating his eyes are darting across the terrain—watching, sensing, listening for anything out of place. This is what makes Therion an unmatched General— he's the most observant man under the Stars.

We see Galreth approaching in the distance, and everything looks as it should—though that doesn't necessarily mean anything.

Children are out in the streets, day trade is bustling as it should, and neighbors seem to be talking to one another uninhibited. It's enough for Therion to visibly relax, and I take his confidence as a sign that I should, too.

We ride the long way into the village, avoiding any highly visible routes, and not long after, the inn comes into view, the weeping eye insignia scrubbed from the building, and all looking restored.

Therion lets out a bird call—something he's proficient in, and has developed his own language for with the leaders he trains across Aevryn—and the sound of scuffing and scurrying feet fills my ears.

The innocent and wide eyes of the stable hand peer out from behind the gate, and he drags it open for us to enter into the inn's courtyard once more.

Inside, Merrik stands and stretches his hulking frame, as if he's been sitting and waiting for a while. "Good to have you back, son," he says in a gruff yet warm timber, and runs his hand down Nyx's flank as we pull up.

Jax, Torvyn and Finn are also waiting, expressions laden with anticipation and curiosity. It's Jax who speaks up first, "Cutting it pretty fucking fine, Kael. It's almost dusk."

"What do you want me to say, Jax? It took as long as it took for a fucking reason," weariness has seeped into my tone and my words come out as a snap. "Now, make yourself useful," I say, handing the reins to Jax, and dismounting seamlessly off the back.

I reach for Elyssara's waist, and before she's even had the chance to move, I lift her from Nyx and place her gently on the cobblestones. At ground level, her eyes are at the same height as my chest. I tilt her chin upward, dragging her gaze to mine. *Gods, she's beautiful.* Her gaze drifts over my face, across my chest and shoulders, lingering a second too long. She bites her lip, and I know exactly what she's thinking.

I lower my voice, letting it drop into something rough, something meant for her alone, "You keep looking at me like that, darling, and I won't care who's watching when I make good on what your eyes are asking for."

The blood rushes to her cheeks then, but she steels herself, refusing to feel embarrassed. "You make me feel..." she falters, breath catching. "Stars, I don't even know how to explain it."

Therion brushes past us then, and in an almost whisper, he says, "I've accepted this, but it doesn't mean I want to watch you mentally undressing each other all the fucking time, or listen to you talk about your cute little feelings." His words come out harsh, but there is no denying the smile he is fighting. He walks away brusquely, and Elyssara chuckles in his wake.

"Mavyrn's right—he's a grumpy bastard," I say. We both laugh then, but it doesn't last long.

"I hate to interrupt," Jax wags her finger between us, "whatever *this* is, but we have business to tend to."

"Fuck's sake, Jaxxy. We spoke about this—*be nice*," Merrik stresses the last words, as if he has indeed spoken about this. Likely a lot.

Jax rolls her eyes but reluctantly—and thankfully—backs off. Merrik has always had a way of getting through to her that none of us have ever been able to. It's why I paired them up to infiltrate the Dravari guard. She's chaos, but he is somehow able to rein her in.

"We need to move quickly. Word from the unit in Vyrhal is that the Royal Guard are exceeding our timing predictions. They know we'll be trying to cross The Joining, and they're coming to intercept before we make it to The Wastes. We have to leave tonight," Torvyn speaks with the confidence of a battle-hardened leader who's been in these situations many times before.

"Fuck," I drag my hands through my hair. I turn to Seren, knowing she's the key to the next leg of our journey. "We need to take a look at the next part of the prophecy and know exactly where we're going. *Now*," urgency coats my words.

Seren nods with efficiency and conviction—she's been doing that more and more. "I'll need help to sort through the books with such little time. Ronyn and Elyssara know how I work, they can come with me," she says with the grace of a leader, and I can't help but agree that it's a smart call.

Elyssara's radiant jade-green eyes lock onto mine—brighter, deeper, more alive with every relic we claim—wordless but screaming everything she can't say. There's a hesitation there, a pull, like she doesn't want to leave. I nod anyway, forcing the encouragement she needs, even as my chest tightens, the ache deepening with every damn time we're apart. Whatever this is between us, I need answers. And soon.

Elyssara follows Seren reluctantly, and I spin on my heel, pulling up a crate around the table while the rest of them do the same, and we all do what we do best—plan our next mission.

"So, give us the rundown," Merrik is straight into action, as usual.

I opt for quick and ruthless, "We're changing plans."

The group erupts in similar fits of displeasure. A cacophony of "I knew it's" and "this will never work's". I allow them their moments, but ultimately, they will get in line or I will fucking put them there.

Jax looks downright disgusted at the change of plans, and seething, her face dripping in disdain, she spits, "The council will never go for this, Kael."

"We've never had a chance at actually bringing down The Decay! We'll break the curse, extract Nalya ourselves when they're vulnerable, take back what's ours." I've been planning how I'll counter their resistance for hours coming down the mountain, and this is the best bet I can make.

"That's a suicide mission and you know it—we've never even broken through the castle grounds!" She's panting, rage permeating every part of her, "And that's assuming she's even there!"

"We will find a way," I say.

"You're fucking delusional!" Jax throws her arms in the air, spittle forming in the corners of her mouth.

"That's what I said," Therion concurs.

I throw him a venomous look to shut the fuck up and keep his opinions to himself.

"Alright, alright," Merrik's calming presence cuts through the chaos—forever the voice of reason. "Let the lad plead his case, you lot."

A darkness rumbles through me then, and the air turns ice cold and still. I know without looking that my shadows have come out to play, because all eyes are locked on me and they've all stopped breathing. I look straight into the eyes of each of them, "Firstly, don't you ever fucking forget who you're talking to. Secondly," I pause weighing the merits of sharing this, "she's Skaedor's heir."

Silence. Stunned.

Jax's mouth opens—of course she's going to say something snide —but I slam my hand on the table. Shadows lash out like smoke, cold tendrils curling around the legs of the table, coiling up arms before snapping back into me. Deadly and sharp. "Don't," I say directly to Jax.

"WHAT!?" the words reverberating through my skull, as Torvyn, Finn, and Merrik look to me to elaborate.

"And—" I try to continue.

"Holy fuckin' Stars, there's more?" All calmness has vanished from Merrik's tone.

"She has the gods' magic in her," I wait for the remarks.

"What the fuck, Kael? *How*? What does that even mean?" Jax's disbelief is mirrored in the rest of the group, too.

"We don't know yet. All we know is that King Thalmyr and an unknown sorceress exiled the gods, and they left the last remnants of their magic in her."

"Well, fuck Kael. Any other realm-shifting tidbits you'd like to share with the group?" Torvyn's sarcasm never ceases, no matter the stakes.

"Oh, there's more," Therion mutters under his breath.

I give him a callous sideways glance.

Elyssara would skin me alive for telling them this. But fuck it—if I don't, they'll never grasp how deep this runs. And they need to. Because this? This is war.

"I think... we have some sort of," I look to Therion for assurance, who gives me an imperceptible nod, so I continue, "... connection."

"Yeah that's what happens when you fuck, Kael," Jax states drily. "Why can't you just choose someone else? Plenty of girls back home would literally sever their own legs off to get in your bed."

"That's what I said," Therion concurs again.

"Would you all fucking listen? It's not about that. There's something *else* between us. It's something *more*. I can feel it. It feels like she's part of me."

No one dares to speak.

"I think we're bonded in some way," I venture, the words leaving a bitter taste. Saying it out loud makes it heavier—real.

The silence is pregnant. No one breathes. This truth has the potential to reshapes battle plans—kingdoms, even.

"What does that even mean?" Jax presses after a heartbeat, leaning forward.

"I don't know. But it's not just emotion. I can feel her. Her pain. Sense where she is."

Torvyn lets out a low whistle. "So if someone gets to her…"

"They get to me," I finish, the weight of it heavy in my chest.

"So the entire rebellion rests on where you stick your cock? Brilliant, Kael," Jax's frustration bursting through.

"It's not about that," I snap.

"Could've fooled me. You're tied to her now, Kael. Anyone who wants this rebellion gone? They'll go through her."

As much as I hate what she's saying, she's not wrong.

"Well, fuck me sideways, lad," Merrik interlaces his hands and stretches them over his head. "I thought we'd be talking about the compass." He huffs a laugh then, and his levity is a welcome respite from the intensity.

"Yeah, we got it. Well, Elyssara got it. Only Skaedor's heir could touch it," I offer.

"Right, well she's turning out to be quite important in this whole thing, I'll give ya that."

"She's the *key* to it all, and I hope you all fucking understand that," I grit out. "If any of you mention a godsdamned thing about the gods' magic, her role as heir, or the bond to another living soul, I'll skin you alive myself and leave you for the fucking duskprowlers."

They all acquiesce and nod. They may not agree with my choices, but they'll godsdamn kneel to my orders.

Despite the conviction of my words, I feel like I'm in over my fucking head.

I'm supposed to be the one keeping this whole rebellion afloat. The steady hand. The untouchable commander.

But this bond?

It makes me reckless. Makes me dangerous.

Because one blade at her throat, and I'd be on my knees.

CHAPTER FIFTY-THREE
ELYSSARA

MY CHEST ACHES AS I WALK AWAY FROM KAEL, AND I CLUTCH AT MY leather chest plate to ease the pain.

"What is it?" Seren queries.

"It's nothing," I lie. "Just nervous about the next relic. Surely they can't all be in Dravara. I know we'll have to cross The Joining soon."

Ronyn throws his arm around me, and pulls me in tight while we walk back to the rooms, "Scared of a realm full of monsters?" he jeers. "Never stopped you before. We've faced worse, I'd say." That lop-sided grin and his shaggy mop of hair bounce across his forehead, and I can't help but smile back at the big optimistic fool.

"We *have* faced a lot of Bloodbonds and lived to tell the tale," I allow.

"I've even shot a crossbow!" Seren exclaims.

We all chuckle together, and walk straight into Seren's room, where all her maps, books and parchment remain undisturbed.

We settle into a steady rhythm of reading, writing notes, discussing theories, and poring over the prophecy, sipping tea of hibiscus and honey. The peace and nostalgia of losing hours to books and conversation feels at odds with the circumstances, but I relish them, anyway.

As if someone tugs hard on a thread stitched through my chest, I jolt upright. The door opens and the rest of the group walk through. The ache unspools the moment Kael finally steps through the door, his ocean eyes locking onto mine. Relief swells in my chest so fast it's dizzying—like breathing after drowning. *What in the Stars is going on?*

He winks at me and flashes one of those half-smirks that turn me molten.

"So, what have you come up with?" He prompts, directing the question at Seren.

"We're looking at this section here," she says, pointing to the old parchment, its ink smeared and worn. Her finger underlines the verse:

> *In shadowed depths where roots entwine,*
> *The crown reveals the path divine.*

I read the lines again, unease spreading through my veins There's something ominous in the poetry—something waiting in the dark.

We all hunch over, crowding around the parchment, and leaning over towers of books and countless notes tucked between pages.

"I can deduce that this piece of the prophecy refers to the Obsidian Crown, according to this text of *Ancient Lore & Historical Relics*," Seren pauses for dramatic effect, but we all look at her, not at all sure what she's referring to.

She scoffs, but continues. "It's heralded as a Seer of Legitimacy," Seren announces, fingers trailing the brittle edge of the parchment. "The crown doesn't grant power—it decides if you deserve it. It judges the bloodline, the soul, the intention. And it doesn't care for politics or self-righteous claims." She flips through aged pages with practiced speed before landing on a section, her nail tapping the ink. "It's sentient. If it accepts you, it shows you things—histories, visions, things that have been buried. If it rejects you..."

"What happens?" I ask, my throat dry.

Seren hesitates—just for a breath—then meets my eyes. "The rejection is... violent. Fatal in most cases."

"Do we know why it's hidden? Why its part of the prophecy?" Therion questions.

"Because it confirms or denies the rightful kings and queens of the realms," she looks up then, letting the gravity of her statement sink in. "And if it's hidden, that means someone doesn't want to answer to the crown."

"This day just keeps getting better and better, doesn't it?" Merrik says drily, running his hand through his graying beard.

Kael cuts through the pondering group, "Any leads on where it is?"

"My theories at this stage are that it's connected to Shadowweave magic—*shadowed depths* and *the Obsidian Crown* sound too coincidental to not be connected to The Obsidian Serpent constellation, wouldn't you say?" Seren doesn't wait for a response before continuing. "But without maps of The Wastes, and limited information in these books, I have no leads on what it means for the roots to entwine... *Yet*." Determination lines her face, and she continues trawling through pages.

I look up from the table and catch Therion and Kael exchanging a weighted look.

"What do you know?" I ask, an edge to my voice.

"I know where we're going next," heaviness coating Kael's words.

"Care to enlighten the group?" Ronyn quips, but Kael's jaw tenses. For a heartbeat, it seems like he won't answer.

Then, with a grim finality, he mutters, "Home."

The word drops like a stone in my chest. Whatever's waiting there... it's not just about the crown. It's about *him*.

CHAPTER FIFTY-FOUR
KAEL

"And where exactly is home?" Elyssara breathes. Her words come out soft, but there's steel in them—like she already knows the answer won't be good.

"The far east of The Wastes. Thornewood." I don't soften it. She deserves the truth—at least, the parts that won't ruin the plan. Jax looks displeased at the confession, but fuck, Jax always looks displeased.

"The entwined roots are in Thornewood?" Seren presses, eyes wide with that spark she gets when she's on the edge of solving something.

Therion clears his throat, closing his eyes for a beat too long. I know that look—he's lost in memories that still fucking bleed.

"Thornewood sits on the edge of a grove," Therion says, voice low. Surprise twists in my chest—he never talks about this. "It was once a sanctuary for kings and queens to take respite, to gather wisdom." He drags in a breath, the kind that feels like it's scraping against his lungs. "But since the last rightful king died, the grove's gone feral."

Silence swells, heavy and sharp. Even the fucking air feels tighter.

Merrik breaks it, his rough timbre a relief. "It was a sanctuary—sure. But its heart was always for the crowned. And now?" He shakes his head. "She's turned. The roots tangle, trees bend, the paths close, and no one gets through. At least, no one who's come back to talk about it."

"One could argue they went in under-prepared and paid for it," Jax snaps, the weight of lost soldiers thick in her voice.

Elyssara ignores Jax, her jaw ticks, disbelief warping her words. "And that's where the crown is?"

"I don't know for sure," I admit. "But the prophecy points to entwined roots, and there's nowhere else in Aevryn where the land twists in on itself like that. If the crown's hidden somewhere... the grove makes the most sense."

Seren chimes in, flipping through a brittle page. "The crown is tied to legacy and legitimacy—it would make sense for it to be placed in a sanctuary once meant for kings and queens. And if the grove's turned hostile, it's probably because no one worthy has claimed it since."

"Or because someone doesn't want it found," Therion mutters darkly.

"So we're walking into a death maze for a crown that we're not entirely sure is even there?" Elyssara deadpans.

"Pretty much, yeah," Merrik doesn't sugarcoat it.

Ronyn lets out a long, slow whistle. "A moving death maze, a killer crown, and a rebellion hanging by a thread? Sounds fucking perfect." He flashes that reckless grin. "I'm in."

We gather around a frayed map spread across the table, the edges curling from age and wear. The Joining cuts a jagged line across the parchment, the last breath of Dravara's territory before it collapses into inaccurate projections of The Shadow Wastes' terrain. It looks simple enough here—just a slash of ink. But they're about to find out just how much they've been lied to.

Merrik traces a thick finger along the border. "The main crossing's here, but it's swarming with Guards this time of year. Even their best idiots wouldn't leave it unguarded."

"Except they have," Jax cuts in, leaning forward, boots kicked up on the table. "Scouts came back empty. No Royal Guard patrols, no lookouts. It's been fucking silent."

A heavy pause.

"Too silent," Therion mutters. "They're not just absent—they're waiting."

Elyssara's brows furrow. "If they know we're moving, wouldn't they stake The Joining itself?"

"Exactly." I tap the map. "That's why we don't take the open ground. We use the smugglers' tunnels."

Seren hums, rifling through parchment and notes. "The old passages under the cliff side? Are they still intact?"

"Barely," Merrik grunts. "They twist under The Joining, popping up on The Wastes' side. Used to be prime for contraband runs, but not many dare it now. Our rebels are the only ones game enough to attempt it."

Elyssara's eyes flick to me, skeptical. "And the horses?"

"I'll cloak them with Shadowweave. Keep them above ground, hidden." I don't say how draining that'll be. No need to worry them about the risk. "They'll be waiting on the other side."

Therion shakes his head, jaw tight. "You're going to burn through your magic. That cloak's going to drain you before we're even halfway through."

"I'll manage," I say with a finality that kills any further debate.

But Elyssara's sharp gaze lingers on me like she sees right through the lie. "Why can't we just cross with the horses? Can't you cloak us all like you did in The Barrier District?"

I wish I could. "Duskae, your magic was bound and barely traceable then. If you walk amongst Bloodbonds and Aetherstrides, it won't matter if you're cloaked or not—they'll feel you."

She huffs in frustration.

"We move fast," I continue. "The tunnels aren't wide, and they're not forgiving. We hit the exit before the Royal Guard realizes we've slipped under them."

"And if they already know?" Jax's question lands heavy.

A beat of silence.

"Then we deal with them," my words a promise.

Elyssara blows out a breath, her knuckles pale against the edge of the table. "Of course we do."

The plan's in motion fast. The horses are saddled, shadows creeping around them like thin smoke as my magic wraps tight. It takes effort—more than I let on—but I hold the cloak steady.

We ride for hours in tight formation toward The Joining. The path grows harsher with every mile, the ground turning from dirt to cracked stone, brittle under hoof.

No guards. No patrols. Just silence.

It scratches at me like sandpaper—too clean. Too easy.

"Still no sign of them," Therion mutters, eyes scanning the horizon. "Not a godsdamned soul."

"They're waiting somewhere," Merrik agrees, his hand never straying far from his sword. "I can feel it."

The Joining unfolds before us—massive, raw, and brutal—but we stay back a healthy distance to not be detected.

The stretch of land between The Shadow Wastes and Dravara is wide, flat, and savage—an open scar across the realm.

Nothing grows here.

No trees. No grass. Just churned-up earth, riddled with scars of old battles. Bones still litter the ground, half-buried, bleached white against the blood-stained soil—remnants of the countless lives lost in the wars that made this place infamous.

The Wastes to the east—harsh, jagged, windswept.

Dravara to the west—lush but oppressed and poisoned by the rot of its king.

And this? The Joining is the cracked, bleeding vein between them.

The Joining is held by soldiers raised on bloodshed—men who've known nothing but killing, hate, and orders from kings they'll never meet. Separated only by dry, flat land—neutral territory that waits hungrily for the next bloodbath. They've been held here at the center of our lands, fighting battles for kings in untouchable towers, who wouldn't spare them a second thought.

Merrik points to a slope that curves down toward the cliff side.

"Smugglers' tunnels run under there. We slip in, avoid the open field."

I reach out, twisting more Shadowweave around Nyx, forcing the cloak tighter. My temples throb, a dull pulse with every shroud I weave. I'm okay, for now, but the effort to keep these cloaks in place while we're underground will hurt.

"That's going to leave you dry for the fight," Therion warns.

"Then we'll make sure we end it quickly." Another lie. Another gamble.

We move silently from a distance, avoiding the usual locations of scouts and soldiers that typically patrol the outskirts of The Joining, despite none being visible. We dismount at the cliff's edge, still shrouded by the dense trees on the fringe of the Galreth region. The tunnel's entrance stares at us at the bottom of the jagged cliff we need to climb down. It's nothing but a scar in the stone—jagged, dark, and waiting—easily overlooked by passersby. I suspect they're waiting for us at the bottom of the cliff. It's the perfect location— nowhere to go, easy to surround us.

Elyssara glances toward the empty plains, jaw tense. "Still no patrols."

"Which means they know exactly where we're going," Therion mutters.

Her fingers twitch toward her dagger—subtle, but I notice. She doesn't like this. Neither do I.

I tighten my grip on my blade. "Then let's not keep them waiting."

We begin our descent down the rocky cliff, the jagged stone scraping at my palms as I lower myself down. Loose gravel slips underfoot, tumbling into the abyss below. Every movement feels too loud.

At the base, the tunnel gapes open like a broken jaw—dark, cold, and still. I can taste the damp in the air, the copper tang of old blood lingering in the stone.

Elyssara steps to my side, her voice low. "Feels like a trap."

"It is." I don't bother lying.

The wind howls through the pass, fierce and biting—like it knows it's the last wild thing left alive here.

Merrik's boots thud on hard-packed dirt. "Smells worse every time I come here," he grumbles, waving a hand in front of his face. The stench of damp earth and old blood rises thick from the darkened entrance.

Jax's eyes dart around, alert and on edge. "If this place doesn't kill me, the fucking smell will."

"We're not alone," Therion states with certainty, slicing through the arbitrary complaints.

Elyssara brushes past me toward the tunnel, her fingers skimming the boulders. Her jaw's tense, but there's fire in her step.

"You sure this is the best route?" she asks, voice low.

"It's the only route." And it's true. The Joining's surface is a blood-soaked chessboard—the minute we step into open ground, we're fucked.

Therion and I brandish our weapons, moving with stealth through the pass. Ronyn has climbed boulders to find a higher vantage point, arrow nocked and ready to loose.

Elyssara moves with the grace of a warrior, haired intricately pulled back from her face in a warrior's braid—the way she always has it when she knows she'll fight, and it's godsdamned mesmerizing —Jax watching her back with her hands poised and Seren between them, armed with her crossbow. We move as one through the pass, ready to fight our way into the tunnels.

But no one's here.

We can hear the murmurs of soldiers from above—playing cards, drinking, sparring—but nothing else. No hitching breaths, or scrape of metal. Just... silence.

Therion signals to enter the tunnels, and we all follow his lead.

The tunnels swallow us whole—dark, wet, suffocating. The air is heavy, a cloying dampness that sticks in my throat. Every boot step echoes too loud, the sound bouncing off the jagged stone walls.

Before we move through the tunnels, I twist more Shadowweave around Nyx, the magic clawing at me—each shroud feeling like it rips a thread of magic loose inside my chest. My vision darkens at the edges, a cold sweat slicking my brow. But I force it tighter. I can't drop it. Not yet.

The space is tight, the walls rough, gouged with deep claw marks—some old, some fresh. Water drips from somewhere high above, the droplets a stark reminder of the deafening silence.

Therion keeps his sword raised, eyes flicking over every shadow.

Elyssara's eyes dart up the tunnel walls, the sharp angle of her jaw tense. "The echoes are off. Something's wrong."

"I know," I grit out, but we're already too deep.

My grip tightens around my blade's hilt, and I notice Therion's already in a fighting stance, axe poised for use. *He feels it, too.*

The tunnel twists sharply to the right, narrowing even more. The air shifts—subtle but wrong. Too still. No echoes of distant smugglers. No faint shuffle of rats. Just silence.

A predator's silence.

"Where the fuck is everyone?" Merrik rumbles behind me.

I spin just as Therion does, both of us looking back toward the entrance.

Therion lunges, hand reaching through the gap, fingertips brushing metal—then the gate slams down with a thunderous clang. His knuckles scrape against the iron as he yanks his arm back, cursing violently.

But it's too late.

The iron gate slams shut.

Torvyn's face is there—half-lit by the torches—but there's nothing soft in his eyes.

"Torvyn!" Therion barks, slamming at the gate.

Torvyn holds up a hand, his jaw clenched. "I didn't want to, boss. But—" He cuts off, voice rough. "It's Finn. They promised they wouldn't hurt him if I did this." His breathing is ragged, panicked, "I'm doing it for my boy."

The words hit like a fist to the gut.

"You fucking sold us out!" My voice comes out like a snarl, lethal. "They won't spare you, Torvyn. You're nothing but a fucking pawn. Both your heads will be on spikes before the sun sets," I drop my voice low and guttural then, malice lacing every syllable, "and if they don't, I'll put them there myself."

Torvyn's hand lingers on the gate's latch, knuckles white. "I'm sorry, Kael." His voice cracks, barely a whisper. "I know what this means."

"You're already dead," I spit back. "I'll come for you."

His hand lingers on the lock for a breath longer, then he's gone —shadows swallowing him as he disappears into the pass. Therion reaches for the lock, poking his fingers through the iron gate, but he pulls his hand back instantly, gritting his teeth and seething. "Fuck!" he yells. "It's made of lillath."

Magic-nullifying metal.

"Kael..." Seren's whisper is barely a thread, her wide eyes fixed on the shadows shifting ahead. "They're here."

I turn—

And torches are lining the tunnel, shadows stretching long before dozens of Royal Guards emerge, their armor catching the dim light. Their blades gleam—sharpened and waiting.

Elyssara's breath hitches, sharp and fast, but she doesn't step back. Her dagger's already drawn, knuckles white around the hilt. "We're trapped."

"Yeah," I mutter, voice like stone. I slide one sword free, the metallic rasp loud in the suffocating dark. "But they forgot one thing."

The darkness stirs around me—thin tendrils of shadow curling up my forearm, licking the blade.

I smile savagely.

"I'm better in the fucking dark."

CHAPTER FIFTY-FIVE
ELYSSARA

RONYN DOESN'T WAIT—HIS ARROW FLIES, PIERCING THROUGH THE throat of a soldier before he can even raise his sword. The man gurgles, blood bubbling over his lips as he crumples, the crest of King Thalmyr barely catching the dim light before it's swallowed by darkness.

I drop low into a fighting stance and move like a predator converging on its prey.

Steel screams against steel. The tunnels are a cacophony of clashing blades, strangled shouts, and the wet crunch of bodies hitting stone. The copper tang of blood thickens the air, hot and suffocating, as I twist beneath the arc of a sword—its edge grazing the braid at the nape of my neck.

Too close.

I lunge low, dagger flashing up, and feel the sickening split of flesh as the blade sinks between ribs. The guard crumples, blood pooling at my boots—but there's no time. Another one's already on me. I pivot hard, my blade locking against his, the impact rattling up my arm.

The tunnel is a mess of bodies and steel—no room to maneuver, no light but the guttering torches throwing warped shadows against the stone. Every shout, every clash, echoes tenfold, bouncing through the narrow space like a scream that won't stop.

"On your left!" Ronyn's voice cuts through the din.

I duck instinctively as a sword whistles past—missing me by a breath before Ronyn's arrow thuds into the attacker's throat. He winks at me, another arrow already notched.

"You owe me one, El!"

I shake my head at his levity, slashing through the legs of another guard as he charges.

And then I see him.

Kael.

And gods, it's terrifying.

He moves like a storm made flesh—silent, merciless, inevitable. Shadowweave lashes from his hands, curling like smoke, dragging guards into the dark before their screams are cut short. His sword gleams under the torchlight, blood-slicked and merciless, carving through armor like paper.

One guard lunges for him—too slow.

Kael sidesteps, shadow tendrils snapping tight around the man's throat. With a flick of his wrist, the guard's head jerks back, spine bending at an unnatural angle before the shadows slam him into the tunnel wall with a wet crack.

Blood spatters. Bones break. Kael doesn't flinch.

Another comes at him from the side—but Kael's already there, driving a blade upward, straight through the man's jaw. It pierces through the top of his skull with a sickening crunch before Kael wrenches it free.

His jaw is tight, sweat running down his temple, but his eyes—stormy and wild—are locked onto the chaos like he's feeding off it.

There's no hesitation. No mercy.

It's not the way a man fights. It's the way a weapon does.

And for a breath, I'm horrified.

But it's short-lived—because that dark, sharp-edged thing buried deep inside me?

The part I don't like to look at?

It's in awe.

Because he's devastating. Brutal. Beautiful in the way a wildfire is—terrifying and unstoppable.

I don't want him to stop.

But I see it now—the strain pulling at him. The shadows wrapping the horses above ground are eating him alive. His magic frays at the edges, slipping under the strain of distance—but he won't let go.

I slice and bend, maiming and tearing through the next wave without thought, the world falls away and only the kill remains; I'm in the killing calm.

And I relish it.

I relish the way the darkness feels when I let it in.

Bursts of bright white light spear through the tunnel, finding their targets with unerring precision. It takes me a moment to register—Jax is wielding my magic.

Bolts of Lightborne magic fire from her fingertips, obliterating guards into nothing more than fine ash.

I draw inspiration from it—from *her*, from the well of power singing in my chest, clawing at my binds to be unleashed. I siphon small amounts out and send them into the fingertips of my left hand, while my Starforged Blade sings and brands its victims with every slice in my right.

I spear my magic out with one hand and carve into throats with the other—and the feeling is sweet, possessed by rage and fury of years spent in hiding.

I feel invincible.

Every drop of magic the gods buried inside me rejoices in my brutality.

And then it hits—

Pain, sharp and cold, tears through my ribs.

I stumble.

My vision tilts, the weight of the blade in my hand vanishing as the world lurches sideways. The coppery taste of blood fills my mouth—except I haven't been cut.

My heart thunders, but there's another rhythm beneath it—another pain, deeper, older.

Kael.

I can feel him.

His magic is fraying—each tether stretched thin, snapping one by one as he pours everything into holding that godsdamned cloak above ground. I can feel the pull of it, the weight dragging him under like a rip tide.

And worse—

I can hear him.

Not with my ears.

Inside my own mind.

"Elyssara—where the fuck is she?"

The thought isn't mine.

It's jagged. Raw. *His.* Breaking into my mind like a blade through bone.

"Kael—?" I gasp, my hand curling against my ribs where the phantom pain sears.

"Get. To. Her."

His voice, rough and desperate, claws through my mind before vanishing like smoke.

"Elyssara—MOVE!"

Merrik's shout yanks me back to the now.

I barely twist in time—a sword cleaving down where my head had been.

My dagger's gone—lost in the chaos—so I grab the nearest thing I can, a broken pike from a fallen guard, and ram it into my attacker's chest.

Blood sprays hot against my cheek. My hands shake.

"What the fuck was that?" I breathe. But there's no time. The battle rages on, brutal and relentless.

And I still feel him.

Feel the strain of him holding on—barely.

Every time he takes a hit, the ache echoes in my bones.

His pain is mine now.

And he's losing.

A guard lunges for Seren—blade aimed for her unguarded back.

"Seren, down!" I scream, throwing my whole body forward. I

tackle the guard mid-swing, my pike plunging into his side. His blood soaks into my gauntlets, but I don't stop—not when Seren scrambles free, not when another slash grazes my shoulder, not when the phantom pain from Kael's fight somewhere in these tunnels flares again.

His strength is draining fast.

I can feel the tremor in the Shadowweave, the threads threatening to snap.

"Kael, hold on!"

I don't know if he can hear me.

Don't care.

And then—

Like a ghost of a thought, his voice brushes the edge of my mind—

Raw. Ragged. But sure.

"For you? Always."

CHAPTER FIFTY-SIX

ELYSSARA

I see him then.

Kael.

Buckling at the knees. Sword slipping from his grasp. Sweat slicking his skin, his breath coming too fast, too ragged.

"Kael!" His name rips from my throat, raw, desperate—terror overtaking everything else.

I move, carving a path toward him, but I'm too far, the press of bodies slowing me down.

Too slow.

A guard steps forward, towering over him, blade gleaming as he crouches low—aiming straight for Kael's throat.

"No—"

The guard pauses, the tip of his sword hovering just shy of skin. A cruel smile spreads across his face. "Well, we've been looking for you for years, son," he sneers, tilting his blade just enough to catch the flickering torchlight. "And now I've got myself a pretty little Lightborne and a—"

He never finishes.

Because something inside me breaks.

Magic slams into my ribs like a living thing, thrashing, fighting against the binds still caging half of it away.

It wants out.

It wants blood.

The pressure swells—hot and suffocating—boiling in my veins, clawing through every limb like wildfire, hungry and endless. The air thickens, humming with power.

The guard senses it—they all do.

He glances up at me, and for the first time, I see it. *Fear.*

I unspool.

Tear my magic free.

The world splits apart.

Light detonates from my hands, raw and unchained, a force that shakes the ground beneath us.

A scream rips from my throat, guttural and primal, as I flood the tunnels with white-hot Lightborne magic—a storm of celestial power unleashed.

But Kael doesn't burn. As if responsive to my intentions, the magic cocoons him, wrapping him in an unbreakable shield—safe. *Mine.*

But the others?

The ones who tried to take from me?

Who thought they could touch him?

They don't stand a chance.

The light consumes them—shredding through flesh, searing through armor, reducing them to nothing but flickering embers in the air.

No screams.

No time to beg.

One heartbeat, they exist.

The next, they're ash.

And the tunnels fall silent.

CHAPTER FIFTY-SEVEN
KAEL

THE WORLD WAVERS AT THE EDGES, EXHAUSTION PRESSING DOWN
like a blade to my throat. The cloak is still in place. I feel the threads
of shadow stretching thin, unraveling, but I grit my teeth and hold
them. Nyx. Aura. Just a little longer. If I let go now, The Joining's
soldiers would see them—would know.

My breath shudders in my lungs.

And then I see her. *Elyssara.*

Standing apart from the others, magic still humming in the air
around her. Untouched. Unshaken. A star in the dark.

And I wonder if she even knows the weight of what she just did.

Gods. She's fucking powerful.

Therion and Merrik haul me to my feet, sweat still beading
along my skin, my legs nearly giving out beneath me. Every part of
me feels hollowed out, as if the magic siphoned straight through my
bones.

Jax whistles low, arms crossed as she fixes Elyssara with an
unreadable stare. "Well, that was something. Probably could've done
that from the start and saved us the hassle, eh?"

"Jaxxy," Merrik rubs his temples, exasperated. "Can you ever
just... *not?*"

"What? Just saying." She grins. "If we're all done being dramatic, can we go before the next round of bastards show up?"

Therion claps a hand on my shoulder, steadying me. "We need to move, brother. Now. We need to get into The Wastes before anyone else comes looking for... *her*."

His eyes flick toward Elyssara.

She's standing apart from the others, shoulders stiff, hands clenched at her sides. Tortured. Confused.

I fall back from the others, slowing my pace to match hers, giving myself a reprieve.

"So now it's you saving me, Duskae." I try to keep it light, give her something to hold onto. "I think I'd make a decent damsel in distress, don't you?"

I brush my fingers along hers, just once. A grounding tether. She doesn't pull away.

She doesn't blink.

"What... was that?" Her voice is low, almost raw.

I don't have to ask what she means. I know. Because I felt her, too.

Her panic for me. Her darkness.

I exhale. "I... don't exactly know."

Her eyes flick to mine—silver-rimmed, bright with emotion she doesn't quite let fall.

"I felt you," she whispers. "And I think... I've been feeling it for a while."

I swallow hard.

"I know." My voice drops to something quieter. "I feel you, too." And I think it's only getting stronger.

CHAPTER FIFTY-EIGHT

ELYSSARA

THE TUNNEL STRETCHES ENDLESSLY, PLUNGING DEEPER INTO THE earth's crust, swallowing sound, light, and life as it goes.

Kael's breathing is labored, rasps and wheezes escape him, alongside his scuffing feet and skin slick with sweat—evidently still holding the cloak in place over Aura and Nyx. I could tell him to drop the cloak. But I already know—Kael would rather die than risk exposing us. *Stubborn bastard.*

"I'll be right back," I throw over my shoulder to Kael as I run to catch up to Seren, who's still brandishing her crossbow and looks as if she might squash it to death.

"I need to talk to you," I say, and by the erratic jump she answers with, Seren did not hear me coming.

"Of course, of course," she says, flustered. "What about exactly? Are you okay?"

"I'm... confused," I say, brows knitting together. "I... can feel him."

"What do you mean 'feel him'? Like emotionally or..." she trails off.

"Here," I say, tapping my chest. "And I know this sounds absolutely insane, but I think... I heard his thoughts."

Seren's composure shatters—her face turns ghostly pale, and she grips the crossbow like it might keep her upright. "When? How?" she says with intense scrutiny.

Well, if I knew that, I wouldn't be fucking asking.

"I—"

But before I can continue, Therion halts, holding his hand up to stop the group. Kael doubles over, taking respite with his hands on his knees, and Merrik and Jax automatically take up fighting stances.

"Light," Therion states simply, pointing to the end of the tunnel.

"'Bout fuckin' time," Merrik grunts out, wiping sweat from his brow.

The air in the tunnels is stagnant and suffocating, the acrid stench is a reflection of the nonexistent ventilation and festering remnants of smugglers' deals gone wrong. The thought of light, air, and sunshine is a welcome reprieve from the tunnels and my own circuitous thoughts.

"And I'm assuming we can expect another little party of armies, rebels, and pointy things when we emerge?" Ronyn quips nonchalantly.

"Well, now that we know the Lightborne can just blast them, we should be fine, right?" Jax snarks.

I consider biting back, but Jax's need to provoke me is becoming insufferable. Tiresome. Repetitive. Predictable. Perhaps I'll blast *her*. Just a little.

Kael's head jerks toward me. Eyes wide. Shocked. Like I shouted straight into his mind. He gives me an almost imperceptible shake of the head as if cautioning me from following through on my thoughts. And I know it now—*he can hear me, too.*

"For the love of all the Stars in the sky, Jax," Kael wheezes again, his voice barely more than a croak. "Would you shut the fuck up?"

Ignoring everyone's bickering, Therion gets right down to business. "I can't sense anything out of the ordinary, but I'll go out first with Jax," his tone is all command. He looks at Jax. "Channel from me, and we'll head out ahead of the group, secure the horses, clear the area, and ensure we have an exit strategy into some cover."

Jax has a scowl on her face, and I assume she's about to argue—that's what she does—but she gives a tight, reluctant nod and makes her way to Therion.

We all seem to agree that we move silently the rest of the way.

I can still feel him.

The awareness of Kael lingers at the edges of my mind, a tether I never sought, never wanted, but now cannot seem to shake. The realization that he can feel me, too—that he heard me—is something else entirely. A prickle of unease settles at the base of my spine. *What else did he hear? How deep does this connection go?*

I swallow hard, keeping my eyes trained on the faint light ahead, though my mind is anything but steady.

This... this should not be possible. This is another complication in a tangle of problems I don't have time to solve.

But the fact remains: I am not alone in my head anymore.

Therion turns around and places a hand on the small of Seren's back, whispering something into her ear. I notice the way Ronyn flinches at the sight, his lips pressing into a thin line. Okay, I guess we'll talk about whatever *that* was later.

Seren moves quickly towards the rest of us, instructing us to stay here for thirty heartbeats. We wait, bodies stilling against the background hiss of Kael's breathing. Therion and Jax surge ahead, and we wait.

No ambush. No fight. No clang of metal.

We edge out of the tunnels, creeping into a small clearing near an abandoned and dilapidated outpost. I turn to look for Kael, when an arrow sings through the air—

"DOWN!" Ronyn leaps for Seren and me, his body crushing us against the dry, packed dirt.

I look up to see the arrow jutting from the rock, less than the width of a fingernail above Kael's head.

Kael stands up straight, a smirk kicking up the right side of his mouth.

Within a single heartbeat, he drops the cloak over Nyx and Aura who become visible in the clearing, and without credence to his injuries and exhaustion, charges into the lifeless trees.

A lone man breaks from the trees, chestnut hair blowing back as he runs, his sharp, fox-like amber eyes meeting Kael's as they sprint towards each other.

I draw my Starforged Blade and a throwing dagger, about to unleash them when instead of a clash of swords, I hear the clash of chests—an embrace, laughter, levity.

"You missed," Kael teased.

"You know I only miss when I mean to, ya bastard!" the man taunts, but there is no mistaking the fondness in his tone.

"Time to go," Therion breaks the reunion with a terse timbre.

"Don't be like that, ya grumpy ass," the man chides. "Get in here." The man pulls Therion into the embrace, and I can see how at home Therion feels.

I sheathe my weapons again and move to make my way to them when Ronyn sails past, a roguish grin on his face. "I like him."

"Things are about to get a whole lot... louder," Merrik exhales the words, as if already exasperated by the pairing Ronyn and this new man will make.

"Daelen, can't say I've missed you," Jax croons, though she embraces him all the same.

"Jaxxy, still being difficult, I assume?" Daelen quips.

Maybe I like him too.

"You fuckin' know she has, Dae," Merrik growls, clasping Daelen's arm in a warrior's embrace. "It's been too long, brother."

The group take a moment to reunite, affection and camaraderie flowing freely, when Ronyn clears his throat, asserting himself. "You don't know me yet, but I'm the better-looking, more talented, and generally quicker-witted version of whatever you've got going on. Ronyn, at your service."

He extends a hand. Daelen stares at it.

A beat passes—just long enough for me to consider drawing the Starforged Blade again—before Daelen roars with laughter, grabs Ronyn's hand, and yanks him into a handshake-turned-hug.

Daelen looks to his comrades and grins. "I like him."

"Dae, this is Elyssara, the Lightborne, and this is Seren," Therion asserts simply.

Daelen's eyes meet mine, and I swear I sense sadness, perhaps even resignation, in them. He lingers on me before extending a hand, "Elyssara, it's a pleasure." He turns to Seren then, and a warm smile graces his face, as if hoping to disarm her, "I look forward to working with you, Seren."

Before I can respond, Therion shifts, as if sensing something. We all notice, and go straight for our weapons, eyes darting, searching, seeking answers for whatever has put Therion on edge.

Through the trees, a tall man with ashen white hair and pulled back in a simple tail with a leather strap walks with an unsettlingly controlled and powerful gait. The others sheathe their weapons, but they don't relax completely, especially Therion, who looks decidedly uneasy with the man's presence.

The tall, sinewed figure stalks toward us, his blue-gray eyes bore into me, as if my very existence is a burden to him.

"Oh yeah," Daelen drawls, "I forgot to mention that fuckin' Zakarius brought himself along on this little adventure of mine."

"How the fuck did he know you were coming?" Kael grits out, some color and energy returning to him now that the cloak has dropped.

"He's not an Aetherstride, Kael, but he tracked me all the way from camp to here without a single fucking sound," Daelen explains, though his irritation is evident.

"Fuck's sake," Merrik exhales. I tuck the reactions away into my mind for analysis later. *They do not like this man.*

The closer Zakarius gets, the more unsettled I feel. His stormy gaze flicks over me, unimpressed. Dismissive.

Then he exhales through his nose, barely concealing his disdain.

"I see you didn't just find the Lightborne. You picked up a few strays along the way." A scoff, cold as ice. "Not the plan, Kael."

There's something in the way he looks at me that makes my stomach tighten. Not curiosity. Not interest. Not even disdain. *Calculation.*

Like he's assessing risk. Like I'm a problem that needs solving.

Or removing.

A flicker of something cold flashes in his dark eyes—gone too fast for me to name.

I swallow hard, forcing my spine straight.

I notice a subtle shift beside me. *Kael.*

I don't need to look at him to know his body has gone rigid, that he's already picked up whatever passed between Zakarius and me.

His fingers flex at his sides. Just slightly. But enough for me to know that he sees it all.

Kael doesn't respond straight away, as if weighing his words.

He exhales, long and controlled, "I think you forget that I make the fucking rules, Zakarius," his voice pure menace. "And you? You execute them," he pauses for another moment, and I think he's done, but he adds, "like an obedient dog."

Zakarius doesn't react right away. Doesn't bristle. Doesn't scowl. He just... looks at Kael. Long. Unblinking.

Then, ever so slightly, his lips curve—just the barest flicker of something that might be amusement. Might be rage.

"Careful," he murmurs, voice smooth as cut glass. "An obedient dog only heels for so long before it bites."

Kael doesn't take the bait—instead, he shrugs off the threat like it's beneath him.

He smirks, "Bite all you want, Zak. A dog's still a dog."

Zakarius exhales, a slow, measured thing, as if filing Kael's words away for later. "We'll see." A pause, just long enough to feel like a promise. "We always do."

I could slice the tension in the air with my blade, tempers running hot, primal urges to fight rippling off both men.

"Are you two done measuring dicks yet? Or can we get the fuck out of here?" For the first time ever, I'm actually relieved to hear Jax speak.

"Here! Here!" Merrik chants in agreement.

Thank the gods.

As if snapping out of some sort of spell, Zakarius' demeanor changes from stone cold to tactical. "I've mapped a route out of here that will avoid every checkpoint and watch tower inside The Decay."

"Well, lead the way, Zak," Therion encourages, exasperation heavy on his tongue.

Zakarius spins on his heel, movements sharp and controlled.

Not a glance back.

"Try to keep up."

I grit my teeth.

Guess we're going to Thornewood.

Gods help us.

PART III
HOME

CHAPTER FIFTY-NINE
ELYSSARA

NYX MOVES WITH EFFORTLESS GRACE, HIS HOOVES BARELY STIRRING
the dust as he glides across the fractured earth, as if he knows—
down to his bones—that this land is home. The Shadow Wastes are
everything I expected: desolate, barren, a landscape flayed open by
curse and ruin.

The ground beneath us is cracked and thirsty, gaping wounds of
scorched rock and ashen soil stretching in every direction. Wind
howls through skeletal trees, their blackened limbs brittle and
lifeless.

I close my eyes for a breath, summoning the memory of Skaedor's Crest, of the view from that towering height. The image aligns
seamlessly with what lies before me now—this place is a wound.
Gaping. Festering. Stripped of all it once was.

I try to reconcile how these people—Kael, Therion, Jax, Merrik,
Daelen, Zakarius—were born to these lands. How people of such
skill, intellect and *color* can be born of such lifeless monotony.

Everywhere I look, there is just... gray. Not even the sun can
pierce through the gray scale clouds and smoky mist that permanently cloaks the sky here.

Kael's grip around my waist tightens, as if he can feel the weight of my revulsion pressing through the tether.

"Not what you were expecting, Duskae?" he asks, though there is no hiding the tenderness there.

For a moment, I can't speak, can't think of anything to say about this... nothingness.

"It's exactly what I was expecting," I eventually answer, "and that is absolutely terrifying." I partially turn to him in the saddle, eyes locking on each other, "I just can't figure out how *you* are from *here*."

He huffs a laugh, "If that's a compliment, El, I'll take it." His gaze turns more serious then, "You'll understand very soon."

"Okay," I say slowly at his ambiguity.

Zakarius takes us on his perfectly mapped route through The Shadow Wastes, and we don't see a single soldier, outpost or watch tower. Fortunately, the prick is impressively good at his job.

We ride past the husks of what were once homes—ramshackle structures with walls sagging inward, their wooden beams brittle and splintered from years of neglect. Some are little more than weather-beaten frames, their roofs long since caved in, leaving only scarce remnants. I've never seen The Shadow Wastes as anything other than this. Nor have my parents or their parents—the curse extending well beyond our lifetimes and into the recesses of history. But stories of what lived before travel on the wind in whispers. Whispers of what could be again, if only this wretched curse was broken.

The wind howls through the ruins, dragging loose materials and splintered planks across the ground, their scraping echoes reverberating through the emptiness. Doors hang from rusted hinges, creaking endlessly—the sound serving as the anthem to this forsaken place.

Even the wind feels wrong here. A hollow howl through lifeless streets. It doesn't carry birdsong, or the rustling of leaves, or the distant murmur of a world moving forward.

And then, movement.

A shadow flickers behind the remains of a doorway—a hunched

figure, wrapped in threadbare cloth, eyes hollow with fear. Another shifts behind a shattered window, their face gaunt, their skin stretched tight over bones. The moment they see us, doors creak shut, wooden slats hurriedly drawn across windows, blocking us out as if our very presence might bring death upon them.

A child—small, filthy, his ribs visible beneath a tattered shirt—stands frozen in the street, clutching something to his chest. His mother appears a second later, snatching him back into the shadows, vanishing behind a splintered door that slams shut with finality.

One man, draped in rags so threadbare I can see the jut of his bones, does not flee. He just stands in a doorway, eyes hollow, watching us pass. He does not beg. He does not cower. He only stares.

Not with hope. Not even with fear. But with despair that turns my stomach.

They've learned that in The Shadow Wastes, hope is a luxury they can't afford.

My chest aches at the resignation in their eyes—there is no more hope, no more desire to simply get through the day. They have given up.

Even the Virellin slums, as ruthless as they were, pulsed with something. A fight to survive. A hunger for tomorrow. But here? Here, there is nothing but surrender.

Kael's voice rumbles low, interrupting my thoughts, "Are you ready to understand?"

He lurches forward on Nyx, into what looks like more cracked earth. Before I can even think, I shout, "Wait—what do you—"

A tremor ripples through the air, a force I can't name but feel in my bones. My stomach lurches, weight vanishing from my limbs as if the ground itself has fallen away. A gasp rips from my throat—except I'm not falling, not really. But for a moment, I am nowhere. I am nothing.

And then—the world does not shift. It does not change. *It folds.*
Bending. Warping. Buckling. The world twisting in on itself.
One breath, and the air is dry, lifeless.
The next, and I am drowning.

Damp air swells in my lungs, heavy with rain-drenched earth and flowers, so vivid it's dizzying. Leaves glisten, fat droplets of water clinging to emerald canopies that stretch impossibly high, swallowing the sky. Beneath them, the earth is dark and rich, every inch teeming with life.

I stagger, chest heaving. It is too much. Too bright. Too full. My mind cannot hold both places at once. Cannot reconcile the death behind me with the impossible paradise before me.

I rip Kael's arms from my waist, unfolding myself from his embrace and scramble down from Nyx.

My hands tremble. My knees buckle. I sink to the damp earth, pressing my fingers into the rich, fertile soil, as if needing to confirm it is real. Needing to ground myself in something. *Anything.*

I clamber to the blooms, they glow with a soft, impossible light, their violet-blue petals open and abundant, thriving as if the world has never known hunger. Their beauty takes my breath away. My eyes prickle with tears threatening to spill down my cheeks, and this time, I don't stop them. I have stolen these for Seren countless times, risked my life to get a glimpse of them, sold my meagre possessions —my body—for just one, and here they are, wild, free and abundant. I pick one, two, three of the flowers from their stems, marveling at their radiant allure.

Ronyn and Seren drop to their knees beside me, arms wrapping around mine, grounding me in memory itself—like Revryn's loft, like hope. Seren's dusty cheeks show the trail her tears have left, her smile in full bloom, and I think it might be the most beautiful thing I've ever seen.

"A lunafleur for you, Little Star," I croak, tucking the lunafleur bloom behind her ear amongst her tangled web of golden curls, just as I always did. "As many as you like, actually." Seren's breath hitches. Her fingers fly to the bloom, brushing its petals in disbelief.

Her gaze snaps to mine. And I know she's remembering, too.

And it's then, pressing a palm into the earth, clutching the lunafleur to my chest with the other, that I realize The Shadow Wastes were never a wasteland. *They were a lie.*

CHAPTER SIXTY

KAEL

She is beautiful.

Not just in the way I have always known, in the way that turns heads and makes men stumble over their words—but in a way that feels otherworldly.

Her joy is as bright as her magic. It radiates from her in waves, unrestrained and uninhibited, as if she has forgotten, for the first time in her life, how to be anything but *free*.

A mane of undulating auburn frames her face and tumbles down her back, rich as the earth. She moves through the wildflowers with the lightness of someone who has never known a place like this could exist—dragging her hands through the lunafleurs, pressing them to her nose with an audible inhale, eyes alight with something soft. Something I didn't know she possessed.

A goddess.

I don't know if it's the tether—the connection that refuses to quit between us—or if it's simply *her*. But I feel it too. *Her wonder. Her breathlessness. Her awe.*

It seeps into me, as if her emotions have taken root in my own, twining together like vines.

I glance toward our group and find Therion with a subtle,

knowing smile, his gaze lingering on Seren. Merrik is grinning outright, and I know why—*this is why we fight*. This is what we're trying to restore. To lift the curse. To free our people. To return *this* to them.

Daelen slaps Merrik on the back in easy camaraderie, sharing a look of understanding. *This is how it's meant to be.* Even Jax, ever unimpressed, looks momentarily stunned before quickly masking it behind a scowl.

The moment is fragile.

And then, like a blade cleaving through silk—

"We keep going," Zakarius snaps, his voice as cold and cutting as the steel at his hip. "Every moment we stop, we make ourselves easy targets."

The dream fractures. The moment is over.

But when I glance back at Elyssara—kneeling in the grass, laughter still on her lips—I can't shake the feeling that some part of her just found something she hadn't even known she was looking for.

Ronyn spins toward the group, arms crossed, head tilted, that signature roguish grin tugging at his lips.

"I have a few... *thousand* questions," he says, throwing his hands wide as if trying to physically encompass the absurdity of it all. "Like, oh, I don't know—maybe mentioning the existence of an entire hidden paradise would've been helpful? Cryptic assholes, the lot of you."

A startled laugh tumbles out of me before I can stop it, quick and sharp, like something unshackled. Therion barks a real, unguarded laugh—a rare thing from him.

Merrik's rich chuckle ripples through the air, "We protect our land like we protect our people, lad—with our lives."

Seren's mouth falls open. "Wait, what? There's no record of this anywhere!"

I nod. "It's forbidden to keep records here."

She looks ready to combust. "But that's—"

"And," I cut in, "you can wield magic whenever you want—no

mandatory Royal Guard, so no one is keeping track of the magic they sense."

Seren looks like I just told her the sky was a lie. "So, Starborn are just... free?"

Zakarius exhales sharply, disdain twisting his mouth. "She doesn't belong here."

His glare is fixed on Elyssara—not in curiosity, not in scrutiny, but in *contempt*. A silent fury ripples from him, his hands clenched tight over his reins, jaw ticking with the force of his restraint.

He sees only danger in her, a threat to everything he swore to protect—his home, his people, our mission.

His glare is like a blade at her throat. Cold. Controlled.

"She was never supposed to see this. Never supposed to know." Not just anger—fear flickers beneath his scowl, fear for our home, fear for what she might bring.

His gaze flicks to me, sharp as steel. "This is your fault."

The light in Elyssara's eyes dims just slightly. Before she can speak, I do.

"You're right. It *is* my fault." I tilt my head, let my voice go cold. "Because I make the fucking rules, Zak."

I meet his gaze, let the words settle between us, cold and callous. *A challenge.*

Zakarius exhales sharply through his nose, barely concealing his disdain. He doesn't argue. But the tension between us stretches taut, a thread pulled to the edge of breaking.

Not yet. But soon.

Elyssara's expression is neutral now, but I feel her curiosity—an eager, searching thing—pressing at the edges of my mind. A whisper of thought against mine, seeking, prying.

I turn back to the others. "Starborn are free, yes," I concede, "but that doesn't mean Elyssara won't be hunted for her power." I meet her gaze, her piercing green eyes locking onto mine with quiet conviction. "Either to be used as a weapon... or removed as a threat to the throne."

Or fucking breeding like that fucking asshole from the Covenant said.

Elyssara's eyes narrow, and at first, I think it's in fear, but I feel something else. *Resolve.*

"There's a lot to learn, and as much as I loathe to agree with Zak, we should go," Merrik states.

He's right. We mount the horses and commence the last section of our journey home to Thornewood.

We enter the Riverian Jungle—the jungle I spent summers in as a child, ran through with Nalya, foraged in, hunted in, and now, fight for.

The moment we move beneath its emerald canopy, I feel like I can breathe.

The ground, rich and dark, pulses with life, each step sinking slightly into the fertile soil. Towering trees stretch toward the heavens, their trunks thick as fortress walls, their bark webbed with veins of glowing blue—a faint bioluminescence that pulses like a heartbeat.

Vines twist and coil around the massive roots that carve through the earth, weaving an intricate tapestry of green and gold, their leaves broad and waxen, shimmering where sunlight filters through the canopy. Native fruits, plump and glistening, dangle from branches high above, their colors vibrant—deep indigos, searing oranges, and all manner of hues that whisper of magic.

The river runs alongside us, a cascade of molten silver in the moonlight, its surface dappled with the glow of tiny, luminescent fish that dart like scattered stardust.

I inhale deeply, and for the first time in weeks, I feel the weight in my chest loosen. *Home.* The Riverian Jungle is alive in a way that no other place in Aevryn is—wild, untamed, unconquered.

And as I glance down to Elyssara, watching as she tilts her head back onto my chest, eyes wide, mouth slightly parted in wonder, I know she feels it too.

This place is *power.* A secret that has been guarded for centuries —since the curse. A land untouched by the hands of kings and conquerors.

"How is this possible?" She whispers, disbelief and hope tangled in her voice. I know exactly what she means—*how can beauty like this still exist when everything else has turned to ash?*

"The Shadow Wastes are real," I start, "they're just not the whole story."

"Obviously," she says with sarcasm, gesturing her arms around the Riverian Jungle.

I can't help the smirk that pulls at my lips. "Good point." I suck in a long breath, readying myself to reveal my kingdom's well-guarded secrets. But she deserves to know. She deserves to know what we want her to fight for with us. But more than that, I *want* to tell her.

Nyx is smooth underneath us, the rhythm of his gait a steadying presence that urges me on.

"These lands were not always The Shadow Wastes. Centuries ago, the entire land looked like this jungle. The entire place was a paradise," I close my eyes, recalling the stories from my father and his father. Stories of beauty, and peace. "We call these lands Zerynthia."

Elyssara's eyes widen in realization. "Zerynthia," the words come out in an awed whisper. "How did the lands become like... *that?*" She points back to where we'd come from.

"Centuries ago, Zerynthia warred against itself. The Starborn treated the Earthbound as if they were nothing—they took away their rights, their land, their wives," I begin.

"Sounds familiar," Elyssara scoffs.

"The Earthbound fought back with organized armies and attacks. It started a civil war that lasted seven decades. It divided our people and ripped our lands apart."

Elyssara holds her breath, desperately waiting for me to continue. "Then what?"

"The gods stepped in. Or, one god did," I correct myself. "Morrathys."

Elyssara's breath hitches in shock. "God of Death," she offers.

I nod. "Morrathys didn't like the Starborn and Earthbound playing god over death. They used magic to resurrect or destroy at will, corrupting the natural order. Morrathys intervened because death belongs only to him."

"How? How could he do that?" Her desperation is palpable.

"Because it was not the way of the Zerynthian people. We are a people of power, peace and prosperity, and we lost our way," I say simply. "And now, our land is divided by The Decay. Morrathys made The Decay like a mirror, a prison of our own making. The people within it see only desolation, leashed to the curse, never knowing they walk inches from paradise."

She shakes her head, breath sharp and uneven. "Tell me how we end this."

No hesitation. No fear. Just raw defiance.

I turn to her, watching how the light peaks through the canopy and catches in her eyes.

I grip the reins tighter, "We take down Maldrak, and reclaim Zerynthia."

CHAPTER SIXTY-ONE
ELYSSARA

I repeat the words again and again in my mind, trying to reconcile everything I thought I knew. The words ripple through me, strange, new and curious.

Zerynthia.

My heart pounds, thrumming in my veins at this revelation. This jungle feels alive—more alive than anywhere I've ever been. Magic hums through the earth, whispers in the leaves, dances in the light filtering through the canopy like scattered Stars.

This is what freedom feels like.

But beneath my awe, unease curls through me like smoke. Zakarius's glare is like a blade at my throat, icy contempt radiating from him. My stomach knots painfully. The hostility is personal, undeniable, and alarming. But Kael's fierce protectiveness rises behind me, wrapping around my unease like armor. There's something unspoken but palpable between them that they're not telling me, and I'm determined to find out what it is.

I turn slightly, glancing up at Kael, his gaze fixed ahead, jaw tight with determination. A question presses urgently against my lips, words begging to be spoken.

But another feeling rises, softer, quieter.

Trust.

Tell me everything, I think, directing my thoughts to Kael. *Make me believe in your dream.*

A curious, hopeful part of me thinks that perhaps I'll hear Kael just like I did in the tunnel. That I'll hear a soothing echo of his thoughts, but there's nothing but silence as we rhythmically glide along on Nyx.

"The dream," Kael says, breaking the hush, "is to reclaim Zerynthia. Kill Maldrak. End The Decay. Give my people a home again."

The rich timbre of his voice soothes me, but I still feel uneasy.

It feels impossible to turn The Shadow Wastes into anything other than what it is. How will we ever do that? How can I even help?

Kael's voice nudges into my mind, sensing my unease. *We'll restore it, Elyssara. I promise you.* Then his tone shifts, teasing, low and seductive. *But first, allow me to distract you...*

"You can hear me," I breathe, astounded by the occurrence yet again.

That gorgeous smile kicks up on one side, before he speaks in a low rumble, "Oh, I can hear you, Duskae." His palm spreads across my abdomen, sliding slowly downward, grazing my thigh teasingly. "Even before I could hear you, I could *feel* you... everywhere," he breathes the words like a prayer to the Stars themselves.

My breath hitches, and before I can speak, his voice caresses the boundaries of my mind. *You have no idea of the ways I will worship you when we get home, Duskae.* His hand trails back up my inner thigh towards my center, and I gasp.

"Kael—," I murmur weakly, though I don't mean it in the slightest.

"For fuckin' Stars' sake, spare an old man's eyes, will ya?" Merrik grumbles, though amusement sparks behind his exasperation. "I'm too old for this shit."

"And they say I'm the grumpy one," Therion quips, a small smile breaking through.

"Did Therion just make a joke?" Ronyn quips, jaw open wide in mock surprise. "I thought the biggest revelation would be this Zerynthian paradise, not that Therion actually has a sense of humor!"

Daelen's laughter explodes out of him, and even Jax grins widely.

Kael chuckles quietly behind me, his chest vibrating with quiet laughter. He leans closer, voice soft, seductive and meant only for me. "We'll pick this up later, El."

Heat flushes my cheeks, anticipation and embarrassment tangled together. But the moment of levity is fleeting as Kael straightens, suddenly alert, his hand tightening on the reins.

"Quiet," Zakarius murmurs sharply, and Therion has already raised his fist to halt the group. Instantly, every warrior tenses, weapons quietly drawn, laughter dying on their lips.

The jungle falls silent, unnaturally so. The hairs on my arms rise, a shiver racing down my spine. Even the fireflies seem to still, the pulsing bioluminescence of the trees dimming slightly, as if holding their breath.

Kael's voice cuts low through the stillness, a blade of sound slicing the silence. "Something's near."

I reach instinctively for my dagger, pulse quickening. A subtle rustle, a whisper of movement through foliage, and I feel Kael's muscles tense behind me, coiled and ready.

Then Merrik's voice comes steady and certain from my left, "Relax. They're ours."

Shadows detach from the trees ahead—figures dressed in rich leathers dyed deep greens and browns, adorned with subtle streaks of silver and sapphire, blending seamlessly with the jungle.

"Commander," one man says, stepping forward, inclining his head respectfully to Kael, forming the same inverted triangle symbol with his hands that Finn showed me in Galreth. "We've been expecting you."

Kael nods, relief easing the tension in his posture. "It's good to see you, Varian."

Varian glances briefly at me, curiosity glinting in his amber eyes, but he says nothing, turning back to Kael. "The gates are open. Thornewood awaits."

Kael nudges Nyx forward, guiding us beneath a thickening canopy of leaves. My breath catches as the trees part, unveiling Thornewood.

It rises before me—a city crafted into nature itself. Massive trees cradle homes and structures seamlessly woven into the forest, lit by glowing lanterns and delicate bioluminescence. Wooden bridges arch gracefully through the air, interlacing between platforms built into branches thicker than palace walls.

My breath leaves in a quiet exhale.

I've lived my whole life believing there were only two kinds of places in Aevryn: those that devoured you, and those that demanded your soul to survive. But this...

Thornewood is neither.

This isn't just a hidden paradise. This is a civilization thriving within it.

Kael leans in close once more, voice warm against my ear. "Welcome home, Elyssara."

CHAPTER SIXTY-TWO

ELYSSARA

Varian and two other men walk ahead, guiding us deeper into the verdant heart of Thornewood—Kael's home. Small children peek out from homes built seamlessly into the trees, their wide eyes sparkling at the sight of Kael, their commander. Pride shines in their innocent gazes, mirroring the respect radiating from the men and women lining the natural pathways formed by massive, twisting roots.

My astonishment deepens into awe, and something more profound—something akin to yearning—tightens in my chest as I absorb the civilization Kael and his companions have built here. Beyond the city in the trees, veils of water cascade down jagged cliffs, catching the sunlight like liquid jewels before pooling into clear lakes. The constant, soothing rhythm of the waterfalls fills the air with misty coolness, blending harmoniously with the calls of vibrant birds and the rustling leaves.

Kael's thumb traces lazy circles against my waist, pulling me gently back into the present and interrupting my reverence.

And that's when I notice—

Kael's people lined the paths, each dropping to one knee,

forming the inverted triangle symbol. Awe, reverence, and relief mingle openly on their faces, and tears glisten on some of their cheeks.

What is going on? I direct the urgent thought toward Kael.

I feel faint amusement and the gentle brush of laughter in response.

I'm not kidding, Kael. What the fuck is happening?

But before he can reply, a young woman with a vibrant, joyful face and wild, dusty-blonde hair streaming behind her races toward us. Herbs, twigs and potions dangle from a belt at her waist, and dirt smears across her cheek.

"Teddy!" she calls, excitement lifting her voice into an unrestrained shout. "Teddy!"

I glance around, bewildered, wondering who in the Stars she's calling to. The young woman barrels toward Therion, joy lighting her features as she throws herself into his arms, even as he remains mounted on Aura. Therion nestles his face into her sandy hair, which tumbles in unruly waves, gradually lightening to a vivid white at the tips.

When she turns slightly, I glimpse her beautiful eyes—burnished bronze, luminous and familiar.

And that's when it clicks—

Her hair. Her eyes. Even down to her sun-kissed, golden skin. *She's unmistakably Therion's blood.*

Yes, Kael's voice rumbles softly through my mind. *That's his little sister, Rubinia.*

And Teddy? I ask.

That light chuckle returns to my mind again before he says, *a nickname from when he was a boy that Rubi has never let go of.*

That's... oddly sweet, considering we're talking about Therion here, I reply.

Varian clears his throat, drawing our attention. Rubinia quickly releases Therion, smoothing her skirts and lands a playful punch on his thigh.

In an almost regal voice, Varian bellows for the whole city to hear, "Today is a most joyful day, for we are welcoming home true heroes of Zerynthia who, each day, take us one step closer to restoring our homeland to its former glory, power, and freedom!" Varian's voice fills with authority and eminence.

Cheers of fierce agreement ripple through the trees, the people of Thornewood clapping and whistling with great pride. Honor, even.

"Our deepest gratitude to Merrik Havlyn and Jax Dewhirst, whose infiltration of the Dravari Guard has brought critical intelligence to our cause!" Varian continues.

Another wave of cheers crashes through Thornewood. My pulse quickens, trying desperately to track this dizzying new world. I glance at Kael, searching for answers, but his face is an unreadable mask.

Varian lifts his hand, bringing instant silence. "We honor Therion Ashborne, General of War to the Rightful Crown, for securing both the Astral Compass and Elyssara, the Lightborne!"

General of War to who?

My breath catches sharply, and confusion surges. But the cheers become deafening, joyous, and unstoppable before I can process it.

Varian's voice rises higher still, booming through the air. "And above all, we bow to His Royal Highness, Prince Kael Thorne—the rightful heir to the throne of Zerynthia!"

THE WHAT—

My heart stops.

My breath stolen entirely from my lungs.

Prince Kael Thorne?

Heir to the throne of Zerynthia?

Impossible.

My ears ring with the din of the Zerynthian people celebrating the return of their Prince.

My head spins wildly, the world tipping dangerously beneath me. I grip Nyx's mane tightly, anchoring myself as I whip my gaze toward Kael. He shifts in the saddle, sitting up a little straighter and lifting his chin. He settles quickly and turns utterly still, commanding and striking—every inch the prince I never knew he was.

I stare back at the crowd—they're back on one knee, the

inverted triangle symbol pressed to their hearts—and their cheers are deafening.

And yet, all I can do is stare at Kael, heart pounding, feeling as if the ground beneath me has shattered.

CHAPTER SIXTY-THREE

ELYSSARA

My hands shake with fury as Kael urges Nyx on, waving to the people—*his* people—that line Thornewood's paths. He nods his head at every person we ride past, and I internally berate myself for never noticing the graceful, regal way he moves through life.

How the fuck didn't I notice this?

I will explain everything, Duskae, his voice tumbles through me, caressing my mind with gentility, soothing me. And I resent it.

Like I would trust anything that comes out of your fucking mouth, prince. I spit the last word like an insult, spearing it in his direction.

I'm thrilled to see that my title hasn't done anything to quell your defiance and stubbornness, El, he replies smoothly.

Fuck you and your fucking lies, Kael. Again. I've been lied to again.

He exhales slowly, closing his eyes, as if I've wounded him, but almost imperceptibly, he quickly pulls up that cocky mask in place, before saying, *I've always loved that filthy mouth of yours,* in my direction.

The fucking audacity of him.

I remain silent atop Nyx, and Kael doesn't try to goad or soothe me again.

The crowd thins to nothing, and we all dismount from our horses. I cross my arms, and Seren makes eye contact, but I shake my head firmly at her. I don't want to be soothed, approached, or supported. I want to unleash my magic upon this entire fucking place. I am done with being left in the dark.

Kael gestures to follow him, and if I didn't desperately want answers, I would've ignored him, but luckily for him, I have some questions that *will* be answered today.

Kael gestures toward an enormous tree trunk, its bark smooth from countless journeys upward. Carved elegantly into the wood is a spiraling staircase, climbing effortlessly around the wide girth of the tree. Soft, bioluminescent vines wind along the railing, bathing the ascent in gentle, silvery-blue light. As we climb, the sounds of the forest recede below, leaving only the calming rush of distant waterfalls and the subtle creak of wood beneath our feet.

The space opens around us, seamlessly carved into the sprawling branches of an enormous, ancient tree. The walls are woven from interlocking branches, lush leaves, and spiraling vines that allow soft sunlight to filter through, dappling the polished wooden floor beneath my feet.

At the chamber's center stands a massive round table, expertly carved from the cross-section of a single, immense tree. Its countless rings spiral outward, each marking the passage of years, maybe centuries, a history record laid bare for all to see. Surrounding it, seats formed from smooth, sculpted roots curve naturally, encircling the table like an embrace.

Despite the fury still pulsing through me, I can't help but pause, momentarily stunned by the harmonious beauty and regal simplicity of the space Kael and his people have created high among Thornewood's branches.

"Welcome to Council Hollow," Kael murmurs gently beside me, a quiet pride in his voice.

A few people have already taken a seat on the sculpted roots, as if they've been waiting for us—an elderly woman with silver-streaked dark hair elegantly styled, striking soil-hued eyes, rich brown skin, and a dignified elegance that is hard to miss, an older gentleman with white hair and gray eyes that pin me in place with keen observation, and a younger man who can't be older than twenty years who looks nervous and on edge.

"Take your seats," Kael says with command to the room, gesturing to the large table.

Everyone moves in, and he takes the largest seat, which I am assuming is the head of the table, and Therion takes the seat to his right. He nods to me to take the seat to his left, and I roll my eyes, ignoring him, and opt for the seat directly across from him—the furthest point from him.

I'm seated next to the older woman, and she looks towards me, a warm expression on her face, and her elegant robes whispering softly around her as she inclines her head to me with quiet dignity. "I have long waited to see the Lightborne," she murmurs, eyes bright with restrained curiosity. "Welcome, Elyssara. I am Lady Sylvaine Morelle. Should you need to understand Zerynthia's old bloodlines, I am at your service."

"Lady Sylvaine," I say politely, "it's a pleasure to meet you. And, given that I have only just learned that Zerynthia exists, I have no idea what I need to know."

Lady Sylvaine huffs a laugh at that, "Well, I'm here whenever the time comes."

The young nervous man chances a look at me, and I meet his gaze. He immediately darts his eyes away, unsettled. Lady Sylvaine leans over, sensing my curiosity, murmuring quietly, "That's Rowan Nix, our Keeper of Memories. He stores the history of Zerynthia—everything forbidden to be written down—in his mind. Nothing escapes him."

I whip my eyes to her then, "In his mind? How?"

"Rowan is a Mindweaver—it's old Zerynthian magic from the Nix bloodline," Lady Sylvaine answers simply.

"Magic from his bloodline? I didn't even know that was possible," I whisper my shock.

"Starborn magic isn't the only magic, dear. Especially not in Zerynthia."

What the fuck.

Before I could probe the woman further, Varian commands the

room, "The Zerynthian War Council meeting is now in session. All hail Prince Kael Thorne of Zerynthia!"

Everyone, aside from Ronyn, Seren and me, moves to make the inverted triangle symbol, but Kael dismisses them with a wave.

"No need for all the formality, Varian," Kael instructs. "Let's just get on with it."

Apparently, Varian has a flair for theatrics.

Lady Sylvaine clears her throat, announcing she's about to speak. With her voice smooth and steady, rich with quiet authority, she begins, "While you've been away, Prince Kael, we've quietly strengthened ties beyond our borders. Ambassadors from Caeloria have responded favorably to our messages, and even the emissaries of Nymeris seem intrigued by our message that a true heir to Zerynthia has made himself known after all these years."

Varian chuckles softly, folding his hands with practiced ease. "Indeed. I had the honor of receiving correspondence from Caeloria's High Chancellor myself. They remain tight-lipped, but supportive—watchful of our next moves."

The older gentleman with white hair leans forward. He adds thoughtfully, his gray eyes distant, reflecting a quiet wisdom, "Nymeris is wary as ever—they've always been cautious—but the mere mention of restoring Zerynthia has piqued their curiosity. It's clear our struggle has implications beyond our borders."

Caeloria? Nymeris?

The names echo softly in my mind, strange and intriguing. *Just how much don't I know? How far does Kael's reach extend?*

"That's Eldric Bannon, former Royal Advisor to King Aurius Thorne, and now advisor to Prince Kael," Lady Sylvaine whispers in my ear.

Hold on, the crown is passed down through the bloodline?

Kael intercepts my thoughts and sends one of his own back. *It's a monarchy in Zerynthia, El—not a power play like Dravara.*

I nod to him and Lady Sylvaine, but can't peel my eyes away from the meeting.

"Caeloria need to declare their position. We need to know we have their aid when the time comes," Kael commands.

"I'll press further," Eldric confirms.

"Good," Kael says, then he turns his gaze to Daelen. "Dae, any further knowledge of The Decay since we've been gone?"

Daelen sits up straighter, clearing his throat. The first sign of seriousness I've seen. "We've been tracking its movement," he begins. "It isn't a fixed wall of magic—it breathes, it shifts, it *watches*."

A flicker of unease runs through me at his choice of words. *It watches?*

"We sent scouts to the southern border," he continues, "where it used to be weaker, but the passage we once knew has closed. Completely sealed." He shakes his head, frustrated. "The Decay isn't just a barrier—it *learns*. Every time we find a vulnerability, it adapts."

Therion mutters a curse under his breath.

How did we get across then? I send the question down the tether.

Bloodline access. Kael's response comes quickly.

He folds his hands on the table, expression darkening. "And the people who try to cross?"

Daelen hesitates. "Few return. Those who do…" He exhales, gaze flicking to me briefly before continuing. "They don't remember anything. Sometimes, they forget why they even tried. Sometimes, they forget who they are altogether. Enchanted to wipe memory, most likely."

A cold shiver licks up my spine.

"It's worse than that," Varian adds, his deep voice measured but grim. "Some return… *changed*."

Silence falls over the table.

Merrik tilts his head, his expression unreadable. "Changed how?"

Varian exchanges a glance with Daelen before answering. "They speak of things inside The Decay. Shadows with too many limbs. Whispers that tell them to *stay*." His voice drops lower. "One man… he clawed his own eyes out the night he returned. Said he could still *see* them, watching him."

My stomach twists.

Kael exhales sharply. "So, the southern passage is completely closed?"

Daelen nods. "For now. But we're watching it. There are patterns—weak spots, but they never stay in one place for long."

Kael considers what he's saying for a long moment, the room stays silent, waiting for their Prince. "Monitor it, we'll need to move soon."

"Yes, very lovely," Zakarius says mockingly. "Now, are we going to talk about the plan changes, Kael? Or will you keep the fact that we're no longer prioritizing Nalya from the council?"

All eyes shoot to Kael, shock and confusion marring their faces.

Kael narrows his eyes, boring a hole into Zakarius with pure hate, "We will not be pursuing the original plan, and I will take no questions about it in this meeting."

What original plan? I have so many fucking questions.

"She's your sister, Kael! She's rotting in Maldrak's dungeons, and you're—" Zakarius's voice breaks, just for a second, before he reins it back in, jaw clenching so tightly I hear his teeth grind. "You promised her. You fucking *promised*."

His hands slam against the table, rattling goblets, sending a few scrolls tumbling to the floor. No one speaks.

"What do you think he's doing to her right now?" Zak spits. "Torturing her? Raping her? Starving her?"

Kael doesn't move. Doesn't even blink. The air shifts. Shadows ripple from his chair, crawling up the legs of the table, licking at the wood like hungry fire.

"Nalya doesn't want you, Zak." Kael's voice is calm. Deceptively soft. *Lethal.*

Zakarius flinches. But the anger doesn't fade—it sharpens. For a split second, I swear there's something *devastated* in his eyes, buried beneath the rage.

"You don't get to say that," Zakarius seethes, voice lower now, almost trembling. "You weren't there the night she begged me not to leave."

Oh.

"You're an insult to your father's legacy," he spits the words with venom.

The room holds its breath.

Kael drops his voice even lower, even calmer, "Stop trying to play the knight in shining armor for a princess who doesn't fucking want you, Zak." Kael's face twists into something dark and sinister, "Stop pretending that your role here is anything but a debt I owed your father, and accept that you are nothing but a placeholder until someone around here has finally had enough of your shit." The words come out like a promise, as if Kael himself might be that *someone.*

Zak looks as if he's going to combust in fury, his knuckles turning white as he clenches them at his sides.

He stands then, a tempest within that he is barely keeping in check. And just as I think he's about to draw his sword, he turns and leaves the room.

Kael doesn't watch him go. Doesn't flinch. Doesn't move.

He simply leans back, smug, satisfied.

As Zakarius' footsteps recede, the room exhales as if it had been holding its breath. But something sticks with me.

He wasn't just angry. He was *devastated.*

Who was Nalya to him?

"Though I fuckin' loathe to ever agree with the bastard, changing the plan is," Daelen pauses, searching for the right words, "quite problematic, brother." His considered approach settles the room, and Kael's shadows dissipate in the air around us.

Kael exhales deeply and pours himself a goblet of thick crimson liquid. He takes a long pull on the drink and lifts his eyes, looking around the group.

"It's your job to solve problems, is it not?" Kael posits. "Or perhaps there's no use for you." Something in his gaze is fierce and loaded with fury.

"We've been working on the plan for years, Kael—"

Jax barely gets the word out before Kael cuts her off. "Prince Kael," he corrects. His tone is all malice and ice.

Jax looks at him, incredulous, but Kael holds her gaze. A challenge. She looks like she wants to argue, but she doesn't dare. I don't entirely blame her.

Therion, ever the voice of reason, "How about we all take tonight to drink, eat and sleep, and come back to the hollow tomorrow?"

The older gentleman, Eldric, places an affectionate hand on Therion's shoulder, "A fine idea. Council, are we in agreement?"

Murmurs of agreement fill Council Hollow, but it's Kael who has the final word. "Leave if you must, but if you can't bring a new strategy to the table by the time we're back from the next relic, you'll find your seat filled by someone else."

The group rise from their seats, breaking off into small groups to discuss matters, or leaving.

I'm left sitting here, reeling.

My mind spins, my pulse pounds. I came here expecting answers.

I'm leaving with even more fucking questions.

And the worst part? The only person who has answers is the same fucking liar who put me in the dark to begin with.

CHAPTER SIXTY-FOUR
KAEL

I swirl the crimson liquor in my goblet, watching the slow
ribbons of red coat the glass before tipping it back, letting the burn
chase away the weight pressing against my ribs.

It doesn't work.

It never fucking does.

The air in my bedroom is thick with aged oak, smoke, and the
ghosts of that godsdamned meeting. The council was furious.
Rightly so. Everything we've done—every sacrifice, every blood-
stained decision—has been for the plan. And I just tore it apart with
a single sentence.

For her.

I exhale sharply and rub my jaw, trying to stave off the tension
coiling in my gut. Elyssara's anger still lingers in my veins. I felt it in
that meeting. Felt her fire burning at the edges of my mind, her fury
clawing at my restraint.

She wanted answers.

She wanted to rip them from me with her bare hands.

And she will.

I've known her long enough to see the pattern. When she's furious, she comes to me. *Storms to me.* It's always been this way, ever

397

since the moment she snarled at me with dirt under her nails and fire in her eyes in that filthy Dravari tannery. She's like a storm—rolling in hot, leaving wreckage in her wake, shaking the ground beneath my feet before she lets me pull her under.

I tip my head back, watching the shadows coil along the ceiling. Waiting.

Because I know she'll come.

She always fucking does.

The tether between us snaps taut, imbued with fierce determination and fury, and the oak door of my chambers slams open.

Her wet hair clings to her temples, wild and untamed, Star-forged Blade gleaming in her grip like a promise of violence. The woman is fucking stunning, even—especially—in her rage.

"You knew this entire time who you were. Who *I* was. And you still let me walk around like a fucking fool while everyone else knew the truth!" She spits the words like the taste of them disgusts her.

There's no question, just a cold, direct statement of her betrayal.

I steel myself to answer, but she forges on, not waiting for me.

"Did you ever plan to tell me, Kael?" She lets out an exhale that borders on a whimper and her voice breaks, "Or did you get some sort of kick out of keeping me in the fucking dark?"

I rise out of the chair, and reach for her, "El—"

"Don't fucking touch me!" She pulls back from me as if scalded. *Repulsed.*

"I just wanted you to see it for yourself. Zerynthia, Thornewood, my people," I drag my hands through my hair, the last weeks on the road, of keeping myself together, of withholding so much, catching up with me. "I wanted you to see why we're doing this. Why we need you."

"And why the fuck should I believe anything you say, *Your Majesty?*" She drops into a low mocking curtsy, and looks at me with those piercing, emerald-green eyes.

"Just hear me out, El. Please," the words come out pleading, but I don't care. I'll get on my knees and fucking beg if I have to.

She pauses for a moment, exhaling loudly and wiping at her eyes.

Her voice softens, the rage dissipating into something rawer, more vulnerable. "Did you ever think, just for a heartbeat, that maybe I deserve to know what I'm fighting for?" Her gaze bores into me, as if seeing inside my chest, before she adds, "Who I'm falling for?"

Fuck. The words crash into me, carving away the last scrap of restraint and self-control I have left, because despite everything, I'm falling for her, too.

"You deserve to know everything," my words come out like a whisper. *I'm a fucking liar.* I can't tell her everything. She'll never look at me the same.

"So, tell me," she begs, eyes pleading. "You told me I needed to see Zerynthia for myself. That I needed to understand. So help me understand, Kael."

I close my eyes, preparing to relive the worst night of my life, dredging up memories that I'd long since buried. But she's right—I owe her this much.

"You want the truth?" My voice is hoarse. "I was exiled from The Shadow Wastes for the murder of my parents."

Elyssara flinches, as if I've struck her. Her lips part—like she wants to say something, but the words catch.

"They were already dead when I found them." The words scrape against my throat, like shards of glass I thought I'd swallowed years ago.

Her fingers twitch at her sides. The scent of embers sharpens in the air.

"Maldrak was standing behind the guards when they rushed in. Playing the role of shocked noble—he was the fucking executioner. He played me."

A spark hisses from the tip of her blade. But it's not rage anymore. It's something worse.

She believes me.

She stares at me, as if uncertain what to say, so I continue.

"He put me on trial in front of the entire court and painted me as a kinslayer." Elyssara is still silent, staring at me, leaving space for me to breathe, to remember. "Almost every member of that court turned their back on me after that... except for those here—those on the council. They know the truth. They know *me*."

"Why not just kill you?" The words sting, but she looks sincere.

"He wanted me to watch while he took everything from me—my parents, my sister, my kingdom. He wanted to see me suffer."

Elyssara takes a deep breath, composing herself.

"Is this the plan, then? Kill Maldrak? Get revenge? To hell with everything else?" She asks, exasperated.

"My plan is to restore Zerynthia. To carry on my father's legacy. To finish what he started." I say with conviction, reciting the words I've said hundreds of times to the war council.

For a moment, she just looks at me. Not with anger, not with pity, but with something dangerous. *Understanding.* As if she knows the feeling.

Then, her gaze shifts and darkens.

"And what of Nalya? Will you really leave her to rot in those dungeons all for the sake of this plan?"

The air rushes out of my lungs, and the dam containing my fury breaks.

"Everything I've done has been for her!" The words snarl out of me before I can stop them. "Every life I've taken, every battle I've fought, every godsdamned council meeting—"

I'm breathing hard. Elyssara's fingers tighten around her blade.

"Until you."

The words leave me hoarse. Bare.

Elyssara stares at me.

Like she's trying to hate me. Trying to hold onto her fury. Trying to ignore the way my voice just broke for her.

Then, slowly—too slowly—she steps closer.

"You should've told me," she breathes.

"You think I wanted to keep this from you?" My voice is rough, edged with something I can't smooth over. "You think I liked standing there, watching you put the pieces together on your own, knowing that at any moment I could just—" I exhale sharply, shaking my head. "That I could just tell you?"

I step forward, and she doesn't move away this time.

"I didn't want you to just hear it, Elyssara. I needed you to *feel* it. To see it. To stand in these homes, to look into the eyes of people who have lost so much and know that you were the answer to their prayers—not because I told you, but because *you* felt your own power for once."

I drag a hand through my hair, my restraint unraveling thread by thread.

"If I told you back in The Tannery, would you have believed me?" My voice is softer now. "If I said you were more than a street girl with starlight in her blood, that you were meant for something greater, that you could change the entire future of the fucking realms—would you have listened? Or would you have torn yourself apart trying to prove me wrong? Trying to hold onto all the reasons you don't think you're good enough?"

Her breath catches, but she says nothing.

"That's why, El." I look at her then, unguarded. Raw. "Because I needed you to know it before I ever said a fucking word."

A tear tracks down her cheek, "What am I supposed to do with that, Kael?" she whimpers.

My jaw tightens, and I take a step, closing the space between us, "You tell me."

CHAPTER SIXTY-FIVE

ELYSSARA

I SHOULD WALK AWAY. SHOULD STILL BE FURIOUS. BUT STARS SAVE
me—the way this man is willing to break for me cracks me open
and rearranges everything inside me.

You tell me.

His words reverberate in my mind, and I feel cornered by the
truth. Cornered by his ocean-blue eyes that pin me in place with
intensity.

"Why me, Kael?" My words come out desperate, but it's all I
can think to say.

"You're Elyssara, the Lightborne," he says simply, seemingly at a
loss for words.

"So, I'm just a means to an end? A solution to your problem?" I
seethe, composure breaking, and it feels like my heart is ripping
apart. "Am I really so easily discarded? Just another life wasted in
the name of your throne?" I can't help the anger that re-surges
through me.

"No! For fuck's sake, El, no!" Kael's voice is hoarse, his
breathing ragged, and he throws his hands up in exasperation.

"Then what, Kael? What am I if not a convenient solution?"

"You're... the Lightborne and I'm—" He cuts himself off and drags his hand through his hair, frustration winning.

"You're what, Kael? What the fuck are you?" His throat bobs and his jaw clenches, but he doesn't answer. And that silence unsettles me more than any answer could.

I want to turn around and walk away. To leave this room right now and never look back. But I can't help myself. I have to keep pushing him despite feeling as though I'm tearing my own heart from my chest.

"Tell me, Kael. Tell me I'm just a pawn, just another piece on your board. Tell me so I can walk out of this room and pretend none of this meant anything."

We're so close, eyes locked in a silent conversation.

"Fine. Just tell me this, Kael. Why are you still here? Because you need me—or because you want me?" My voice softens almost to a whisper, and a single thread holds my heart intact.

He exhales heavily, closing his eyes.

"I came for you because I needed you," he says, and my lungs threaten to give out. He pauses, breathing ragged, composing himself, "But I'm ready to ruin everything because I want you."

I'm ready to ruin everything because I want you.

I replay the words again and again, searching them for truth in a haze of lies and illusions. *What do I even believe anymore?*

Kael closes the distance between us, his hands wrapping around my shoulders tenderly. "Elyssara, I—" He tries to steady himself, but his hands are trembling, "I can't lose you. I won't," he says the words like a promise.

"That's not your decision, Kael," I say softly.

"What can I do?" He asks, almost pleading.

My heart hammers in my chest. *How many times can my trust be broken before I stop giving it away so freely?*

Despite myself, I *want* to trust him. I want to believe him. And the part of me that knows the weight of keeping secrets from those you love understands. I understand the willingness to sacrifice anything—everything—to preserve a legacy, to keep a promise, to save those we love.

"Tell me everything," I say, wiping the tears from my cheeks and squaring my shoulders. "What else haven't you told me?"

He meets my gaze steadily, eyes dark and vulnerable, throat bobbing, as though he's swallowing down the words he won't allow himself to say.

He steps back from me, and for a heartbeat, I think he's walking away, but he reaches for the first clasp of his chest plate and starts to unbuckle it.

WHAT—

"Let me show you," he says cryptically, seeing my confusion.

Kael unbuckles each clasp slowly, glancing up at me, but my gaze is fixed on his chest plate. With each buckle, more of his sun-kissed golden skin is bared, revealing swirls of black ink in intricate patterns.

I've never noticed it before, or rather, I've never had a chance to see it before, despite our night in the tent on Skaedor's mountain.

He reaches the final clasp, unbuckling it with efficiency, letting it drop with a heavy thud. In the flickering candlelight, inked starkly across his chest, a swirling sea of Stars—constellations spattered across his skin, just like the night sky. So precise they look like they've been etched by the gods themselves.

My breath hitches, and I instinctively reach out to touch it, speechless at the sight before me.

The Lightborne and The Sky must tread as one.

The words return to me instantly, and I whip my gaze to him, shock and surprise defining my features.

"You're The Sky," I breathe. "It's you."

I allow myself to touch his skin—to trace my fingers over the ink marking his chest—and The Sky faintly illuminates with my physical presence. *It recognizes me.*

"It's me, Elyssara," he confirms, voice gentle, tentative. "I'm the one that's meant to be with you," he ventures. "I think it's why I can sense you."

Countless emotions slam into me at once—awe, surprise,

betrayal, hurt—I don't know what to do with it all. My Lightborne marking roars to life, illuminating the room around us in pure, white light. Without conscious thought, I pull my hands back, gather force, and shove Kael's chest with every shred of strength I have in my body.

He stumbles back, surprise taking root in his expression, but I shove him again before he regroups.

"You fucking lied to me all this time!" I scream, voice shrill and hoarse with the effort. "You fucking liar!" The words tear out of me.

I pound my fists into his chest, but sobs wrack my body, stealing my strength.

I feel a faint wisp of cool air coiling around my legs, but I don't care what it is or who is watching.

"I know," Kael soothes, wrapping his arms around me but not stopping my fists. "I know."

"I just want," I say, sobbing and gasping for air, "to be wanted for me."

Kael holds me, wrapping one of his firm, broad hands around my head and the other rubbing soothing circles on my back, "Elyssara, I want you." He tilts my head back, locking eyes with me, "I want you, okay? I want you." I want to believe him, and Stars fucking save me, but I do. I have no reason to believe him, but I do.

"I hate you," I whisper, "But I want you, too."

Then I realize the room is blanketed in darkness, shadows wrapping around us in a protective shield, insulating us from prying eyes and ears and soothing my magic, just as he soothed me.

"I hate that I want you," I say, staring into his eyes, knowing that his arms are the safest and most dangerous place I'll ever know.

He looks down at me with primal possession in his eyes, "It was always meant to be me and you, Duskae." He strokes my hair back from my face, "I meant it when I said it the first time; you're mine." Then, his lips are on me.

Possessive, commanding, and seductive, he claims my mouth like he's breathing after drowning. His tongue sweeps into my mouth, hot and dominant, tasting me, savoring me, devouring me.

I grab his tunic that's splayed open over his chest, bunching it in my hands. I push him away just enough to pry his lips from mine. I can't want this. I will never trust him. Never know if there's not another secret, another layer that he keeps buried inside. I'll never know if I'm anything more than a game.

"You lied to me," I pant, my mind muddled with the scent of him wrapping around me, caressing me, branding me.

He looks at me with carnal lust and something deeper that borders on obsession, "Do you want me to stop, Elyssara?" His hand lightly brushes over my hip, as he flicks his wicked tongue along his lower lip, and my traitorous fucking body goes languid at the sight.

Yes.

"No," I rasp, desperate to get lost in his touch.

He frames my face with his hands, brushing back the strands that have fallen forward, and possesses my mouth with heat and intensity that turns me molten. He moves me backward to his bed, cupping my ass with one hand, and cradling my head with the other like I'm something sacred and breakable all at once. He lowers me down gently and unties my linen trousers and easily slips them over my hips and legs. "Let me worship you, El," he says, the words a promise. "Let me show you how much I want you."

A small moan escapes me, and I fucking hate that he can do this to me.

With slow, seductive precision, Kael removes my tunic and underthings, peeling them from me as if my body is something holy. He lays me bare before him, his gaze roaming every dip and hollow, before pausing at my pussy. I am dripping wet for him. Kael drops his head back and exhales deeply, "I fucking love how wet you get for me, El."

He steps back, eyes still roaming my body, as if committing every inch to memory. "You are fucking perfection."

I whimper then, barely able to contain my hunger for him. I want him to make me moan, to make me come apart beneath him, to make me forget everything that's at stake. *Everything he's done.*

"Will you let me fuck you like no one has ever fucked you before, Elyssara?" His voice a primal growl.

My pussy is dripping wet, my arousal running down my inner thighs. I give him a small nod.

"I'm going to need to hear you say it, El. Let me fuck you," he commands.

I let out a huff of frustration, impatience and hunger wearing me down, "Fuck me, Kael," I rasp the words, desperate for his touch again.

"That's my girl," Kael unties the laces of his leathers, the long, hard length of his cock springing free, and I can't help but moan at the sight.

"Can I taste you first, Duskae?" he asks, arousal thick in his words.

"Yes," I pant.

Kael drops to his knees at the end of the bed, his sky marking glowing faintly and on show. He lowers his head between my thighs and licks right up my center until he reaches my clit. With just the right pressure, he circles my clit, but I'm desperate for more friction. More of *him*. I lift my hips, grinding them into his mouth. He moans, savoring me, "I love it when you fuck my mouth, El."

He devours me again, groaning in pleasure at the taste of me. *Worshipping me.*

His encouragement emboldens me, and I grind my hips again, hungry for more, and I can feel the wave of climax building. But he pulls back with a smirk, "Not yet, El. I want you to come around my cock."

Kael's calloused hands grip my hips and slide me up further on the bed, making space for him. He reaches for a pillow and lifts my hips, placing the pillow underneath my ass so I'm angled for him.

He spreads my thighs wider and kneels between them as if I am prayer incarnate.

"You're so pretty when you moan for me, Duskae," Kael says with a hint of restraint in his voice. His hands tremble as he slowly slides them down my legs, careful not to rush, trying to relish this.

"I need you closer," I rasp, breathing still ragged from pleasure, desperate for him.

He's gorgeous. His upper body on display—cut muscles from

years of honing his body for battle, veins visible in his forearms as he grips me, and that vee that ripples down to his groin. My nipples harden at the sight of him, every beautiful, chiseled line of muscle that accents his body.

His cock twitches in anticipation, hard and beading with moisture. "And I need you, Elyssara," he says like a promise. "There's nowhere you can go where you won't be mine. Where I won't want you."

My body goes languid at his words, and a small whimper escapes me. Kael presses the head of his cock to my pussy, slow, waiting, despite his barely leashed hunger, "Are you ready?"

"Yes," I say in a breathy moan.

His cock slides inside me slowly, and my breath hitches as he stretches me and I mold around him, desperately trying to accommodate his size. The pace of my breath increases at the stretch which feels like both pleasure and pain.

"Are you okay?" He asks with genuine concern. I can see that he's trying to take his time, trying to go slow with me but his grip around my thighs tightens, hands still trembling with barely contained hunger.

I answer by grinding my hips and taking his cock deeper inside me. Kael's expression turns feral, taking my grind as permission to continue.

He looks into my eyes with intensity and sincerity that borders on possessive, and the weight of the moment crashes into me. I see Kael in a way I've never seen him before. He has let me in, let me see the truth of who he is and all that he holds dear. It's not the first time we've had sex, but it's the first time we've had sex as our true selves. The thought only stokes the flames of my desire, and I can't help but grind my hips, desperate to entwine our bodies even more.

Our eyes are locked, a million words passing silently between us. He pulls back to the very tip of his cock and slowly slides back in. I gasp in pure bliss, his cock filling me and hitting parts of me that ripple pleasure through my body. "Oh gods," I cry out.

"I told you the first time, El. My name is the only name that should be on your lips when I'm fucking you," he says as his thumb finds my clit and he drives into me again.

"Kael," I moan.

"That's better, Duskae," he says with arrogance that I can't help but find fucking irresistible.

Kael keeps his thumb on my clit and flattens the span of his massive hand over my stomach and presses down with firm yet careful pressure.

He pumps his cock in and out of me, keeping the pressure on my stomach, and rapturous pleasure takes over my body. *What in the Stars?* I moan his name, cupping my breasts, and rolling my nipples between my fingers.

Kael watches intently, still pumping into me with steady, rhythmic thrusts, "Fuck," he grits out, his eyes wild with feral lust.

He increases the pressure on my stomach and the intensity of my pleasure increases, trapping his cock in that same spot that makes me see Stars. "Give me more, Kael," I request, wanting to break open beneath him.

"You have all of me, El," he replies raggedly, his body gleaming with sweat, but his pace picks up, nonetheless.

My orgasm builds frenetically, and so, too, does my breath. "I'm going to come," I cry.

"That's it. Come for me," he says, voice gravelly.

Our bodies entwine, moving together rhythmically, reading each other's movements seamlessly. I grind into him, and he thrusts into me with smooth, deliberate strokes, and I clench around him.

"Fuck," Kael growls, and his restraint finally shatters.

He grips my hips tightly, almost bruising in their desperation, he groans, slamming into me again and again. All restraint gone, Kael's thrusts are frenzied and feral, and he pushes me beyond the brink of pleasure into pure fucking ecstasy.

The walls of my pussy pulse around him, and rapturous, vibrating clenches of pleasure obliterate me. "Kael," I sob, closing my eyes to focus solely on the unhinged bliss wracking my body, jolting through me like a powerful, unbridled current.

I open my eyes to the sight of Kael's orgasm crashing into him like a wave breaking on rocks, carnal and unleashed. His body shudders, cock twitching inside of me as I feel his warm come filling me. "Elyssara," he grits out, the muscles of his arms bulging with effort, veins pumping. His control, broken. His restraint, shattered. *For me.* He looks like a god.

He withdraws his cock, his gaze shoots to my pussy and lingers there. His lips are slightly parted, as if admiring what he sees. "I love seeing my come dripping from your pussy," he says, his voice pleasure-addled. "You are so fucking beautiful."

I am wrecked. My body trembles, my legs shake, and my mind is far too scrambled to speak.

Kael huffs a laugh at my languid form, and says, "Let me take care of you, El." All I can manage is a weak nod, as a small groan escapes my lips.

Kael rolls onto his back next to me and pulls me onto his chest, tucking me into the crook of his arm. Our bodies curl together.

My breathing begins to settle as I get comfortable on the expanse of his chest. My eyes flutter closed. I'm weightless. Drifting. And all I can think is how safe I feel in his arms, and how that might be the most dangerous thing of all.

As sleep threatens to take me under, Kael kisses the top of my head affectionately and says, "It will always be me and you, El."

CHAPTER SIXTY-SIX
KAEL

THE SOUND OF BIRDS CHIRPING GENTLY PULLS ME FROM SLEEP, AND I reach out my hand, seeking Elyssara. The sheets are still warm, and her scent lingers, but she's gone. Her absence is a physical ache that I feel in my chest. *Where did she go?*

The sun filters through the curtains of my chambers, and the low hum of Thornewood floats through the air.

I pull on my leathers and tie my boots efficiently before stepping out of my room and into the day.

This tether in my chest gnaws at me to find her. After last night, it coiled into something satisfied. Steady. But with her gone, it's fraying again, pulling taut in search of her.

I weave and duck between branches and trunks, letting the tether lead me to her.

It doesn't take long before the sound of familiar voices greets me, and I follow the sound up the winding wooden stairs to Council Hollow.

The room is buzzing with frenetic energy, mainly because Rubi seems to have met Seren, and their shrill, high-pitched squeals are almost deafening.

"They've been like it all morning, lad," Merrik offers while handing me a steaming cup of coffee—the pleasures of home I've missed dearly. "Women and their godsdamned giggling," Merrik adds as an afterthought.

Elyssara has her back to me, poring over a thick text with Therion, while Jax and Ronyn argue over something that is, no doubt, inconsequential.

"Prince Kael," Daelen drops into an exaggerated bow, a smirk lining his features, clearly referencing my request to be called such at last night's council meeting. *Asshole.*

I make my way to Elyssara. As I approach, I pull her hair to one side and brush a kiss on her neck, breathing in the subtle scent of sandalwood that clings to her skin. "Good morning, beautiful," I say, keeping my voice low so only she can hear.

She turns her face to me, cheeks flushing bright red, and gives me a coy smile that makes me want to fall to my knees at the way I can make this fierce, violent woman blush.

"Nice of you to finally join us, Your Majesty," Ronyn quips. "I suppose you're used to having people do everything for you, though." Ronyn's face is pure audacity, goading me.

"That's the first accurate thing you've said all morning," Jax banters.

Therion approaches, clapping his hand to mine and embracing me. He drops his voice so low it's almost inaudible and says, "Looks like you," he pauses for a heartbeat, searching for the right words, "*smoothed* things over with Elyssara." A ghost of a smile appears on his face.

"To a point," I confirm. *Fuck, there's only so much smoothing over my cock can do.*

We break apart, and I move to my usual seat at the head of the table. It's not an official council meeting, but we have matters to tend to. "So, the Obsidian Crown. What's the plan?" I incline my head to Seren, seeing as she usually has all the information.

"After conferring with others from the council, we believe the crown is in Starlit Grove—"

Someone behind me clears their throat, and I look around to find Rowan at the outskirts of the room. "If I may, my prince?"

The Mindweaver steps forward. Rowan is barely twenty summers old, but his gift allows him to archive, recall, and preserve memories, conversations, historical events, and even complex details in perfect clarity. He can call forward anything he's ever heard, read or seen. All of those with Mindweaving abilities were killed during Maldrak's purge to wipe history. Rowan's lineage, the Nix family, was once prominent in my family's court, renowned specifically for their gift. But now, we only have Rowan.

He's lean and scholarly with sharp, watchful eyes and flaming red hair. His astuteness has built him a reputation in Thornewood as an invaluable addition to Zerynthia. If only he acted like it. Rowan's mind is sharper than a blade, but he wears his genius like a burden, not an honor.

"Of course, Rowan. What do you know?" I say.

Rowan's eyes begin to change with subtly shifting hues reflecting active memory recall. His irises shimmer faintly, searching his mind's archives for the answers we need.

"My prince, Starlit Grove will not permit anyone to enter unless they have a rightful claim to a throne. That is why those who enter, do not return," he keeps his voice tight and respectful.

"Which throne, specifically?" I clarify.

"That answer is unclear. As far as I can ascertain, any."

Interesting.

"And I'm assuming you've spoken to Seren?" My gaze shifts back to her.

She smooths down her skirts. "I spoke to Rowan this morning, and our information is a match. If you do not have a rightful claim to a throne, Starlit Grove will remove you, *violently.*"

"So, I'll guess we'll send Kael in first and just see what happens," Ronyn rouses.

I roll my eyes, but don't fight the smile that marks my features. "No need to waste your breath, Ronyn," I say, sipping my coffee. "I was always going first."

Elyssara's gaze settles on mine, unreadable. A breath passes between us, thick with something unspoken. Then, slowly, I wink.

I will protect you at all costs.

Rubi leans forward then, "I don't even bother trying to heal those that attempt it. Just give them some liquor and wait for the end." She kicks her feet up on the table and raises a goblet in salute.

"Fuck's sake, Rubi. It's barely even morning, and you're drinking?" Therion chastises.

"These meetings are dull, Teddy. I thought I'd make it more exciting. I could always go foraging for some of those exotic mushrooms Kael used to like," she quips with a wink.

Therion grumbles something incoherent, and I try to school my features.

"The Grove does not suffer pretenders," Seren asserts. "If it finds you unworthy, it does not simply turn you away—it swallows you whole."

"So dramatic, girl," Jax patronizes.

"Not a figure of speech," Rowan interjects, his voice flat. "It quite literally devours them. The roots are sentient. Once they take hold, they do not let go."

Jax's face goes preternaturally still at Rowan's words, and they hang in the air.

"As I suspected," I confirm. "So," I set my cup down, leaning forward. "How the fuck do we get through?"

Rowan exhales, his irises flickering with shifting memories. Then silence. A long, weighted pause.

Too long.

Finally, his voice is quiet. Grim. "There are no records of such a thing, my prince."

A chill licks up my spine.

Silence stretches, heavy and suffocating.

"Then we carve a fucking path."

CHAPTER SIXTY-SEVEN
KAEL

THE MID-MORNING AIR BITES WITH A CRISP EDGE, DESPITE THE SUN'S warm glare.

Leather creaks, steel slides into sheathes, and the scent of the fresh Riverian earth swirls around the clearing as we prepare the horses.

The energy and buoyancy of earlier this morning is gone, replaced with the quietness that always comes before risk and unpredictability.

Elyssara stands up straighter, smoothing down the unruly strands of vibrant hair that have sprung free from her braid. "Only Kael and I are going," she announces, and all eyes turn to her.

"Absolutely fucking not," Therion counters, tone unwavering.

I stifle a chuckle—they're both as stubborn as each other.

Rowan hovers awkwardly on the outskirts of the clearing, desperate to be useful. He takes a small step forward, and tentatively speaks, "Logically speaking, Elyssara and Prince Kael are the only ones with any validity to enter. That is, if Queen of the Vaythari counts." He shifts uncomfortably on his feet, "The rest of us will just be mulch."

Ronyn raises an eyebrow, "Mulch?"

"Chewed up, unceremoniously digested food for the sentient roots," Rowan explains as if it should've been obvious.

"Right," Ronyn grimaces. "Thanks for clarifying."

"I'm General of War—I'll escort you as far as possible. It's not up for discussion," Therion's voice is a low rumble, and I know there's no point arguing. The man has protected me with his life—and axe—since we were mere boys.

I nod curtly.

"I go where El goes," Ronyn asserts, though his bravado is palpable.

"I would expect nothing less," I allow.

Elyssara sighs, "Fine, but that's it!"

I catch movement to my left through the trees—the sun glaring off polished steel. Zak breaks through the tree line, a snarl already forming on his lips.

"Fuck's sake," Merrik breathes quietly, and I don't blame him. Zak's father was a good and loyal man—part of my father's council of advisors, who was killed in Maldrak's takeover—but the only thing he has inherited from his father is his strategic mind. Zak is loyal to one thing, and one thing only—himself.

Elyssara stiffens at the sight of him, jaw clenching.

"Don't be like that, Lightborne," he says snidely. "I promise to make the journey unforgettable," his lilting tone drips with sarcasm and sets me on edge. "Plus, maybe I don't trust you with the heir to the throne of Zerynthia." He tilts his head to the side, challenging us to make an argument.

A hush falls over the group. Even Rowan stops fidgeting.

Elyssara's lips tighten, but she says nothing. Neither do I. But I'm not fooled. Zak's protectiveness has nothing to do with me, and I know it. He's got another agenda, and I'll find out what it is one way or another.

If he so much as *looks* at Elyssara the wrong way, he won't make it back.

"What the fuck could you possibly bring to the table for this journey, Zak?" Therion probes, cutting an imposing figure by standing up straighter and letting his frame tower over Zak. "Aside from the ability to piss people off with nothing more than your existence," he adds with a penetrating glare.

Jax snorts. Her sense of humor is dark and unassuming, but she's loyal to a fault.

"Intelligence," Zak quips. "While you've been off drinking ale and bedding women in Dravara, I've been here," he gestures to the jungle around him, "analyzing the jungle's rhythms, finding the rip in The Decay, watching the way The Grove moves."

The rip in The Decay? Therion and I exchange a quick glance. Not even Daelen knew about that.

"Oh, didn't know about the rip, *my prince?*" He says the last words with haughty arrogance, but I let it slide.

"When?" I keep it simple.

"The day before the last full moon," he explains, "the sky beamed with bright light and then we heard it. It was like thunder."

That was when we were at Lyssar Temple, Elyssara speaks down the tether to me, surprise coating her tone.

It was, I offer in response.

The blade ignites and the veil is torn.

The words from the prophecy reverberate in my mind.

Noticing the surprise on our faces, Zak continues, "Rhyven tracked it and has been watching it ever since." He pauses, as if weighing whether he should continue. Cautiously, he says, "People from The Wastes have been walking through it. Confused, lost. They end up dying, of course—no water, no food. If there's nothing keeping them in, or we can't bring it down all together, they die. Bit of a problem."

Merrik drags his hand through his hair, understanding the gravity of the situation.

"Fuck," is all I can think to say.

"Yes, fuck." Zak agrees sarcastically. "Admit it, Kael," he says, voice dripping with arrogance. "You need me."

I loathe to see any value whatsoever in Zak, but this is why he's here. He's strategically fucking brilliant. His brother, Rhyven, is an

Aetherstride, and Zak is a Bloodbond. Together, they are precise, intelligent, and lethal. Zak's loyalty, on the other hand, is questionable at best.

"For the moment," I allow, and I mean it. He's one lingering gaze at Elyssara away from being kindling for the fire.

I help Elyssara onto Nyx and swiftly swing myself behind her. I brush my hand over her waist, grounding her, grounding myself. A silent promise: *I've got you.*

"Let's go," I say quickly. I've had enough of this conversation. "Seren, Rowan," I say, eyeing the scholars, "I need you to work on the next relic and have answers by the time we return." They nod stoically. "With the rip in The Decay, our timeline just collapsed. We don't have the luxury of time anymore."

CHAPTER SIXTY-EIGHT
ELYSSARA

THE JUNGLE IS STILL, TOO STILL, AS IF IT'S WATCHING US. The further we get from Thornewood, the more palpable its sentience. Even the air shifts—heavier, quieter, expectant. The trees' bioluminescence brightens with our presence and dims as we move past, confirming what I've known in my bones since arriving—it senses us. It senses *me*.

No one speaks. No one dares to.

We simply ride, watching, waiting, alert.

I look down at my chest and see the compass dangling between my breasts. The dial of the compass points straight ahead, never deviating from our destination. It *wants* me to go there. The compass drives me forward, urging me to keep going.

Ronyn surges his chestnut mare forward in line with us, "So, what's the plan, El?" His roguish grin kicks up the corners of his mouth, and he adds, "Aside from not dying, of course."

I huff a laugh, "That's about as far as I've got when it comes to the plan." I pause for a heartbeat, reminiscing on the sheer recklessness of all the raids, stealing and brawls we encountered—or incited—in Virellin. "But you know I don't need one. Blind stupidity is as good a plan as any, right?"

"That's my girl," Ronyn agrees. "It's worked for us all these years. Why stop now?" Throwing me a wink over his shoulder, he trots ahead to catch up to Therion. Kael stiffens behind me, his hands clenching around the reins in front of me.

What is it? I ask through the tether.

He doesn't respond, and just as I go to probe him again, his voice rumbles back down the tether: *you're not his girl.*

Kael, don't be ridiculous. You know he doesn't mean it like that.

The tether quiets, but his jealousy buzzes like static under my skin.

Kael's possessiveness has become more intense over the last few days. It coils tighter every time someone else even utters my name. I don't know if it's just Zak's presence that's setting him on edge or something deeper.

"I know," he finally says out loud with an audible exhale, releasing the tension from his posture. "But I want the world to know you're *mine.*" He presses a hand to my thigh, infusing his strokes with hot need, "And you know I don't share."

Before I can reply, the air thickens, and the steady hum of insects ceases instantly.

Therion turns and gives Kael a sharp nod.

We're here.

The trees part, the vibrant canopy gives way to an unnatural darkness, where obsidian trees rise like monoliths. Too tall. Too dark. Too oppressive.

The trees reach skyward, and loom downward. *Watching.*

The glow beneath us dims into nothing—even the moss is too afraid to breathe. As if even the light dares not enter.

Ahead, through the veil of vines, it awaits.

Starlit Grove.

My breath hitches at the sight in front of me—the contrast of the onyx trees is offset by the twinkle of vibrant silver bioluminescence that runs through the trunks of the trees like starlit veins.

It truly is a grove of starlight. I rush to remind myself that despite its intimidating beauty, this grove is a seer of legitimacy. A judge and executioner for those it doesn't consider worthy. A shiver licks up my spine at the thought.

Kael, sensing my unease, soothes me down the tether, *I'll keep you safe, El. Nothing will touch you.*

I swallow thickly and slide off Nyx, never taking my eyes from the Grove's looming canopy.

Kael dismounts with fluid grace, and turns to Therion, "You know what to do if today doesn't go to plan." It's not a question, but a statement. They've talked about this already—the possible outcome.

Therion nods tightly, "I'll be at the edge of The Grove. I'll only move in if you give me the signal."

The weight of this moment presses down on me, gnawing at me.

"Morrathys can't have you today, El," Ronyn's words are heavy but loaded with sincerity. It's rare to see Ronyn without his signature cavalier attitude, which is why it hits so much harder when he drops it and chooses candor instead. "I'll be right here."

"Best let the Lightborne go first, Kael. No telling what might sneak up behind you," Zak's vindictive words slice through the heartfelt moment.

"No," Kael responds smoothly, and I'm mildly impressed by his restraint. "I go first, Elyssara follows on my signal."

"You don't come back, Kael, and Nalya is as good as dead," Zak seethes.

"If Elyssara doesn't come back, so are you," Kael replies sharply. "You're only useful to me if she's alive, Zak, and don't you fucking forget that."

Kael spins to me, and holds out his hand. "Ready, your high-ness?" he banters, all signs of malice are replaced with levity, as if we're not just about to walk into a death maze.

I slide my hand into his.

My palm is steady.

My heart is not.

"Let's see if The Grove believes the prophecy."

CHAPTER SIXTY-NINE

ELYSSARA

WE STEP FORWARD, LEAVING THE GROUP AND THE JUNGLE BEHIND US. As if sensing our approach, the ground beneath us groans—an ancient, guttural sound that reverberates around us, vibrating up my spine. Kael's hand grips mine a little tighter, affirming in its presence.

We approach the obsidian trees with veins of starlight, and then I feel it—we cross the invisible threshold, suffocating and breathless, as if we're now encased within The Grove's walls.

My chest tightens, and magic stirs in my heart, traveling down to my fingertips—poised.

We step hesitantly through the grove, boots landing silently on the damp, mossy floor. Vines hang low overhead, ancient tendrils slithering like serpents, reaching out to us as if reading us, sensing us, testing us.

I brush them away, ducking beneath them, but with every contact, faint whispers curl through the air like smoke. Calling to me, luring me to follow. Unnerving in their sentience, the vines swirl around me like lost spirits that never made it out.

"Don't listen, El, they're testing us," Kael instructs, voice tight.

I don't respond, I just keep my eyes ahead, following the

compass, trusting its navigation down the countless winding paths of starlight, vines, and moss.

But then I hear it—the groan from earlier roars to life, shaking the ground.

The earth beneath us splits in two.

Roots burst from the forest floor like serpents, gnarled and twisting. They shoot toward us in a blur, fast and vicious, aiming for Kael.

He leaps to the side, the jagged, grotesque root narrowly missing his torso.

In a heartbeat, Kael unsheathes his dual swords and steps closer to me. But it's no use. The roots twist again, this time aiming to hook his ankles. With lethal efficiency, Kael slices through the roots.

The earth beneath us trembles, and the path ahead distorts, warping into a twisted tangle of roots and vines with no way through.

I chance a look at the compass, but the dial is spinning wildly. It is out of control and unable to combat The Grove's living intelligence.

"This way!" Kael calls, running toward the only open pathway.

I follow, my breath heavy with exertion.

I take five steps—

"STOP!" Kael bellows.

I slide to a stop and look skyward as one of the dark trees creaks and groans before toppling with a crash.

BOOM!

The huge tree trunk lands mere inches from my face and is so vast I can't see over it.

Are you okay? Kael's distressed question tumbles down the tether.

Yes, I reply sharply. *What now?*

I need to find a way to you, he says.

Hold on, I've got an idea. I pause for a heartbeat before adding, *Step back, Kael.*

I can feel his unease through the tether, but I push him away.

I move towards the trunk and place my hands on its beautiful, starlit bark. I close my eyes, summoning my magic to my fingertips again, and let it seep slowly into the bark. It's sentient—*maybe it needs to feel me. Know me. Know we mean no harm.*

For a moment, The Grove stills. The groaning ceases, and the gentle quivering from the ground dissipates.

Then, the roots revolt.

A deafening shriek pierces the air, and the ground beneath my feet bucks as if rejecting me.

Vines burst towards me from above, roots burst from below and the whole grove roars in outrage.

I can't afford gentleness anymore.

I summon magic to my fingertips, and though I have no precision with my aim, I don't need it—I blast Lightborne magic, hot and intense, towards the trunk. *I need to get to Kael.*

The onyx trunk splinters apart and disintegrates in front of me, and that's when I see it—

"KAEL!"

He's ensnared by a tangle of roots that coil tightly around his torso, savagely yanking him off his feet and dragging him backward toward the gaping maw of a hollow tree.

I draw my Starforged Blade and command my magic to my hands again, desperately sprinting toward Kael.

Why aren't the roots attacking me?

I'm almost there, almost by his side, when the sound of grinding wood fills the air. The pathway I'm on twists, caving in on itself, leaving me in a heap on The Grove's floor, my path to Kael consumed by roots and vines that seek to separate us.

In such close proximity, Kael's swords are no use. He's reaching for the dagger in his boot, but the roots pin him in place.

The maw of the hollow tree is dripping with a sticky, green liquid as if salivating.

Kael! I scream down the tether, but it's no use. The roots are not only wrapped around his limbs, but his throat, too.

Panic threatens to seize my heart. My heartbeat pounds in my ears, and my mind is foggy, shrouding me in confusion and fear.

Fuck. Not like this. Not him.

"NO!" I scream aloud, voice cracking with raw desperation. A surge of power slams through my body, fierce and blinding.

"Let. Him. Go." The words come out like a command.

The air snaps. The vines recoil. The roots freeze mid-motion. The Grove shudders.

Kael drops to the ground in a heap as the tendrils retreat like chastised beasts, slithering back into the home from which they came.

Kael's breath comes in harsh pants as he pushes himself upright, eyes wide, fixed on me.

I'm shaking. Magic still churns beneath my skin like a storm barely held back. But that wasn't magic. That was... *me*.

And The Grove knew it.

CHAPTER SEVENTY
KAEL

SHE COMMANDED THE FUCKING GROVE. MADE IT SUBMIT TO HER like a dog, just like the Vaythari's duskprowlers at Skaedor's Crest, beasts known for kneeling to no one.

The Grove is a sanctuary. There's no trace of the wrath it unleashed—only starlit moss and mythic trees that light the way.

Elyssara's compass points straight ahead, and the pathways occasionally move and adjust, but never with malicious intent— more like a protective mechanism.

Elyssara leads the way—one hand wrapped around the compass, the other around her blade. Her long, copper braid trails down her slender back, strong with muscle from weeks of travel and fighting. Her hips sway with the grace of a warrior, her steps sure and steady, as if she hasn't just taken on a sentient grove and won.

I can't help but stare. She's fucking captivating.

I should be thinking about the path. The relic. The danger. But all I see is her.

We continue walking in comfortable silence, though anticipation for whatever lies ahead tints the air with tension.

"Well," Elyssara's voice cuts through my thoughts, "it looks like we won't be mulch." Her tone is light, but I feel her apprehension through the tether.

I huff a laugh, "Perhaps not today, El."

"It accepted us," she answers, beaming now.

"Duskae, it accepted *you*," I counter. "I think it's just tolerating me."

She giggles, and the sound is sweet. Every nerve in my body comes alive at the sound.

A small gasp slips from Elyssara, and she rushes forward, stopping swiftly after a few strides.

"The crown," she whispers reverently.

The Obsidian Crown sits atop a twisted pedestal of onyx forged from the trees themselves, wrapped and pinned by vines. It's as dark as a starless night and looks almost identical to the weapons we source from the volcanic forges of Vyrhal. The crown is inlaid with three starlit shards, like something adorned by gods and goddesses.

Elyssara steps closer, unafraid and commanding. As if sensing her arrival, the vines unbind from the crown and slip down the onyx pedestal.

I'm frozen, not out of fear or apprehension but out of reverence for her sheer power. It's as if her body remembers something her mind hasn't caught up to. She reaches out, wrapping her hands gently, humbly, around the crown.

Her hands don't tremble. She simply lifts the crown without ceremony or fanfare and places it atop her head. *She's fucking beautiful.*

Instantly, the grove groans again, but this time, it doesn't lash out. Every tree bows inward. Every light flares. The groan turns to a rumble—the very ground reorganizing itself in her presence. Even the air crackles in celebration. As if nature itself is kneeling to her.

She turns to me, eyes wide with awe, and light flares from them. Brilliant. Blinding. Divine.

The air ripples with a deluge of energy, fanning out from Elyssara and expanding through The Grove.

Then, she's gone.

CHAPTER SEVENTY-ONE
ELYSSARA

I'm falling.

Tumbling through the sky, free-falling through worlds. Time. Sound. Space. Light. *Reality.*

All I see is an endless expanse of night sky with a spattering of Stars.

I'm falling, floating through a void, a horizon-less expanse of dark and light, neither here nor there.

Where am I?

I can feel something—*someone*—brushing at the edges of my mind, trying desperately to find me. But I can't reach, I can't find my way to them.

A spark erupts around me, bright and blinding.

The void begins to change, expanding and transforming around me into a scene.

I'm no longer falling—I'm *watching.*

The scene comes to life before my eyes.

A young woman—barefoot, hair like mine—runs through a darkened forest. She carries a young child in her arms. The child's wild russet hair whips in the wind, sticking to the tears on the child's cheek. The woman wears a beautiful gown, smeared with dirt and blood, ripped and tattered. Her eyes dart behind her, her breath panicked and shallow. *She's being hunted.*

She stumbles, tripping on the forest floor. She crashes to the ground, holding her child to her chest, and whispers, "Lesara, run. You must run." She sets the child down with urgency and frantically takes off her silver marriage cuff, shoving it into the child's hands. "He won't stop hunting us. The monarchy has fallen—we are a threat to his reign as long as we live. You must disappear. Take this," she wraps her hands around the child's, cupping the cuff between them. "Keep it. You'll know when to use it."

A chill runs through me. The cuff looks like—

"Now, run! Do not look back, Lesara!"

Lesara. My mother. This is my mother.

My mother looks into the eyes of her own mother, tears running like a stream down her swollen cheeks, but she nods and tucks the cuff into the folds of her dress, lifts her skirts, and runs through the forest without glancing back.

My mother was a Dravari princess. Which makes me—

The vision shifts.

A great stone chamber unfurls around me—walls carved from black rock veined with silver, lit by the glow of a floating ring of symbols suspended in the air like a constellation. At its center stands a man cloaked in royal violet and ash-gray—Thalmyr. I'd know his face anywhere. *The villain of Virellin.*

Younger than I expected. And devastatingly handsome.

But power coils around him like smoke. Hungry. Possessive. Twisting his handsome features into something grotesque.

In front of him, a woman kneels.

She glows—not with magic, but *divinity*. Skin kissed with sunlight. Hair like soft golden threads. And eyes that hold the sorrow of Stars.

"Nyrielle, say your vows," he commands, his voice a honeyed facade that I immediately detect as subterfuge. *Nyrielle.* Goddess of Light and Wonder.

She looks at Thalmyr with devotion and adoration in her eyes.

I gasp in recognition. *She loves him.*

Her voice trembles as she speaks, though it's strong enough to shake the walls. "I give it freely—my blood, my vow, my heart. Let it bind us," she says with purpose and intent.

She reaches for his hand, slicing her palm and offering it up. Her golden blood spills like liquid sunlight into his.

He smiles that sickening smile I've seen hundreds of times from the forgotten side of The Lightborne Barrier in Virellin.

And I *know*—deep in my gut—that it's not love. For him, *it's strategy.*

He steps back, eyes dark with purpose. He looks behind him to a cloaked figure, gesturing for them to move forward, "Do it, Daphinia." Her arms raise, and the ring of floating symbols ignites, glowing red. A circle of ancient runes carves itself into the stone floor, pulsing with forbidden power—chains of shadow coil around the air.

"No," Nyrielle whispers, realization dawning too late. "No, Thalmyr—what are you doing?"

"You gave me your heart, goddess," he says coldly. "And now I sever yours from the realm, along with all the other so-called gods I've never bowed to."

She screams. Her form fractures—splintering into light and sound and agony. A shockwave blasts outward, and I see a vision— the gods, all of them, bound in place by the force of the ritual. Frozen mid-motion. Screaming in silence.

They're torn from the skies. Ripped from the rivers. Wrenched from the forests.

Nine of the gods and goddesses are thrown to the floor of the stone chamber. Frozen, incapacitated by whatever spell Thalmyr has them under.

But in their final suspended moments—before their bodies are dragged into oblivion, before their voices are swallowed by the void —they act.

Not with words. Not with war. But with memory. With will. *With magic.*

Their essences, fractured and fading, pulse outward—nine

divine threads of light seeking sanctuary in the physical world. They reach for what they can: sacred places, sacred objects, sacred blood-lines. The oldest stones. The roots of ancient trees. The blades of fallen Stars.

The relics. They reach for the relics.

Beautiful golden light is cast around the chamber like a spider's web of divine magic.

Thalmyr turns to the cloaked figure—Daphinia—again, urging her to act.

But the gods and goddesses of this world don't relent. They continue weaving their magic, infusing it into the physical world—their final sacred rebellion.

They don't leave weapons. They leave keys.

Keys to awakening.

Keys to reclaiming what was stolen.

Keys to what comes next.

Daphinia slices through Thalmyr's palm, blood pooling in his hand.

He takes three long strides to the center of the circle of runes and allows a single drop of blood to fall from his hand.

The blood lands on the chamber floor, and within a single heart-beat, the gods are cast out—flung into a prison between realms. *Trapped.*

Whatever Thalmyr did—this spell—exiled the gods from our lands, leaving us to our wars, our suffering, our slow unraveling beneath power-hungry hands. *A godless realm.*

Thalmyr. He just stands there. Breathing heavy. Smiling.

A basin behind him begins to glow—fed by the tether he carved between realms. Their essence flows through it like leashed light, channeled from exile to empire.

I'm panting. Unable to center myself amongst the visions. I clutch my chest as if my hands can relieve the pressure there.

But before I can even take another breath, the vision fractures.

Light rips apart and reforms as stone walls emerge once more, but this time the chamber is not vast and ceremonial like before—

it's jagged, damp, and ancient. Hidden. It feels buried beneath years of dust and blood.

Dark iron torches flicker with green flame.

An altar sits at the center of the room, and around it, chalked in crimson sigils and carved bone, is a summoning circle.

A man kneels at its heart.

He's older, cloaked in royal navy trimmed with silver, a faint crown glinting in his golden brown hair. He looks familiar—his profile stern and shadowed, strong and noble.

Kael.

No... not Kael.

This is his father.

King Aurius.

I watch as he reaches into a small iron bowl and paints three lines of blood across the stone. His voice trembles as he chants, not with fear, but desperation.

"God of Endings. Guardian of the Final Gate. Morrathys, hear me. I do not summon you to command, only to beg. Spare my people. Break your curse. Return balance to Zerynthia."

The shadows swell.

A second man steps into the circle, silent until now. He bears Aurius's face—sharper, crueler. A brother.

They exchange no words, only a knowing look.

Then the circle ignites.

The runes flare green and black, and the altar shakes with power. A shape unfurls in the shadows. Ancient and beautiful— terribly so.

Morrathys. The tenth god.

Skin like moonlight, smooth and pale, stretched over a frame too tall, too still. Hair as dark as a raven's wing falls around his shoulders, and his eyes—gods, his eyes—are fathomless pools of night.

He does not walk—he *descends*. Graceful and slow.

"I am not yours to summon," Morrathys grits out, voice like breaking stone. "But I have watched. And I have listened. And now I have come."

He steps into the circle. The torches snuff out.

The room holds its breath.

Aurius stands to speak again—but he is not given the chance.

The second man moves.

Steel flashes.

A blade pierces Aurius's side.

The King gasps, stumbling forward, gripping the altar for support. "Brother..." he rasps.

Then, louder—broken and bitter, "Maldrak..."

I freeze.

Maldrak.

Maldrak is Kael's uncle.

The usurper. The man who exiled Kael and stole his throne.

The moment Aurius collapses, Maldrak steps into his place. His hands still slick with royal blood, he raises them over the altar.

"I offer blood to bind," he says, calm and cruel. "Not for mercy. Not for balance. But for dominion."

Chains of smoke whip from the altar, wrapping around Morrathys like tendrils of iron.

He struggles—shrieks—and the walls of the chamber splinter with the force of his resistance. But he's already caught in the snare of the ritual. Bound by the ancient law that governs even gods.

Maldrak places his hand to the altar, and the spell seals with a flash of green flame.

The torches relight. And Morrathys goes still.

Not dead.

Enslaved.

I watch in horror as Maldrak carves a symbol into the altar with the point of his blade—a twisted, jagged 'M'.

The Mark of Morrathys. Of death.

Then he presses the blade to his forearm and slices it open. With his blood, he brands the first soldier standing behind him—marking him with that same symbol.

The man collapses, writhing.

Then... rises.

His eyes are empty. Obedient. *Leashed.*

Behind Maldrak, dozens more soldiers await.

One by one, he brands them.

Each time, Morrathys's bound essence surges through the mark, latching onto the soldier, turning them into something else—*not dead, not living, not free.*

An army of revenants.

Not loyal by oath.

Loyal by brand.

My stomach turns. My vision spins. I can't breathe.

The last thing I see before the vision begins to crack is Aurius's crown, stained with blood, resting on the altar like a warning.

And Maldrak's eyes.

Looking toward the throne not as a burden... but a birthright.

As the chains finish binding Morrathys in shadow-light, Maldrak doesn't even look back at what he's done. Instead, he turns to his soldiers—those branded with the Mark of Morrathys, eyes void of will—and says coldly, "Take him to the Temple of Endings. Seal it. No one opens it unless I command it."

And just like that, the God of Death vanishes from the world— not exiled to some distant realm like the others, but buried right here in Zerynthia. Slumbering. *Waiting.*

The scene before me fades, and I am falling through the night sky again.

I let myself fall this time. The visions race through me, crashing through my mind as I drift through starlight.

My mother. The marriage cuff. Thalmyr. Aurius. Maldrak. The blood spell. Nyrielle. Morrathys. The Mark.

My chest rises too fast. Falls too hard.

Nothing is as it seems.

The air around me rumbles, sending a ripple through my body.

I gasp at the sudden jolt.

The crown releases me.

I collapse to my knees, heaving, body trembling.

I look up, and Kael's eyes meet mine from across The Grove.

Suddenly, I'm not sure which part of the vision scares me more —what's been done, who I am, or what I'm destined to do.

The air thins. The Grove tilts.

I drop to the ground, limbs shaking.

My chest burns bright, searing pain dragging across my skin. Points of the Eye of Lireal carving into my skin, branding, claiming, permanent.

And then—darkness swallows me whole.

CHAPTER SEVENTY-TWO
KAEL

I DON'T KNOW WHAT SHE SAW IN THOSE VISIONS, BUT SHE LOOKED haunted. *Tormented.*

I've nestled her limp frame against my body for the ride back to Thornewood, and she hasn't stirred at all. Her breathing is steady, though I keep attempting to access her through the tether, and she feels vacant.

With the setting sun dropping below the treeline, we pull into Thornewood and are greeted by Rubi, Seren, Daelen, and Rowan. They surround us, looking expectant and eager.

I nod curtly.

"We'll rest," I announce. "And convene in Council Hollow when the moon reaches its highest point." My words are commanding.

Zak's brother, Rhyven, approaches the group. He's not part of the council, but he's been a good and loyal man over the years. While Therion and I have been searching for Elyssara, Rhyven has stepped up to track and hunt for the people of Thornewood. He has his father's head and heart, which unfortunately didn't extend to Zak—*he* is only skilled with the mind.

"I hope your return signals another relic secured, Your Highness," he says sincerely, bowing slightly in deference. No matter how many years go by or how many times he's heard everyone else call me Kael, his preference for propriety wins. Zak rolls his eyes, and the tight exhale he lets out doesn't go unnoticed.

"Elyssara was judged as worthy and valid by The Grove *and* the crown, yes," I choose my words wisely, directing them to Zak. "She is a rightful Queen of this realm," I add, my words precise and cutting.

"What brilliant news, my prince. We've hunted wild boar in your absence in hopes of celebration. Tonight, we feast." Rhyven's smile is genuine and warm. His loyalty to Zerynthia—and the crown—is steadfast.

"Good," I say, nodding in approval. "Rest, eat, drink, and tonight, we convene under the moon's peak," I spin on my heel, Elyssara heavy in my arms, desperate to get her to my room. She needs rest.

"I'll send Rubi for Elyssara," Therion shouts to me as I make my way to my room.

My room still smells of her—vanilla and sandalwood are etched into my blankets and pillows, hanging in the air like even her scent knows she belongs here, with me.

I lay her down gently, brushing loose auburn strands from her face. Her breathing is shallow, increasing in pace and intensity. She's dreaming. Or perhaps, she's reliving the visions. Her movements mirror her actions in The Grove. I gently shake her shoulders. "Elyssara," I breathe.

A small whimper escapes her, brows furrowing in distress, "Elyssara, wake up!"

I gently tap her cheek, becoming more urgent, "El! You need to wake up!"

Her eyes spring open, and she gasps for air, pressing into her elbows to sit bolt upright. Sweat beads on her brow, breath rushing in and out of her.

I pull her into my chest, holding her, "It's okay," I assure her. "You're safe. I'm here."

Her breathing begins to calm, the tension in her muscles slowly dissolving under my touch.

She looks up at me with wide green eyes, thick with relief yet edged with something else. Something conflicting.

"He's your uncle," her words come out like a whisper as she averts her gaze.

I know exactly who she means without further explanation.

I let out a shaky breath. "Yes," I allow, though the word tastes like ash. "In name only." I pause for a heartbeat, gathering myself. "He stopped being my uncle the day he betrayed my father."

She stills, lifting her gaze to mine again, and looks at me knowingly—the visions have already told her.

"Why didn't you tell me?" Her voice breaks on the last word. *Because I didn't want you to think I was like him.*

"Because it doesn't change anything. He's bled our lands dry. Forsaken our people. Taken my throne. Imprisoned my sister. It doesn't matter who he is," I say, my voice low and brutal. "He dies."

Her penetrating stare bores into me, and then she nods, "He dies." She opens her mouth to speak, but words don't come. She hesitates, snapping it shut again. I can feel her apprehension through the tether, but I give her time to consider her words. She looks at me intensely and finally says, "You're nothing like him, Kael." She says it like a truth, not just a comfort.

"He's my kin," is all I can offer, because although I fucking hate the wicked, cruel man, our blood is the same no matter how much I wish it weren't.

"No matter your blood or the sky you were born under, we all have a choice in who we become," she says with conviction. "Kael," she turns her entire body to me, giving me her full attention and physical presence, "*you* are a good man."

I can see that she believes it. Believes that I'm a good man.

But she hasn't seen what I'll do yet. Who I'll become to end this.

"Careful, El. You almost sound like you believe you have a choice in all this," I force a smirk, chasing away the dark.

She huffs a laugh, a genuine smile taking over her face. It soon dissipates as she's reminded of all that's happened.

"I've done bad things, Duskae," I say with a shake of my head.

Her eyes meet mine. "For good reasons, Kael," she says with genuine warmth.

"We both have," I agree.

She nods, and I hope she's starting to forgive herself for all that's come to pass in her life.

She swallows thickly, pausing thoughtfully as if weighing her words carefully. Finally, she speaks, "Do you know that he keeps Morrathys entombed in The Temple of Endings? That he's bound Morrathys to himself?"

Surprise ripples through me. "Morrathys is here in the physical plane?" I know that Morrathys is leashed to Maldrak somehow, but entombed? *That's definitely new information.*

She nods. "Maldrak's entire army is leashed with some mark on their necks as well. They're almost... inhuman," she says, disgust twisting her face.

I don't speak. Not right away. Because something in her expression—patient, waiting—tells me there's more. And I need to hear it.

"Tell me," I say instead. "Everything."

She nods, just once. And then... she begins.

CHAPTER SEVENTY-THREE
ELYSSARA

I tell him everything.

The cuff. The fallen monarchy. My bloodline. My mother.

The gods' betrayal. Nyrielle. The god-magic relics. Thalmyr. Daphinia. Maldrak.

Every breath the crown dragged from me. Every truth it unearthed.

Everything.

The words unspool from my mouth, flowing freely as I consolidate everything the crown thrust upon me.

I don't know what terrifies me more—reliving the horrors of the visions or the cold, dark fury that comes over Kael as he listens.

Night has fallen around us, darkness seeping in through the knots and hollows of the tree Kael's room is cradled in. My stomach growls in hunger, and tiredness aches through my bones.

Kael leans back against the pillows, pulling me into his chest—tucking me into the crook of his arm like I belong there.

He brushes a kiss into my hair, but his voice—low and dark—still cuts through the quiet.

"They'll all die."

Despite the exhaustion that gnaws at me, my hatred, vengeance, and fury flood my senses, "Every fucking one of them." My voice is gritty and raw.

"I love it when you're violent, El," Kael says, voice gravelly and rough. "You're not the kind of woman who hides behind pretty dresses and propriety. You're the kind of woman who leaves a mark on the world with her blade, her mind, *and* her heart."

His words cleave through the fragile casing around my heart.

Not because they're cruel.

But because they're true.

I can't speak, tears threaten to spill down my cheeks, and my throat goes thick with emotion.

I've spent so long dulling my edges.

Biting back my rage.

Playing small so I wouldn't scare the people around me.

Saving the real me for the dark streets of Virellin—and putting on a pretty, palatable mask in the harsh light of day.

But Kael doesn't flinch at the fire in me.

He leans into it.

Like he finds *home* in my darkness.

He sees the fractured parts of me—and holds them together.

He sees them, and he *stays*.

I tuck myself into his chest, into the warmth of him, and for the first time... I start to believe.

That maybe there is so much more life beyond the prophecy.

That maybe I don't have to bury who I am to become who I'm meant to be.

Kael unfurls me from his arms, covering me with a blanket, "Stay and rest, Duskae." His voice is tender and warm, "I'll return with food and ale."

"Okay," I agree in a whisper, voice raw with emotion.

I watch as the towering warrior—my Prince of Zerynthia— heads for the door. The armor across his broad shoulders catches the moonlight seeping through the window, illuminating him in silver. He looks back at me briefly and winks at me with that infuri- atingly handsome smirk, before closing the door after him.

For the first time in what feels like weeks, I am left alone to my own thoughts.

Perhaps in another world, at another time, I might've made a home here, nestled amongst the trees. Seren seems to have found a friend in Rubi, Ronyn would find a role here in the rebellion, and me? Well, waking up next to Kael, living beyond the prophecy... it's a reality I never thought I could have. Never let myself believe I *could* have.

My thoughts are interrupted by a sharp knock at the door. I climb out of bed, dragging my aching bones and tired muscles to the door.

I throw it open, lips curling into a smile. "You really can't stay away for too long, can you, my prince—"

Zak.

Not Kael.

His fists clenched, knuckles white with the pressure. His mouth is twisted into a sneer, and his nostrils are flared as if he's barely leashing his fury.

"Lightborne," he snarls, pressing one of his wide palms flat on the door, barring me from closing it.

I slide my hand down to my thigh inconspicuously, feeling for my dagger, and feign nonchalance, "Your Prince has gone to the feast momentarily, but he'll be back soon. What can I do for you, Zak?

I feel for my blade again, but I know it's not there. I can't sense its presence or feel its weight at my thigh. Kael must've taken my thigh holsters off while I was unconscious. *Fuck.*

He takes a step towards me, but I hold my ground, keeping my rising panic in check.

"You are getting in the way, Elyssara," he seethes.

I try desperately to make a plan to either get to my blades, or diffuse him, but I'm blank, my mind still hazy from losing consciousness.

"What exactly am I getting in the way of, Zak?" I spit the words at him.

His breathing is ragged, his teeth bared, and I can smell the faint hint of alcohol on his breath.

He steps closer, and for a moment, I think he might strike. Then he says it—quietly, cruelly, "He will never get Nalya as long as you are alive."

"Kael loves his sister. He will not leave her to rot!" My pitch heightens, no longer able to quell my panic. Though Kael hasn't told me his plans to rescue her, I know he wouldn't leave her. Not for me. Not for anyone.

"He was always too much like his father—*soft, weak,*" the words flood out of him as if they've been pent up for years. "Too eager to look after every poor charity case that comes begging."

Something inside me snaps, and my magic springs to attention. I try to summon it, but it's like reaching through thick water—my magic is there, but it won't obey. Something about it feels sluggish, slow. Still, the air cracks around us, and my fury roars to life.

I take a step towards him, closing the gap between us, "What makes you think she'd even want you, Zak?" I say the words with mocking malice, every word chosen to inflict pain. "She'd take one look at you, at what you've become—arrogant, jealous, deceitful—and turn away. Perhaps Maldrak's cell would even be preferable to her?"

His jaw twitches. *Good. I've struck something real.*

I keep going, "You're already dead, Zak." I smile—bravado masking the terror in my bones. I've dealt with brutes before. Rage makes them sloppy. And it's the only edge I've got. "When *he* hears about this, you have no chance. You're a walking fucking corpse, Zak."

He tilts his head. A slow, predatory smile creeps across his face.

He takes another step towards me, pushing past the door, and kicking it shut. "Or, perhaps, your beloved prince will never hear about it at all," his voice is low, almost a whisper.

"Fucking try me," I drop low into a fighting stance, ready to fight without a weapon. Revryn's words float through my mind.

Before you ever pick up a blade, remember this: you are the weapon.

He moves to strike, but I'm faster, I kick out with my foot, slamming it into his ankle. He swallows a cry, but barely flinches. *He's a Bloodbond.* Realization crashes into me. They're known for their battle fury, endurance and regeneration, so there's no way I'll win on strength alone.

"Come here, you little bitch," he growls.

I try to summon my magic again, but it's subjugated by my exhaustion from The Grove.

The moonlight glints in the corner of my eye and I chance a look—my thigh holster sitting on a small table next to the bed.

If I can just get there—

Zak sees the opening and wrenches my head back by my hair.

I cry out. I'm overpowered and weaponless. *Think, Elyssara. Think.*

"He should've fucked you and discarded you right from the beginning," he spits. "The only thing you're good for." The greed and entitlement in his eyes tells me everything I need to know. I've seen this look in the eyes of self-righteous men before. Usually in the early hours of the morning after a long stint at the tavern. Entitled men that think they have the right to use and discard the bodies of women for their own debased pleasures.

I grit my teeth, and this time, I summon vengeance. If I can't have my magic, I know vengeance will always come when I call. I throw my elbow back behind me as hard and as fast as I can, catching him in the throat.

He growls in frustration, coughing, and reaching for his throat with the hand that was gripping my hair. *Now is my opportunity.*

I run for my thigh holster, the Starforged Blade illuminating, as if it knows I'm calling it. I stretch out my hand, feeling the cool hilt on my fingertips—

"I don't fucking think so," Zak croons, as he wraps his arm around my neck, his forearm crushing my windpipe.

He drags me across the room, his spare hand finding the laces of my leathers. He wrenches them down, pushing them past my hips, hands groping at me with liberties that are not his, his forearm still cutting off the air from my lungs.

I try desperately to scream, to kick my legs, to throw my elbow back again, but it's useless. I rasp. My vision splinters. He's too strong. I'm pinned. We crash into the side of the bed, and I do the only thing I can think to do.

Kael, I rasp down the tether. *Zak—*

And then, darkness.

CHAPTER SEVENTY-FOUR

KAEL

"You've outdone yourself, Rhy," I say to Rhyven, swallowing down another mouthful of wild boar. I wash it down with ale.

"It's my pleasure, my prince," he inclines his head politely.

"Rhy, please," I'm almost begging at this point. "We've known each other since we were boys. Just call me Kael," I laugh.

His cheeks flush, but he smiles good-naturedly.

"Or if you prefer, you can always call him bastard, asshole, fool, or perhaps even a cu—"

"Daelen!" Seren admonishes. "No, you absolutely cannot call him that!"

The group bursts into laughter. Even Therion can't keep the smile off his face.

"See, I knew I liked him," Ronyn says, elbowing Daelen in the ribs in camaraderie.

"I say, it's completely okay to call him any of those things," Rubi pauses for a beat before adding, "when it's accurate."

"Which is often," Merrik whispers conspiratorially to the group.

Rubi lifts a tankard, mischief on her lips, "Cheers to that."

It's been a long time since I've sat around a fire with my people.

My mind drifts to Nalya, imprisoned in Maldrak's dungeons, wasting away, likely clinging to life.

I shake the thoughts from my head. I've spent too many years not living because I didn't feel worthy of it while Nalya isn't living at all. But tonight, I let myself enjoy this. The company, the ale, the meat, the beautiful woman asleep in my bed.

I take another bite and feel a whisper at the edges of my mind. A gentle scraping against my mind, so weak, so soft, that I second-guess myself.

I take another sip from my tankard, the pulse at the edges of my awareness, getting more insistent.

Then, the tether snaps taut, pulling tight in my chest. *Kael!* Elyssara screams down the tether. *Zak!*

That's all I need. She called my name—and *his*.

Something's horribly fucking wrong.

Therion notices my shift instantly, "What is it?"

"Elyssara," I say before drawing my sword and heading straight for my room.

"Right behind you, brother," he says.

I don't thank him. I don't look back.

I bolt.

Lethal rage pulses through me, and the need for blood takes over.

I take the stairs three at a time. The door's ajar.

I burst into the room and almost crumble at the horrifying sight in front of me.

Mottled skin blooms across her throat.

Scratches and cuts lace her thighs—marks from hands that didn't belong.

Blood clings to her fingernails. She fought.

Zak's slitted eyes land on me, and he moves to open his mouth.

He doesn't even get a scream out before my blade finds his ribs.

I don't remember moving.

Only my need for blood. My fury. *Her.*

I withdraw my blade. But I can't stop.

My blade finds his chest.

His shoulder.

I slice through his abdomen, gutting him like a pig for the spit.

Strong arms wrap around my chest from behind, "He's gone, brother." Therion's voice cuts through my blind rage just long enough to reach me.

Zak's body crumbles to the ground and the world around me roars back to life.

I nod briefly, just to let him know I heard.

I drop my sword, blade clanging against the wooden ground, rushing to Elyssara.

Her leathers hang off her in shreds, baring skin that was never his to touch. I cover her with my cloak, shielding what he tried to steal. "Get out!" I yell, commanding the others who have followed, weapons drawn in preparation. "String him up in the village square!"

She's limp in my arms, and I can't help but soothe her despite knowing she can't hear me.

"I've got you. You're safe now. I'm here."

CHAPTER SEVENTY-FIVE
KAEL

THE MOON HANGS HEAVY AND BRIGHT—ALMOST AT ITS PEAK.
Watching. Waiting.

I asked Merrik to watch over Elyssara in my room and sent Rubi to heal her, though I know the worst of the attack won't be physical.

I stride into Council Hollow, and the war council members have already taken their seats. There's a heaviness in the room. A palpable tension.

They all stare at me, breaths held. Assessing.

There's no time to grieve. No time to feel the full weight of everything. Not when war looms.

Therion, Jax, Varian, Daelen, Rubi, Lady Sylvaine, Eldric, and Rowan. Ronyn and Seren stand on the edge of the room, faces solemn. I invited them here tonight—Seren is our best planner, and Elyssara needs Ronyn wherever she goes; that much is clear.

I sent word for Rhyven to join us, too. I need to know if he's a threat after everything that happened with Zak. He's the last one to arrive, looking regretful, and he averts his gaze when I try to make eye contact.

I clear my throat, "I've called the war council together tonight for a few reasons." My voice is commanding and unwavering—a skill I learned from my father. "Much has come to light since our journey to Starlit Grove, and I owe you all an update. Secondly, we need a comprehensive plan for the next journey to the fourth relic," I pause for a heartbeat. "And finally," I turn to Rhyven. "We need to discuss the events from earlier this evening." I stare at him unflinchingly.

Without hesitation, he kneels with the symbol of Zerynthia pressed between his hands—like a man asking not just for forgiveness but for a future, "I beg for your mercy, my prince."

I regard him with the full weight of my scrutiny, my stare unrelenting.

"Zak chose his path. And paid the price," I let the loaded words hang in the air for a beat. "But I won't have this council splinter further, and I won't be questioning where your loyalties lie again," he lifts his head, his gaze meeting mine. "If you've something to say, speak now, Rhyven."

He inhales, steadying himself, but his trembling hands don't escape my notice. "All I ask, Your Highness, is that you give me an opportunity to prove my undying loyalty to Zerynthia and my fealty to you," he stammers the words.

I look around the room at the war council—Eldric, who has been on this council with my father since before I was born and who has always been a wise and just servant, nods his acceptance and approval. Lady Sylvaine nods tightly, and her approval carries merit—she's masterful in court politics and judging one's character.

Therion doesn't move, still weighing Rhyven's words and integrity.

Varian nods predictably, though his judgment lacks the weight of the others. There's always an angle with him.

Jax shakes her head, though I expected that. Jax is critical and often beyond reproach, even if wrongdoing is by association alone.

Daelen nods, and though he can be brash and shameless, his opinion is one I respect.

"Please, my prince," Rhyven begs. "Don't judge me by my brother's actions. I know better than anyone how overindulgent and misguided he could be. I beg you—see me for who I am, not who I'm tied to," he pleads the words, voice cracking in desperation.

I look to Therion again. His nod is nearly imperceptible—so faint I almost doubt seeing it. But it's enough for me.

"Very well," I say with a nod. "You'll get your chance to prove your loyalties, Rhyven, but they'll need to be earned." Despite being Zak's brother, he's also his father's son. Brannon was a good man, a loyal soldier, and most importantly, a Zerynthian through and through. Rhyven is no different—though his loyalty will soon be tested by the sight of his brother's body hanging in the village square.

"Thank you for your mercy, Your Highness," Rhyven stands, backing towards the door as if hoping for a swift exit.

"I don't offer mercy. I offer an opportunity to prove your loyalties," I announce. "Sit down," I say with fierce command.

He nods quickly and stammers, "Of course, of course. Anything you need."

He pulls out a chair and sits, though his nervousness is apparent. I don't blame him—I'm not known for being overly forgiving.

"Seren, Rowan—what of the next relic?" I gesture to Seren to sit down.

Seren clears her throat delicately, placing the old piece of parchment on the table and sliding it forward. "We're looking at this section here," she says, pointing to the lines that read:

> *Where ruins burn and the Flame-heart sleeps,*
> *The dragon stirs in the soul it keeps.*
> *And in the skies where wild winds sing,*
> *Beast and bond form a timeless ring.*

"And what have you discovered?" Lady Sylvaine asks.

Seren's face shifts from innocent and pure to scholarly and wise in a heartbeat. Her brows furrow in concentration, and she begins, "My mother used to tell me a bedtime story about the *sleeping flame.* She said it lived beneath the ashen ruins of a city that vanished. A city so old, even the maps forgot it." She looks around at the room, and we've all leaned in, elbows resting on the table, eagerly awaiting her discoveries. "She used to say, *'The flame remembers. Even if the world does not.'* I thought it was just a tale."

Rowan interjects smoothly, "Seren told me about this tale, wondering if the sleeping flame was connected to the Flame-heart from the prophecy, so I Memory Walked thousands of records looking for threads and archives relating to it," he pauses for a heartbeat, looking straight at me. "I found something... unexpected. Something big."

I incline my head, trying to mask my eagerness. "And?"

"There's an ancient myth that speaks of the Flame-heart as a dormant soul of a dragon," he lets the words hang in the air. No one speaks, all of us holding our breath in collective curiosity. "The Flame-heart is not a literal beating heart, but the preserved soul of an ancient dragon that carries the will and memory of the most powerful dragon."

"I can add to this myth," Lady Sylvaine announces, her voice firm and confident—a reminder of her decades advising kings— and I can't help but raise my eyebrows in surprise. "Don't give me that look, boy—I advised the last three kings. There are things I was never meant to forget," she says, giving me a wry smile. "The ancient dragons were soul-bound to the Dravari royal line—not just as their allies, but their protectors," Lady Sylvaine says with such conviction that I'm inclined to accept it as the truth.

"Are you telling me that the dragons aren't really extinct?" Ronyn asks quizzically from behind Seren.

"I'm telling you that their extinction is largely fabricated, yes. Many were killed, but others went into hiding when the Dravari throne fell," Lady Sylvaine confirms. "Now, they're sleeping, dormant. I don't know where. They're wiped from Dravara's memory along with everything else of importance, no doubt—they'd pose a great threat to Thalmyr."

Ronyn drags his hands through his shaggy brown hair, eyes blown wide in surprise. "Well," he drawls, "fuck."

Fuck, indeed.

"How do you know how the Dravari monarchy fell?" I ask,

genuinely curious to know how this unassuming courtier knows so fucking much.

She looks at me sardonically and says, "How do *you* know how the Dravari monarchy fell?"

The sneaky old woman.

I smirk. *Now I know why my father liked her and kept her on his council despite many opposing her position.*

I pause for a moment, weighing the merits of sharing this. "Since Elyssara informed me that she is the lost Dravari heir according to the Obsidian Crown," I reveal, feeling the weight of the admission settle heavily in my chest.

The room stills. The council is silent, processing the information.

"You couldn't just pick a regular woman with no royal lineage, bound magic, or fucking soul-bonded dragon, brother?" Daelen whistles, dragging his hand down his face.

"Yeah, what he said—except she's my best friend, so pretend I didn't," Ronyn quips.

I smile at Ronyn and Daelen—they're trouble when they're together.

I quickly drag my gaze back to Rowan and Seren, "We'll get to Elyssara in a moment, but first, how do we find these ashen ruins of a city?"

Rowan sits up a little straighter, "The only information I can pull from my archives is that there is a lost kingdom that can be accessed through an enchanted waterfall somewhere in Zerynthia where the Flame-heart sleeps. The only detail I could decipher during the Memory Walk was an ancient rune carved into a rock beside the falls—one I've never seen in any other record." Rowan shrugs as if what he's said isn't fucking world-changing.

I don't miss the way Lady Sylvaine huffs out a shaky breath— apprehensive, maybe. Perhaps what's hidden doesn't want to be found?

Rhyven raises his hand, "I believe I can actually help with that, my prince." He swallows thickly, his unsettledness still obvious, "I've tracked elk to the ends of Zerynthia and have seen a waterfall with a rune."

"And I can read the runes," Seren adds enthusiastically.

I nod, taking in the information, weighing it all. "And how exactly is the Flame-heart preserved?"

Seren's eyes flick between Rowan and me, slightly uncertain. "We don't really know," she admits. "But we assume it's kept in some sort of vessel, but Rowan found no archive, and I have nothing in the few books I was able to bring," Seren concedes.

I tap my chin in thought, eyes dropping to the table.

Eventually, I lift my gaze, pinning Rhyven with my stare. "Rhyven, I guess it's your chance to prove your loyalty—we leave for the waterfall when the sun rises."

CHAPTER SEVENTY-SIX
KAEL

I don't finish up in Council Hollow until the early hours of
the morning.

I told the council everything about the visions at The Grove—
everything about Elyssara.

The council had their hesitations about Elyssara initially, but
now they understand—we need her. We need her to defeat
Maldrak, to bring down The Decay, to remove Thalmyr as a threat,
to have any chance of rescuing Nalya. She knows more than we
could ever discover on our own. But more than that, *I need her*.

Every logical voice in my head knows that I shouldn't be feeling
whatever I'm feeling for her. In another reality, we'd be sitting on
opposing thrones, negotiating peace treaties from across the continent, bartering trade prices via messengers. We were never meant to
be together. Never meant to feel this *pull*.

Fuck, the Stars know it. I know it. But I'm a selfish bastard. I've
lost the people I love the most, and I won't lose her. Not a fucking
chance.

I leave Council Hollow and head straight for my room where
Elyssara rests.

I knock softly on the door, peeking my head into the room, not expecting to see Merrik with his sword drawn and aimed at my throat.

"It's just me, you old bastard," I chide playfully.

"Well, you'd have my balls in a vice if I didn't protect the lass with my fuckin' life, wouldn't ya?" He counters mockingly.

I huff a laugh. "I would," I concede. "How is she?"

Rubi stands up from Elyssara's bedside, a belt filled with herbs and tinctures hanging from her waist, face serious for once. "Physically, she's fine," she states simply. "But it's her mind and her heart that may take more mending."

I nod. I'd already assumed that.

"I've given her some willowbalm to help her sleep, and tended to her cuts and scratches," Rubi says in a hushed voice. "She's resilient," she says softly, pausing. "Almost too resilient."

I know. She's learned to brace for the fall before it comes.

"She's been through a lot," I say, voice low.

"She was calling out for her mother," Rubi adds. "What do you know of her?"

I exhale heavily, gesturing to Merrik and Rubi to move away from the bed. "I've already told the council, so I may as well tell you both now, too. She's the Dravari heir. Her mother was killed by Thalmyr," I say clearly and concisely.

Rubi sucks in a sharp breath, clapping her hands over her mouth to cover her gasp.

"Fuck," Merrik grits out, placing his hands on his hips in astonishment.

"She's also soul-bound to the dragons, and the last one's soul is preserved in a vessel in a lost kingdom," I let the weight of my words hang between us. I know how ridiculous this sounds. I know how far off-track we've gone, but I can't help but feel that this is precisely where I'm meant to be, anyway.

"I need a fucking drink," Rubi groans, rubbing her temples.

"You've got to be kiddin' me," Merrik says. "Lad, I know how you feel about her, but isn't this getting...," he weighs his words, carefully selecting them, "you know, a bit beyond any semblance of a plan?"

"She *is* the plan," I say tightly. "Merrik, I won't lose her. I will not let anyone hurt her. I won't use her."

He shakes his head as if he's about to dissuade me, "Look, I like the girl, and I know you have feelings for her—"

I cut him off, "It's more than that. We're tethered somehow. I can't explain it, but it's... like she's part of me."

Merrik looks exasperated, but I know he has a big heart. My father trusted him. Confided in him. He groans, internally warring with himself.

"Merrik, I need you to come with us to find the vessel. Most of the council are coming, aside from Eldric, Varian, Lady Sylvaine— we'll need your guidance and intel," I say. "And I need you to look out for Jax."

"Ugh," he grumbles, hesitating, and scrubbing a hand over his beard. He pauses for a long moment, "You know I'll go wherever you tell me, ya little brat."

A laugh escapes me, and I slap him on the shoulder. "You, too, Rubes. We need a healer among us, especially with how Elyssara is."

Rubi has practically lived in the infirmary in Thornewood for years, tending to every ache and pain from children to the elderly. Seeking pleasures in the wild mushrooms and experimenting with brewing her own liquors. I knew she'd jump at the chance to come. "Fuck yes," she says, pumping her fists in the air. She needs this—an escape, a purpose, a fight worth joining beyond tonics and healing balms.

"I thought you'd be excited," I laugh.

"And what are we getting excited about?" a voice croaks from behind us.

Elyssara.

"You're awake," I rush over to her, taking a seat on the bed.

Merrik and Rubi slip out of the room, leaving Elyssara and me alone.

"How are you?" I blurt the words out, scanning her body for injury.

"I'm... okay, I think," she says, closing her eyes, assessing. She winces as she shifts in bed, then masks it with a question "What happened in the meeting? Did Seren have a plan for the next relic?"

What I say next will almost be as much a revelation to her as finding out she's the Dravari heir.

What I'm about to tell her is about so much more than the return of the dragons or the next key to unbinding her power. This is personal. Familial. *Emotional.*

"They did good work—we're leaving to find it at first light, depending on how you recover," I begin gently.

"I'm ready," she says sternly, convincing me.

A small smile stretches across my mouth, "I knew you'd say that." I pause, softening my tone even further, "There were some significant revelations, El."

"Oh?" She pulls herself up to sit.

"The Flame-heart from the prophecy is the preserved soul of the last dragon who is dormant. Sleeping," I explain, and she looks at me wide-eyed. "And the dragons are soul-bound to the Dravari bloodline," I add. "They're bound to *you*, El."

She doesn't speak. Doesn't blink. Just stares at the wall like the world has tilted sideways again. And maybe it has.

I reach for her hand, not just to comfort her—to remind her I'm still here.

Her fingers entwine with mine, and her gaze slowly comes back into focus, meeting mine with her realization.

"The dragons are real," she murmurs, voice almost a whisper.

"They are," I say softly.

"And they're... *mine*?" she asks, eyes wide with wonder.

"As the last living Dravari royal, yes. They're yours," I say. "We don't know how we awaken them from their dormant state, we don't even know where they are. We just know that somehow, the soul of their leader is preserved in a lost kingdom," I explain. "And we're going to find it for you."

She nods slowly, but I can still see the storm behind her eyes— the weight of what this means sparking like a tempest beneath her skin.

"Then, let's go find my dragon."

CHAPTER SEVENTY-SEVEN
ELYSSARA

THE RIVERIAN JUNGLE blooms around us as THORNEWOOD
shrinks in the distance. Nyx's steady gait beneath me calms the fire
still humming through my veins since Zak.

I know I'll have to face what happened at some point. But not
today. Not now.

Kael's arm wraps around me in a protective embrace, his hard
muscles anchoring me here with him.

I am safe. I am safe. I am safe.

Rhyven leads the way, his eyes darting left and right, just as
Therion's do when he's tracking and sensing in the way only
Aestherstrides can do. Occasionally, he looks around, letting his eyes
land on me before quickly averting them. I'm unsure if he's sizing
me up like a predator does to prey or if he's genuinely concerned
for my well-being. Likely the former.

Therion has Aura sitting on Rhyven's tail, barely giving him
space to lead on his tawny mare. Watching, assessing. I have no
doubt it's on Kael's command, but somehow, I think Therion would
be doing it, regardless.

We ride for what feels like an eternity. The luminous, vibrant
jungle blurs into itself, lunafleurs morph into moonmilk blossoms,

and miravine lilies bloom into duskwater irises until the world around me becomes a kaleidoscope of colors and phantom scents— each bloom pulsing faintly with life beneath the canopy.

The sun gives way to the rising moon, and the Stars begin to twinkle through the thick canopy above. We ride into a clearing, and Rhyven turns to the group, "We'll camp here this evening. We'll feed and water the horses, and I'll hunt for us." He nods to Kael in deference, and Kael nods back.

We all dismount from our horses and begin setting up camp for the night.

I sense someone approaching and turn swiftly, just in time to see Rhyven mere feet from me. "I'm sorry to startle you, Elyssara," Rhyven says with sincerity, arms raised in surrender. "I was hoping to catch you before we departed for the journey, but you were... recovering." He winces as he says the last word, looking at me regretfully. Rhyven waits for me to respond, but I just stare at him. Unblinking. "I want to offer you my most sincere and heartfelt apology for the actions of my brother. Zak was...," he pauses, searching for the right words, and I flinch at the mention of his brother's name. "He was ambitious and bullheaded. He had a very particular way of seeing the world and how it should be, and I've been on the receiving end of what happens when it doesn't go his way," he offers, hanging his head repentantly.

White hot rage surges through me. As if Rhyven is the victim here.

I know it's cruel, but I say it anyway, "I hope, at least for your sake, that those particular traits don't run in the family."

He huffs a laugh, "I suppose I deserved that. Unfortunately for Zak, he seemed to develop those traits of his own accord." Rhyven looks at me with humility and something akin to pride, "My father raised me to be a good man, Elyssara. A noble, respectful man and I aim to honor his memory by living like someone he'd be proud of. You can rest assured that Zak's traits will die with him."

Despite every instinct screaming to hate him, I can't ignore the quiet ache in his voice. We are not our kin. And maybe... he's trying to prove that more than anyone. We should not be judged by the actions of those around us but by our own merits. As far as Rhyven goes, he's never wronged me.

"I'm glad to hear it, Rhyven," I say, softening my tone slightly, though I can't entirely keep the bitterness from them. "I appreciate you taking the time to apologize."

"As I've said to His Highness, I look forward to proving my loyalty," he states. "Starting with capturing us all a hearty dinner," he beams a smile at me, bowing slightly, and spins on his heel, nocking an arrow in his bow, before disappearing into the jungle.

I accept his apology, but wariness of him still lingers.

While the others set up camp, Jax attempts to teach me how to control my magic enough to light a fire—much to her chagrin. The conversation is light and playful, and the weight of the world feels like it lifts temporarily from my shoulders.

These people that I was raised to fear are beginning to feel more like the friends I was never allowed to keep. Kael smiles easily around them, obviously relaxed and unguarded in their presence. I've seen Kael in battle. I've seen him command. But this—this boyish grin, this light in his eyes—it's the version of him no one else gets to see. And he's letting me see it.

Rhyven stumbles into the clearing, a river elk slung across his back, nearly crumbling under its weight.

Daelen licks his lips, "Despite your brother being an absolute twat, I'm very fucking happy you came, Rhy, if for no other reason than I'd be very hungry without you."

Rhyven's cheeks flush, a shy smile tugging at his mouth. He throws the river elk down onto the ground and pulls out his skinning knife.

"And of course, everyone is stoked I came because..." Ronyn reaches into his saddle bags, pulling out three silver flasks, "I brought Ashbrew!" He brandishes the flasks and his signature lop-sided grin and adds, "And because of my insanely good looks, of course."

"I'll take the flask over the looks," Therion jests, snatching the flask from Ronyn.

"I wouldn't mind both," Jax says with a sensuous purr, winking at Ronyn and setting his cheeks aflame with embarrassment.

"Jaxxy," Merrik chastises, shaking his head, but he can't keep the smile from his lips.

"Teddy! Pass it to me—the only liquor I have is for festering wounds," Rubi pleads petulantly.

"Absolutely fucking not," Therion quips, pursing his lips. "Not after last time you had Ashbrew."

"What happened last time?" I ask with a sly smile, my tone practically begging.

"Teddy's being a baby," she says to me, then turns back to Therion. "It wasn't that bad. I had quite a bit of fun, actually."

Therion rolls his eyes, exasperated, "The last time we drank together, Rubi picked wild mushrooms and told us they were safe to eat," he explains. "Let's just say she was wrong," he narrows his eyes at her, obviously still holding a grudge.

"I wasn't wrong, Teddy. I *lied*—there's a difference," Rubi teases.

"Therion ran around Thornewood naked, pretending to be a duskprowler," Kael chimes in, that smirk of his dimpling his cheek.

Seren gasps, clapping her hands over her mouth, "Oh I'm sorry," she stammers. "That sounds... interesting," she smooths down her skirts, trying to distract us from her flushed cheeks that have sprung to life. Therion notices her blush, and an almost imperceptible smile graces his lips.

"See? We had a good time," Rubi shrugs nonchalantly. "Things can get dull around here—I like to shake them up."

"Nothing is ever dull with you, Rubes," Therion grumbles, but there's no mistaking the fondness in his tone.

Laughter ripples around the fire, and for a moment, I forget the prophecy, the power, the pressure. For a moment, I'm just Elyssara. I'm just here... with them.

Laughter, liquor, and light conversation float around the fire while Rhyven prepares the elk.

I listen to stories about Kael as a young boy and all the mischief he and Therion got up to. He listens and laughs, entwining his fingers with mine, unabashedly claiming me as his in front of his friends. His council. His kingdom.

I feel the tears welling in my eyes. *Is this what it feels like to grow up with friends? To be part of something? To be chosen? To belong?* I let myself believe—just for a breath—that this will last. I get lost in my thoughts of belonging, of family, of having someone know you as a child, and to still know you as an adult, and all the nostalgic stories and memories you'd build together. The idea is foreign to me, having hidden myself for as long as I can remember.

Rhyven interjects, "You know, Elyssara, His Highness used to tell stories of who'd be at his side when he one day ruled." He looks at Kael, a conspirator's grin spreading across his face. It was the first time I'd seen him look at Kael this way—like a friend rather than his prince.

"For fuck's sake," Kael cringes, which only makes me want to hear it more.

"For all the Stars in the sky, please tell me," I plead eagerly.

"What was it, Therion?" Rhyven looks to Therion for confirmation.

Therion smirks slightly, "Something about a woman who felt more comfortable with a blade in her hand and blood marring her face, I believe."

Kael groans, burying his head in his hands.

"That's right," Rhyven agree. "And something about a woman who wanted to fight at his side, not hide in his tower."

Kael barks a laugh, no longer able to hide his embarrassment.

"Looks like he found her," Rhyven says, raising the flask high in the air. "To Elyssara, the woman who does not hide."

"To Elyssara!" The group bellow in unison. My eyes are locked on Kael's, unable to look away from him.

"To Elyssara," he says softly, and something loaded hangs in the air between us that feels too good to be true.

CHAPTER SEVENTY-EIGHT

ELYSSARA

We find a steady rhythm over the next five days—easy
conversation, hunting, a meal beneath the rising moon, and a flask
of liquor that burns all the way down to my belly.

The group falls into a natural dynamic—Therion and Rhyven
lead, track and hunt, Jax provokes Merrik in ways that make him
cringe and grumble in frustration, Daelen and Ronyn laugh and
share inappropriate jokes, and Rubi makes Seren blush with wild
stories of experimental herbs, pranks and tales of Therion and Kael
as young boys.

It leaves Kael and I trailing at the back of the group, sharing
stolen kisses, long embraces, and stories about who we've been
before each other. We spend a lot of time in silence, simply enjoying
the convergence of our world and the people in it.

The beauty of The Riverian Jungle is mirrored in the people
around me—so full of color, life and magic. The contrast between
this place is stark compared to the dying streets of Virellin, thick
with rot and the reek of The Black Stream.

I feel as if fate has dragged me here, pulling me along with invisible strings, urging me to the next place, the next relic, the next

moment. But now that I'm here, I feel like I'm choosing it—to stay, to live, to see this through, whatever the cost.

My thoughts are swallowed whole by the sound of rushing water. I sit up straighter in the saddle, and Kael leans forward, brushing his lips across my neck, "I think we're about to find a lost kingdom, Duskae."

Gooseflesh ripples across my skin at his touch, "And some dragons," I add.

He hums his agreement, and Therion and Rhyven urge the horses on, brushing under low-hanging vines that cloud our view ahead.

My chest tightens. The air here feels charged—like the space between lightning and thunder.

The hushed sound of water turns into a roar as we sweep through the vines, and the view steals my breath.

Water cascades over layered rock like glass, veiling the cliff side like moving glass, ancient and alive. The falls pool in the crystal-clear turquoise waters below that shimmer under dapples of sunlight, while lush greenery hangs overhead, framing the falls.

Dragonflies flit across the water's surface, and land on moss-laced stones that border the pools. Mist clings to my skin, and the air smells of petrichor and damp earth.

Despite the beauty in front of me, my eyes don't stay on the pristine waters—they go searching, scanning the area for the rune Kael told me exists here.

There.

Seren inhales sharply.

"Threshold to the forgotten," she whispers, her voice ethereal and distant, eyes locked on the rune. Her eyes are wide, glassy—like memory has brushed past her skin.

"Holy fucking Stars, it exists," Ronyn mutters in awe, as if he never really believed it would.

"I'll scout ahead," Rhyven announces, already drawing his swords and slipping into that low, predator-like stance he adopts when danger might be near. Kael gives him a tight nod.

"Do we have any idea how we actually find this threshold to the forgotten, Seren?" Kael asks.

She closes her eyes, tilting her head slightly, like she's listening for a melody none of us can hear. "In terms of records from Rowan or my books, no," she admits. "But..." Her brows pinch faintly. "I can feel it... calling to me."

The group exchanges glances, uncertain. "Little Star, what do you mean?" I ask.

"Do you remember at Lyssar Temple? When I could hear the song of the wind without knowing how?" she says, and I nod slowly. "It's like that. But stronger. Like there's a melody in the water, or the wind. A memory. Like it's part of me."

My breath catches. *Part of her.* The way the light seems to linger on her skin here, how the wind keeps brushing her hair into her eyes —it's as though the waterfall itself is trying to remember her.

I glance down at my chest, half-expecting to see the Astral Compass gleaming in the sunlight—but it's gone. Hidden. Along with the blade and crown Kael and I secreted away before we left Thornewood. The ache of separation from them is unfamiliar, but the blade Revryn forged still hangs at my thigh. It has never failed me.

"What is it calling you to do, Little Star?" I ask gently.

Seren's voice trembles. "To follow the water home."

The words settle between us like mist—soft, reverent, full of something ancient.

"Then we follow the water," Therion says without hesitation.

CHAPTER SEVENTY-NINE

ELYSSARA

Rhyven returns with a nod, satisfied that the area surrounding the falls is clear. No sign of threat—at least, not the kind we can see. We take only small rations of food and water, then make our way toward the cascade.

I don't know what waits beyond the threshold to the forgotten, but I know one thing with unshakable certainty: whatever it is, it will change everything.

I force my breathing into an even rhythm as we climb, each step dragging me closer to something I can't name. The rocks are slick with moss and spray, the sound of the waterfall growing from a hum to a roar that devours thought.

The cascade rises before us like a wall of living glass. It cuts the world cleanly in two—*this side*, and whatever lies on the other.

Though the setting is tranquil, the water crashes with astonishing force, throwing mist across our path and soaking through armor and skin alike. It slicks my palms, clings to my lashes. My braid hangs heavy down my back, already a tangled mess.

I scramble up the slated rock, jagged edges biting into my palms, feet slipping as I clamor for purchase. Just when my grip begins to fail, strong hands seize the back of my armor and haul me over the ledge.

I collapse on my hands and knees, lungs dragging in air, heart a thunderous drum. My fingers dig into stone. I'm shaking, soaked through, and utterly breathless.

Kael crouches beside me, one hand steady on my back.

"You alright?" he asks, voice low and warm.

"I am," I manage.

Around us, the others stumble into view—sodden, scraped, wide-eyed. Even Therion looks like he's been dragged through a downpour.

"Is it not slightly concerning," Ronyn starts, peeling wet curls from his face, "that we look like this and the adventure hasn't even *started* yet?"

"I thought you were always up for a plan without a plan, brother?" Therion quips, clapping Ronyn fondly on the shoulder.

Ronyn's roguish grin creeps across his face. "Which is why," he announces, dripping with cavalier charm, "I'll be going first—into wherever the fuck it takes us."

He strides towards the cascade, sopping wet curls hanging raggedly down his neck, opens his arms wide and plunges himself through the sheet of water with his head held high.

I sprint toward the falls, heart in my throat. "Ronyn!" I scream. "Ronyn!"

Seren is beside me in an instant, her scream tearing from her throat, "Ronie!"

Kael's hand settles on my shoulder. "We were all going through, anyway, El." His voice is steady, grounding, calm. "I'll go next, okay? Make sure he's alright."

I nod, tucking Seren under my arm, pulling her into my side.

"The bastard's got balls, I'll give him that," Daelen remarks from behind us.

"Or a very small brain," Jax scoffs back.

I tune it all out, focussing solely on Kael.

"I'll meet you on the other side, Duskae," Kael says tenderly, eyes on me as he walks backwards into the cascade which swallows him whole.

I suck in a sharp breath, my lungs catching on the absence—the not-knowing carving something raw through my chest.

"You need to go, El. Can't have you last with no one to cover your back," Therion says, practical as ever. "Hold Seren's hand—go through together."

Seren and I lock eyes, and clasp hands. "Together," I agree.

"Together," she whispers.

We walk towards the cascade—the end of one world, and the beginning of another—and ignore the war drum beating inside my chest. I tighten my grip on Seren's hand and charge into the unknown.

The mist coats my skin, and I feel the first crash of water hit the top of my head, and then I'm falling.

Tumbling.

Weightless.

Light. Color. Sound. Wind. They whip and swirl around me, blurring into a tunnel of weightless chaos.

I realize, suddenly, that I've been somewhere similar before—Mavyrn's gateway of threads.

Where's Seren? I look around, but I don't see her. I can't see anything but the kaleidoscopic colors and light that blur in my vision.

I feel like I'm falling upwards and downwards at the same time, disorientation causing my chest to tighten with panic.

I am safe. I am safe. I am safe. I repeat the words to myself over and over, until a hard pull gnaws at me, as if it's dragging me up. Or maybe down. It's as if I'm being pulled from the gateway.

I brace myself, waiting to be flung from the gateway into another world.

Seren—where is she?

A sudden, wrenching pull yanks me from the gateway, pulling me from the portal into the world beyond. Instinctively I suck in a long inhale, holding my breath—

I am plunged into freezing cold water that bites at my skin, sending tingling impulses through my body. I open my eyes to look around but it's as black as the night sky without Stars.

I don't know which way is up, but my lungs beg for air, so I start swimming. I claw through the water with everything I have.

My heavy boots and armor stop me from moving efficiently, but I don't care. I have to find my way. I have to find my friends. Panic crushes my chest, lungs squeezing tight in exertion and desperation.

I search the waters for any signs of—

Light.

I see light.

I do the only thing I can think to do, and force words down the tether, *Kael, where are you?*

The response is instant, *I'm here, El. Follow the light. It's for you.*

I keep swimming, relief flooding through my veins as the light gets brighter but my chest feels like it's being crushed by a boulder.

I break through the water, gasping for air, reaching for any sign of the ground. My hands find the cold stone ground, and I drag myself out as far as I can, but only make it halfway before my arms give out, so I let my chest lay limply on the stone, lungs burning. I lift my gaze, and the gleaming silver tip of a spear hovers inches from my face.

Ronyn stands beside a woman, casually tearing into a chunk of bread like he hasn't a care in the world.

He rips off a bite, then drapes an arm around the woman still aiming a spear at my face, like they're old friends, "Don't be like that, I told you there'd be more of us."

What the fuck?

"And this?" he adds, gesturing to me. "This is the one I told you about—my best friend. The rightful heir. The Zhari. Ring any bells?"

Thankfully, the spear is removed from my face, and I'm dragged out of the water by Kael and Ronyn.

Seren, Jax, Merrik, Rhyven, and Therion stand in a group nearby, all looking drowned and disheveled. *How did they get here before me?*

As if hearing my thoughts, the spear-wielding woman with skin of deep bronze, straight, onyx hair down to her waist and a leather strap pulled tight around her forehead looks to me, and says with a thick accent I can't place, "Everyone has a different journey into the unknown, Lightborne." *She knows who I am.* "The more resistance one has to the unknown, the longer and more painful the journey."

I nod, unsure what else to say to her.

I stumble forward a few steps and lift my gaze.

My mouth parts in awe as the beauty of my surroundings crash into me.

Intricate caverns, with glittering stalactites like glass chandeliers adorn the roofs. Glowing moss climbs the walls in veins of turquoise and violet. The soft echo of slowly running water from gently flowing rivers and aquamarine channels drifts through the air like a melody. The rivers cut paths through stone streets, glowing from below, casting the caverns in a turquoise glimmer.

Hollowed bridges, worn smooth by ancient feet arch over the channels.

These people—whoever they are—live in underground caves with structures that have been built straight from their hands.

It's beautiful.

The caves are dark, save for the glow of the waters, and the few torches that cast shadows that dance along the smoothed stone walls.

Where are we?

As if hearing my thoughts again, the onyx-haired woman says, "Welcome to The Lost Kingdom of Cindralis, Lightborne."

CHAPTER EIGHTY

ELYSSARA

The onyx-haired woman turns and strides forward with controlled, graceful movements. Her spear taps the ground with every step, her shoulders pulled back in quiet, unyielding confidence.

We follow without question, flanked by her kin, spears gleaming and ready.

Seren edges closer, gripping my hand. I glance at her.

Glimmering stone flickers faintly beside her, winking with each step like a memory trying to wake.

The woman glances over her shoulder. Her gaze snags on the light, lingers a breath too long, then snaps forward.

Seren stumbles, her hand slapping the wall for balance. And the stone ignites.

Light blooms around her hand in a burst of white and turquoise, the wall responding as if it knows her.

The woman watches silently. Then turns. Says nothing.

We move on.

The caverns wind tighter. Children peer out from behind curved walls. Strangers stare too long. Recognition flickers in their eyes like a secret passed down through generations.

The woman slows again, casting another look toward the glimmering wall just ahead of Seren.

Seren releases my hand and quickens her pace, closing the gap between them. I recognize that look on her face—desperate curiosity, hot and wild.

She clears her throat. "What do you know? Why is it doing that?" She gestures sharply at the glowing stone.

"These walls hold memory," the woman replies, her tone almost bored. "They whisper to those who carry the blood."

"The blood?" Seren echoes, voice lifting an octave. "What does that mean?"

"You're Veilborn." She flicks her night-black hair over her shoulder with practiced indifference.

"Veilborn?" Seren is nearly shrieking now, her brows furrowing in disbelief.

The woman exhales sharply, annoyed. "Yes."

"Why do these walls respond to me?" Seren demands. "Why do they know me?" Her voice drops to a whisper. "Why do I feel like I belong here?"

The woman's gaze sharpens. "Veilborn blood does not forget its homeland."

Homeland.

She turns to me. "Yes. Her homeland. The girl is born of Cindrali blood."

Seren steps forward, fire in here eyes. "The girl is me. Tell *me* of my homeland."

"I owe you nothing, child," the woman says coolly. "But she—" she jabs her spear toward me, "is Zhari."

She slams her spear into the ground twice.

The sound echoes like thunder through the stone. Just like the Vaythari. The rhythm reverberates in my bones.

The Vaythari are their sister tribe. *Their kin.*

The weight of the belt Syphra gave to me at my hip feels heavier now—like it knows what I'm about to say. My voice cuts through the cavern.

"I *am* your Zhari," I say, loud and clear. "Now tell me of the Veilborn."

The woman's posture shifts. Her voice deepens.

"Veilborn are rare," she begins. "A hidden magic born only of the Cindrali. We alone can sense them."

She turns fully to Seren.

"Keepers of the liminal. Protectors of the ancient. Veilborn walk between worlds—the doors between realms once belonged to them."

Seren's breath catches.

"They feel what others ignore," the woman continues. "Hear the music of the wind. Read the language of the unseen. They touch the soul of the forgotten."

Ronyn's voice cuts through the silence. "Therion *said* she had magic." He elbows the onyx-haired woman again. "He bloody knew it. Called it weeks ago. Tvira, this guy is the best Aestherstride in the realms." He shoots Therion a wink. Therion's expression doesn't flicker. "No offence, Rhy." He shoots Rhyven an apologetic glance.

"Tvira?" I ask, brow arching.

"Yep." Ronyn beams. "El, this is Tvira—leader of the Cindrali tribe, lost underground for a few hundred years, legendary warriors, sacred secrets, all that."

"And how exactly do you know Tvira?" I ask, incredulous.

Ronyn shrugs. "I think I just popped straight through the water-fall or something. Waited hours for the rest of you, so Tvira gave me food. We got to talking. You know how it goes, El."

I do know. Because this is typical fucking Ronyn.

"Ronyn has no resistance to the unknown," Tvira's tone is loaded with meaning. "He welcomes it." *Unlike me.* She didn't need to say it—the implication was heavy enough.

"So, now that Seren's officially magical and we've all had our moment—can we eat? I'm starving," Ronyn says, rubbing his belly in exaggerated motions.

"You may eat with your friends," Tvira says, "but I will take those two with me." She points to Kael and me, eyes narrowing, "I have someone who has waited a long time for you."

CHAPTER EIGHTY-ONE
ELYSSARA

Kael and I trail Tvira who walks with the grace of a honed warrior. Her hair ripples elegantly down her back with the sway of her hips, and it glints with the light of the mossy walls.

We walk in silence, but Kael's smooth, low tone rumbles down the tether, *I've got you, El. No matter what.*

I know, I reply swiftly. *It's just so much to process.*

We'll figure it out, he pauses for a heartbeat, *together.*

Together, I affirm.

Tvira's steps slow as we approach a small cavern with the flickering light of a fire greeting us at the entrance.

Tvira slams her spear down, as if this is how the Cindrali announce themselves. "Nehvara," she calls into the cavern, the smell of sweet smoke and herbs drifting out to us in the halls. "The Zhari walks among us once more," Tvira declares with gravitas.

I exchange a look with Kael, whose hand has not left the hilt of the blade sheathed at this side since we arrived, and he shrugs as if to say '*I have absolutely no fucking idea what's happening.*'

I sense movement inside, and after a few heartbeats, an older woman with the same skin of deep bronze and ink-black hair—though it's speckled with gray from age—appears at the entrance.

"You may leave us," she says to Tvira assertively, though not unkindly, and Tvira simply nods and walks away. The older woman with creased skin around her eyes and deep set grooves in her cheeks from decades of smiling, edges toward us. She drags her gaze across our faces, in a curious, intrigued manner, eyes loaded with meaning. Something about her presence is disarming, because Kael's hand falls to his side, obviously put at ease by her warm, grounding nature.

"The Lightborne is here," she greets us warmly, her rich brown eyes lingering on my face wearing an expression akin to awe or maybe even relief.

She tightens the woolen wrap around her shoulders, squeezing it to her chest, "Come in, please. I've been waiting for you."

We enter what appears to be her living quarters—an inviting rug with blankets layered on the floor for cushions are placed around a low-burning fire. It's simple, but somehow, it feels homely. She gestures for us to take a seat, her warm brown hands enveloping my own, thumbs brushing my knuckles, and squeezes them with tenderness.

The woman—Nehvara—moves to a smooth surface carved from the stone itself, and gathers drinking mugs that appear well-used, and brings them over. "I'll pour us some tea," she says gently, gesturing to the old kettle hanging above the fire. "It helps to calm the nerves." She looks at us with a knowing smile, apparently aware of my apprehension.

"That sounds lovely," I reply in a whisper.

Nehvara passes me a mug the color of clay, "Drink deeply, dear. You look like you need it."

She looks to Kael, gaze assessing, and says, "I know you don't think you need it, but you're wrong." Her knowing smile meets her eyes, and Kael takes a long sip from his mug.

We sit in awkward silence for a while, and I start fidgeting with the edge of my leather armor, desperate for something to do with my hands. I wait, trying to allow space for the woman to share why it was so imperative we came straight here. But my patience snaps— I let out an impatient huff and say, "We're here bec—"

"I know why you're here, Lightborne," Nehvara cuts me off. "And we'll get to that," she says slowly and deliberately. We settle back into silence, though I'm on edge. *Why am I here if she won't talk to me?*

Kael looks perfectly comfortable, sipping his tea and allowing the fire to warm his bones.

"How long has the tether been active?" Nehvara asks with curiosity, looking between us.

Kael and I share a brief look, before I turn back to Nehvara. I know exactly what she means. "About two weeks, I believe." *Since the moment I heard his voice in my head when I thought he was dying.*

"The first time I saw her," Kael says. I whip my gaze to him in surprise, but he's staring at Nehvara.

"The Sky called her home," Nehvara murmurs softly to herself, eyes closed, "and she listened."

She pries her eyes open, gaze landing on me. "The Lightborne and Sky must tread as one," Nehvara recites in an eerie tone, and I swear that just for a moment, the fire dims, casting Kael's face in flickering shadow—half-light, half-dark. Her voice drops low, seriousness etching her features. "The threads between you were spun in starlight long before your first breaths. But a tether is only a tether when it is chosen."

"We didn't choose this—it just happened," I countered, confusion rippling through me.

"The tether is not woven yet, dear. What you're experiencing now is simply an invitation," Nehvara says flippantly and I have no idea what she means.

"An invitation to what?" Kael demands, leaning into Nehvara's words.

"Into your Starbound Tether," she says simply.

What in the fucking Stars?

I look to Kael, then back to Nehvara, bewildered.

"The Starbound Tether is a rare fated connection between two souls. I can feel it between you," she closes her eyes, placing her hand over her heart, and inhales the rich herbs and spices from her tea. "I can see it, too."

The invitation Nehvara spoke of, it hums in the space between us now. Waiting to be answered. Or rejected.

"You can see what?" I ask. "Can Seren see it?" If Seren can see the unseen, maybe she knows whatever Nehvara does, too.

"I can see the golden threads that connect you. Mind to mind. Belly to belly. It's why you can feel each other's emotions, hear each other's thoughts," she makes it all sound so simple. "There is only one missing—that's how I know you have not yet chosen."

I can barely breathe, my chest rises and falls too quickly. "Your hearts," Nehvara says.

Kael doesn't speak, but his fingers graze mine, tracing gentle circles on the back of my hand. A tether not yet chosen, but there all the same.

"You have not chosen to give your hearts to one another. When you choose this, you will be Starbound for eternity. Always connected. Unbreakable. Always aware of the other's presence, feelings, thoughts. *Bound*," she says the last word with finality.

"What happens if we don't choose it?" I ask cautiously. "If we don't give our hearts to each other?" I can barely hear my own voice —blood rushes through my body, pulsing in my ears.

"Then the tethers will fray, and the bond will be lost," she says, and my stomach knots with dread. *I can't lose him.* "And you will defy the prophecy, of course."

"How do you know this?" I demand. "Who are you? *What* are you?" My words come out like a rasp, scratching my throat on the way out.

"I'm a Cindrali Seer—I hold wisdom in one hand and foresight in the other," Nehvara's face is still laced with warmth and tenderness as she speaks, as if she draws no pleasure from seeing me spiral uncontrollably. Even so, I can't stop the way my breath rushes in and out of me, panic settling into my bones. This is all too much. Too much pressure, too much at stake.

"What else do you know?" I ask, unable to let my curiosity relent.

She turns to Kael, eyes penetrating, as if unfurling his soul right here, "I think the question is—what does *he* know?"

Kael winces, visibly flinching under the weight of her gaze, but remains silent and stoic.

"What did the winds sing to you, Sky?" Nehvara presses.

I will protect Elyssara at all costs. I remember the truths the winds sang to Kael. I remember the way his devotion to my safety made the walls around my heart submit to him. *I remember.*

Kael closes his eyes, tips his head back and exhales deeply, as if steeling himself for whatever comes next. "The winds told me that I would need to destroy Elyssara," he pauses, hesitating on the words unspoken, and I think my chest might cave in. "Or she'd remake the world."

The world around me blurs, and my breathing turns ragged and frantic as truths collide.

"What?" I pant, unable to reconcile what I'm hearing. A silent scream tears through my mind. The words echo in the marrow of my bones. *Destroy me?*

Kael turns to me, grabbing my hands in his, "Look at me, El. Look at me," he commands, voice a desperate plea.

Tears roll freely down my cheeks, and I try to pull my hands from Kael's, but his grip is unwavering. "I don't care what is written in the Stars, Elyssara," his voice thick with emotion. "I will tear down every star in the fucking sky. I will defy them every day for the rest of my life if it means never hurting you." I lift my gaze to his, chest heaving in devastation, "I will rewrite the Stars with my bare hands because I will never destroy you. I will never hurt you. You are mine, from now until the Stars claim me." His voice is conviction incarnate and an ember stays alight in my heart.

A sob tumbles out of me—I can't bear it. I can't take the ache in my chest. *I scream.* I scream for the walls that he has torn from my heart, that threaten to rebuild. I scream for the lies intended to protect me, that annihilate me later. I scream for everything I feel for this man, that is too much for my wounded heart to hold.

Kael squeezes my hands, desperately trying to keep me tethered here—to this moment, this place, *him.* I still, for just a heartbeat, locking eyes with the man who can cut me deeper than any blade.

The scream dies in my throat, the firelight flickering through the veil of my tears. And in the quiet that follows, his voice finds me.

Soft. Broken. Undeniable.

"I love you, Elyssara. I think I've always loved you, even before I knew it. And I will never stop." The words are a vow. A promise. An answer to an invitation. An anchor in the middle of a storm.

I whimper, crumbling into his arms like a child's doll.

Sobs wrack my body, purging my pain, my heartache.

Because despite myself, Kael is The Sky, and I know *home* is in his arms.

CHAPTER EIGHTY-TWO
KAEL

I hold her in my arms until every tear has been shed, because I know I've hurt her. But I'd do it again if it meant getting this time with her without her seeing me as her destroyer.

I know I'm a selfish bastard—I fucking know it—but I don't regret it. I won't repent for giving us time to feel *this*.

The trembling has stopped, and the last tear has fallen, but still, she lies in my arms beside Nehvara's fire. I've stroked her hair, traced idle circles on her back, and assured her again and again that I will never destroy her. She will never fall at my hand. I might be fucking insane, but I will battle every star in the sky of this forsaken land to save her if I have to.

The stillness is disturbed by the gentle clang of Nehvara's necklaces as she moves towards us at the fire again. She picks up the kettle hanging over the fire and refills our mugs. "I *did* say you'd need it," she teases softly, though there's no bite in her words.

I let out a breath that's not quite a laugh, not quite anything at all, but Elyssara doesn't move.

I know she needs time with this, but we need answers. *I* need answers. "So tell me—who should I believe? The sighing winds of Skaedor's Crest, or the prophecy that's been choking us since day one?" My question is genuine, but there's no mistaking the bitterness in it.

Elyssara finally lifts her head, reaching for her mug, my question having piqued her interest. Her eyes are swollen and red, and her braid has unraveled, strands falling wild around her face—untamed and beautiful, like the storm she's always been.

I have gone over this again and again with Therion. *How can the prophecy say one thing, and the winds of truth say another?*

"Both—the winds and prophecy say the same thing, Sky," Nehvara answers smoothly. She stills, lifting her mug to her mouth and taking a long pull. "The problem is, you have not seen the full prophecy."

Elyssara's breath hitches, her back stiffening instantly.

"Are you fucking kidding me?" I grit out, and my hand goes to the blade at my hip instinctively.

Nehvara closes her eyes regretfully, "No. Whatever you have seen is incomplete, Sky," she shakes her head, reaching into the leather satchel resting on the floor behind her.

"Here," she pulls out a piece of parchment with small, neat handwriting and passes it over the fire.

Elyssara leans in, and we read it:

> *In the twenty-fifth summer beneath Lireal's Eye,*
> *The Lightborne shall rise where the Stars deny.*
> *Bound to the Sky, yet free from the flame,*
> *She carries the light—and an unspoken name.*
>
> *Five keys await to unbind her light,*
> *Where shadow and star must share the night.*
> *Beneath the temple where fears take form,*
> *The blade ignites and the veil is torn.*
>
> *On starlit peaks where the heavens sigh,*
> *The compass rests 'neath the watcher's eye.*
> *In shadowed depths where roots entwine,*
> *The crown reveals the path divine.*

Her skin shall glow with threads of light,
Each relic found will burn more bright.
Piece by piece, the Lightborne wakes,
To bend the dark, the veil it breaks.

Where ruins burn and the Flame-heart sleeps,
The dragon stirs in the soul it keeps.
And in the skies where wild winds sing,
Beast and bond form a timeless ring.

The Lightborne and Sky must tread as one,
Their union unlocks what must be undone.
Vengeance shall blaze to balance the scales,
And justice shall rise where all else fails.

When relics awaken and powers combine,
The chains will fall, and the Stars shall align.
Her destiny looms, unknown and untamed,
To balance the world or shatter the frame.

And then, I realize: there's more that we've never seen before.

But light unbound can blind the land,
A ruin born from an open hand.
The heavens will break, the Stars shall weep,
A blow must strike, or darkness keep.

The Lightborne shall rise, and truth shall ignite,
Unless the Sky destroys her light.
One truth must break, one vow must sever,
Or silence and shadow shall reign forever.

"It's me," Elyssara whispers, "I will be the ruin of Aevryn."

"I will never let that happen, Duskae," I soothe. "You're too good, El. You carry too much light to be what they fear—you would never harm this world."

"But I will," she breathes. "The Stars have foretold it."

"No—"

"There will come a time where you must decide between your own will, your heart, and fate," Nehvara interjects. "You must continue walking the path of prophecy, dears. For on the other side of it, who knows what will be?"

"Don't *you?*" I snap.

The old woman laughs, "All I know is that the Flame-heart has been stirring, awaiting your arrival here, and the Flame-heart stirs for no one."

Elyssara leans in, wiping her eyes as if to clear them, "The prophecy says it's sleeping—so, how do we *awaken* it?" Her voice is raspy from screaming, and I wince hearing it.

"You must find the Flame-heart a worthy vessel to take form within," Nehvara says.

A worthy vessel for a fucking dragon?

Before we can speak, Nehvara continues, "The Flame-heart is not just any dragon, Starbound. The Flame-heart is the soul of Tarrakai—the most powerful dragon in history. His form is gone, but his soul lives on in the Heart of Ashara—a jewel." She holds her hands over her heart in reverence. "For Tarrakai to awaken in dragon form, he will need a worthy vessel—someone brave, who holds love for the Dravari line, loyal," she explains. "You will take the Heart of Ashara and we will not stop you, but you will not awaken Tarrakai until it's time."

The words settle like stone in my stomach. *Stars, let the vessel not be her.*

"How will I know when to awaken him? How do I even do that?" Elyssara pleads.

"You will know," Nehvara says with conviction, but I'm lost in her cryptic mysticism.

"And what happens to the vessel when it's time to awaken Tarrakai?" I ask.

But Nehvara stands swiftly, draining the remnants of her mug and gestures for us to stand, "That is all for today. Tomorrow, I'll take you to the Flame-heart."

"One more thing," Elyssara pleads. "How do we help you? How do we reunite you with the Vaythari? I made a promise to them," Elyssara asks, desperately clinging to the good she can do in the world.

"Awaken the Flame-heart and all will be restored in time. Not today, and not tomorrow, but soon," Nehvara says, and the fire dims to nothing, leaving us in darkness.

CHAPTER EIGHTY-THREE
KAEL

THE FIRE CRACKLES LOW, THROWING LONG SHADOWS AGAINST THE slick moss-covered walls in the main cavern of Cindralis.

The Cindrali people gather in small groups to scoop some sort of stew into their bowls from a dented old pot over the hearth.

"El!" a buoyant voice travels through the dark, reaching us on the outskirts of the cavern. *Seren.* "El!"

"Little Star," Elyssara says affectionately, pulling Seren in for a warm embrace.

"What's wrong? Why are your eyes all puffy and red?" Seren squeezes Elyssara's arms, worry furrowing her brow. She spins her gaze to me, narrowing her eyes, "What did you do?"

No one speaks to me like this, especially not a small, blond girl who barely comes up to my chest. A chuckle escapes me, and I lift my arms in mock surrender, "It's a long story. I'll explain once everyone's here."

She slaps me lightly across the upper arm and swiftly turns her back, leaning into Elyssara who can't hide her enchanted smile any longer.

We go with Seren to find the others, who are pulled in close around a small fire, bowls of stew long-since eaten, and two fresh bowls awaiting us.

"Thank you," Elyssara says politely, her usual fierceness devoid from her tone.

"Let me guess," Ronyn begins, "you can shapeshift into a wolf, Therion's actually a god, and Daelen has the power of invisibility—how'd I do?"

Daelen barks a laugh, and Therion shakes his head, though I glimpse a faint smirk on his face.

Elyssara's mouth twitches up at his comments. "You're such a fucking moron, Ronie," she admonishes.

"Well," Jax prompts, "out with it. Where'd you go and what do you know?"

Fucking Jax. Always so subtle.

"Do you ever think that a slightly more," Merrik weighs his words, "*gentle* approach would endear people to you a bit more, Jaxxy?"

"Not really, old man. Go have a nap—we have plans to discuss," she shoots back, gesturing to the rest of the group.

Rubi takes a swig of something pungent from a mug, hissing through her teeth in the aftermath, "Brask," she explains, holding up her mug. Therion shakes his head at her, already looking exasperated. *Typical.* "What?" She exclaims. "They tell me a mug every night stops illness—I'm just testing the theory, like the brilliant healer I am, Teddy." She takes another sip from the mug, wagging her eyebrows up and down at Therion.

He mutters something imperceptible under his breath, probably a prayer for patience—or maybe just a curse aimed at Rubi's liver. The two of them have been this way since we were kids. Somehow, it calms me. It reminds me what we fight for.

I look at Elyssara and she's smiling, talking to her friends with ease, and eating stew, and the sight of it puts me at ease.

"I don't mean to stop the fun—" I start, but I'm cut off.

"Yes you do, Kael. You always get in the way of our fun," Rubi teases, pouting like a petulant child.

I roll my eyes playfully at her, before continuing, "We met with a

Seer named Nehvara who holds the gift of both ancient knowledge and foresight."

Seren's face lights up and her eyes instantly lift to mine, "Did she say anything about me?"

The desperation in her expression fucking kills me.

Elyssara leans in, wrapping her arm around Seren. "No, Little Star. I'm sorry—Nehvara told us... well, she told us what she wanted to tell us and nothing more."

"Oh," Seren says. "It's okay. It's not important right now, anyway." Her gaze drops. Therion lifts his hand, as if he's about to reach for her, but puts it back down. Seren sniffs, fighting whatever emotions she's barely keeping in check, "What about the Flame-heart?"

Grateful for the topic change, I recall what Nehvara said. "The Flame-heart is the soul of Tarrakai—the most powerful dragon in history—and at some point... *soon*, we will need to find a vessel for the Flame-heart to awaken," I pause, searching for the right words, "*within*."

"Within?" Daelen asks, incredulous. "As in, a fuckin' dragon will live inside someone?" He asks, throwing his hands in the air. "With all due respect, my prince—fuck that."

I fight a laugh that is desperate to escape, because truly, *fuck that*.

"Nehvara didn't say what would happen to the vessel, just that we'd *know* when and how to do it when the time was right," I offer.

"Well, that's some cryptic shit if I've ever heard it," Daelen shakes his head in disbelief or rejection. Either way, I can't blame him.

"Fucking seers—always so dramatic," Jax rolls her eyes, expression bored.

"And the rest?" Therion asks, ever the pragmatist.

Are you ready? I ask down the tether.

Elyssara looks at me, emerald-green eyes pinning me in place, and she nods.

"Elyssara and I are...," the words catch in my throat, heavy with meaning that we haven't figured out yet, "bonded." I fumble over the words, but Elyssara sits up straighter, pulling her shoulders back.

"We're Starbound—our bond is written in the Stars. A fated tether of mind, body and heart," she explains, and the power in her words makes me think that perhaps she actually wants this.

"No Starbound tethers have been recorded for hundreds of years," Seren says in awe. "I thought they were a myth," she breathes.

"We're still figuring it out," I say, trying to give Elyssara time and space to process everything.

"What does this mean, Your High— I mean, Kael?" Rhyven asks. "How exactly does this work, especially if you are to take back the throne?"

His question hangs in the air. Not because I haven't thought about Elyssara ruling by my side, but because she's the Dravari heir —she has her own throne to take back. And because there is so much more at play here than solely what *I* want.

Despite the tangled emotions in my chest, I keep my answer simple, direct. "I don't know. The tether has not been... fully chosen yet. Nehvara described it as *an invitation*," I explain.

"I see," Rhyven says, his expression furrowed in thought. "And how do you... *accept* the invitation?" He posits the question carefully.

"We don't exactly know that either," I say truthfully.

Rhyven nods, accepting my answer.

"That actually sounds right," Ronyn says, and I look at him, confused. "Not knowing anything is kind of our *thing*."

"It actually *is* our thing," Therion agrees.

"In that case, it's probably a good time to let you know that there's one more thing that we didn't know," I say, pulling out the parchment from Nehvara with the complete prophecy.

I smooth the parchment out on the stone floor, the firelight catching the ink like it's burning.

I read the last lines aloud.

> *"But light unbound can blind the land,*
> *A ruin born from an open hand.*
> *The heavens will break, the Stars shall weep,*
> *A blow must strike, or darkness keep.*

The Lightborne shall rise, and truth shall ignite,
Unless the Sky destroys her light.
One truth must break, one vow be severed,
Or silence and shadow shall reign forever."

"We were missing the final two verses," Therion murmurs, voice low with shock.

The words hang heavy in the air. Like smoke. Like ash.

No one speaks.

Not even Ronyn.

The fire crackles. Somewhere across the cavern, a bowl scrapes against stone. But in our circle, there is only stillness.

And now we know what's written in the Stars.

And what we may have to break.

CHAPTER EIGHTY-FOUR
KAEL

TVIRA TAKES US TO THE BATHING POOLS—HUMID AIR FROM THE
warm, bubbling pools creates a chorus of drips from the cavern's
ceiling that sounds melodic, relaxing. The pools are empty, still and
serene.

Elyssara whimpers at the sight of them, and I don't blame her.
We've been on the road for several days, and the thought of
submerging myself in warm crystalline waters is enough to make me
shuck off my clothes without thought for who's around.

"A change of clothes," Tvira says sharply, gesturing to a neat
pile of folded clothes sitting on a carved ridge in the cavern wall.
"Robes to dry off," she says in her typical clipped tone, pointing to
linen robes the color of wheat that she's flung on the stone floor.
"Javi will take you to your resting place later," Tvira spins on her
heel with efficiency, leaving the hot pools with no further
explanation.

I guess we'll meet whoever Javi is later.

My leather vest is thrown to the floor already, so I pull off my
tunic. Elyssara's eyes land on my chest, and her breath hitches as if
she's mesmerized.

She closes the distance between us and runs her hand along the constellations marking my chest. They illuminate under her touch, recognizing her as home.

"El," I whisper, "I know I didn't tell you about the sighing winds, but—-"

"I know why," she says fervently, cutting me off. "You chose me —over the Stars, over fate, over your people," her eyes are glassy, and her throat bobs with emotion.

"And I would choose you again, every single time. I fucking refuse to be bound by what the Stars decide to write. We can write new stories for ourselves, Duskae," I tilt up her chin and brush a kiss to her lips—she tastes like starlight incarnate. She kisses me back with hunger, opening her mouth for me in a tangle of tongues, and every brush of her fingers feels like a constellation waking beneath my skin.

She pulls back, looking up at me with wild hair and those untamed eyes, "Are you ever going to tell me what that even means?" A smile dances on her lips, but sensuous hunger laces her gaze. "Duskae, I mean. I used to think it was an insult," she admits.

I exhale, brushing a wild strand from her face and cupping her cheek. "In old Zerynthian lore, Duskae is the Goddess of the Unfated. A beacon of free will. Of choice," I say tenderly, pulling her in closer.

"That sounds unlike any of the other gods and goddesses," she says softly, eyes twinkling with curiosity.

"It is. They hated her for it. They erased her from the myths because she threatened their hold on fate. She was the one thing they couldn't predict. Couldn't control. Never saw coming. So they destroyed her," I hold her gaze, tightening my hold on her.

Her breathing is ragged, shaky, but her gaze is reverent. "She is the Goddess of Choice, Elyssara. Old lore says she left a shard of herself in the world, a spark that would one day awaken when the world was again on the edge of collapse," my voice is low, intent. "You're the one they never saw coming—the one who commands The Sky. You're the spark, El."

Her breathing deepens, but her eyes never leave mine. Her gaze bores into me—wide, wild, shining—and tears begin to well. "Then we should choose each other," she pants. "In defiance of it all. For ourselves," the words come out like a prayer. A promise. "Remove your clothes," she whispers, urgent.

We undress in silence, the only noise the steady melody of the dripping ceilings.

She's bare and breathtaking—soft in all the places I crave. Every inch of her calls to something primal in me—want, yes, but reverence too. Like touching her wrong might shatter something holy.

Her skin glimmers, the pool's reflection casting rippling shapes across her skin. The Eye of Lireal illuminates under my gaze, and I take my eyes lower to her soft breasts, rising and falling with her breath.

I drag my gaze down the curve of her hips, drinking her in like a man starving—until I land at the apex of her thighs.

She slips her hand between her thighs, drawing a finger through her center. She stalks towards me with a primal hunger that threatens to buckle my knees. She wipes the finger across my chest, the glistening evidence of her arousal painted across my Sky marking. "I'm so wet for you, Kael," she whispers, and grabs my hand.

She tugs my hand, pulling me toward the steps into the hot pools. She leads the way, her ass and hips swaying like a fucking goddess before my eyes. My cock is already hard, and it pulses at the sight of her.

She walks down a few steps of the hot pools before turning back to me, "Sit down, my prince," she purrs seductively.

I swallow thickly, bewitched by the woman before me. Her power, her confidence, her raw sensuality that has me in a fucking chokehold.

Elyssara's gaze is locked on mine—unwavering and commanding. She sinks to her knees on the step, water lapping against her lower back. She leans forward, still not breaking my gaze, breasts hanging in the pool.

"I choose you, too," is all she says before taking my cock in her hand. She grabs me by the base, and takes the tip in her mouth, swirling her tongue around it.

I drop my head back in pure ecstasy, the feeling of her mouth on my cock has Stars in my vision.

She slides her mouth down my cock, almost reaching the base. I reach the back of her throat and she moans.

The sound of her moaning with her mouth around me has my release already building. "Fuck," I grit out.

She lifts her head, lips swollen from sucking me, "I want to worship you, Kael."

"You don't need to, El," I manage. "You don't have to do this."

"I *want* to do this," she says quickly, no hesitation in her tone. "Let me," she says, and pushes me back so my elbows rest on the step behind me.

She wraps her hand and mouth around my cock again, pumping her hand and sliding her mouth up and down. "I fucking love seeing your mouth on my cock, El," I say, voice gritty and raw. She moans at my words, and I look further down—her breasts bob under the water, illuminating them, and I can't take it anymore.

"I need to fuck you, El," I groan.

She lifts her head, eyes full of lust and heat, but she says nothing. Simply pulls her body from the water and straddles me.

She grabs my cock, placing it at her entrance, eyes glazed from arousal.

"You're so fucking beautiful, Elyssara," I say the words like a promise. *My Starbound.*

She lowers herself onto me, and a small gasp escapes her.

"Are you okay?" I ask, concerned.

"I'm more than okay," she whimpers. "I love how you fill me, Kael," she says softly, and the words threaten to undo me right there.

She begins to rock back and forth, grinding her clit on my body while she takes me deeper. "You take me so well, El," I say, voice thick and low. "You're taking all of me like such a good girl," I encourage, watching her ride me all the way to my base.

Her breath picks up, ragged and shallow. Her pussy clenches around me, and I can feel her climax building. She grinds harder, the lines of her stomach rippling with her, the pools reflecting off her in a way that makes her look like a fucking goddess atop me.

I reach my hand forward, placing gentle pressure on her clit, and she cries out in pleasure.

Her eyes fling open, locking with mine, "I love you, too," she says, her words breathy and carnal, and I almost come at the sound of them.

I love you, too.

Her words reverberate through the cavern walls. *She chooses me, too.*

Something gold flickers in the water, just beneath the surface. Not reflection. Not light. *Us.*

Golden threads emerge from the water, unfurling around us, through us, within us.

The threads pulse brighter—gold light spilling from her skin to mine, from mine to hers.

But she doesn't stop. Her body moves rhythmically, erotically, and her hands trail up her body, cupping her breasts, massaging them while she rides me. She's lost to passion, to lust, *to love.*

The golden light pulses from her chest to mine, plunging beneath her skin, and embedding it in mine, too.

Her moans become more intense, more breathy, and I can feel her climax, as her pussy pulses and contracts around me.

"I love you," she breathes again, and I'm undone. I spill into her, shuddering as we come together.

"I love you," I repeat back to her, my words tumbling out in a groan, and the golden light erupts in a spattering of shimmering flecks in the cavern. *They look like Stars.* I bracket her hips with my hands as she goes languid atop me, her climax wrung from her body.

I lift my gaze to the cavern around us, "Whatever this is between us, El," I say, staring at the golden specks illuminating the dark cavern. "It's more than prophecy," I murmur.

Her eyes stare in awe at the space around us. "We're Starbound," she breathes, and I think it's the most beautiful thing I've ever heard.

CHAPTER EIGHTY-FIVE
KAEL

now strapped to her waist—one that wasn't there yesterday. I have
no idea where the others slept, but it seems we all had the same idea
to meet here first thing.

Nehvara looks between Elyssara and me, and nods tightly, "It's
done, then. Good. You'll need each other now more than ever."

Elyssara and I share a look—she smiles shyly, and I return a
wink.

Rubi strolls up behind Elyssara and brushes past her with a
smirk, "I could tell you had that well-fucked look, Kael." She lets
out a long whistle, tosses a wink, and plops onto a stone ledge to tie
her boots. The woman is always disheveled.

Therion groans at his sister.

"El doesn't quite have the same look, though, does she, Rubi?"
Ronyn asks, throwing a conspiratorial look to Rubi who shakes her
head dramatically. "Not up to the task, Kael?" Ronyn wags his
eyebrows.

"Poor little prince can't perform," Rubi pouts.

I huff a laugh, and grab Elyssara's hand, pulling her into me,
dismissing them with a shake of my head.

"You both feel different," Therion observes seriously, furrowing his brow. "I don't know what it is yet."

"Pretty sure it's love, brother," Merrik deadpans.

"We're Starbound, now. The tether is complete," Elyssara shares, nuzzling into my shoulder, and it surprises me. She seems... *proud.*

"Because you fucked? I thought that already happened," Jax says indifferently. "What's so special about this time?"

Fucking Jax.

"Jaxxy," Merrik admonishes with a sigh. I don't know how the man does it—his patience is unnatural.

"That's not what solidified the tether, you fucking ass," I say to Jax. "It's..." I trail off, unable to find the words.

"Choosing to love each other, despite knowing we were never meant to," Elyssara finishes for me.

"Should I... offer congratulations? Is that appropriate in this circumstance, my prince?" Rhyven asks sincerely.

I fight the urge to laugh at his constant need for diplomacy. "I don't think so, Rhy. You're good to just carry on as you were."

He nods, stepping backwards with two strides, and clasps his hands behind his back.

I turn just in time to see Seren stalking up to me, her pointer finger colliding with my chest, "Do not hurt my friend, Kael Thorne. Do you hear me?"

I can't help myself—I laugh. The sweetest woman in existence just threatened me. I try to leash my laughter, but fail miserably, "I will not hurt your friend!" I pull it together, and add, "Nothing would bring me more pain than hurting Elyssara." It seems to satisfy her because she nods curtly and turns swiftly, walking back to Ronyn, who is still raising his eyebrows at me.

"Enough," Tvira announces, striding towards us from a dark corridor. "The Flame-heart deserves your reverence," she says, as if reprimanding young children. "We follow Nehvara into the vault," she commands. "And we do it in silence."

There's no room for arguing in her tone, and we all obey.

So bossy, Elyssara mocks down the tether, which sounds louder and clearer than it has in the days before.

Or maybe she just knows what she wants, I reply. *We both know how I love a woman who knows what she wants.*

Nehvara turns her head to us slowly, a small smile gracing her face as if she's somehow privy to our conversation through the tether.

Nehvara keeps walking through the dark caves of Cindralis, taking us deeper and deeper into its underbelly. She carries a lantern that barely enlightens the space enough to see a few steps ahead, and the humidity in the air is cloying.

We walk in single-file, sweat beading on my skin, for what feels like hours, but no one speaks. No one dares to with Tvira walking at the rear, her spear clanging the ground with every step.

Elyssara turns to me, her face glistening with sweat, she opens her mouth to speak—

"We're here," Nehvara announces, stopping in front of a stone archway.

"The Heart of Ashara is sacred. *Holy.* We have been guardians of the Flame-heart for a long time, waiting for the Lightborne to walk the realms to claim what's rightfully hers," she says, her words reverberating off the stone walls. "You will know when and how to awaken the Flame-heart. There will come a time when you will be faced with loss, and you will know," her cryptic words wrap around us, and Elyssara's breath hitches.

"The Flame-heart asks for your blood, Lightborne. That is all," Tvira says coolly from the back of the group.

"My blood?" Elyssara asks.

"Come," Nehvara commands, gesturing to Elyssara to move to the front. Nehvara unsheathes her small knife, palming it with deftness—like she's used it before... *skillfully.* She spins the knife around, holding out the hilt to Elyssara. "A slice across the palm, a drop of royal Dravari blood on the jewel," she instructs with simplicity.

Elyssara looks around at me and holds out her hand for me to join her. "Yes, yes. Take your Starbound," Nehvara says mockingly, though I can tell she means it fondly.

I take her hand and step through the threshold—and the air shifts immediately. Even thicker—charged with a power so old it hums against my skin. Crackling like a warning, or perhaps a welcome. The chamber is vast and circular, carved from dark stone like the rest of Cindralis, but here, rivers of molten embers run through the walls like veins, casting the chamber in a fiery red glow.

It flickers and dances, casting moving shadows across the chambers. In another situation it might be eerie, but here, with her, it's beautiful.

At the center of the room, a single stone pillar rises from the floor—worn smooth by time, reverently polished. Upon it rests a red velvet cushion, and nestled atop it, The Heart of Ashara. *The jewel of the Flame-heart.*

A chain of gold, delicate yet strong, spills over the velvet. In the heart of the pillow, a swirling red and orange jewel is encased in a claw-like setting of solid gold, each curve precise, talon-like.

Elyssara edges closer, moving slowly, deliberately. As we get closer, I realize the jewel moves, as if it's a living thing. A sacred, holy thing, desperate to awaken. Red and orange meld together, crashing into each other like waves.

"It's beautiful," she whispers in awe.

"It's yours," I reply smoothly, reminding her that she is the rightful Dravari heir. Soul-bound to dragon-kind.

A small gasp escapes her as she stands before the pillar. "Mine," she whispers, as if reminding herself. The air crackles around us, ancient magic drenching the chamber.

She moves her hand to the gold chain of the Heart of Ashara, moving to pick it up, her fingers graze the metal lightly.

"Ow!" She shrieks, pulling her hand back sharply, and cradling her hand in her chest.

I move to her side swiftly, "What happened?" I demand.

"It felt like a bolt of lightning under my fingertips," she says, her fingers branded with a swollen red welt.

"Blood, dear. It needs your blood," Nehvara croons from the archway.

"Right. Blood," Elyssara murmurs to herself.

She holds Nehvara's knife in her right hand, hovering it over the palm of her left. The knife is small, ceremonial, runes etched into the hilt that I don't understand.

With a single cut across her palm, crimson wells up, vivid against her skin.

She doesn't speak, but she doesn't hesitate either.

She holds her hand over the Flame-heart, letting a drop of blood fall directly onto the jewel—the Heart of Ashara.

Where ruins burn and the Flame-heart sleeps.

I remember the words.

The instant it hits the Heart, the room *responds*.

The molten veins flare to life, blazing brighter, filling the chamber with a vibrant glow. The pillar hums in unison. *Ready.*

Elyssara steals herself, ready to try the necklace again.

She ghosts her fingers over the chain, testing, assessing.

She goes straight for the jewel, scooping her fingers under it to lift it into the palm of her hands.

The Flame-heart illuminates, and simultaneously, so, too, does her skin marking. The Eye of Lireal on her chest stirs awake, constellation blooming to life, the etching spreading further across her chest with permanency.

She looks to me, wonder filling her eyes, and it steals the breath from my lungs.

Elyssara clasps the Heart of Ashara around her neck, letting it hang delicately on her chest.

"Beautiful," I say, and she smiles, scrunching her nose in genuine, unabashed happiness.

If there was ever a moment I believed in fate, it's this one.

The room settles back into its mellow glow, the crackle of magic in the air simmers into a steady hum.

We walk to the archway, where the group gathers around for a look at the Heart of Ashara.

"It is done, Lightborne," Nehvara declares. "You've set in

motion a cascade of events that cannot be stopped." Her voice is pragmatic—but beneath it, something tightens. Ominous. *Certain.*

We settle back into our single-file line, and make our way back to the gathering area.

Ronyn breaks the silence, "So that's the fourth key," he says.

Murmurs of agreement thread through the air.

"And there's no mention of other relics in the prophecy?" He says, as though he's trying to figure something out.

The group gives him more non-committal murmurs of confirmation, but I hold my tongue. Realization dawning on me.

"But doesn't the prophecy say there are five relics?" He looks around, arms outstretched in question, but no one speaks until, slowly, I see it click for them, too. "So what the fuck is the fifth relic?"

CHAPTER EIGHTY-SIX

ELYSSARA

RONYN'S QUESTION HANGS IN THE AIR, AND THE SILENCE STRETCHES.

What is the fifth relic? Why doesn't the prophecy speak of it?

No one has the answer.

Not yet.

We reach the gathering chamber once more, alive with Cindrali people cooking, cleaning, sipping tea together.

Though we've retrieved what we came for, it doesn't feel like a victory. Not entirely. These people are still trapped—separated, lost, forgotten.

Tvira stands tall and stoic, holding my gaze for a long moment as if it were a silent farewell. She inclines her head slightly—the only sign she acknowledges that we won't see her again, at least not until we've awakened the Flame-heart and restored Cindralis.

"This is where we part ways," Nehvara says. "You have what you need. Now, the path is yours to walk."

I clutch the necklace at my chest, remembering why we came. The pressure of the prophecy, impending war, Kael's sister. All of it crashes down on me instantly. I squeeze my eyes closed, drawing in a long, steady inhale.

"The more you resist, the more difficult the journey," Tvira croons, and though I'd like to bury one of my daggers into her thigh, she's right. I can't escape this. And deep within, I don't actually want to. I owe this to my family. I owe this to my bloodline. *I owe this to Aevryn.*

I nod curtly. Our farewell is simple. No ceremony. No blessing. Just a sharp incline and the soft rush of water echoing from the narrow tunnel ahead.

We move toward it—toward the cold, bottomless abyss that brought us in.

Back to the world above.

"Swim down. The threshold does the rest," Nehvara explains, though it barely feels like one.

"Swim down," Ronyn repeats, laughing hysterically at the ridiculousness of the explanation. "Allow me, ladies and gentlemen... and Daelen, a god among men," he quips before leaping head-first into the freezing waters, and swims down without another thought.

"He's obviously a brilliant judge of character," Daelen jokes, the grin on his face cocky and brazen. Then again, it almost always is.

"We'll go," Therion declares, reaching for Seren's hand.

One by one, everyone leaps into the waters, and doesn't return. *That has to be a good sign.*

Kael kisses my forehead, "I know you need to do this alone, El." He winks at me, "I love you." Warmth blooms in my chest.

It's just me. Me and these fucking waters and this godsdamned Gateway of Threads.

"What's it going to be, Lightborne? Resist? Or free fall into the unknown?" Tvira probes.

I've waited for this prophecy for most of my life. I've starved in the streets of Virellin just to get a chance at doing precisely what I'm doing now. I've fought it at every turn—resenting the choices, the weight, the journey. *But no more.*

I walk to the water's edge, the chill from below licking at my feet. I stare into the dark chasm, and my own face stares back at me. My mother's face. Her eyes. Her untamed hair. And her unbreakable spirit.

My unbreakable spirit.

I turn around, balancing delicately on the edge, and let myself go, free falling into the abyss. The waters rise to meet me like fate itself—cold, swift, inescapable.

I lock eyes with Tvira, and I swear I see her smile before the waters swallow me whole.

CHAPTER EIGHTY-SEVEN
ELYSSARA

I STUMBLE TO THE GROUND, DRENCHED AND BREATHLESS, THE waterfall thundering behind me like a gate slamming shut. My palms scrape wet rock, chest heaving. I glance back at the rune still glowing faintly beside the cascade.

I made it.

"Much faster this time, El. I've only been here about an hour, I'd say," Ronyn calls out with a grin.

"Fuck off," I mutter, though my voice is half-cough, half-wheeze —lost under the ripple of laughter that spreads through the group like wildfire.

Rhyven pushes forward, a crease between his brows. "Well, don't just leave her on the ground—she's the Dravari heir, for Star's sake," he snaps, fussing like an anxious steward. His movements are tight, and his tone is sharper than usual. Something's got him wound up.

But one look at Kael, who's still doubled over in laughter, and I can't help it—I crack too, the tension sloughing off my shoulders like a deadweight.

"I'm okay, Rhy. *Really.*" I push to my feet, dripping and dizzy but standing.

"You look like you could do with some brask," Rubi says, sauntering up like she didn't just emerge from a death-defying magical Gateway. She holds out a battered flask, smug as sin.

"Rubi, are you fucking serious right now?" Therion barks, aghast.

"How in the Stars do you *have* that?" I gasp, laughter bubbling out of me, raw and uncontrolled.

"What?" she says innocently, turning to Therion. "Tvira was quite willing to help me out, actually." Her grin is all teeth and trouble.

Therion mutters something savage under his breath.

"Tvira was the one who gave you brask?" I repeat, blinking at her like she's conjured it from thin air.

"Oh, Tvira gave me *lots* of things, if you know what I mean," Rubi says with a conspiring wink, wagging her eyebrows like a complete menace.

"We *all* know what you mean, Rubi. Now put the fucking brask away," Therion snaps, exasperated.

But I can't stop laughing. None of us can. It's the flavor of laugh that catches in your throat. The kind you get as a child when you've just gotten in trouble but can't stop the laughter from exploding.

"Excuse me," Rhyven cuts in, his voice too tight, too formal. Embarrassed, perhaps? Or something else? His cheeks are flushed, jaw set like he's holding something in. "I'll go scout ahead. Ensure our travels back to Thornewood are safe."

Kael gives a curt nod, the smirk still playing at his lips. Rhyven doesn't wait for further approval—he turns and disappears down the slope in a flash of silver steel.

"I think we should get Rhy drunk on brask when we return," Ronyn muses. "Or what about those mushrooms, Rubes? I'd *pay* to see Rhy act like a duskprowler."

We descend the slick, slated rock face in single file, boots skidding, fingers clutching at twisted vines and slippery edges. Water drips from our clothes, hair flat to our skin, every breath dragging in the thick, misty air. The waterfall roars behind us like a reminder of everything we've just traversed.

At the base, Therion halts so abruptly that I nearly run into him. His head tilts, his nostrils flaring. That stillness wraps around him again—the way it always does when he's listening to something the rest of us can't hear.

"Someone's coming," he murmurs, voice like steel.

He draws his axe without ceremony, and Kael mirrors him, blades whispering free from their sheaths. In an instant, we shift from wet, exhausted travelers to a pack of warriors ready for battle.

Branches rustle. Tension tightens.

"It's me, my prince. Just me." Rhyven emerges from the trees with his hands raised, breathing hard, his pale hair damp and clinging to his forehead.

We all exhale as one, though the unease still lingers like mist.

Kael lowers his swords an inch, eyes narrowing. "All clear?"

Rhyven nods, but it's too fast. His gaze flicks from Kael to the treeline and back again. His shoulders twitch like he's about to bolt.

"All clear," he says again. "Though... the river's flooded. We'll need to loop around, hit the western ridge. It's a short detour."

"That ridge is exposed," Therion says, already scowling.

"Only for a moment," Rhyven insists. "Then we cut back through the stone glen. We'll be sheltered again before anyone even knows we're there."

Something in his tone makes the hairs rise on my arms.

Too eager. Too rehearsed.

I open my mouth, the warning forming in my throat—

"We'll do it," Kael says, sharp.

"Kael," Therion warns, the edge of his axe glinting.

"We'll scout ahead at the crest," Kael adds, firmer now. "If it's not safe, we pull back."

Therion doesn't like it. That much is obvious. But he nods, tight and reluctant.

So do we all.

Even though the air tingles with warning.

Merrik urges his mare beside us, "Lad, we can just camp here for the night. Wait for the river level to drop and return home the way we came."

Kael pauses for a heartbeat, weighing his options, "Rubi's been away from the infirmary for almost two days, Mer. The relics are there unguarded. Our hunters are away—there's no food. We can't stay away any longer than we've already been."

Merrik grimaces. He knows Kael's right—that he has a point. But he doesn't like it. He grunts in displeasure but leaves it alone.

"It's just up here," Rhyven calls from the front, Therion trailing him closely, tracking in the way he does.

Kael looks to Merrik and shrugs, "We're here now—let's get home."

Therion stills up ahead, holding up his hand to stop, his tall frame tensing. A predator ready to strike.

Everyone halts instantly, but Rhyven is further ahead. He can't see Therion and keeps going.

"Something's wrong," Therion murmurs, but there's no mistaking his words. "We're not alone."

"Fuck," Kael grits out, but doesn't hesitate to slide his swords from the scabbards at his back.

My hand hovers over the blades at my thighs, senses alert and ready.

Therion hisses his name, low and urgent, but Rhyven doesn't flinch. Doesn't turn. Doesn't hear.

Or pretends not to.

Therion gestures to all of us to dismount and doesn't hesitate to brandish his axe.

We all leap down at his command with no hesitation. No waiting, just action.

Ronyn has an arrow nocked in a heartbeat, and Jax's magic flares at her fingertips. Daelen and Merrik are crouched low with broad swords at the ready, and Rubi pulls out a sickle blade from her belt, which I'd always assumed was just a harvesting tool.

Seren, brows furrowed, aims her crossbow, and this time, she doesn't look frightened—she looks prepared.

"There's no sound," Therion states. "No birds, no insects, no wind," he says. "This isn't right."

Even the wind is holding its breath. The jungle is too quiet. Not dead—*waiting*.

Then the first arrow flies.

It whistles through the silence, embedding itself in the bark of a tree inches from Jax.

A second follows—this one grazing Daelen's upper arm.

Kael's voice slices through the hush. "AMBUSH!"

The command rips from his chest like thunder, and all hells break loose.

All at once, the trees erupt.

Dozens—no, more—of masked warriors spill from the shadows. Not wild, not disorganized. *Trained*. Moving in formation.

I leap into action, the sound of steel singing in my ears.

My dagger finds the flesh between the ribs of a soldier moving towards Seren. I withdraw my blade, slick with dark crimson blood, almost black, and that's when I see it—*the Mark of Morrathys*.

"It's Maldrak's army!" I bellow, but don't stop moving.

I charge into the fray, ready to rip through soldiers who dare to come after my friends.

Jax's magic flares around us, blooming outwards to cast the jungle in a vibrant white light. *Lightborne magic*.

Soldiers fall at her hands, dissolving into dust on the jungle floor.

Therion's axe doesn't swing—it cleaves. Each strike lands like a death sentence. No flourish, just brutality. He's not fighting for glory. He's ending threats. He's slicing through men with precision and calculated fury. He unleashes an avalanche of brutal attacks—sliced throats, cracked skulls, mangled bones. He senses movements before they happen, calculating in less than a heartbeat, and killing in a single breath—he's made for war.

I fight like the warrior Revryn prepared me to be—I cut through flesh like silk, my blades the beginning of their afterlife.

Ronyn picks off Maldrak's men with unerring accuracy, moving like a blur of stealth and finesse.

But it's Kael that takes my breath away. He moves like shadow incarnate, not a man, but a force—swords spinning with deadly precision, each strike choreographed in violence and grace. His blades sing through the air, leaving behind trails of silver light as if the Stars themselves mourn each soul he sends to the Final Gate.

His shadows crawl along the earth like hounds loosed for the hunt—wrapping around ankles, necks, slicing breath and bone. But it's Kael's eyes—cold, unyielding, divine—that silence even the boldest soldiers. He doesn't look at them like enemies. He looks at them like ends.

Markings of the night sky peek over his armor, veins and muscles tense with exertion as he deftly wields his swords, his piercing blue eyes the last thing these soldiers will see in this world.

Kael. My Starbound. My ruin and my salvation.

I should be terrified—but I'm mesmerized.

A soldier with veins as dark as night rippling out from his blood-shot eyes rushes me. His mouth twisted in a snarl, a shiver licking up my spine at the sight—a *Bloodbond*. I drop low, instincts screaming at me to incapacitate him first. I pull my arm back, ready to embed my blade in his groin.

But invisible hands wrap around my wrist, twisting my arm with inhuman strength.

Pain screams up my shoulder, a jagged blaze of fire. My blade clatters uselessly to the dirt.

"KAEL!"

"I've got the Lightborne bitch!" The man behind me snarls, his breath rancid, festering.

Chains clink behind me, and another soldier materializes holding heavy silver chains. *A Shadowweave cloak.* They've been hiding in plain sight.

I hiss in pain.

They wrap the chains around my wrists behind my back. I cry out in agony as they sizzle against my skin, and the tether to Kael snuffs out, going completely silent. The tingle of my magic that hums under my skin quiets, and I feel... empty.

"KAEL!" I cry, and that's when I see it.

Jax, Merrik and Daelen are already on the ground. Faces pressed to the forest floor, knees digging heavy into their backs, cutting off their air.

Five men crowd around Kael, dragging him to his knees, chains hanging from his wrists, too. He fights, snarling at the men who played a cowardly game.

Seren is dragged down by men twice her size, knees pressing into her delicate back, shoving her body into the dirt, "They're lillath chains, El. They nullify magic." She wheezes the words, and a soldier presses their boot to her neck to stop her from talking.

"NO!" I cry, desperation pressing down on my chest, clawing at me to do something. *Anything.*

Ronyn's bow is crumpled and broken, lying splintered under a looming tree.

Panic seizes me. I can't see him.

Ronyn!

We're vastly outnumbered. More soldiers with the Mark of Morrathys break through the treeline, descending on us in droves.

Kael's roar of defiance ripples through the jungle, a battle cry, but the cowards who hold him down in chains of lillath land a hit on his jaw, and blood trickles down his chin. "You fucking cowards!" He grits out, his jaw clenched in unhinged resistance.

A strangled grunt escapes me as I throw my head back, connecting with the soldier behind me.

"You fucking bitch," he snarls, and the blunt force of his hilt cracks into my head.

My vision blurs, but in the distance, I can make out a figure lying unmoving in the dirt.

I beg my sight to clear.

Come on! Come on!

It clears enough to take in Ronyn's limp frame, a cracked and bleeding split in his head.

NO!

But I can't do anything.

Because that's when I see him.

A tall, imposing figure cloaked in black strides through the treeline, gold chains hanging from his neck in a show of blatant ostentatiousness. His ocean blue eyes are the same hue as Kael's, but that's where the similarities end.

"Ah, it's so good to see you again, nephew," he croons with an arrogant smile.

Kael spits blood onto the ground in greeting, drawing his mouth back in a snarl.

"You always were an untrained animal, Kael. Your father raised you to be weak—always acting with your soft hearts instead of your brains and blades," Maldrak growls.

Kael's breath hitches, but not at the insult. His eyes dart to a rocky outcropping beside Maldrak, and then back again, flicking back and forth. Confusion, or terror, or something else entirely fall across his face.

I can't see.

I fight desperately against the lillath.

What the fuck is over there?

Kael groans, fighting against the restraints, but the soldiers push him down, a blade at his throat. A soldier with a leather strap fixing his hair in a long, tangled tail of dirty blonde hair leans down to Kael, whispering something that makes Kael's jaw clench.

"We had a deal, nephew. Or should I call you *prince?*" Maldrak mocks.

Kael doesn't respond, veins bulging in his neck at the tension.

"I'm just so glad you could make it today, nephew. I thought you wouldn't come. After all, I know you thought you could change your plans without my knowing," Maldrak sings, but there's no denying he's toying with Kael. "But then, it's so fortunate that we have a mutual friend who could keep me informed."

The crowd of soldiers jostle around, parting to make way for someone moving to the front.

"Rhyven," I whisper, barely believing my eyes.

"RHYVEN!" Kael's voice is murder incarnate.

My heart cleaves in two. *He fucking sold us out.*

"Did you think you wouldn't pay for what you did to Zak?" Rhyven growls, animalistic fury taking over his body, his fists clenched at his sides with barely leashed rage.

"You fucking rat!" Kael screams, and I can hear Therion and

Daelen snarling into the dirt with boots and blades keeping them in place.

"Why?" I breathe, almost inaudibly.

"*Why?*" Rhyven snarls, his voice cracking under the weight of his hatred.

"Because you are no one. You are nothing. You don't belong to Zerynthia. You don't belong to us. You were a curse from the moment you crawled into our world—an infection we should have burned out long ago."

His chest heaves with barely leashed rage.

"You ruined my brother. You ruined my family. You made us *weak* when we needed to be *strong*—and now look where we are."

His voice lowers into something even uglier.

"Zak was right. We should have let him rip you apart when we had the chance."

A desperate roar rips from Kael's throat. A soldier charges toward Kael to shut him up, but he throws himself forward. Shoulder launching in a frenzied arc that uppercuts the soldier under the chin. All I hear is the sickening crack of bones before the dirty blonde soldier swipes at Kael with the back of his hand.

Kael drops to the ground.

"NO!" I cry, desperate to get to him.

The soldiers drag him back to his knees, blood and dirt mingling on his face, hair falling forward into his eyes.

"Let's not get distracted here, children," Maldrak says calmly. "We came to make a deal, did we not?"

The dirty blonde soldier leans down, whispering something into Kael's ear, and his eyes dart to the rocky outcropping again. *What can he see?*

He shakes his head in defiance, but says nothing.

"We made a deal, didn't we, nephew?" Maldrak pushes again, calculating, calm.

"Yes," Kael grits out.

I whip my gaze to him.

What?

But he keeps his eyes ahead, fixed on Maldrak.

"Care to share what that deal was, *prince*?" The last word is thick with venom.

Kael doesn't speak. His body is pinned in place, except for his eyes, still frantic, as they race between the rocks and Maldrak.

"Did we not make a deal for the Lightborne in exchange for your dear sister?" He mocks.

The air is stolen from my lungs.

I can't fucking breathe.

What is happening?

"Well?" Maldrak probes.

There's a long pause, and I can't breathe. My chest rises and falls too quickly. My hands tremble in the chains.

"Yes," Kael confirms. "We have a fucking deal," the words come out like a rasp.

My gut roils. Its contents threatening to spill out.

"I would *really* love to hear you say it, nephew. Just so the Lightborne is clear about the terms."

Kael swallows thickly, eyes darting, but he refuses to meet my gaze.

"Elyssara for Nalya," he admits, and I unleash a scream that rattles the world.

CHAPTER EIGHTY-EIGHT

KAEL

She screams—sharp and raw, the kind that doesn't sound human.

The kind that rips the world in half.

Her scream cuts through the air, in the same way it cuts through my heart—swift, devastating.

She struggles against the chains, snarling and growling in defiance as the soldiers drag her to her feet.

"You don't want to back out, do you?" Maldrak lilts.

I look to Nalya—frail, skeletal, scarred—and the knife poised at her throat beyond the rocks.

I can't let her fucking die.

"Say yes, and she dies, *my prince*," the soldier behind me whispers into my ear with a snarl.

"No," I say but it fucking kills me.

I do what I swore I wouldn't. I look at Elyssara, struggling, fighting, tears of fury running like rivers down her cheeks.

"You fucking did this," she shrieks, her voice raspy from screaming. "The prophecy was right, Kael. You *have* destroyed me," she screeches, her eyes wide with shock and disbelief. "You have fucking destroyed me," she cries, sobs wracking her body.

The Lightborne shall rise, and truth shall ignite,
Unless the Sky destroys her light.
One truth must break, one vow must sever,
Or silence and shadow shall reign forever.

I've destroyed her. I've broken my vow to never hurt her. I've carried out my part of the prophecy.

I squeeze my eyes shut, as if darkness might erase the sight of her breaking.

As if anything could.

I look to Rhyven, and something flickers in his gaze. Remorse, perhaps? Or regret? The flicker is gone before I can be sure, but I pin him with my stare, the taste for blood on my lips. "You do not come out of this alive, Rhyven," I bite, my voice low, lethal. "I will hang you next to your brother in the town square and I will not repent," I vow, the words a promise.

Elyssara's screams mingle with Seren's, sisters torn apart, as the soldiers drag her across the jungle floor while she fights, kicks, screams for her freedom.

"I'll take care of her for you, nephew," Maldrak sings through the broken cries. "She'll birth a dynasty from the magic the gods left behind in her veins—and I will turn their gift against the world they sought to save." My hands itch for steel. Hunger for shadows at my fingertips. "Our children will outlive us all. And the world will kneel —not just today, but for a thousand years to come."

I bite my cheek, a metallic tang coating my tongue.

I'll fucking kill him.

"She'll make me an army of gods, Kael—we'll conquer every piece of land until there's nothing left for anyone else," he says as if he's won. As if this is the end. "My Queen," he says wistfully, and the words wreck me, cleave me in two.

He knows.

He knows about the gods' magic.

A cloaked sorcerer steps forward, arms raised, light bleeding from their palms in ribbons of fire and thread. The air warps, crackles. Magic stretches open the world like a wound. The light grows, expanding in threads that seem alive, humming. *A Gateway of Threads.*

The gateway opens to reveal the land beyond—Maldrak's kingdom—and the soldiers step through, piling into the portal in droves.

Maldrak drops into a mocking bow, stepping through the gateway with the look of victory on his face.

Her shrieks tear through the air. And then—her eyes find mine. Wide. Wild. Shattered. "You destroyed me," she breathes, like the final curse of a dying star as she's swallowed whole by the gateway.

I can't breathe. The prophecy strikes like a sword through the ribs.

> *The Lightborne shall rise, and truth shall ignite,*
> *Unless the Sky destroys her light.*

And I have done exactly what the Stars demanded.

The soldiers force me to the ground, and I don't fight it. *She's gone.*

They drag Nalya out from behind the rocks, her frame fragile and despondent, and shove her to the ground next to me. The Mark of Morrathys stares back at me from her neck, onyx veins stretching out from its center. *She's been marked.*

The last of the soldiers moves through the gateway, and the sorcerer—whoever they are—follows, closing the portal behind them.

Elyssara.

She's gone.

And I will burn through gods and galaxies.

I will raze realms.

I will bring down the fucking Stars to get her back.

ACKNOWLEDGMENTS

This story has whispered to me for years—begging, pulling, pleading to be heard. To write it, I closed a successful business, restructured our family life, and stayed up far too late for far too many nights, traveling to distant lands only I could see. But here she is—a tale woven from people I adore, worlds that once lived only in my imagination, and starlit magic I believe we all carry inside us.

Firstly, let me start with my husband—the inspiration for Kael, my grounded, salt-of-the-earth anchor, and the greatest champion for my writing (and for me in general). Thank you for encouraging me to burn everything down to write this, for reminding me that I should make magic out of this life we share, and for inspiring those spicy scenes I know we have all come to love and admire (pun, intended).

Secondly, thank you to my beautiful, supportive friends who have encouraged me without a single moment of doubt.

Hollie, thank you for being the very first safe sounding board that listened to my dream of world building and fantasy writing on that roadtrip, who continually reminded me that this was the path, who inspired me with her own best-selling books, and who told me to go for it when this was just a secret dream inside a locked box in my heart.

Thank you to Mikka, Megan, Nat, Sophie, Holly, Kathy, and Larni, who encouraged me, supported me, cheered me on, and reminded me of my greatness when I feared I'd blown up my entire life for a failed mission.

Thirdly, thank you to my brilliant, thoughtful, helpful beta readers and social media community who gave me feedback, told me to keep going, trusted my wild new direction, and backed me from the very first time I uttered this preposterous idea. Jules, Katie, Bess—your loving support and feedback shaped this story in such a beautiful way, and I'm eternally grateful. Coral and Tash—thank you for your help in naming Zakarius and Daelen; it's so special to bring characters to life with the help of those rooting for my success.

Next, Tricia. My emotionally attuned, deeply connected, and wildly intelligent editor, who refined this story with masterful insights. Thank you for tending to my story with tenderness and a light touch—you came in with the clear intention of helping me tell my story with more precision, and never tried to change it, and instead, you trusted this channelled piece of work, and for that I am eternally grateful. Thank you for holding me emotionally through this process, which resembled a hellish roller coaster—you handled it with grace and love. I am so deeply grateful for your contribution.

Almost there, I promise.

My family. Thank you to my parents, who told me to pursue this path with reckless abandon, even when it didn't make sense, who believed in me as a storyteller from the very first moment I held a pen in my hand, and who told me to prioritize my calling over everything. Thank you for your belief in me.

My girls—Billie, Riley and Luka. Every time I look into your eyes, I am reminded of why I must pursue the path that makes me the most happy, alive and radiant. Thank you for reminding me to truly live for you.

And finally, to you. Readers, supporters, past clients, my online community, people from the local cafe, school mums, fellow story-tellers and creators—your presence here means I can continue to do what I love. Without you, I am just a woman on a computer. With you, I am a woman who tells stories for a living. Thank you for being part of the wind that carries this story.

I can't wait to share the second leg of this journey with you (and every leg thereafter).

Brit x

LOVED THE SKY CALLED HER HOME?

Please consider leaving a review on **Amazon** or **Goodreads**. It helps *so much*—not just for visibility, but to help other readers find their way to this story.

Want more?

Sign up to receive behind-the-scenes extras, bonus scenes, launch event details, and exclusive ARC invitations here: https://www. bjwildewrites.com/

Want a taste of Book Two?

Read on, my friend.

THE DARKNESS REMEMBERED
HER NAME

Book 2
The Song of Stars Trilogy
A sneak peek

CHAPTER ONE

ELYSSARA

I think it's been four days since I was taken, but I can't be sure. Days have blurred into nights, and the only measure of time is the meal—if you can call it that—thrown into my cell. I don't know when, but it seems to be once a day.

The dungeons reek of piss and unwashed bodies, and the air is thick with imminent death, punctuated with pained groans of whoever else dwells down here.

My eyes have adjusted to the dark. I can see the slick, grime-covered stone floors, the outline of bodies curled up on rat-infested cots. But worse than that is the sound. The sound of keys jingling as the guard approaches. The heavy thud of boots descending the stairs. A warning of what's to come. Because I know what happens now—someone will be taken, and they'll never return—only replaced by a new body. *It might be me today.*

I push myself to sit—a woeful attempt to prepare myself—but the sharp pang of pain through my ribs cripples me, and I drop back onto the cot. They're probably broken. I hiss a curse, and my lip splits again. The crusted blood from days earlier breaks apart to make way for the river of crimson that spills from my lower lip.

We're a game to the guards. If they don't take us, they brutalize us in our cells for savage enjoyment—a spectacle to everyone else in the Kryntar dungeons. We're either forced to endure it or forced to watch it. I'm not sure which is worse.

The thudding boots are closer now, the jingling of the keys racketing through my mind.

"Get up, Lightborne," a female voice croons. "It's your turn today."

"Why not just do it here?" I croak, my voice hoarse from disuse. "Make a hero of yourself while I'm in chains."

I know I shouldn't provoke her, but bitterness is not so easily buried.

"Not today. Death must be earned, too. Especially by a Dravari whore." She spits the words with disdain.

"Better than being a leashed dog for a King ruling a wasteland," I retort.

The woman steps close enough for the bars of my cell to cast shadows across her face, and drops her voice into a low whisper, "But still far better than being a forgotten princess of a lost throne. Or a kinslayer and prince who rules nothing but a treehouse."

Kael.

My breath hitches, and I recoil. A cruel smile plays on her lips, and she knows she's struck something real within me.

He betrayed me. He fucking gave me up. He played me. And yet I still cling to the fragile hope that he'll come for me—that it was all part of the plan. I know I shouldn't. But hope is a cruelty of the mind—a mirage in the desperate dry of the desert.

"I would rather be no one at all than be complicit in Maldrak's plans," I grit out, pain still flaring in my ribs.

The woman turns the keys in my cell's lock, and the heavy door groans open. She strides across the cell and sits on the cot's edge. She raises her hand, and I brace myself for impact, but her fingers graze my cheek, pushing my dirty, blood-soaked hair behind my ear.

"Oh, I'm not just complicit, darling. I organize this entire operation for Maldrak," she mocks with a lilting tone. "And, don't worry,

Lightborne. You will beg to be no one when we're finished with you."

My heartbeat quickens. My skin prickles with unease. Panic threatens to consume me, but I've been prey before. I soothe myself the way Revryn taught me:

Tell me something you can smell, see and feel, little one.

One heartbeat at a time.

One foot in front of the other.

One moment is all you have.

"But today is your lucky day, Lightborne. His Majesty would like to dine with you this evening," she says, still stroking my hair with tenderness so at odds with her words.

I startle. *He what?*

"We need to clean the filth off you—make you look slightly less like a Dravari gutter rat."

I move to push myself up again, but before I've even made it to my elbows, her fist curls into a ball and collides with my ribs.

I muffle an agonized groan. I will not let her see me hurt. I will not break.

I breathe through my teeth, "Fuck you."

Her eyes light up at my defiance—as if breaking me will be her own personal mission.

"Come on, Gutter Rat. Time for dinner."

ABOUT THE AUTHOR

B.J. Wilde writes emotionally immersive romantasy woven with ancient magic inspired by nature, multidimensional heroines, and the kind of men who ruin you for anyone else. A lifelong lover of folklore, myth, and the wild, she draws inspiration from misty forests, ancestral memory, and the quiet pull of Mother Nature.

When she's not writing, she's chasing sunlight through the trees, lifting weights, walking the coast, sipping lattes, researching forgotten goddesses, chasing her beautiful daughters, or creating space for deep creative work through her online community of writers and artists.

She lives on the Gold Coast with her husband and their three daughters—her greatest teachers in love, wildness, and wonder.

The Sky Called Her Home is her debut novel.

Connect with her at www.bjwildewrites.com or on TikTok/Instagram @bjwildewrites.